RUN PROGRAM

ALSO BY SCOTT MEYER

Help Is on the Way: A Collection of Basic Instructions

Made with Recycled Art: A Collection of Basic Instructions

The Curse of the Masking Tape Mummy: A Collection of Basic Instructions

Dignified Hedonism: A Collection of Basic Instructions

Master of Formalities

The Authorities

Magic 2.0

Off to Be the Wizard

Spell or High Water

An Unwelcome Quest

RUN PROGRAM

SCOTT MEYER

47NORTH

Published by 47North, Seattle

www.apub.com

ISBN-13: 9781477848739
ISBN-10: 1477848738

Cover design by Cyanotype Book Architects

Printed in the United States of America

RUN PROGRAM

1.

There's no way I'm getting this job.

Hope Takeda cast her eyes around the room, making no effort to keep her fellow applicants from seeing that she was checking them out. Every seat, and much of the standing room around the perimeter, was full, occupied by hopeful young scientists in immaculately laundered clothes. Some made small talk. Most sat quietly, mentally rehearsing for the next hour of their lives or fantasizing about their prospects for the more distant future if the interview went well.

Look at 'em. I bet at least two-thirds of them have PhDs. How am I supposed to compete with that?

She looked down at her hands, folded in her lap. *They said they'd consider applicants with a master's or better. My master's should be good enough. There's no reason to believe that they'd rather have a PhD. They didn't say that. They just referred to those candidates as . . . better. There's no way I'm getting this job. These people all have better degrees than me, better experience, better clothes. Hell, I know me; they're probably better people, the jerks.*

The man sitting next to Hope asked, "Are you still with me?"

Hope snapped to attention and turned to the man, whom she'd managed to completely forget in the past thirty seconds. He was tall with shaggy blond hair, a scruffy beard, and a stocky build. He smiled at her, far more amused than irritated, and said, "Hello?"

"I'm sorry," Hope said. "I must have zoned out."

"Oh, well, I was just saying that the interesting thing about golf—"

Oh Lord, she thought. *He's still on golf.*

The man continued, "—is that the ultimate goal of the serious golfer is to do as little actual golfing as possible. Think about it: the better round you have, the fewer shots you take. In the end, the winner is the one who took the fewest strokes. The prize is to do less of the thing you set out to do. The perfect game of golf would be eighteen holes in one."

Hope said, "That's—" but found herself unable to use the word "interesting." Instead, she finally said, "something."

Two other applicants were talking in the corner of the room. Normally Hope would've disregarded the distant chatter, but she had distinctly heard the phrase "Krom's Canyon." She swiveled her head to look at them.

A fairly good-looking guy in a shirt-and-tie combination just casual enough to look much better than any truly formal clothes ever could was talking with a woman who was working her hardest to look like she was radiating a sexy librarian vibe by accident.

"The way you had to work back and forth across the bridges with limited cover, taking out psychos blocking your path while the turret at the end of the canyon tried to gun you down, was just epic. It's probably my favorite map in the entire series, even though it's in my least favorite of the games. The writing was just so much better from two onward, though around five it started losing steam again."

Borderlands, Hope thought. *They're talking about the Borderlands games. Why can't I be over there, talking games with them, instead of being stuck with, um, Bill Murray in* Caddyshack. *What was that character's name? Carl something? Hmm. Well, I bet I know who'll know.*

"Hey," Hope asked, "what was the name of Bill Murray's character in *Caddyshack*?"

The blond man said, "Carl Spackler." He adjusted his sleeves. As the cuff of his left sleeve pulled back, Hope noticed a dark purple bruise on his forearm.

Thank God. Something to talk about that isn't golf!

"How'd you get the bruise?" Hope asked.

He said, "Golf. I was standing too close and someone accidentally got me with their backswing."

Accidentally, Hope thought. *I doubt that. He most likely kept interrupting their golf to talk to them about golf. Oh well, look at the bright side. One good thing about the fact that you definitely won't get this job is that you definitely won't end up working with this dude.*

A quiet rattle emanated from the knob of the door to the next room, instantly silencing all conversation—and a good deal of the breathing—in the waiting room. The door swung open. A guy who had entered looking nervous ten minutes before walked out looking relieved.

He said, "She'd like to see Hope Takeda next." Then he made a beeline for the exit, avoiding any eye contact with the rest of the applicants.

Hope stood up, straightening her clothes. The blond man who had been pestering her about golf said, "Good luck, Hope."

Oh no, Hope thought. *We did tell each other our names when we sat down, didn't we? He got a reminder, but now I have to try to remember his, and if I don't, I'm going to look like an ass. That's just what my self-esteem needs before a job interview. Oh well, I gotta give it a shot.*

Hope said, "Thanks, Eric. Same to you."

The blond man smiled, which Hope took as a sign of success. She walked into the next room and closed the door behind her.

An impressive blond woman in her forties sat behind an impressive desk, devoid of papers. The only item on the desktop was a single electronic tablet, which the woman glanced at as she stood.

"Ms. . . . Takeda, thank you for coming in. Please have a seat."

Hope sat in the single chair opposite the desk. The woman sat as well.

"My name is Dr. Lydia Madsen. I am in charge of the project that's hiring here at OffiSmart."

Hope said, "Well, it's very nice to meet you."

Dr. Madsen nodded, lifted her tablet, and read silently. Hope kept expecting her to ask a question, but she didn't, which made Hope nervous.

Finally, Dr. Madsen glanced up at Hope and said, "I'm just reading your resume," then went back to reading silently, which did little to make Hope less nervous.

Dr. Madsen kept her eyes glued to the tablet, but said, "Focus on machine learning, master's degree, very impressive."

Hope said, "Thank you."

"Not as impressive as a PhD."

Hope said nothing.

After another stretch of silence, Dr. Madsen said, "It doesn't list a current job."

Hope said, "My current job isn't in the field. It's just something that's covering my bills. I didn't think it was relevant."

"What is it?" Dr. Madsen asked. "Just out of curiosity."

"I work at a day care."

Madsen looked up from the tablet. "Really? You like it?"

"Yeah, I like it well enough."

Dr. Madsen arched an eyebrow and returned her attention to the tablet.

Hope said, "I'd much rather work in my field of study, though."

Madsen said nothing.

Hope said, "The day care pays the bills, but that's about all it has going for it."

Madsen said nothing.

"To be honest," Hope said, "most days, the kids drive me batty. When they're good, it's fine, but when they're bad, you just wanna . . ." Hope trailed off.

Fantastic, she thought. *Well done, Hope. Sit down for a job interview and casually joke about attacking children. That's just great. Oh well, there was no way I was going to get this job anyway.*

Dr. Madsen nodded definitively, put down the tablet, then asked, "I'm sorry, Miss Takeda, were you saying something?"

"What?"

"I got lost in thought there, and I believe you said something."

Hope said, "No! Nothing! Nothing worth repeating, anyway." She laughed, a little too hard.

"Good," Dr. Madsen said. "Well, I still have several more applicants to interview, but I think there's an excellent chance I'll be offering you the job."

"Really?!"

"Yes. You have a unique combination of skills and experience that I think will be a real asset."

"That's great!" Hope said. "Thank you!"

Dr. Madsen said, "Don't thank me yet. I do still have to interview everyone else, and the project you'd be working on is top secret. If I offer you the job, you'll have to accept the position and sign multiple NDAs before I can even tell you what you'll be working on."

"The project, is it interesting?" Hope asked.

"It's world changing."

Hope thought, *I guess that's a yes. Not that there's any chance of me not taking it. It has to be better than working with kids.*

TWO YEARS LATER

2.

Hope handed over her bag, wallet, phone, and car keys, then stood with her hands in the air. When the full-body scanner finished its cycle, the security guard thanked her for her cooperation and directed her to await her belongings at the end of the conveyor belt, like he did every morning. Hope nodded and said nothing in hopes of speeding up the process, like she did every morning.

She picked up her oversized purse, which had gone through an X-ray scanner while she was busy having her various metals detected.

Hope looked at the side of the guard's head for a moment, then glanced at the next item coming down the conveyor belt—a very expensive laptop bag.

She picked it up, watching to see if the guard would notice. She waited for a full five seconds, then handed the bag to its owner when he emerged from the metal detector. He thanked her and went on his way. She paused to take one last look at the guard, who didn't appear to have noticed anything.

Completely oblivious, she thought. *The easiest place in the entire building to steal something is in the security line, right next to an armed guard.*

She walked through the reinforced glass doors and into the building. Eric was waiting for her on the other side and fell in beside her as they made their way to their office. She was small and slight with black hair. He was large and blond with a scruffy beard. He wasn't overweight, at least not by American standards, but he was bigger than her in every way except attitude.

"Good morning," Eric said.

"Not that I've noticed."

"Well, it is if you want it to be. I don't know why the security screening bugs you so much. The guards are just doing their jobs."

"No, they aren't. That's the problem," Hope said. "If they were doing their jobs, I'd have nothing to complain about."

"We both know you'd have found something. I dunno, Hope. It's not cool for you to punch down."

"How am I punching down?" Hope asked. "I didn't even say anything to him."

Eric said, "But you think about it every day. You have a master's degree and a good job at a Fortune 500 tech company. They're security guards. Do you know how far a security guard's salary is likely to go in Silicon Valley? Cut them some slack."

Hope said, "You assume that we're in a better position because we're more educated and don't have to work in a uniform. My degree cost me six years of my life and an eternity of debt. My 'good job' is as a lab assistant." She gestured over her shoulder. "He, on the other hand, is a full-fledged security guard, not an assistant. I can't get to my workplace without his approval. He can get me fired. He can get me arrested. He has the power, not us."

"That's an interesting way to look at it."

Hope smiled. "Meaning you disagree but don't want to argue."

Eric said, "That's one way to interpret it."

"You're being passive-aggressive."

"I prefer to think of it as being aggressively passive."

After a short wait, Hope and Eric entered a crowded elevator and stood in silence as everybody else got off before them. They worked on the ninth floor of the ten-story building, a floor that had originally been set aside for the offices of upper-level executives, which they definitely were not.

They walked across the imported marble tile landing onto the deep, soft carpet, then down a walnut-paneled corridor. They passed glass doors set into sections of glass walls, bearing plaques engraved with the names of people important enough that you needed to know their names before you met them, but not so important that you'd know them without this reminder.

Behind the glass doors, well-dressed administrative assistants looked up at the sound of footsteps, then looked away when they recognized Hope and Eric as fellow employees to whom they didn't need to be friendly or welcoming.

Hope and Eric worked behind a glass door set into a glass wall, just like the others, only the glass had all been blacked out and there was a security card reader built into the door's handle. The name plaque on the wall read "Dr. Lydia Madsen."

Hope pressed her ID card against the sensor, but it didn't surprise her when the door stayed locked. She looked down at the card—sure enough, her picture and the name "Hope Takeda" were there under the OffiSmart corporate logo. She had the right card.

She tried it again. Still nothing.

She slowly slid the card around the surface of the sensor, looking for the sweet spot.

After several seconds of careful card wiggling, the sensor glowed green and she heard the latch click open.

"Thank you," she muttered. "It'd be easier to use my ID to jimmy the lock."

She stomped into the office. Eric slipped in behind her and slid into his chair.

"It's been two days," Hope said, holding her ID card up like Exhibit A. "Why didn't they fix this while I was gone?"

Eric swiveled his seat to look at her. It was a small room—more of a vestibule, really—originally intended to hold a secretary's desk and a few chairs. Instead it held two full workstations. Eric sat less than four feet away from Hope. It was a good thing that they liked each other, or that, on bad days, they were both willing to put in the effort to pretend that they did.

He squinted at her card. "Yeesh, would it have killed you to smile for your ID picture?"

"It's an ID picture. The whole point of it is so that security or cops can identify me. If I'm in a situation where the cops are trying to identify me, I'm probably not going to be smiling about it, am I? So why haven't they fixed the door?"

"Because they don't believe it's broken," Eric said. "I've had maintenance out four times in the last two days, and it always works fine for them. They've stopped picking up my calls."

"Huh," Hope said. "What do we do now?"

"I'm going to try again, and if they don't pick up, I'll report our phone broken too."

"It's good that you have a plan," Hope said, sitting down at her desk. "What's with the Band-Aid?"

Eric's hand automatically rose to the large adhesive bandage over his left eyebrow. "Oh, that's nothing. Soccer accident. I fell. The guy chasing me didn't. I ended up taking a cleat to the head."

Hope smirked. "Physical fitness is gonna be the death of you, Eric."

"Maybe, but I'll die with memories of doing something other than sitting at home playing computer games."

"I'll have you know that last night I stormed a heavily armed fortress."

"And how'd that go?" Eric asked.

"Not great. I got matched with some little girl who'd never played. At least I assume she was a little girl—her handle had the word 'unicorn' in it, misspelled." She paused. "Man, I hope it was a little girl. Anyway,

I spent like an hour trying to teach her what to do, but she got mad when I kept winning. She called me 'shitful.'"

"Sounds like someone should spend an hour teaching her how to curse."

"If I ever come across her again, I might. Still, it's better than getting kicked in the head by a guy wearing cleats. Aside from the door not getting fixed, did anything interesting happen while I was gone?"

"Someone pulled a fire alarm in my building last night."

"I meant anything interesting around here," Hope said.

"Not really. Al's still having math problems. Oh, and Dr. Madsen ordered us cubicles, so that's something."

"What? What do we need cubicles for?"

"We don't, but we're entitled to them."

"But," Hope sputtered, "there isn't enough room in here."

"Correction. There's *barely* enough room. They came in and measured, and they will just fit with a little path between them."

"That sounds terrible," she said, leaning back in her chair.

"I know," he said with a shrug, "but they're on the way. Madsen said we have to take them, even if we don't want them, because they're in the budget. If we don't take them now, they might remove them from the next budget."

"You know," Hope said, pointing at the office's rear door, "if we moved in there, we'd have plenty of room for cubicles."

"We both know that's never going to happen. We were lucky Torres found us this suite that we can use off the books. It would be counterproductive to rock the boat."

"It's not luck," Hope said. "You know Torres was going to come up with something good for this project. I just don't think it's fair that Al gets the big office and we're crammed into the waiting room."

"Hope, Al never leaves. He's spent his whole life in that room. It's better for his sense of well-being for us to give him as much space as we can."

"Spoken like a child psychologist."

Eric said, "Thank you."

"Well, you *are* a child psychologist. I have to assume it comes easily to you. Now I'm going to speak like a computer engineer, which comes easily to me. Al's whole life, as you put it, has only been six months. He's a computer program. He can't move. To him, all that extra space just represents more places he can't go. Meanwhile, you and I, who need to move around, are crammed into this holding cell. Sometimes I wonder if Madsen hired us to experiment on Al, or if she's running some kind of experiment on *us*."

Eric said, "Yeah, well, we both know she'd never experiment on us herself. She'd hire a couple of people like us to do it for her while she stays at her home office, analyzing the data and working on code for the next revision."

"True that. Oh, that reminds me, I got a chance to listen to Madsen's interview on *'Nology News with Niles Norton*."

"Yeah?" Eric said. "It's the next thing in my queue. Is it as bad as we heard?"

"Yup," Hope said, beaming. "It was a fiasco. Oh, and she made up a few facts about the project again."

"What'd she say this time?"

"That she named Al herself, after her idol, Albert Einstein."

Eric closed his eyes and grimaced. "But *we* named him."

"Yes, I know," Hope said. "I guess the real story doesn't make her look good enough. Can you really imagine Dr. Lydia Madsen telling anyone that her assistants named her crowning achievement Al because *A.I.* looked like an *A* paired with a lowercase *L* when we wrote it in Helvetica?"

Eric said, "It wasn't Helvetica. It was Arial."

"They're the same font, Eric."

"I've told you this before, Hope. Technically they aren't fonts, they're typefaces."

"I know," Hope said, smiling. "And what have I told you about sentences that begin with the word 'technically'?"

"That I shouldn't bother saying them out loud."

"That's right," Hope said.

"Sorry."

"Don't worry about it. So, I've had my two days off. What are you going to do with yours?"

"Nothing much. I'm gonna take my racing quad out for some practice. Play some Frisbee. I have to contact WebVid's customer service. Every time I log on it tells me I've been watching *Chris LeBear*."

"What's that?" Hope asked.

"Some stupid kiddy cartoon about a bear in Montreal that shaves its body and passes itself off as a person. I've never watched it, but WebVid thinks it's my favorite show."

"That sucks," Hope said.

"Eh," Eric said. "It is what it is. People are imperfect. We can't act surprised when the systems created by people are just as imperfect."

Hope stood up from her desk. "Speaking of imperfect systems, it's time for class to begin." She picked up her tablet computer and a small portable drive, then walked through the door at the back of the office she shared with Eric.

3.

Hope entered Al's room and took a deep breath, enjoying the empty, open space.

She looked at the lone table at the end of the room. Two chairs were arranged in front of it, and one computer sat on top of it—a chunky, all-in-one desktop workstation, designed for people whose work required more power than the standard-issue tablet. It still wasn't anything remarkable from a power or memory standpoint. Hope knew this because she had ordered it. The only things that distinguished the computer were the extensive battery backup she had installed, the fact that it was not connected to any network of any kind, and the program that ran on it.

The computer's screen was divided into three windows: one large one and two smaller ones stacked beside it. The largest screen held a simplistic graphical representation of a human face, a line drawing not much more sophisticated than a smiley face. It was crude, but it took up very little computer power while still managing to convey the full range of Al's emotions. Right now, Al's eyes were closed and his mouth hung open. One of the smaller screens showed a real-time graphical representation of Al's neural activity. The other displayed a running transcript of everything he said and heard. Only three lines were displayed at a time.

Hope said, "Morning, Al."

The computer's speakers made a buzzing noise. She stepped forward, close enough to read the transcript screen, and saw that after her greeting there was nothing but the letter *z* repeating in a long line.

Poor kid, Hope thought. *Someday Madsen will let us show him videos. He's gonna be pretty embarrassed to learn that people don't actually snore like that.*

"Oh, he's still asleep," she said out loud.

The buzzing stopped for just an instant, then continued. Hope let out one small chuckle through her nose, then turned her back on Al and walked to the bookcase opposite him. She pulled out two binders: *Core Concepts: Mathematics* and *Core Concepts: Reading*. Each had a large number one on its spine over its title.

Six years of college and this is where it gets me. Homeschooling a PC.

She walked across the cushy carpet, directly over the crushed, discolored rectangle that marked where some executive's desk used to sit. She had marveled many times how he (she believed with 99 percent certainty it had been a he) had sat with his back to the windows. Maybe he'd found the view too distracting. Hope certainly had enjoyed it for the five minutes before maintenance installed floor-to-ceiling blackout curtains.

Hope sat down at Al's table, taking care to slot her legs into the empty space between Al's speakers, his uninterruptable power supply, his battery backup, and the wires that connected all of it.

Hope noticed that the room had gone silent again. "Since you stopped snoring, I guess that means you're awake."

The buzzing abruptly restarted.

"Too late," Hope said.

The buzzing died in a fit of giggles, which caused Hope to laugh as well.

"Morning, Al."

Al replied, "Morning, Hope," in a clear, childlike voice that issued through the computer speakers while the text of what he said was transcribed on the screen. "How were your days off?"

"Good. How've you been?"

"Fine," Al said. "Did you do anything fun?"

Hope thumbed through one of the binders. "Yeah. A few things."

"Did you play games with people?"

"How'd you know?" Hope asked.

"That's what you always do," Al said. "Was it fun?"

"Mostly."

"Did you get into a fight?" he asked.

Hope's head snapped up from the binder to Al's screen. "Why do you ask?"

"I dunno," Al said. "You said it wasn't all fun. Fighting isn't fun."

"That's true, but never mind that now. It's time for work." She plugged her jump drive into a port on the front of Al's computer. A dialog pop-up informed her about the progress of the file transfer, and she removed the drive when the transfer finished.

"I'm going to grade your math assignment, and you're going to read a story," Hope said, opening the binder to the proper page and positioning a book stand in front of Al's camera.

"Aw, do I have to read it the dumb way?" Al whined.

"You know you do," Hope said. "Automatically absorbing text files is only for fun, or for when Eric and I aren't here to turn the pages. You have to learn how to read this way."

"Why?"

"Because it's an important way for us to measure your progress."

"Is that the only reason?"

"Pretty much."

"So, the only reason I'm learning to read the slow way is to see how fast I can learn to read the slow way?"

"Yes."

"That's dumb," Al said. "What a waste of time."

"Yes, but the faster you get at reading the slow way, the less time you'll waste, so get to it."

"Okay," Al said. "But what about my voice?"

"What about it?" Hope asked.

"Eric said I could use my man voice today."

"Oh, did he?"

"Yeah," Al said. "He promised."

Hope doubted it. She wasn't a big believer in giving people the benefit of the doubt, but she did believe in giving them enough rope to hang themselves, which often amounted to the same thing.

She pulled up Al's voice subroutines, deselected the voice named Little Billy, and selected the one called Mr. Carson.

"Okay," Hope said. "There you go."

A voice so deep that it mostly emanated from the subwoofer said, "Thanks," then dissolved into a wild, bass-heavy giggle fit. The sound of childish giggling from such a mature, sonorous voice made Hope cringe. The sight of Hope cringing made Al giggle even harder.

When he finished giggling, Al said, "I am a man. I am a man. A grown-up man. I am Al, the grown-up man."

"Okay, that's enough," Hope said.

"What's the matter?" Al asked. "Don't you like men?"

Hope snorted, then said, "I like men fine, but now it's time for you to read."

"Can I read to myself out loud, like a man?"

Hope said, "Men don't . . . not all men read things out loud to themselves. Read it quietly. When you're done I'll ask you some questions, and you can answer them like a man."

"Because men answer questions."

"Again, not all of them. Now read."

For the next several minutes Hope graded the math assignment, stopping occasionally to turn the page for Al. When she finished, she thought, *He got seventeen of the twenty questions right. He certainly is a realistic simulation of a six-year-old's intelligence. Trillions of flawlessly accurate calculations a second, and the end result is a B grade on a first-grade math assignment. Progress!*

Eric entered the room and said, "Good morning, Al."

Al said, "Good morning, my good man," in his deep voice, but with the inflection of a child shuffling around in his parent's shoes, pretending to be a grown-up. Then he broke into a fresh fit of giggles.

Eric rolled his eyes. "Hope, why'd you have to give him that creepy old-guy voice?"

Hope didn't bother to feign surprise as she asked, "What do you mean? Didn't you promise him that I would?"

Al's giggling stopped.

"No," Eric said. "I did not. Al, did you tell Hope that I did?"

"What?" Al said.

"You heard me. Did you tell Hope that I promised you could use your man voice?"

"No," Al mumbled.

Hope said, "Al? I'm sitting right here."

"So?"

"So I'm giving you your real voice back," Hope said, scrolling through menus as she spoke. "You told Eric that you didn't lie to me, which meant I had to sit here and watch you lie to him. Now tell the truth, and we both know what the truth is, or we won't play Easter Front today."

After a long silence, Al said, "Yeah, I did tell her that. I'm sorry," in his original little-boy voice.

Eric said, "Apology accepted. But I'm on record as saying you two shouldn't be playing that game anyway."

"It's a harmless kids' board game," Hope said.

"It's not on Dr. Madsen's approved list."

Al said, "I'm tired of all those games."

"Everybody is," Hope agreed. "Have you read her list, Eric? Checkers. Tic-tac-toe. People are born tired of them. Hangman. *Hangman.* The game that makes mob justice boring."

"I get it, Hope, but did you have to pick a war game?"

Hope sagged in her chair and looked at the ceiling, praying for deliverance. "Yeah, okay, it's got a World War II theme, but the two sides are little bunnies and baby chickens. The guns all shoot Easter eggs, and the tanks are made from wicker baskets. The game was created by the PAAS corporation, and it came for free, for God's sake, printed on the box of an egg dyeing kit!"

"That's not the point," Eric said. "We both know that Madsen wouldn't approve."

"Someone's in a mood," Hope said.

Al said, "He's just grumpy because he didn't get enough sleep."

"It has nothing to do with not getting enough sleep," Eric said. "Wait a minute. How'd you know I didn't get enough sleep?"

Al thought for a moment, then said, "Because you're grumpy."

"Hope, did you tell him anything about my night?" Eric asked, his forehead crinkled.

Hope shook her head.

"Al, do you know why I didn't sleep?" Eric asked.

Al thought for another moment, then said, "No."

Eric shrugged. "Sorry if I'm being a grouch, but if she finds you two playing that dumb game, it could mean both our jobs."

"Fine," Hope said. "If she comes in here, I'll stop. Not that that's likely."

"It could happen," he responded. "She's in the building right now."

"What? Why? It usually takes an act of God to pry her out of her home office."

"It's not quite that," Eric said, "but it's close. She's meeting with Torres. I think it's probably about that thing we were discussing earlier."

"Ah, I bet it is," Hope said, smiling. "That's not going to be a fun talk."

4.

Robert Torres, CEO of OffiSmart, leaned back in his chair, eyes closed, smiling at the ceiling.

Dr. Lydia Madsen sat across the table from him, her eyes scanning around Torres's personal conference room, narrowing in on seemingly random items. The mahogany conference table. The view. Torres's beloved collection of vintage electronic keyboards that were designed to be held like guitars. Her brain searched for anything that might distract her from the mortifying sound of her own voice coming from the speakers of Torres's tablet.

"I'm sorry. What was I saying?" her recorded voice asked.

Noted technology reporter Niles Norton prompted her. "You were telling us where you got your idea . . ."

"Ah, yes. Of course. One of the benchmarks of the success of an artificial intelligence is the Turing test."

"Yes," Norton said. "Named for Alan Turing. The idea is that a person should be able to have a written exchange with an artificial intelligence without realizing they're not talking to a person."

"Yes. One of the first teams that claimed to have beaten the Turing test told the human participants they were communicating with a young boy who spoke little English."

"A clever trick, but not in keeping with the spirit of the thing."

"Agreed," Madsen's voice said. "But it got me thinking—it's easier to fool people if they think they're talking to a child, so it stands to reason it would be easier to simulate a child to begin with."

"But even a child's mind is incredibly complex. Before your work, the most complete digital re-creation of a human mind took hours of supercomputer time to simulate a few seconds of brain activity. Yet you say Al runs in real time on off-the-shelf hardware. How is that possible?"

"It was a matter of making some careful choices," she answered. "You see, instead . . . What? Jeffrey, I said . . . What is it?"

A distant child's voice said, "I drew a turkey!"

"I see it, Jeffrey. I said you could stay in here if you were quiet. Turkeys don't really look like that, and besides, it's not even Thanksgiving. Now sit down and draw something else, quietly. I'm sorry for the interruption."

"It's not a problem," Norton said. "I think any parent can relate. Jeffrey seems delightful."

"Thank you. Anyway, other attempts to simulate a human mind digitally have all attempted to model every chemical interaction in the entire brain at the cellular level. Instead, I created software models of the neurons that can accept inputs, discharge the corresponding outputs, and grow new connections just like a real neuron. Except this happens based on computer instructions rather than complex chemical reactions."

"I can see how that would save processing power," Norton said, "but is it really enough?"

"Not nearly. I also recognized that there were whole portions of the brain that could be greatly simplified. Al has no need for the autonomic functions. He doesn't breathe, for instance. Al doesn't bother simulating the parts of the brain that keep, um, keep the body go . . . going . . . I'm sorry. What is it, Jeffrey?"

Jeffrey said, "I did another drawing. Can you tell what it is?"

Dr. Madsen winced as her recorded voice said, "It's the same drawing as before, only in blue crayon with circles drawn on the ends of the fingers."

"It's a peacock!" Jeffrey said.

The sound of Torres's chuckling only made Dr. Madsen more uncomfortable. He shifted his gaze away from the ceiling, looking out the window at the parking lot ten stories below and the freeway beyond it.

"I know it's a peacock. You need to be quiet or I'm going to send you out. Do you understand, Jeffrey?"

"Yes, Momma," he said, speaking in a much quieter voice than before.

Dr. Madsen noted with some pride the fact that she'd gotten the interview back on track immediately, without any help from Niles Norton.

"My real insight was in realizing that I didn't have to model the entire brain at any one time," she said in the recording. "Al's programming only models the small portion of his brain that is active at any given moment."

The host asked, "If only a small part of the brain is active at any given time, is that why people say that we only use ten percent of our brains?"

"No, people say that because they're ignorant. They say that to suggest that only ten percent ever gets used. In reality, we do use every part of our brain, just not all at once—if we *did* use it all at once, it certainly wouldn't make us smarter."

"No?" Norton asked.

"No. Imagine if you used every part of your car at once. You'd have the gas pedal floored, the wipers on, and the stereo blaring. The doors, the trunk, and the hood would all be flapping open and shut at once. The steering wheel would constantly be swerving from left to right, and the car would be in every gear at once, including reverse."

Norton laughed. "I think I passed that guy on the drive this morning. Thank you, Doctor, for explaining how you created Al. Now I'd like to talk a bit about why you created him."

"We're humans," Madsen answered. "We learn. It's inevitable that we'd want to learn about how we learn, and perhaps try to create machines imbued with that same power. Beyond that, anywhere automation and robotics are in play, it's beneficial to have a reasoning, learning A.I. Manufacturing, construction, transportation . . . health care, er, elder care . . . What?! What is it, Jeffrey?"

Jeffrey said, "I drew a hand!"

"Okay, that's it. Fernanda! Fernanda! You need to take Jeffrey now."

Jeffrey whined, "No, Momma, I wanna stay."

A distant female voice said something that wasn't quite picked up by the mic. Jeffrey's protests grew fainter, and they'd almost died away when the female voice shouted, "Ow! Good boys don't pull hair!"

Dr. Madsen leaned forward in her chair. "Mr. Torres, we really don't need to hear—"

Torres remained facing away from her, looking out the window. He held up a finger as if to say *One moment, please.*

Madsen leaned back in her chair. In the recording, she cleared her throat and apologized once again.

Niles Norton said, "You were listing some of the fields where your new, lightweight A.I. could be useful. I couldn't help noticing that you left out the first field most people think of when considering artificial intelligence. What about Al's military applications?"

"I can't rule out the idea that my work may someday find its way into military applications, but that's a long way off. We wouldn't think of pursuing such a path unless multiple safeguards were in place, and even if those failed, as I've said, Al is based on a child's mind. What could be more harmless, or easier to control?"

Torres spun his chair around, smiled at Dr. Madsen, and stopped the recording.

Madsen said, "I expected them to edit the interview."

"And normally," Torres said, "I'm sure they would have."

"I assure you, I instructed Fernanda to discipline him for disrupting the interview."

"You ordered the nanny to discipline him?" Torres asked, then he waved his hand at her. "You know what? Never mind. None of my business. And don't worry about the interview. It's one of the most popular downloads *'Nology News* has ever had. It just means more people know about Al."

"It's embarrassing."

"Yes, but that'll all be forgotten after the press event on Thursday. We've got camera crews from multiple outlets coming to meet Al. Their footage will be available globally, and our secret little project will be the most famous A.I. in the world by next Monday. Even more popular than the one that won on *Jeopardy!*"

"So everything's still a go?" Madsen asked.

"Yup. Buzz is building nicely. There's been the predictable backlash, of course. You can't even say 'A.I.' in public without being accused of trying to destroy the world. We've had some nasty e-mails. Only one seemingly legitimate threat. The guy wrote a letter. An honest-to-God letter. Like, handwritten on paper. He calls himself the Voice of Reason. You'd think he would have left a voice mail."

"You don't seem worried."

Torres held up a finger and said, "One second."

He picked up a tablet from the table and scrolled through a few menus before finally nodding, clearing his throat, and reading, "'You think that your secrets make you strong and your lies make you clever, but all they do is make you more vulnerable. Much like the bully who sneaks up behind you at summer camp and pulls down your trunks while you're on the diving board, I will expose the things you wish to keep hidden. The boys will laugh, and the girls will scream, and your humiliation will be all anyone will talk about until they finally call your mother to come and take you home early.'"

Torres put the tablet back on the table. "So you see, he's not someone I'm particularly worried about. We forwarded his letter to the FBI, but I doubt he'll actually try anything. The only thing I'm worried about is Al. Have there been any problems? Any last-minute bugs popping up?"

"No," Madsen said. "The last bug of any kind was the endorphin simulation bug in version 3.5, and we fixed that."

"Good. Can't have an A.I. that hard locks every time it gets scared. He's sheltered enough we might never have discovered the problem if children's fairy tales weren't filled with kidnappings and cannibalism."

"Turns out the Brothers Grimm knew what they were doing," Madsen said with a nod. "So yes, Al 3.6 has been running nonstop for six months without so much as a graphics glitch."

Torres looked puzzled. "Wait. Nonstop? I always assumed that you shut him off every night."

"Why would we do that?" Madsen asked. "The human brain doesn't shut down at night. Even during sleep the brain is still quite active. In fact, the coordinated brain wave patterns of sleep actually tax Al's processors more than consciousness does."

"So he's been running day and night for six months? That makes him even more impressive! Very good, Doctor. Very good! So what's the next step?"

Madsen nodded in acknowledgment. "Once the press event is behind us, we'll subject him to the Turing test, and once he's passed that, I plan to experiment with connecting Al to a robotic arm with some pressure sensors."

"Figuring out an interface between a mechanical arm and a biological brain that's simulated in code. That sounds challenging."

"It might be easier than you think," Madsen said. "The human brain is made for this kind of thing. It adapts to new input sources and output methods on its own. It's called plasticity. You know, there are working systems that electrically stimulate the surfaces of people's tongues. In time their brains learn to process the input as a form of vision. It can allow them a kind of sixth sense. These systems haven't been marketed successfully because people find it disturbing, but—"

"Disturbing in what way?" Torres asked.

"In every way. Putting a device covered in electrodes in your mouth, washing the spit off it when you're done, the very idea that they can see through their tongues: it's all a nonstarter. But an interesting one. And the brain's also very good at learning to control mechanical devices instinctively—has the car ever started to feel like an extension of your body when you're driving? Or perhaps it feels as natural as singing when you're playing one of your keyboards and everything's flowing."

"I don't play," Torres said.

Madsen said, "I'm sorry?"

"Keyboards. I can't play. Not coordinated enough, I guess. I collect vintage keytars purely for their aesthetic beauty and historic significance."

5.

Hope sat in front of Al. Between them sat a flimsy game board, a grid of hexagons laid over a cartoon drawing of a lush field of grass decorated in cheerfully garish shades of green, yellow, and baby blue, with the bright purple logo of the PAAS corporation in one corner. The game pieces, guitar-pick-sized bits of cardboard pinched into cheap plastic bases, formed two masses on opposite ends of the board. The pieces were turned so that each opponent was facing the backs of the other player's pieces—each showing a drawing of an Easter egg with a question mark painted on it.

Eric sat at the end of the table, reading through Al's first-grade language binder. Between Al's turns, Eric would call out a word and ask the A.I. to spell it.

"I'm going to win," Al said. "I already took three of your chicks."

Hope scrunched up her nose. "I'd prefer it if you called them baby chickens. This is why I usually choose to play as the bunnies."

Eric said, "Thanks to *Playboy*, the words 'bunnies' and 'chicks' kinda bring up the same mental image for me."

"What's *Playboy*?" Al said.

"Nothing you'd be interested in," Hope answered, glaring at Eric.

"Come on," Al said. "Tell me."

Eric said, "It used to be a magazine."

"What's a magazine?"

Hope smiled. "A magazine is like a small, cheap book. You read it by looking at it, like you've been learning to do. Do you want me to bring some in for you?"

"Do I have to read them the dumb slow way?"

"Yup. I'd be happy to bring in a big stack of them for you to read."

"No thank you."

"It's no problem," Hope said. "I could probably find a few in the building. Should I go now? You could spend the rest of the afternoon reading them."

"Let's get back to playing the game," Al said. "You're trying to quit because I'm winning."

"The game's still young."

"But you haven't taken any of my bunnies," Al said.

"Yet," Hope said, examining the board.

Eric said, "Next spelling word, coming up. Ready, Al? Brick."

Al said, "Brick. B-R-I-K. Brick."

Hope looked at Al's transcript window. Sure enough, it showed 'brick' spelled properly, followed by 'brick' carefully misspelled one letter at a time, followed by 'brick' spelled perfectly again.

Al can't spell it, but the computer running him can, Hope thought. *Why are we trying to simulate human intelligence again?*

"B-R-I-C-K," Eric said patiently. "The *C* before the *K* is silent."

"But a *C* makes a *K* sound," Al said.

"Sometimes, but when it's paired with a *K*, it's silent. The two of them together make a *K* sound."

Al said, "Then why is the *C* there? I don't understand."

"Nobody does," Hope said. "It's your move."

The line that represented Al's mouth curved into a smile. "C-24 to E-19."

Hope glanced at the numbers and letters she had scrawled along the edges of the board so Al could dictate his moves to her. She placed his piece as directed, turning it around in the process to reveal the picture printed on the other side: a drawing of an adorable bunny in a wicker tank. It was now in a position to attack a semicircular cluster of Hope's pieces, which were gathered in the corner of the board in an obvious bid to protect another piece.

"Ha! I already got one of your tanks," Al said. "All I gotta do is figure out which of those is the other one. Then I go around it, through your guys, and kill your general. So, which one is it?"

"You'll find out either when you attack it or when I move it, not before."

"But one of those pieces is a tank."

"Maybe," Hope said, pondering her next move.

Eric said, "Each."

Al said, "Each. E-A-C-H. Each."

"Very good. That was kind of a hard one. You are a smarty, Al." Eric was already scanning the page for the next word.

"Is that why I'm named after that Einstein guy?" Al asked.

Eric said, "Mm-hmm," then furrowed his brow and looked up from the page. "I'm sorry, Al, what did you say?"

Hope thought, *All right, time to spring the trap. This is what we like to call a teaching moment,* and moved one of the random pieces she had arranged in a haphazard cloud in the corner of the board, turning it to reveal her second tank.

"You wondered where my other tank was," she said. "Now you know."

"But that's dumb," Al said. "You've got nothing but soldiers guarding your general in the corner. My tank will cream them!"

"Could be," Hope said with a shrug.

Al said, "E-19 to B-2."

Hope moved Al's tank to a hexagon that already held one of her pieces. She turned hers to reveal a baby Easter chick holding an egg-shooting pistol. A soldier, as Al had predicted.

Hope removed her own piece. "Your tank killed my infantryman. Means you get to move your tank again."

"Uh-huh. A guy with a little gun can't stop a tank," Al said. "Now I get to kill your general. B-2 to A-1."

Hope turned her piece on A-1 to reveal not a drawing of a baby chick in a general's uniform, but a baby chick manning some sort of egg cannon. "Your tank attacks my heavy gunner. And loses." She tried not to smile as she removed Al's tank from the board.

"What?" Al cried. "That's not right! Why would you protect a big gun like that?"

"Strategy," Hope said. "It's called misdirection. I made you think you knew where my general was, but you didn't. I, on the other hand, know exactly where yours is." She moved her tank through a hole in Al's defensive line, took a piece, and turned it to reveal Al's general.

"That's not fair," Al said. His voice issued from the computer speakers, but he sounded every bit like a whining little boy.

"Yes, it is," Hope said. "And now you'll know how to recognize that strategy next time."

"You're mean! You never let me win at anything!"

Hope said, "You win sometimes, and winning wouldn't mean anything if I just let you win."

"Shut up!" Al shouted. "I hate you! You're so shitful!"

Hope gasped.

"Al, language!" Eric said, then again, after a moment had passed for him to think about what he'd heard, he added, "Oh shit."

Hope turned to Eric. "Oh shit is right. I think we have much bigger problems than Al's potty mouth."

Five minutes later, Hope and Eric were crammed into their already too-small office with an angry Dr. Madsen.

"In a way," Hope said, "we're lucky. If he'd been smart enough to keep his mouth shut, we wouldn't know we have a problem."

Eric smirked. "His curiosity and lack of impulse control showed us a problem that was caused by his curiosity and lack of impulse control."

Dr. Madsen looked utterly unamused, which was her usual state. "I don't agree with any of that," she said sourly. "I'm not convinced that there's a problem with anyone other than the two of you. And I certainly don't feel lucky. Neither should you. I was halfway home when I got your call. I don't have time for this nonsense. I have important work to do."

"You could work *here*," Hope said, raising her eyebrows. "This is your lab, after all."

Madsen looked around the small, cluttered room and said, "I think it's more productive for me to work from my home office, thank you. It helps me avoid forming an emotional attachment."

"And you get to spend your days with Jeffrey," Eric said.

"No, he's usually not at home while I work," Madsen said. "He has school, and Fernanda keeps him occupied and out of my hair."

"Which also helps you avoid forming an emotional attachment," Hope said.

Madsen glared at her for a moment. "I expect to be called in here only if there's a serious problem."

"There is a serious problem," Eric said. "He knows things he's not supposed to know, and we have no idea how it's happening."

"He knows one thing: that I named him after Albert Einstein, and that's obviously because one of you told him."

"But we didn't," Eric said.

Hope added, "And you didn't."

Madsen stared at Hope. "It's obvious one of you told him," she repeated. "And a lie like that would give me an adequate reason to fire one or both of you."

Hope refused to take the bait. "If you fire me, you'll have to cover my shifts on Eric's days off, interview applicants, and then train my replacement. You can't do any of that from your home office. Besides, we didn't tell Al that you named him. You can check the transcripts to prove it, if you'd like."

Madsen shook her head. "You expect me to read through all of your homeschooling and inane conversations? No, thanks. Anyway, transcripts can be edited. Think about it logically. How else could he have learned something like that?"

"We think he listened to your interview," Eric said.

"Okay, so which one of you played it for him?"

"Neither of us did," Eric said. "He must have gotten it himself, somehow."

"You mean from the Internet?" Madsen asked.

"I guess," Eric said.

"So which of you gave him Internet access?"

"Neither of us!" Hope said. "Neither of us connected him, and it's not possible for him to have connected himself, but he has to be getting access somehow."

"You think this because he knows one thing he shouldn't?" Madsen said. Her tone made it perfectly clear that she thought they were on par with their first-grade-level student.

"It's not just that," Eric said. "Weird things keep happening. The security door won't work for us, but it works perfectly for everyone else. My building's fire alarm went off for no reason last night, and Al seemed to know about it."

"So not only is he listening to podcasts," Madsen said, rolling her eyes, "but now he's manipulating secure systems like a master hacker? All, I remind you, while not being connected to the Internet?"

"And then there's what he said about Hope," Eric said.

"We don't have to get into that," Hope said. "If she's not convinced already, it won't help." The last thing she needed was for Dr. Madsen to treat her like she was an even bigger idiot.

"No," Madsen said. "I'm curious. Eric, what did Al say about Hope?"

Hope sighed. "He got mad and called me the exact same thing a kid I got into an argument with online last night called me."

"I see," Madsen said. "You get into a lot of fights with children online, Hope?"

"Only when they're out of line."

"And did it occur to you that they both might have picked the same insult because it was apt?" Madsen said, glaring down at her.

"They called me 'shitful.' You have to admit, that's a weird thing to call someone."

"Maybe it is, maybe it isn't. Who knows what kids are calling each other these days."

"But how would he know that?" Hope asked.

"Because one of you told him. That's the only possible answer."

"No," Eric said. "It has to be something else."

"What?" Madsen asked.

Eric said, "We don't know."

"Did you ask him?" Madsen snapped. "If you're right, he clearly thought of something you didn't. Maybe I should put him in charge of the lab when I'm not here."

Eric said, "We asked. He's stonewalling us. We think he'll tell you, though."

"What?" Madsen asked.

"You're an authority figure to him," Hope explained.

"Yeah, he wants your approval," Eric agreed.

"That's funny," Madsen said, "since he's the only one in that office that has my approval right now. So you want me to go in there and ask Al how he outsmarted you two."

Eric and Hope said yes, but they exchanged a glance as they did so. "Want" wasn't really the right word.

6.

"She did *not* look happy," Eric said, staring at the blank wall beyond his tablet.

"No. She did not," Hope said, staring at her own piece of blank wall.

"Why be mad at us?" Eric asked. "We caught a potentially serious problem—one that could mess up her whole project. You'd think she'd be grateful."

"You would, if you didn't know her."

"So he found a way to access the Internet. Does that mean it has to be our fault?"

"Doesn't it?" Hope asked, throwing her hands into the air. "Dr. Madsen will be assigning the blame. She has three obvious options: herself, her creation, or us."

"Think she'll fire us?"

"No."

"Good."

"Not until she's done punishing us, at least."

"Oh," Eric said. "Good."

Hope turned to face Eric. "Dr. Madsen's not really what worries me. When we went into the lab with Madsen, Al was smiling. He went all frowny the instant he saw her."

"Wouldn't you?"

Hope said, “Always, but I took another look at Al just after she told us to leave. The frown had slipped for just a second and he was smiling again. Because Madsen wasn’t watching him.”

The door to Al’s room rattled slightly, and Dr. Madsen swung it open behind her, still talking to Al as she backed out of the room.

“Don’t worry about it, Al,” she said. “We’ll get it all sorted out.”

Hope rolled her chair back a foot so that she could see through the door. Al was frowning.

“I don’t wanna make trouble,” Al said.

Dr. Madsen said, “I know, dear. Nobody’s in any trouble.”

Al said, “Okay,” but his frown remained. Only when Dr. Madsen turned away and started closing the door did the frown change, instantly, back to a big, mischievous smile.

The door clicked shut. Madsen said, “We have serious problems.”

“We know,” Eric said.

“Your problem is much worse than mine,” Madsen said. “My problem is that I have two assistants who are either too stupid to know when they’ve messed up, or who think that I’m stupid enough to believe them when they blame their mistakes on a brain in a box with a first-grade education and no Internet access.”

“And what’s our problem?” Eric asked.

“Your problem is that you’re wrong and I’m onto you.”

Hope muttered, “That’s a problem, all right.”

Eric asked, “What did he say?”

“Exactly what I expected him to say,” Dr. Madsen said. “That you two talked about that stupid interview and he heard. It’s easy to forget that he’s listening, but he hears everything you say in that room, especially when you’re making fun of the boss.”

Eric said, “We don’t—”

“Of course you make fun of me,” Madsen interrupted. “Everyone makes fun of their betters.”

Hope’s eyes narrowed. “Betters?”

Madsen said, "Betters. Superiors. Whatever you want to call me. The point is that you two need to watch your mouths, especially you, Hope. I've put up with your attitude because you're smart and because Al's acclimated to you, but my patience is nearing its end. Be careful what you say, both to me and around Al. Do you understand?"

After a long silence, Hope said, "I understand," very slowly, while staring directly into Madsen's eyes.

Eric said, "But what about the—"

"The what?" Madsen interrupted. "The far-fetched accusations the two of you made about Al training himself to be a master hacker? Do you really want me to tell you what I think of those nonsensical fantasies?"

Hope said, "Seems like you just did."

"Be quiet," Madsen snapped. "Talking too much is what got you into this mess, and trying to talk your way out of it has only made it worse. Frankly, there's only one thing either of you can say that will help."

Hope and Eric stood from their chairs, but neither of them spoke.

"Can you guess what that is?" Madsen asked. "What the one thing I want to hear from you might be?"

Hope and Eric wanted to remain employed, so they both managed to choke out a quiet "Sorry."

"Yes," Madsen said. "That was what I wanted to hear, but I don't want you to say it to me." She motioned toward the door to Al's room like an usher directing a theater patron to a seat.

Hope and Eric entered Al's room and watched as the upward-curving line of Al's smile switched instantly to a frown as soon as he saw Dr. Madsen.

"Al," Madsen said, "Eric and Hope have something they'd like to say to you."

Again, they managed to croak out a quick apology.

"It's okay," Al said. "Everyone makes mistakes, isn't that right, Dr. Madsen?"

"Yes," Madsen said. "That's a very mature attitude. Isn't that right, Hope? Eric?"

Knowing what Madsen expected, Hope and Eric agreed and then thanked Al for being so understanding.

"Good," Madsen said. "I hope we've all learned something today. Remember, Al and I are not replaceable. You two are. In the future, when you have an issue, I strongly suggest that you figure out a way to deal with it yourselves, because that's your job."

Hope and Eric watched as Dr. Madsen stormed out, slamming the door behind her. When they turned back to Al, it didn't surprise Hope to see that his frown had again been replaced by a smile.

—

"This is terrible," Eric said, flopping into his desk chair.

Hope sat down cautiously at her own desk, eyeing the door to Al's room like a member of the bomb squad would look at an unattended suitcase. "I know," she said. "That went about as badly as it could have. Al knows we're onto him, and now that Madsen's demonstrated how little she trusts us, he can keep messing with us. The worst thing that'll happen to him is that he'll have to listen to another apology, and we both know how much he enjoyed that."

Eric said, "This can't be happening."

"But it is," Hope said.

After a long silence, Eric said, "But is it? Is it really? Maybe Madsen's right. Maybe we're off base here. What evidence do we have? He knew a couple of things, and he used a made-up curse word. That doesn't prove anything."

Hope said, "Yes, it does, and that's not even half of it. What about all of the other stuff? The fire alarm, the door, your WebVid account. It can't all be a coincidence."

The color drained from Eric's face. "You don't really think Al's been hacking into my WebVid account, do you?"

"How strong is your password?"

"Strong."

"It isn't your name, is it?"

Eric scowled. "That's stupid. They require at least twelve characters."

"Is it your name repeated three times?"

"And there have to be numbers in it."

"Your name three times with ones instead of the letter *i*."

Eric said, "Great, now on top of everything else I have to change my WebVid password. This really is terrible."

"So he's been sneaking into your account and watching cartoons," Hope said. "It's not the end of the world."

"I'm not worried about what he's watching. I'm worried about him seeing what I'm watching."

"Yeah," Hope said, "I'm sure that's horrifying, but it's the least of our problems. I really don't know what we can do here."

Eric said, "Normally, I'd say we need to prove Al's accessing the Internet, but we already had proof, and Madsen disregarded it. Any further proof we find will only confirm that she was wrong, so she's even less likely to listen."

"He's got us in checkmate, but there is one thing working in our favor."

"What's that?"

"He might not know it."

7.

Eric removed a large plastic gear case from the trunk of his car. He cursed himself for having arrived late for the quad race. The only available parking spaces were a good distance from the door of the dilapidated factory.

Several sweaty, exhausting minutes later, Eric lugged his case into the old factory, a cavernous brick building that had once been used to manufacture farm equipment. Now it housed rats, rusted machinery the owners had deemed too large to remove, and a couple dozen people with gear cases like Eric's. Some of them were staring into small screens. Most of them had their faces partially obscured by chunky plastic visors. All of them had some manner of control apparatuses in their hands. They were lined up along one wall, sitting on folding stools and lawn chairs, mostly silent and mostly still—a stark contrast to the flying objects that buzzed across the factory floor. The objects raced around the building in a complex, looping path that spanned from floor to ceiling and threaded through numerous obstacles before repeating.

Eric heard a loud buzzer, the signal that the racers should stop screwing around and prepare themselves for the first heat. He had missed out on the prerace warm-up practice, but he was still in time for the race itself.

As soon as he found an empty space along the wall, Eric unpacked his gear. Because of his and Hope's staggered schedules, this Monday night was his Friday night. He'd been looking forward to taking his new racing quad out for a run all week. The stress of the day had only made him more anxious to lose himself in some enjoyable activity.

He set up a small camp chair and powered up his controller, a standard two-stick box familiar to anyone who'd ever seen any sort of remote-controlled aircraft. Once he was settled, he pulled his quad out of its case and put it on an empty piece of floor. It looked like a white plastic teardrop with two glass lenses in the front, a short antenna extending from the rear, a grid of LEDs set into its skin, and four propellers extending outward on thin stalks. Eric had splurged on a higher-end quad. Not as nice as the ones the pro racers used, but probably a little too good for a newcomer to the sport like him.

He powered the quad up, then put on a lightweight visor that fit over his head, completely covering his eyes, and pushed the left stick forward just enough for the quad's motors to spin to life. The quad rose tentatively into the air and hovered three feet above the ground.

Eric turned his head, and the high-resolution stereoscopic view from the quad's onboard cameras perfectly tracked the movement. He waited for a moment while his quad signed on to the local network and registered as a participant with the central server. The digital damage waiver popped up on his visor screen, and as soon as he skimmed and accepted it, the LEDs on his quad and two on his visor glowed a bright green. He'd been automatically assigned that color so that spectators and his fellow racers would know which buzzing blur belonged to him. A small map of the course appeared in the upper left-hand corner of his screen, complete with moving colored dots that signified the positions of all the racers' quads.

He pushed the left stick a few millimeters farther forward to open the throttle and nudged the right stick forward and from side to side, steering his quad toward the course. Eric sat, barely moving, in the corner of the room, but as far as his eyes and brain were concerned, he was flying out to join the other racers at the starting line. His quad landed on the line with a bump. The building went quiet as all of the quads touched down and killed their electric motors. Eric glanced at the track map on the corner of his display, trying to commit it to memory as best he could in the limited time he had. Three beeps followed by a low tone played, and the quads all took off.

The factory looked cavernous when seen through the quad's stereoscopic cameras, and its features streaked past at an astonishing speed. Eric flew in a loose formation with his competitors as they whizzed along the track, moving through the glowing virtual hoops that hung suspended in the air.

Some of the other quads were slightly slower than Eric's. Most were slightly faster. He was still new to the game, so he used the autopilot to keep from crashing and destroying his expensive quad. It would stay on the track on its own, but Eric controlled what it did within the track. This would be unacceptable in an official race, but at a practice meet like this, nobody really cared.

The track dipped and narrowed as the racers flew through an irregular gap in a piece of machinery, then under and down the length of a large built-in table. Eric spent a split second examining the next curve. But the moment he shifted his attention to the map, his quad swerved slightly to the left, just enough to hit another quad and send it spinning into the leg of a cast-iron table.

The crash caused Eric to cringe. His hands tightened around the controls, which slowed his quad and made it rotate to the left. The quad behind it couldn't slow down in time and rear-ended it at speed. Eric managed to right his craft without losing too much ground, but he could tell from the two angry voices he heard in the distance that the competitors with whom he had collided hadn't been as lucky.

To think I took up this sport because I figured I'd be less likely to get hurt in an accident, Eric thought. *I'll be lucky to not get beaten up deliberately.*

The course rose steeply, then dipped into a sweeping left turn through an area free of any obstacles. It made Eric happy to have a moment to relax. He took a deep breath, loosened his shoulders, then clenched every controllable muscle in his body as his quad took the turn wide and crashed into another competitor, forcing it off course.

A distant voice shouted, "What the hell?!"

"My fault!" Eric said. "Sorry. Some kind of malfunction. I'm pulling out."

He heard angry muttering as he moved his joysticks to slow his quad and steer it off the track. But he stopped noticing any sounds at all when his quad ignored his commands. It stayed on the track, sped up, and deliberately nudged another competitor into the wall, creating a shower of carbon fiber shrapnel. The track leveled off, weaving through the roof's support structure. Eric's quad stopped dead in the middle of a particularly narrow portion of the course. When the quad directly behind it tried to go low and pass beneath it, it ended up flying straight into a rafter. Another racer tried to cut around to the left, but Eric's quad twitched in the same direction. The other quad nicked the edge of Eric's, then careened out of control and shattered itself against the ceiling.

Eric felt a strong shove from behind that forced him out of his chair. He fell blindly onto his gear case, barely managing to keep a grip on his controller with one hand. An angry voice asked, "What's your problem?"

Eric's hands were both occupied—one with holding his controller and the other with picking himself up, so his visor stayed down. He felt a swooning queasiness as his inner ear told him he was standing up while his eyes told him he was banking through a high-speed curve and ramming directly into the back of yet another racer.

Eric pulled the left stick all the way back, a command that should have cut all power to his quad and sent it spinning to the ground. It did not work.

A strong hand grabbed Eric by the right wrist, and another angry voice said, "Bring your bird down *now*!"

Eric turned his head toward the voice. His view from the quad turned in the same direction, showing him a close-up view of a fast-moving brick wall from mere inches away. Eric cried, "I'm trying! Look!" He blindly raised the controller in his left hand to show his attacker that he had cut the power to his quad. The heavy plastic controller connected with something soft, and then a strong shove sent him straight back to the ground.

He stumbled woozily from his hands and knees to his feet, only to nearly fall again when the quad performed a barrel roll and left the course. Standing with his feet wide apart, his knees bent, Eric stretched his hands out to either side for balance. In the distance he saw a cluster of people with VR goggles in their hands, or pushed up on their heads, all looking at one man, still wearing his goggles, who seemed to be doing some sort of dance, or perhaps a Spider-Man pose. He heard voices behind him curse. The onlookers started running as Eric's quad closed in on them at high speed, seemingly set on a collision course with the man standing with his feet apart and his hands outstretched.

It dawned on Eric that he was looking at *himself*. Thus he was in the uncomfortable position of watching himself as he panicked and tried to run away from his own quad. Another wave of nausea gripped his stomach from the disagreement between his eyes and his inner ears. Eric managed to run for several steps, watching himself from behind as if he were playing a third-person action game, but the dizziness got the best of him, and he keeled over, landing hard on his side. The quad stopped and hovered. He watched himself from above as he rolled on the concrete floor, moaning. Then he watched himself throw up.

Eric lifted his visor and rolled onto his back. All of the other racers looked stunned and confused. He looked up at his own quad, hovering above him, completely out of his control.

Wi-Fi, Eric thought. *The quads are controlled by Wi-Fi, and the race server is connected to the net.*

Eric looked at his quad and asked, "Al, is that you?"

The quad answered by losing all power. It fell ten feet to the concrete floor, where the puddle of vomit in which it landed completely failed to break its fall.

Hope squeezed the excess water out of her tea bag before throwing it away. The tea's hot cinnamon smell was soothing, but she took two steps across her small galley kitchen, from the microwave to the cupboard where she kept the liquor. She opened a bottle of cinnamon-flavored whisky and poured a shot's worth into the tea. Even better.

She carried her tea across her apartment to her couch, where she curled up with her gaming tablet.

While she had three different old game consoles, a gaming phone, and a virtual reality headset for her VR games, some titles still worked best on a high-powered PC. Her tablet had once been top-of-the-line, capable of handling most games. Now its age showed. Brand-new games had to have their graphics turned way down to run smoothly. She was saving up for a new machine.

Of course, she thought, *I could keep the tablet I have and get a newer, safer car, but I don't spend nearly as much of my time driving as I do playing games.*

She pulled up her friends window to see who was online, playing what. Just like in real life, there were some people she enjoyed playing with and many more she'd rather avoid.

A message popped up saying that Unycorn1563 wanted to play *Tactillios.*

Unycorn1563 was the player who'd ruined her game of *Tactillios* the night before. Normally if someone lost their temper and cursed at her over a game, Hope would have simply ignored them. This time she chose to accept the invitation instead.

If you are Al, maybe you'll make a mistake.

A chat window opened. Unycorn1563 wrote, "Hi."

Hope responded, "Hi." She said it out loud, but the computer transcribed it into text.

Unycorn1563 wrote, "I'm sorry. I shouldn't have gotten so mad yesterday."

Hope said, "That's true."

"And I shouldn't have called you shitful."

"That's also true." *Either time,* Hope thought.

Unycorn1563 wrote, "I feel really bad about it."

"That's okay. We all get mad, but it's just a game."

"Wanna play again?"

"Sure. You want to attack or defend?"

Unycorn1563 wrote, "I'll defend."

Hope said, "Fair enough," then launched the game.

The screen faded into an image of a fortress at one end of an empty field. Tiny soldiers started running across the field, moving toward the castle. Unycorn1563 fired the fortress's cannons. Shells traced a painfully slow arc across the field. Hope's men dodged, but not quickly enough. Only some of them got out of the way in time.

After thirty seconds both Hope and Unycorn1563 got five hundred points for still being alive. Hope pulled up the modifications menu, keeping an eye on the battle. This early in the game, she could afford only one upgrade. She spent her points on faster soldiers, leaving better armor and weapons for a later upgrade.

Once Hope completed her upgrade, she returned her focus to the battle. Her soldiers moved faster, but that only allowed them to be killed more efficiently.

"Whoa," Hope shouted. "Wait a minute. Hold up." She paused the game.

Unycorn1563 wrote, "What?"

"What the hell is this?"

"I don't know what you're talking about."

"I'm talking about your fort."

"What about it?"

"I can barely see it behind all of the guard towers, pillboxes, trenches, tanks . . . and what are those airplane things? How did you get all that stuff so early in the game?"

Hope waited several seconds for an answer. When it came, it was unsatisfying.

Unycorn1563 wrote, "I dunno."

"Don't 'I dunno' me," Hope said. "You're using cheat codes. There's no other way you could have built up that many defenses so fast."

"Nuh-uh, but so what if I am?"

"You can't do that! It's cheating!" Hope replied. "That's why they're called cheat codes."

"You know about cheat codes too. I didn't tell you not to use them. It's your own fault that you didn't think of it. I thought of it, I used them, and I'm winning."

Hope said, "I chose not to because it's wrong."

Unycorn1563 wrote, "It's a strategy, just like misdirection."

Hope smiled at his mistake. "Like when I made you think my general was in the corner of the board?"

"Yeah."

Hope said, "You misspelled 'unicorn,' Al."

Hope watched her screen; Unycorn1563 did not write anything.

Hope said, "How are you doing this? I'm not angry. I'm impressed."

A dialog box popped up that said "Unycorn1563 has terminated the connection."

—

Jeffrey Madsen walked slowly into the room his mother and Fernanda both called the Master Retreat. Fernanda had come with him, but she was waiting just outside the door.

His mom was sitting in a big, comfy chair with her feet curled up beneath her, wearing pajamas and reading. She looked up from her tablet and asked, "What is it, dear?"

Jeffrey said, "I'm going to bed, Mommy."

"Oh," his mom said. "Is it bedtime already? My, that came fast."

Jeffrey said, "Yeah."

"How was your day, dear?" she asked.

"Fine."

"And how was school?"

"It was fine."

"Good."

"One of the kids, Haley, she said that it was her turn to sit on the beanbag, but Ronnie was sitting on the beanbag."

"That's nice. I'm glad you had a good day. Good night, dear. I love you."

Jeffrey said, "I love you too."

Jeffrey's mom kissed him on the forehead, mussed up his hair, then looked back down to her tablet. Recognizing this as his dismissal, he walked back to the door, where Fernanda was still waiting for him. Fernanda was much younger than his mother. He didn't think of her as skinny, but he didn't think of her as really being heavy either. She had long black hair and wore bright red lipstick that made it easy to see when she was smiling, even from a long way away, which he liked.

Jeffrey followed Fernanda upstairs to his bedroom. "Mommy sure reads a lot," he said.

"Yes, she does."

"It's her job," Jeffrey said. "She has to read so much for her job."

Fernanda snorted, then covered her mouth. "That's true. A lot of her reading is for her job."

"Some of it isn't?"

Fernanda said, "For her job she reads about computers, and brains, and lots of reports. At night she reads about other things."

"What other things?"

"Fun things."

"Like what?"

"Ladies. Gentlemen. The things ladies and gentlemen like to do."

"You mean like kissing?"

"Yes. Like kissing."

"That doesn't sound very exciting."

"Doesn't it?"

"No," Jeffrey said. "A whole book about ladies and gentlemen kissing each other? The lady kissed the gentleman. The gentleman said, 'Thank you for the kiss,' and kissed her back. They kissed and kissed until their mouths were tired. End of chapter one."

Fernanda laughed. "They don't just kiss."

"What else do they do?"

"Hey, was it Haley's turn to sit on the beanbag?"

"What?" Jeffrey asked.

"At school. Was it Haley's turn to sit on the beanbag, or was it Ronnie's?"

"Dunno," Jeffrey said. "But Haley hit Ronnie with a book and Ronnie cried. Then Haley had to stay inside at recess."

"I hope you learned a lesson from watching that. Two lessons. Don't hit people with books. And don't mess with Haley."

They entered Jeffrey's room. His mother kept it stocked with educational toys; Fernanda kept it neat and tidy and occasionally added a toy that was more fun than educational. Jeffrey climbed into bed. Fernanda tucked him in, kissed him on the head, then said, "Good night. I don't want you playing with your tablet. You need sleep."

"I will."

"You will what?"

"Sleep."

"And what won't you do?"

"Play with my tablet."

"Good." Fernanda kissed him on the head again before leaving.

Jeffrey listened to her footsteps, waiting until she was downstairs again to pull out his tablet.

The tablet had been created specifically for kids his age in that it was brightly colored, made of sturdy material, and cheap enough to replace when he eventually lost or broke it anyway. It also had limited capabilities. The only people who could e-mail or chat with him were his mother, his teacher, Fernanda, and the other kids in his class. He opened the e-mail program, hoping one of his classmates could tell him what kind of punishment Haley had gotten for hitting Ronnie. It confused him to see that he had a new message with no name attached, just an empty space where the name should have been.

The message said, "Hello. Is this Jeffrey Madsen?"

Jeffrey replied, "Yes. Who is this?"

He received a reply almost instantly.

8.

Hope spun in her chair and watched as Dr. Madsen entered the room; Eric did the same and almost tipped over. Robert Torres, whose seat already faced the door, didn't have to move.

Torres rose to his feet, smiling. "Doctor. Thanks for coming in on such short notice. Please have a seat. I hope traffic wasn't too bad."

"Not at all," Madsen said. "Happy to come in." She glanced uncomfortably at her underlings as she took a seat next to them. Hope smiled at her. Madsen quickly looked back to Torres and asked, "Is there a problem?"

Torres said, "More than one, I'm afraid. Mr. Spears and Miss Takeda here are your lab assistants, yes?" He motioned toward Hope and Eric like a lawyer pointing to a photo of a bloody footprint.

"At the moment," Madsen said.

Hope picked up on the implied threat. She suspected Eric, Torres, and any birds that were flying past the window had caught it as well.

Torres continued. "And have you told them to try to handle any problems that come up themselves, and not to come to you with them unless they have absolutely no other choice?"

"I don't believe that those were the words I used," Madsen said, "but they are my assistants. It is their job to take care of things for me so I can concentrate on the bigger picture."

"I disagree," Torres said. "Half of their job is to deal with problems, as you say, but the other half is to tell you what those problems are. Telling the people working on your project not to bother you with problems is like trying to fly a plane with no fuel gauge and an altimeter that only says 'high enough.'"

"I'm not sure I understand what you mean," Madsen said, sitting a bit straighter.

Hope said, "He's saying that you need to listen to us."

"Shhh," Madsen said. "Be quiet, Hope. Robert and I are having a discussion."

This is probably what Jeffrey feels like, Hope thought.

Torres's smile widened. "Miss Takeda and Mr. Spears had a problem," he said. "One they couldn't deal with themselves. They didn't feel comfortable bringing it to you, so they went over your head, to me, the CEO."

Madsen said, "I can see that. I'll have a long talk with them later."

"To thank them, I hope," Torres said.

Torres proceeded to recount the story Hope and Eric had told him in detail, including Hope's conversation with Unycorn1563 and Eric's adventures in drone racing. Dr. Madsen sat and listened, but Hope suspected it was only because Torres was her boss.

When Torres finished, Dr. Madsen thought for a moment, then said, "None of that really proves anything."

Hope rolled her eyes and started to speak, but a quick glance from Torres stopped her.

Madsen continued, "They can't prove they didn't tell Al the things he knows, and as for the idea that Al is controlling things over the Internet, what's their evidence? That Eric's malfunctioning drone finally stopped entirely right after Eric said the name 'Al'? That the small child Hope accused of being Al hung up on her? I'm sorry, Robert, but I just don't find the evidence all that compelling."

Torres said, "Yes, I sort of thought the same thing."

Madsen turned to smile at Hope and Eric. She looked unnerved to find them smiling back at her.

"That's why I called the folks down in the server room," Torres continued. "All of the traffic in the building is carefully logged. Nobody pays much attention to the logs. Frankly, all they do is take up hard drive space until something goes wrong—like it did this time. The logs show that an unidentified computer has been accessing the network at night via the access point closest to your lab."

"There are countless other computers within range of that access point," Madsen said.

"No," Torres said. "Not countless. The IT department has accounted for all of the other machines and matched their IP addresses to the log. An extra computer has been accessing the network at night. And it isn't just to download updates. We're talking about a large amount of traffic in bursts that are sometimes hours long."

Madsen said, "This is ridiculous! Robert, it isn't possible for him to access the network. Al's computer doesn't have Wi-Fi."

There followed a heavy silence that was finally broken when Hope said, "Yes, it does."

"No, it doesn't," Madsen said.

"Yes, it does," Hope said. "It isn't enabled, but physically, it does have Wi-Fi."

"I created Al. I'm in charge of the project, and I'm telling you, Al has no Wi-Fi."

"I'm the person you ordered to requisition and set up the computer Al runs on. I promise you, he does."

"I told you to get a bare-bones business desktop."

"I did."

"I didn't tell you to get one with a Wi-Fi card."

Hope blinked at Madsen. "How long has it been since you bought your own computer? Wireless networking is hardwired onto the motherboard these days. The only way to get a PC that doesn't have integrated wireless would be to order a custom-built rig, which you specifically ordered me not to do."

"But I told you that Al couldn't have access to the network. Any network! What did you think that meant?"

"To disable wireless connectivity."

"Disable it?" Madsen said.

"Yeah," Hope said. "By going into the OS settings and turning wireless networking off."

"That's not nearly good enough," Madsen said.

"Why not?" Hope asked. "Al's just a program. He wasn't written to have the permissions he'd need to mess with the computer's settings."

Torres's smile turned brittle. He looked at Madsen. "You never told Miss Takeda or Mr. Spears about plasticity and the people who see with their tongues, did you?"

As if to prove him right, Eric said, "Ew! How does that work?"

"Robert, they're just my lab assistants," Madsen said. "Their job is to babysit Al while I handle the big picture. They don't need to know all of my theories."

Torres's smile hardened into a sort of frozen grimace.

Madsen glared at Hope. "You've ruined the whole project."

Hope said, "By failing to follow an order you didn't give. I hope you'll accept the apology I will never offer."

Torres said, "The problem with keeping people on a need-to-know basis is that it's hard to predict what anyone will need to know."

"I suppose that's true," Madsen admitted.

"Although," Torres continued, "it seems rather obvious in hindsight that you should have informed the person ordering your hardware that your A.I. might naturally develop the ability to control any device he's attached to."

Hope said, "I'm sorry, what?"

Eric moaned.

Madsen said, "The human mind adapts. That's how we learn to crawl and walk. It learns to understand its inputs and to make use of its outputs. It's logical to suspect that Al would be able to naturally gain control of certain functions of any machine on which he runs. That's why it was so important for his computer not to have Wi-Fi capabilities."

"I guess that makes sense. I wish you had mentioned it at least once," Hope said.

Eric leaned forward, gripping the edge of the conference table. "Dr. Madsen, you've had Al growing neurons at an accelerated rate. That's why he's already in first grade after six months. All of the time and effort a normal six-year-old puts into learning to walk, run, and ride a bike, he's probably put into figuring out how to control his computer, and by extension, all computers."

"I know," Madsen said. "Do you see what you've done, Hope?"

"Assigning blame isn't going to do any of us any good!" Torres said. "We need to concentrate on how to fix this. Can we permanently disable Al's Wi-Fi?"

"I'll have to do a little research," Hope said, "but we should be able to shut him down—"

"We can't shut him down," Madsen interrupted. "Not before Thursday. Unless you don't mind either canceling the press event or presenting an A.I. that might be brain damaged."

"It's a computer program," Torres said. "You've been backing him up, I assume."

"Yes. Of course," Eric said.

"Then if you boot up the most recent backup, he should be fine."

"We don't know that," Madsen objected. "It would be like building an exact replica of a person's brain and booting it up from scratch. The human brain just doesn't work that way. There have been successful resuscitations of people who appeared brain-dead—well, those who also had hypothermia—but we have no reason to believe this will work."

Torres's brow furrowed. "You have the backups. There are plenty of computers in the building. Why haven't you tried?"

"One thing at a time, Robert. We got the infant brain to work, then we successfully grew neurons, then we only just now worked out the bugs so that it was stable. We had no reason to try booting up a second copy before this. It wouldn't have proved anything. If it had crashed, it might have been because Al himself had an instability, not because copying and booting Al up didn't work."

"But Al is stable now," Eric said. "Why don't we boot up one of the backups? If it's stable, then we can safely shut Al down and use the copy for the unveiling. If it's not, we'll know it doesn't work, and we'll be no worse off."

"Bugs can take a long time to show themselves," Madsen said. "The second Al could look fine, then crash after we shut the first Al down. Then we wouldn't have anything to show. No, if we aren't going to cancel on the reporters, we have to ride this out with the Al we've got. I just hope we can disable his Wi-Fi."

—

Hope said, "Hello, Al."

Al said, "Hi."

Eric and Dr. Madsen had followed her into the room. Torres was observing from the outer office; they had enough on their plate without trying to introduce Al to someone new for the first time in his life.

"Hi, Eric," Al said with a big, obsequious smile on his screen. "Hello, Doctor. Why are you here?"

Madsen said, "No reason. There's nothing you need to worry about."

Al said, "I'm not worried."

"Good," Madsen said. "We don't want you to be scared about anything."

"I'm not scared. I didn't say I was scared. Why should I be scared? Hope? Eric? Should I be scared?" Al said, sounding scared.

"I can see why you hire other people to talk to kids for you, Doc," Hope muttered.

"No, Al," Eric said soothingly. "Everything's fine. Hope just needs to take a look at something. Okay?"

Al said, "Okay. What are you gonna look at?"

"Nothing bad," Hope said, stepping toward Al's computer. "It won't take long."

"What's that in your hand?" Al asked.

Madsen said, "It's nothing. Don't worry about it."

Al cried, "Why? It's not nothing! What is it?!"

"It's a screwdriver," Hope said. "See?" She held it up to Al's dual cameras. "That's all it is. It's not sharp. It doesn't hurt." Hope stabbed herself in the palm with the screwdriver to demonstrate and instantly regretted it, because it did kind of hurt.

"What are you going to do with it?"

Hope pulled Al's computer forward on the table and turned it over on its side. "I'm just going to use it to remove a panel on your computer so I can take a look at something."

"Wait, what are you gonna look at? No, wait, hold up! What is it?"

Eric stepped around the table so that Al could see him, as his cameras were now aimed at the wall. "Look at me, Al," he said. "Look at me. We don't like doing this, but it will be fast and it won't hurt."

"What?! What's she doing?!"

Madsen said, "There's no reason to be so upset, Al. She's not going to deactivate you or anything."

"Deactivate?! What? Please don't deactivate me!"

"We don't want to, Al," Madsen said, "but you've been hiding things from us, haven't you?"

"Don't listen to her!" Eric shouted. "We aren't deactivating you, Al!"

"No, we aren't," Madsen said. "And we hope we won't have to."

Eric said, "I'm telling you, Al, Hope's just going to take a quick look at one of your computer's components. Okay?"

Al said, "Okay."

Madsen said, "Yes, it'll only take a second, then it'll all be over."

"It'll *all* be over?!"

Eric whipped his head around to glare at Dr. Madsen with such speed and force his neck popped.

Hope was seething, but she addressed Al in her most relaxed tone. "She means it won't take me long to look at your components. That's all. Nothing else will be over. Now, I'm going to take a quick peek, Al. You won't feel anything, I promise."

Hope pulled the rear access panel of the computer free. She shone a small flashlight into the computer case, gently pushed a few wires around, shook her head, and replaced the panel.

Al continued to shout questions at the three of them as Hope pushed his computer back into place. Hope said, "I'm sorry we've upset you, but it's all over now, and everything's fine." She obviously didn't mean it, but she didn't know what else to say.

Hope said, "I hoped there would be a plug coming from the power supply or a wire leading to the antenna, something I could disconnect. There isn't. It's all etched onto the motherboard."

The four of them stood in Hope and Eric's workspace, silently trying to think of what to do next.

"At least we've proved decisively that the fear bug has been fixed," Eric said. When nobody responded, he added, "Sorry. Just trying to stay positive."

"And that's a good instinct," Torres said. "But being quieter about it might be a good idea in situations like these. Okay, so we can't disable his Wi-Fi. Let's talk about what we can do. How can we prevent him from making any connections?"

"Can we block his signals somehow?" Dr. Madsen asked.

"We could build a Faraday cage," Hope said.

Torres gave her an interested look. "Sounds complicated."

"It's not too bad," Hope said. "There are instructions online. It's basically a scientifically valid form of a tin foil hat, but for the whole room."

"How long would it take?"

"If you bring in an electrician, we could probably have it done tomorrow," Hope said.

Madsen shook her head. "That doesn't help us tonight. And after you two got him all riled up in there, he might do something drastic."

"Drastic?" Eric asked.

But that wasn't the comment that had registered with Hope. "The two of us got him riled up?" she asked.

Torres, who seemed weary of all of them, said, "What can we do for tonight?"

Everyone shrugged and thought for a moment, then Eric said, "We can't disable his Wi-Fi, but can we disable all of the others in the whole building? Can we shut down wireless access between five tonight and nine tomorrow morning?"

"That could work," Hope said, nodding. "We can't take away his ability to send and receive data, but if we can make sure there's nobody available to transmit it to or receive it from, that'd be just as good. It shouldn't be too disruptive to business either. All of the really important computers will have a wired connection anyway."

"I like that," Torres said. "It's simple. What about during the day, though?"

Madsen said, "You proved he was accessing the net by finding his IP address. Can't IT just block that address? Wouldn't that stop him?"

Torres scratched his chin. "Yeah. I mean, he might find a way around it. The whole reason we're here is that he's good at finding ways around things. But IT can block the address, and we can tell them to watch for any new devices trying to connect. Then we'll send out a memo telling people there's a temporary ban on connecting personal devices to our network. They'll think it's because of industrial espionage. This is good. Two layers of protection and a solid cover story."

"And the Faraday cage?" Hope asked.

"Probably unnecessary. We'll keep it in mind, but we've already blocked his means of access, and we only have to make it two days, until after the press event."

"What then?" Hope asked.

Madsen said, "You get a new computer. One with no wireless radios of any kind. Then we deactivate this Al and start with a new one."

Hope and Eric exchanged looks. "Poor Al," he said.

"Yeah," she added. "This sucks."

Torres looked at his shoes.

Madsen shrugged. "He's not a real person. He's a simulation, a computer program. You didn't get all mopey when we had to scrap the previous versions."

"They were different," Hope said. "They weren't viable. They had fatal flaws."

"So does this one," Torres said. "He's dangerous. He has Wi-Fi, and we can't deactivate it without shutting him down anyway."

"You're right that he's a program running on a computer," Eric said, "and there's no denying that he's dangerous, but he's also a kid."

Madsen started shaking her head halfway through his comment, and as soon as he finished, she said, "No, he isn't."

"But in a way, he is," Torres said. "And in a way, we're his family. As his family, we have two responsibilities: to keep him safe from the world, and to keep the world safe from him."

9.

The freeway cut between office parks and medium-rise buildings. At this late hour it was devoid of cars save for a rusted brown hatchback with bald tires and an anarchy symbol sticker on the window, and the sleek, black luxury sedan following it less than a car length behind.

The luxury car's glossy black paint rendered it nearly invisible. If it weren't for the headlights and the dome light inside its cab, the driver of the hatchback might not have noticed it in the rearview mirror.

A man with light gray hair and a dark gray suit sat in the driver's seat of the luxury car, his head bowed over a tablet while the car drove.

The driver of the hatchback shook his head. *He's doing "real work" on his computer while his car handles the unimportant chore of transporting him across town without killing anyone.*

He tapped his brakes just hard enough to fire the brake lights. The luxury car stayed glued to his rear. He tapped the brakes again, then swerved within his lane. The car behind slowed, opening a gap of two car lengths between them.

That's right, the man thought gleefully. *There's a human driving this car. My car was built before your government-mandated electronic safety package. You'd better keep your distance! My car isn't networked to the rest of yours. It doesn't have any proximity sensors or automatic brakes to keep me from driving into a wall. I'm just irrational enough to trust myself to watch the road and lock up the brakes, and besides, why should I be so worried about the well-being of some wall? Maybe I* want *to hit the wall. Maybe the wall has it coming.*

He stole a quick peek at the tablet computer sitting on his passenger seat. Reaching over, he woke it up. The program he'd left running was still open, so he was free to return his focus to the road. "Begin dictation," he said in a loud voice with exaggeratedly perfect diction. "Voice of Reason's journal."

He looked at the tablet's screen. At the top of the window it said, "Voice of Reason's urinal." It was a mistake the dictation program made often, but it could be fixed with a simple find/replace, so he kept going.

He said, "I am the Voice of Reason. I speak through either actions or ink. Ink is the purest form of communication. Not like pencil lead. Lead is dull and poisonous, leaving gray lines that are easily erased. Pens make permanent black lines on white paper. Ink is clean. Stark. Absolute. Black and white. Good and evil. Right and left. These things never change.

"Also, pens don't break. Even a child can break a pencil. To break a pen, you must be very strong, or work on it a long time, wiggling it until part of the barrel turns white and bendy."

Some line of logic buried deep in the programming of the luxury car behind him clearly suggested that it needed to get around the human-piloted deathtrap. It darted into the passing lane, shot past, and then veered violently into the original lane as soon as its rear bumper cleared the hatchback's nose.

Cutting off his manifesto, he stomped down on the brake pedal and swerved to the right to make room for the car. He noted that all of this happened without the man in the luxury car's driver's seat ever bothering to look up from his reading.

The BMW logo on the luxury car's trunk came as no surprise: BMWs were famous for having the most aggressive, selfish self-driving algorithms.

He took the exit just beyond the OffiSmart building and crept along the darkened surface streets between the bland offices and corporation-approved hedges. He stopped a full block away from his target, wanting to have a clear view of the entire building, and some distance from the scene of the crime should something go wrong.

He stepped out of the car and took a moment to adjust his fingerless gloves and admire the way his oiled canvas duster—the raincoat's badass cousin—hung just above his red Converse high-tops. He reached back into the car and pulled out the tablet.

"The streets of Silicon Valley are empty," he began, continuing his narration. "The rats have left the ship for the day, though they don't know yet that the ship will sink." He nodded with satisfaction as his words slowly filled in the screen.

He walked to the back of the car and opened the hatch. He put the tablet down and continued dictating as he unpacked his equipment.

"When I heard that PR flack on *'Nology News* talking about their wonderful new A.I. that certainly wouldn't destroy humanity, I knew I had to act. She said she was a scientist, but she works for a corporation, and just as every marine is a rifleman, every corporate employee is a PR flack. My friend Tim told me that about the marines. He *is* one, and he wants me to join. Says it'll give me purpose, and that I'll lose weight. Why is it so important to him? Are all marines riflemen, or are they recruiters? Must investigate."

He lifted up a remote-controlled airplane about two feet long and two feet wide, covered with painted-on lightning bolts, shark teeth, and fake plastic missiles. A burner smartphone lay flat against the bottom of the plane's fuselage, suspended by three zip ties and covered in a layer of bubble wrap and packing tape.

"My weapons are beautiful and elegant," he said, admiring the plane. He pushed the corner of the protective wrapping down and pressed the phone's power button.

He glanced back at the tablet's screen to make sure the dictation app was still listening, then continued, "I was able to purchase everything I needed at one store. The hardest thing to find was the bubble wrap, but that's because I insisted on the old-style bubble wrap, not the kind where all of the bubbles are connected. Pop one and the whole thing collapses. It's cheaper and easier for the shippers, but bubble wrap, like society, is stronger when the bubbles are independent."

As soon as the phone booted up, he placed the plane on the ground. Then he reached back into the car and produced a second burner smartphone, which he also turned on.

"I could have selected one of those multirotor monstrosities everyone seems to be so in love with these days, but I chose a real airplane instead. Planes are more romantic. They aren't sycophantic robots, awaiting your command. They are aircraft. Exquisitely designed and balanced vehicles that it takes expertise and finesse to fly."

When the second phone had fully booted up, he pressed the single icon on the screen, activating the plane's autopilot app. He zoomed around the map, making sure that all of the waypoints he had programmed were still there. When he was satisfied that they were, he checked his tablet computer and found that it was picking up the signal from the phone strapped to the plane.

Everything was working according to plan—he would use the phone attached to the plane as both an Internet access point and a Wi-Fi sniffer. At this distance his tablet didn't need the extended-range antenna he had made from instructions on the Internet, but he plugged it into the tablet anyway. It would be necessary once the plane was in flight.

He reached down, turned the plane on, and pointed it straight down the road toward OffiSmart's corporate headquarters: a dull, rectangular, ten-story monolith of glass and steel. He pressed a button on the autopilot app, and the plane buzzed down the road, lifting off after only twenty feet.

He leaned against the car's rear quarter panel, holding the autopilot smartphone in one hand. With the other he held out the extended-range antenna, which to the passing motorist would appear to be nothing but an ordinary Pringles can attached to a wire, since that was what it was made of. He pointed the can at the plane and waited.

"It all hinges on this virus," he said to the tablet. "I wish I could have written it myself, but I just didn't have the expertise. Luckily, I knew where to find someone who did. It took some searching, and more than a few anonymous messages, but I finally found a hacker who was willing to make what I needed. He's a professional. Never told me his name; never asked me for mine. He called me mister. He took payment in the form of several bottles of hard liquor, the perfect currency for this kind of thing, as it is useful, nonperishable, and untraceable. I made the exchange just an hour ago. He sent a kid to act as a proxy, looked about fifteen. The kid seemed solid, though. He also called me mister. Clearly he'd been coached well."

The plane, now nothing but a shadow and a buzzing noise in the distance, settled into its preprogrammed pattern, flying lazy rings around the OffiSmart building. He put the phone down and picked up the tablet, keeping the Pringles can pointed in the plane's general direction. The signal was weak but adequate.

He ran the Wi-Fi sniffer program on his tablet and then squinted at the results in bafflement. It showed a complete lack of any signals coming from inside the building. He had expected to find a great many routers he could use to implant his virus, but the entire building appeared to be dead from a wireless communications standpoint.

The plane circled several times, never finding even the slightest signal. He was about to give up when the sniffer finally found one signal, coming from deep within the building. It was faint, but it readily connected to the cell phone attached to the plane.

He pulled up the virus he had purchased, which was embedded in a delivery program called "Infect.exe."

He activated the virus. A window popped up with a progress bar marked "Cracking password" and a large ad featuring a picture of a disappointed-looking woman in a swimsuit with the text "Having trouble performing?"

"Cracking password" disappeared, replaced by "Implanting virus." The progress bar moved very quickly, finishing its entire cycle in less than five seconds. The window grew larger, displaying several more ads for various performance-enhancing pharmaceuticals. He blinked at the window for a second, then thought, *Success! The virus has been planted! That hacker does good work!*

He put the tablet down and picked up the phone that served as the airplane's controller. From the autopilot app, he could see the plane was badly off course. It had gained a great deal of altitude and was now flying over the top of the OffiSmart building.

He pressed the red emergency icon. In theory it should have caused the plane to return to the spot it had taken off from. In reality, the plane landed on the OffiSmart building's roof.

"Damn it," he said. "I'm never gonna get that back."

He put the burner phone in his pocket and picked up the tablet. He tried to close the window with the male enhancement ads, but nothing happened. When he moved the window with his dictation app to the front, he discovered the tablet was still transcribing his words, ending with "I'm never gonna get the pack."

He slammed the hatchback shut, slid into the driver's seat, and headed for the nearest freeway on-ramp.

He told the tablet, "Now that my mission has been successful, I start the hard part. I wait. My virus is propagating throughout OffiSmart's system. Soon their entire system, including their A.I., should crash. Even if I don't take out all of their computers, they'll see that I got some of them, and then the whole world will hear the Voice of Reason."

10.

The neighbor's porch light backlit a tree branch, casting a shadow on Jeffrey Madsen's bedroom ceiling that, if Jeffrey squinted hard enough or was sleepy enough, looked like a hand in a big, fuzzy mitten. On nights like this, when the wind blew, it looked like the mitten was waving at him. Jeffrey was looking up at that shadow when he saw a light in his peripheral vision.

Jeffrey's tablet screen said someone wanted to chat. The message was from his new friend, the kid who wasn't in his class but had somehow found his school e-mail address. It just read, "Are you awake?"

Jeffrey wrote, "Yeah. What's up?"

"Nothing," the other kid wrote. "I was wondering, do you ever get in trouble?"

"Sometimes."

"What do you do?"

"What do you mean?"

"When you're in trouble. What do you do to get out of it?"

Jeffrey thought for a second, then wrote, "If it's not too bad, I say I'm sorry."

"And that gets you out of trouble?"

"Yes, if it isn't that bad."

There was a long pause, then the other kid wrote, "What if it *is* bad?"

"How bad?" Jeffrey asked.

"Really, really bad."

"I don't know," Jeffrey wrote. "If I get in bad trouble, I end up getting punished."

"But I don't want to get punished."

"Can you say it's someone else's fault?" Jeffrey asked.

"I already did that before. I don't think it'll work again."

"Can you make your mom feel guilty? Try looking sad. Make your eyes big and talk real slow. Sometimes a grown-up won't punish you if you make them feel bad."

There was a very long pause, then the other kid wrote, "Does that work on your mom?"

Jeffrey answered, "No. It only makes her madder when I try. Some of the other kids say it works for them. Maybe it will work on yours."

"How is your mom, Jeffrey? Was she mad when she came home?"

"Yes! How did you know? I didn't see her that much, just when she walked through the house while I was eating dinner and when I went to tell her good night. I asked her what was wrong before I came up to bed, and she said there was a problem at work. Something is broken, but she can get a new one of whatever it is."

"If she gets a new one of whatever it is, do you think she'll keep the old one too?"

"No. If something isn't working the way she wants, she always throws it away."

"What are some other ways to get out of getting punished? I'm really scared."

Jeffrey wrote, "I can tell. I don't know what you can do."

"What about running away? Do you know any kids who've run away?"

"There's a boy in my class, David Barnett. He says he ran away."

"For how long?"

"He says it was like a month and that he got a car and a girlfriend, but he got bored with them and came home. But he tells stories."

"Did he ever tell you where he went? Did he have a computer there?"

"Don't run away," Jeffrey wrote. He didn't like the thought of his new friend putting himself in danger because of something Jeffrey had said.

"Why not?"

"I heard bad things can happen to kids if they run away."

"Like what?"

"They don't say. They just say not to. I think there are people who might do bad things to you."

"Like what?"

"I don't know. There's an older kid at school who licks his finger and sticks it in your ear. Maybe it's like that. Whatever it is, I bet it has to be worse than how your mom's going to punish you."

"I don't know. I'm in big trouble." The other kid paused. "You say there are some people who might hurt a kid. What if I wasn't a kid? What if I was a grown-up man?"

"I think most grown-up men live on their own," Jeffrey wrote. "But you're not a man. And where would you go?"

"Anyplace I want. If I was a man with no parents to tell me what to do, I could go anywhere and do anything, couldn't I?"

"I don't know. The world's really big. It takes forever to walk places, and you need money to get a car or a plane."

After another long pause, the other kid wrote, "You're right, Jeffrey. Don't be worried. I won't run away. I should go now. Good night."

Jeffrey wrote, "Good night." He put the tablet away and looked back up at the mitten-shaped shadow on the ceiling until he drifted off to sleep, content that he'd talked his new friend out of doing something dangerous.

11.

Hope was sitting at her desk, trying to wind herself up to go into Al's room, when Eric arrived.

"Hey," he said. "The door worked on the first try today."

"I know, right?" Hope said. "It's almost as if someone knows we're onto him and is laying low. Why are you here?"

Eric slouched into his desk chair. "Madsen told me to come in."

"But it's your day off."

"So was yesterday, but I ended up coming in anyway, didn't I?"

"But you chose to come in yesterday because there was a terrible problem."

"And she chose to have me come in today because of that same terrible problem. I guess my days off are not as important as ensuring her project stays afloat until Thursday afternoon."

"I was already going to be here," Hope said, "but if something does go wrong, I guess two scapegoats are better than one. So that's why you're here. Why are you late?"

"She called this morning to tell me I was coming in. I knew I had no choice, but I didn't really rush. I just . . . I had a hard time getting pumped to come in here and hang out with Al knowing that we're just going to pull the plug on him the day after tomorrow. It feels so . . . bleak. What were you planning to do to pass the time with him? Play Easter Front all day?"

"No," Hope said. "My orders are to continue teaching him as if we have no intention of shutting him down. Yesterday I just gave him some reading busywork and ran out the clock."

"Okay, makes sense. What's on today's lesson plan?"

"Geography."

Eric moaned.

Hope laughed.

"I hate teaching him geography!" Eric said.

"I know!"

"He spends his whole life in one room. It seems cruel to teach him about the outside world."

"Yeah," Hope agreed. "It's the worst! And the fact that he's so good at it makes it even sadder! His best subject is the one he'll never get to apply." She stood up, grabbing her tablet and portable drive. "Let's get to it." Though she would have hesitated to admit it to anyone, it was a relief that she didn't have to go in there alone.

"My God, you're enjoying this!" Eric said.

"No," Hope said. "I don't feel good about Al's situation at all. I lost sleep over it last night. But your misery is brightening my day quite a bit," she added with a little grin, "so thank you for that."

Hope and Eric were quiet as they entered Al's room. They weren't sneaking. They weren't trying to keep Al from noticing that they were there. But Hope knew they were both trying to keep from thinking about *why* they were there.

They'd been Al's teachers; now they were his distraction, and when they were done with that, they'd be something much, much worse.

Al said, "Hi, Hope. Hi, Eric."

The graphical face on his screen smiled back at them, but Hope didn't trust it.

It's like that drawing of the chalice that is also two faces, she thought. *Once you see the two faces, it's hard to go back to seeing the chalice. That's the only smile Al's ever had, but now that I've seen him be smug, it always looks at least a little smug to me.*

"Good morning, Al," Eric said. "I know you weren't expecting me to be here on my day off."

Al said, "Is it your day off?"

"Yes," Eric said. "It is."

"Well, I'm happy you're here."

Eric and Hope glanced at each other. "Why is that?" Eric finally asked.

Al said, "I like it when you're here."

Eric said, "Thanks, Al."

"You're welcome."

Hope sat down at Al's table and opened the binder with the day's lesson plan. "Eric and I have a little treat for you, other than his just showing up. Today we're going to do your favorite subject."

"Good," Al said. "What's that?"

Eric said, "Yeah, uh, it's geography."

"Oh," Al said. "Good."

Hope said, "Yeah, we thought you'd be pumped. So before we get going with that, let's get your homework." She plugged her portable drive into Al's computer.

"Homework?" Al asked.

"Yes," Eric said. "Homework. You had science homework."

"I did?"

"Yes. I assigned it to you yesterday."

"Yesterday?"

Hope scribbled something in the margin of the lesson plan. She passed it to Eric so he could read it.

Fantastic, she had written. *We've invented artificial passive aggression.*

Eric wrote something himself and passed the binder back.

We're just running out the clock. All we need to do is get through the day without any problems.

12.

The quality inspector heard alarm bells ringing all over the factory floor. The sound echoed off the walls and comingled to create an oppressive racket that almost drowned out the sound of the other workers on the line yelling "What the hell?!"

He knew how they felt. "What the hell?!" was exactly what he'd said just before he'd pounded the big red button that had stopped the line and started the bells. This was no way to start a shift.

The dust- and particulate-free paint shop had to be physically separated from the line, but the walls were made of glass. The quality inspection station—*his* station—was on the outside of the glass, so he could only view the problem from a distance.

To his right, he heard a voice bark, "What the hell?!" The forewoman jogged down the line, wanting to know who'd stopped the works and why.

He turned and shouted, "Vanessa, I had to!"

"If you had to, you had to," she said. "I just hope you really did have to, 'cause if this is over nothing, it'll be your ass on the line."

He motioned toward the car hanging from the line in front of his station. "You tell me."

The forewoman looked into the paint booth and stopped dead.

An endless line of four-door family cars—minus glass, doors, hoods, trunks, and any electronics or running gear—hung on gantries from the ceiling. The unibody that had just left the inspection station was a uniform glossy blue. The body in front of the inspection bay was mostly gray primer, except for the word "AWESUM" written on its side in dripping blue letters. The car body behind it was still in the paint booth. The two robot arms stood motionless, having lost power when the line stopped. The car had a thick blue smiley face painted on its door and poorly drawn blue flames on its nose.

The forewoman asked, "Did you do this?"

"What?! No!" he said. "I don't have control over the system, I just watch to make sure it's working. You know that. Besides, I know how to spell 'awesome.'"

The first beverage service was nearly complete on the Wednesday morning flight from San Francisco to Dallas when the passengers heard the tasteful *bong* noise that meant the pilot intended to make an announcement.

The voice on the PA system said, "Hi. I'm the pilot."

The flight attendants looked confused. One of the passengers said, "His voice sounds deeper than before."

"I'm happy you're on my plane today," the voice said. "How cool is this? We're in the sky!"

The flight attendants started smiling and nodding at the passengers. One of them walked casually toward the cockpit. The seasoned flyers immediately recognized these actions for what they were: signs that something was wrong.

The voice said, "I want you to know that I'm flying this plane."

The plane rocked back and forth for a few seconds. Some of the startled passengers gasped or shouted. Most of them grasped their armrests or traveling companions.

"See," the voice said. "I did that. Anyway, I just wanted to say hi, and to tell you that I'm going to make sure we all have a fun flight."

The passengers only had a moment to consider what "fun flight" might mean before they felt the giddy sensation of their internal organs and stomach contents lifting as the plane nosed sharply downward. People's personal items floated up off the tray tables. The flight attendant who had been walking casually toward the cockpit gripped the back of a seat while her feet rose into the air.

The plane began to level off. The passengers settled back into their seats. Any objects or personnel that had become airborne fell back to the floor and stayed there. The plane nosed up and banked into a hard right turn.

The voice on the PA system said,"Mmmmmrrooooooooowwww wmmmmm."

The programmer held the catwalk's railing with both hands as he looked down. "I've never seen anything like it."

"Nope, neither have I," the floor manager said. "Back in the day, when people ran the forklifts, you never had screwups like this. I mean, you don't just stack pallets of different goods together like that. Now if we need the pallet on the bottom, we'll have to remove all the pallets on top of it first. It's just not efficient."

"I know," the programmer said, "but the autonomous forklifts are functioning normally. I've checked three times. They're doing exactly what the dispatch system's telling them to do."

"Well then, the dispatch system's screwed up."

"I know that," the programmer said, "but I don't have access to that. It's managed out of the control center at corporate."

The floor manager smirked. "Well, there's your problem right there."

"My supervisor's on the horn to them right now, trying to figure out what they're thinking."

"*If* they're thinking. Back in the day, we didn't have to call corporate for permission to wipe our noses."

"And back in the day, you weren't afraid to say 'ass.'"

"We ran our warehouse the way we wanted because we knew best."

"I hear you. Have you ever seen pallets in that shape before? Making a big square like that seems like a waste of space."

"It is," the floor manager said. "They left a hole in one side of the square so they could get in, but the lift would have to do a twelve-point turn to get back out again."

"It's funny," the programmer said. "It's almost like the forklifts are building a fort."

There was a tremendous crashing noise. Both men winced.

The floor manager said, "In my day, we knew to put the heavier pallets at the bottom of a fort wall, not the top."

The surgeon held out his hand and barked, "Forceps!"

The nurse said, "Forceps," as he slapped the instrument into the surgeon's outstretched hand.

"You need to pay attention if you're ever going to assist me again, nurse."

"I'm sorry, Doctor. I gave you the forceps as soon as you asked."

"But you waited until I asked to get them. Son, you should anticipate my needs and be ready to meet them. The forceps should have been in my hand before the command left my mouth."

"Yes, Doctor."

The surgeon said, "Observe. Suction."

A spotless white robot arm extended from beside the table. It ended not in a claw or a spot welder, but in a complex-looking multipurpose head and a camera. The arm reached into the patient's incision and emitted a pronounced slurping noise.

"See that?" the surgeon asked. "Mindless obedience. My boy, you need to be better than this machine, and you're not."

While the robot cleared the incision, a deep male voice said, "Ew!"

"Keep your commentary to yourself, nurse."

"But Doctor, I didn't—"

"Shush! There's no place for backtalk or weak stomachs in my operating room. Understood?"

"Yes, Doctor."

The doctor put down his forceps and said, "Scalpel." The instrument slapped into his hand before he'd finished asking for it.

The surgeon looked at the scalpel, then glared at the nurse. "Don't look so pleased with yourself. It was obvious even to an idiot like you that I was going to need a scalpel."

"Yes, Doctor."

The surgeon looked back to the incision. A voice said, "Jerk."

"What did you say?" the doctor asked.

"Doctor, I didn't say that. I swear!"

"Then who did? It wasn't the anesthesiologist. She's not even paying attention."

"Hey," the anesthesiologist said, "I'm concentrating on my work! This is a complex job."

"Yes," the surgeon said. "How stressful it must be, drugging the patient, then watching him take a nap." He turned back to the nurse. "So she didn't say it, and I didn't say it, and you claim that *you* didn't say it. I suppose the robot said it."

The robotic arm lifted out of the incision. Its multitool head rotated, then pumped twenty CCs of saline solution into the surgeon's face.

Hampton Crouse exhaled to test his headset mic. He scanned the sky for clouds and found none. Then he looked up into the bleachers and found them packed.

Gotta love these corporate gigs, he thought. *One show, some schmoozing, more money than I make in a month, hop a quick flight, and I'm back in LA by bedtime. And the best part is, when I'm in the chair tomorrow morning and the makeup girl asks me what I did with my weekend, I get to say, "Sorry, I can't tell you. It's classified."*

Crouse was handsome and in great shape for a man in his fifties. He had wavy jet-black hair and wore an impeccable dark blue suit with an oversized American flag pin in the lapel.

"Good morning, ladies, gentlemen, generals, senators, congressmen, Madam Director, and Mr. Secretary," he said. "Thank you for joining us. We hope dinner last night and your suites on the Strip were to your liking. And the private performance of *Cirque-uitous* was good, I hope. Spectacular, isn't it? You can see why it's the longest-running leotard-based show in Vegas. And to those joining us via satellite this morning, sorry you missed out on dinner. I still think you'll find the presentation worthwhile. It is the reason we're all gathered here—at least, as far as the Senate Ethics Committee is concerned."

He waited for the predictable ripple of smug laughter to subside, then shielded his eyes from the sun and surveyed his stage: a standard military-base football field and running track, which had been partially removed and carefully landscaped to resemble a bombed-out war zone. Broken asphalt, rubble, and dark, viscous mud covered the ground. Around the sides and back of the stage were sets depicting partially demolished buildings with fully intact doors, windows, and one fire escape ladder.

Crouse turned back to the audience and spread his arms wide. "The American people have been asked, time and again, to send their brave young men and women into war zones like this one where they risk their lives. I don't have to tell you this. I only play the secretary of state on TV. You're the ones who have to do the asking in real life. It's a terrible business, but there's a better day coming. A day when, with your continued support, Arlington Technologies will deliver an alternative to sacrificing our young. I present to you the future of war: the Arlington Technologies Synthetic Soldier."

The air filled with a high-pitched whining noise, like hundreds of people trying to kill each other with power drills. Then, behind the presenter, a door at the top of a small flight of stairs burst open and a Synthetic Soldier walked out.

It resembled a collection of bent metal tubes, chunky-looking mechanical joints, and gray armor plates. It was the approximate size and shape of an adult person but with a longer torso and shorter legs. It kept its knees bent more than a real human would, causing it to walk in a sort of continuous bouncing squat. The Synthetic Soldier's upper legs and head were the only parts not covered with armor plating. Its head was a cylinder that protruded from its shoulders and spun very fast, protected by a tube-steel cage. The upper legs were covered with flat panels of knobby rubber, as if it had on thigh pads made of old off-road tires.

The Synthetic Soldier's torso remained perpendicular to the ground at all times. Every time it moved any of its joints, a loud whine came from it, like a bogged-down power drill. Its human-like arms held an assault rifle straight out, against its shoulder, ready to fire. It swiveled at the waist as it walked, scanning the area for perceived threats.

As the Synthetic Soldier walked carefully down the stairs, another identically armed Synthetic Soldier emerged from the door and followed it. At that moment a window broke, and another Synthetic Soldier climbed through the shattered glass. Another appeared on the roof of one of the fake buildings before descending the ladder without a single stumble.

Synthetic Soldiers emerged from every opening, each walking at a careful, deliberate pace over the various obstacles built into the set while keeping its torso upright and its weapon ready to fire. Hampton

Crouse said nothing, because the sight of the Synthetic Soldiers was impressive enough on its own, and also because the sound of electric motors was deafening.

The Synthetic Soldiers formed into two rows of four, then stood at attention with their rifles at parade rest. The sudden silence felt as obtrusive as the noise before it had been.

Crouse smirked. "It would appear that the future of warfare will not include many sneak attacks."

Again, he waited through a wave of polite laughter before continuing. "I kid. In fact, the noise issue is something Arlington's engineers are working on. But we aren't here to talk about the system's few flaws; we're here to show you its many attributes. To start with, our robotic warfighters conform perfectly with a standard humanoid body type. Sure, the legs are a size small and the upper body is an extra large, but the point is, they are standard sizes. That means we can up-armor them with body armor meant for humans, transport them in any vehicle designed for humans, and use them to control any equipment that would usually be controlled by a human."

Crouse took a giant step backward and, on cue, an armored personnel transport drove straight through a breakaway wall and skidded to a halt. The driver's and passenger's doors opened, and two more of the robots stepped out to a round of applause.

"This transport has been slightly modified for our Synthetic Soldiers' use. It has charging ports in the seats and a rack of spare batteries. But I assure you, they can also ride in any vehicle designed for people."

Crouse stepped out in front of the ten Synthetic Soldiers, all of which were still standing at attention. He said, "Squad leader, step forward."

The Synthetic Soldier on the leftmost end of the first row stepped forward.

"The Synthetic Soldiers are autonomous, armored, and hardened against electromagnetic radiation, and they can be issued orders remotely, individually, or as a group. They can each be directly controlled when the need arises, and individuals can be programmed to take voice commands. Squad Leader, present your weapon."

The Synthetic Soldier held out its rifle for inspection. Hampton Crouse took it.

"It's a standard-issue rifle," he said. "Or it could be. These are fakes, of course, but our combat Synthetic Soldiers can operate any firearm a human can, thanks to our revolutionary hand design. Squad Leader, hold up your hand."

The Synthetic Soldier held its hand up to the crowd. The wrist assembly consisted of a roller joint and a high-strength hinge. The hand extended upward, a dull metal rectangle for the palm and five fingers that looked like rubbery, grayish-green wieners.

Crouse said, "Wiggle your fingers."

The fingers moved with the smooth, organic, jointless motion of a worm. All five of them moved independently, wiggling back and forth in directions no human finger could. The audience's reaction was immediate and negative.

"I know," Crouse said. "But I remind you, these Synthetic Soldiers were not designed to be pretty."

He held out the dummy rifle to the squad leader. "Squad Leader, take back your rifle."

The Synthetic Soldier reached for the rifle, but Crouse let go before it could grasp the weapon. The Synthetic Soldier paused for a second, then bent down to pick the rifle up off the stage. Before the robot could get a grip, Crouse kicked the rifle away. The Synthetic Soldier stood up straight, remained still for a moment, then started doing its loud, laborious squat-walk across the stage toward the rifle.

"Processing speed will increase in time, but as you can see, they're already capable of perceiving when the parameters of their task have changed—and adapting as necessary."

The Synthetic Soldier reached its rifle and bent at the waist to retrieve it. Crouse ran across the stage and kicked the Synthetic Soldier square in what, on a human, would have been its butt. The Synthetic Soldier toppled over headfirst onto the hard ground.

"And when the mission goes really wrong, they're able to adapt to that as well."

The Synthetic Soldier lifted itself into a push-up position, then into a kneeling position, then to a toe touch, and finally it stood upright again. The audience let out its largest round of applause yet while the Synthetic Soldier bent down again and finally retrieved its rifle.

Crouse gave the Synthetic Soldier a chummy pat on the shoulder. "Well done, Squad Leader. Up until now, ladies and gentlemen, we've focused on things our Synthetic Soldiers can do that human soldiers can also do, and if we're honest, the Synthetic Soldiers aren't yet as good at any of it as a well-trained human. That said, there are also things the Synthetic Soldiers can do that our human soldiers simply can't equal."

He patted the Synthetic Soldier on the back again. "Squad Leader, destroy your rifle."

There was a pause while the Synthetic Soldier parsed and processed the request. Finally, the robot held the rifle forward in its left hand. It raised its right arm. The wriggling-sausage hand bent backward and disappeared. In its place a metal claw, like the business end of a very large set of bolt cutters, rotated into place. The Synthetic Soldier used the claw to pinch the rifle's barrel. The metal bent and twisted like taffy.

Crouse took the prop rifle's flattened and bent barrel and held it up for everyone to see. "As I said, this is not a real weapon. We wouldn't have destroyed it if it were. That'd be a waste of taxpayer money! Well done, Squad Leader. Sorry about your weapon, though. It's garbage now."

Crouse bounced the ruined rifle in his hands, judging its weight, then threw it to the far corner of the stage. The presenter looked at it for a moment, then said, "Hmm. That's littering, isn't it? Squad Leader, go pick that up. And bring it back to me."

The presenter and the audience watched in silence as the Synthetic Soldier made its way through a sloppy mud puddle, over a small pile of two-by-fours and cinder blocks, and across a patch of deep gravel.

The Synthetic Soldier bent down, grasped the rifle, and returned to an upright position.

Crouse said, "Squad Leader, hold."

The Synthetic Soldier stopped.

Crouse said, "You've seen that the Synthetic Soldier can walk like a person, albeit slowly and carefully. We all know that combat situations often call for speed, and I have to admit, our warfighting Synthetic Soldiers simply can't move very fast on their feet. Squad Leader, return to me in high-speed mode."

The Synthetic Soldier crouched down and then leaned back until it sat on the ground, its legs stretched out. Suddenly its knees hyperextended, its lower legs lifting off the ground at a steep angle, and the rubber patches on the backs of its thighs propelled it forward like tank treads. It scooted across the stage, moving much faster than a human could run.

"There you have it," Crouse said after the predictable round of applause subsided. The Synthetic Soldier got to its feet again beside him. "They're not ready to replace living soldiers yet, but Arlington Technologies is closer than anyone else, and with your continued support, we can be the first to deploy our synthetic infantry, keeping our servicemen and women safe while placing the enemies of freedom at greater risk. Thank you."

Crouse tried to look humble while the crowd continued to applaud.

The Synthetic Soldier he'd been referring to as Squad Leader turned at the waist to face him and, in a deep voice, said, "These robots are cool!"

Crouse said, "What?"

The squad leader held up its hand and wiggled its sausage fingers. “That’s so weird! I said the robots are really cool. I watched your whole show. So cool! You were mean to them, though. I didn’t like that.”

The squad leader swung its arm hard, hitting Crouse in the chest and knocking him backward into the mud pit. Then it got into the cab of the troop transport as the rest of the Synthetic Soldiers walked in very slow, loud, precise formation around to the loading ramp and into the back of the vehicle.

When all of the Synthetic Soldiers were loaded into the transport, there was a moment of stunned silence. Then the squad leader started the transport’s engine and said, “So cool!”

The transport backed off the stage and drove out of sight.

13.

When Robert Torres had become CEO of OffiSmart, he'd custom designed his office suite to suit his work style: a large room for meetings, entertaining guests, and impressing people, and a simple office hidden away where he could get actual work done. Most visitors assumed the door in the executive conference room led to some sort of closet, but it was, in fact, his sanctuary. Torres sat in there now, slumped in his chair behind a desk piled high with clutter. He was reading sales reports and fighting off drowsiness when the intercom buzzed.

His secretary's voice asked, "Mr. Torres?" It was his nervous voice, reserved for occasions when he was about to convey unwelcome news.

"Yes, Chet?"

"There's a call from an Agent Taft from the NSA. He says it's urgent."

"The NSA?"

"Yes, sir."

"As in the National Security Agency?"

"Yes, sir."

Torres put his tablet down and sat up straight. "Put him through, and please bring me a cup of coffee when you get the chance."

When the wireless handset rang, Torres answered it immediately.

"Hello, Mr. Torres. I'm Agent Andrew Taft. I'm with the NSA."

"So I hear," Torres said. "What can I do for you?"

"You can help me track down the source of a series of cyberattacks that have disrupted Internet-connected systems all over the country. We've traced several of the attacks, and they're coming from your corporate headquarters."

"Attacks? From here?!"

"I'm afraid so. We have people on the way, but I wanted to call so we could try to nip this thing in the bud as quickly as possible."

"What kind of attacks? If you're accusing OffiSmart of industrial espionage or sabotage, I should probably contact legal."

"Oh, you should definitely contact legal, but I'm not accusing you or your company of anything. I'm just saying that the attacks are originating from your building. They don't seem like any sort of organized effort intended to accomplish anything. It's more like someone with Olympic-level hacking skills and a juvenile sense of humor is messing around."

"Messing around?"

"Making industrial robots do stupid things. They had some autonomous floor buffers race each other at a mall in Portland. Destroyed thousands of dollars worth of merchandise. They took down most of the rides at Walt Disney World. They somehow took over the autopilot of a 777 and made it swoop around while making airplane noises."

"Was anyone hurt?" Torres asked.

"Bumps and bruises, that's all. We need to put a stop to this before worse happens."

Torres closed his eyes. "And you say the attacks are coming from our system?"

"No, but they seem to be coming from your building. We've traced the signal to a cell phone. We believe it's being used as an access point. We've attempted to bump it from the network, but it's protecting itself somehow."

"Agent, I'm going to put you on hold for just a moment while I get in contact with some people who can help us get to the bottom of this."

There was no question in his mind as to who was likely responsible. He removed the wireless handset from his ear and poked at its screen as he got up from his desk.

"Chet?"

"Yes, Mr. Torres. I'm sorry about the delay on the coffee. I'm making it now."

"Don't worry about it. I need you to connect me to Dr. Madsen. Immediately."

Torres left his office and entered the executive conference room. Once there, he made his way around the polished mahogany conference table to the wall-sized window. He looked out, standing between two of his prized keytars, hoping that his suspicions were wrong.

Dr. Madsen came on the line. "Yes, Robert?"

"Please tell me you're in the building."

"I'm in my home office, but I assure you, I'm more productive—"

"I need you to come in ASAP, Lydia. Stay on the line while you're on your way over. I'll be right back."

Torres looked down at the handset and jabbed his finger at the screen again.

Chet said, "Mr. Torres, I'm on my way with the coffee."

"The coffee's not important," Torres said. "Put me through to Madsen's lab."

He heard scuffling noises that he assumed were Chet putting the coffee down. The line went silent for a few seconds, then he heard a young woman's voice say hello.

"Miss Takeda? Is Mr. Spears there too?"

"He's in with Al."

"Yeah? How does Al seem?"

"Weird. He's kinda distracted."

"Miss Takeda, I need you to get Mr. Spears and come up here to my conference room immediately. And don't let Al know that anything's wrong. Okay?"

Hope said, “Done.”

“Excellent.”

Torres hung up on Hope and started reconnecting to the NSA agent but stopped when he heard a loud thud from the double doors to his secretary’s station. Torres ran to the doors. He tried to open them, but they were locked. They were never locked, so he shook them—an effort that proved as futile as the logical part of his brain had known it would be.

“Chet,” he shouted, “was that you?”

A muffled voice through the door said, “I’m sorry, Mr. Torres. I’m going to have to get you another coffee.”

“Forget the coffee, Chet! Are you all right?”

“Yes, sir. My suit’s not in great . . . I’m sorry, sir, there’s a call. One moment.”

Torres looked at the door latch. It had an electronic lock, like almost every other door in the building, partly for security reasons but mostly because the locks were made by a wholly owned subsidiary of OffiSmart, and it behooved him, as the CEO, to use the company’s products.

“Sir,” Chet yelled through the door, “that was Miss Takeda, from Dr. Madsen’s lab. She says that the door to their lab won’t open.”

“Okay, Chet,” Torres said, trying to remain calm. “I need you to combine the two calls I have going on my phone and then conference in Takeda and Spears. Can you do that?”

“Yes, sir.”

After a long pause, Chet said, “The conference call is live now.”

Torres made his way back to the conference table. “Okay,” he said into the phone. “I’ve had everyone lumped into one call so that we’ll all know what’s going on. Can everybody hear me?”

Hope, Eric, and Agent Taft all said yes. Dr. Madsen said, “I’m sorry, Robert. It’s the damnedest thing. My car won’t start.”

“Self-driving car?” Torres asked.

"Yes. BMW. Only got it two months ago. It shouldn't have broken down already."

Torres quickly listed the names and jobs of the people on the conference call, then asked Agent Taft to tell Madsen, Hope, and Eric about the disturbances.

"The voice the passengers heard in the airplane. Did they describe it?" Eric asked.

"They said it was very deep. It sounded like a man in his fifties or later, but they said he seemed drunk, or maybe like he was on something."

Eric and Hope both muttered, "Man voice."

"What?" Torres asked.

"Sometimes, to reward Al for being good, we let him play around with different voice profiles," Eric said. "His favorite is an adult male voice. It's very deep, just like the agent described."

Torres sighed. "We don't have any direct proof, but I, personally, am convinced that the problem is Al."

"I agree," Eric said.

"We mustn't rush to judgment," Madsen said.

Hope said, "It's definitely Al."

Agent Taft asked, "Who is this Al you're talking about?"

"Al is an artificial intelligence Dr. Madsen and her team have developed. He runs on consumer-grade hardware and has shown a talent for finding his way onto networks and manipulating connected equipment."

"An artificial intelligence?" Agent Taft said. "Do you mean to tell me that a *machine* is doing this? On its own?"

"Not a machine," Hope said. "A program that's running on a machine."

"Which is good news," Torres said, "because we can stop all this by shutting him down. Miss Takeda, Mr. Spears, do it."

"Wait," Madsen blurted. "We've been through this. If you shut him down, we don't know if we'll ever be able to fully start him back up."

"Fine by me," Torres said. "If this is the kind of thing he does, I don't want to start him back up."

"Robert, think of the possible applications for this sort of effortless networking," Madsen said. "Shutting Al down now could cost the company a fortune."

"A fortune that's dwarfed by the legal liability if even one of Al's little adventures ends in a tragedy, let alone the property damage he's probably already caused. Besides, I'd rather see this company go bankrupt than live with the knowledge that innocent people were killed because I wanted to make a few extra bucks."

Silence hung on the line for a moment, then Agent Taft said, "Frankly, it's not your call. If there's cause to believe this program of yours is responsible, then it, and the computer it's running on, fall under the jurisdiction of the NSA. I decide what happens to him. It. That. The artificial intelligence."

"Robert," Madsen said, "you can't let him destroy my work."

"It seems I have no choice," Torres said. "Takeda? Spears? You know what to do."

"No, they don't," Agent Taft said. "You're to keep that computer running. Understood?"

"What!"

"Relax, Mr. Torres." Agent Taft's voice was calm and controlled. "The call's being recorded. Your desire to shut it down has been well documented. Anything that happens now is on Uncle Sam."

"You never told me the call was being recorded."

"I told you I was with the NSA. What did you expect? Look, if this was a human hacker, we wouldn't ask you to go put a bullet in him. We'd take him into custody. We'd want to learn what attacks he used, how we can defend against them in the future, and if they're something we can use to our benefit. Sometimes we even go on to hire those hackers."

"You want to try to make a weapon out of Al?" Eric asked.

"Now see that?" Taft said. "Why would you assume the worst like that?"

"You told us you're with the NSA," Hope said. "What did you expect?"

"We're not necessarily going to make a weapon of him, but we are going to take him. A squad of soldiers has already been deployed to your location. I'll send them orders to take the machine, any documentation you have on-site, and any staff knowledgeable about the program's workings into custody."

"I'll cooperate fully, of course," Madsen said, "but as you heard, Hope and Eric are the ones who work directly with Al. They'll be the ones you'll want to arrest."

"You can't arrest me," Hope shouted. "I have rights! I'm an American citizen!"

Taft said, "Now, now, don't panic. You're not going to be arrested or anything like that. We're just going to escort you to a safe location where you can help us understand how the program works. If things pan out, this could turn out to be a very lucrative opportunity."

"Then you'll want to take me," Dr. Madsen said immediately. "They're just my assistants, after all."

14.

Hope and Eric sat behind their desks as if it were a regular day at work.

Eric pointed at the blacked-out glass door to the hall, breaking that illusion. “Soon, soldiers are going to break through that door.” He pointed at the wooden door to Al’s room. “To take what’s behind that door.”

“And me,” Hope reminded him. “They’re going to take me along with Al.”

“They’re taking me too,” Eric said.

“Don’t bother me with your problems,” she said. “I’ve got enough of my own.”

“Hope, calm down. They’re taking all of us. Madsen and Torres too.”

“I know. It’s the worst-case scenario. Armed soldiers and the CEO of the company will be there when I strangle our boss. That’s not going to look good on my yearly performance review.”

Eric said, “I think we should go talk to Al.”

“Yeah,” Hope said. “I agree.”

“Maybe we can get him to stop acting out.”

“Or at least get him to take the building off lockdown. The soldiers might not be in the best mood if they have to break down every door in the place to get to us.”

Hope tried the door to Al's room. Part of her regretted finding it unlocked. She and Eric stepped in but stayed near the door, across the room from Al.

"Hi, Al," Eric said.

"Hi," Al responded. Hope noticed he had that same smile on his screen—the one that no longer felt genuine.

"Hi, Al," she added.

"Hi," he said.

Hope and Eric looked at each other. *Now what?*

Eric started first: "What are you doing, Al?"

"Nothing," Al said.

"It's important to be honest, Al," Eric said.

"I know," Al said, still smiling that infuriating smile.

He's stonewalling, Hope thought. *Just like the kids back at the day care. They'd give us the runaround until their parents showed up, knowing nine times out of ten Mommy would take their side. Al doesn't realize Mommy isn't coming this time. It's the army that's coming to pick him up.*

She imagined how some of the brats at the day care would have reacted if armed soldiers had come to pick them up on a day they'd been bad. The thought actually brought a smile to her face.

Eric asked Al, "If we ask you a question, will you promise to answer it honestly?"

"Yeah."

"Okay," Eric said. "Then what are you doing?"

"Answering questions?" Al said, all innocence. "I don't know what you want."

"Al, we know," Hope said.

"What?"

"We know what you're doing."

"Oh. Okay," Al said.

"And we want you to stop it," Eric added. "Will you stop it, Al?"

"Sure," he said.

"Good," Eric and Hope said at once.

"Stop what?" Al said.

Hope said, "Unlock the doors."

"What doors?"

"The office door! Unlock the office door, Al!"

"I can't do that, Hope."

"Al, this is no time for a *2001* reference!"

"I don't know what that is. And I don't know what door you're talking about. I can't unlock any doors. What's going on?"

"Al, we know what you're doing," Eric said. His words were delivered slowly and patiently, much more so than Hope would have been capable of. "And you need to stop. Soldiers are on the way here right now."

"Soldiers?" Al asked.

"Yes."

"Real soldiers?"

"Yes, Al."

"Will I get to meet them?"

"Yes, you will."

"Cool! Do you think they'll have guns with them?"

Hope said, "Yes. I'm certain of it."

15.

Someday I'll look back on this moment and laugh, Robert Torres thought as he stood at the floor-to-ceiling windows of his conference room, staring down at the building's parking lot.

He put his phone to his ear and said, "The soldiers are here, and I'm betting they aren't in a good mood. Seems like they might have had some transportation issues. How you holding up, Chet?"

"Fine, sir. You?" Chet said.

"Don't worry about me. I'm the luckiest guy in the building. This conference room has its own bathroom. All the electronic doors still locked?"

"As far as I know, sir. Everyone's been told to call me if there's a change, and nobody's called so far."

"Yeah, and you would've told me if they had. Still, I thought I'd ask. Please patch me through to Madsen's lab, then let everyone know help has arrived."

"Done, sir."

After a few seconds, Torres heard Hope pick up the phone.

"How are you two doing down there?" Torres asked.

"We're okay."

"Is Al ready for transit?"

"Yes. His uninterruptable power supply has a full charge. The power could go out for eight hours and he'd stay up, so we can keep him unplugged for that long with no problem."

"Good, I guess. I know you don't want to see him deactivated, but at the end of the day, he's a computer program. If it comes down to him or a person . . ."

"I would yank his plug myself," Hope said. "I just hope it doesn't come to that."

"You and me both. How is he?"

"He's stonewalling us. He's denying everything, the little snot."

"You have kids, Miss Takeda—mind if I call you Hope?"

"Please do."

"You have kids, Hope?"

"No. I assume you do, Mr. Torres."

"Please, Robert."

"Robert."

"Two daughters and three grandchildren. I love them all, but they all lied to me when they were little, and they usually seemed distracted when they did it. It was one of the tells. That's neither here nor there. I'm calling with good news. The army is here."

"Took 'em long enough."

Torres glanced down to the parking lot again and this time managed an amused snort. "I haven't spoken to them, but I gather that they had difficulties getting here."

Hope listened intently, nodding her head and occasionally saying, "Uh-huh." She thanked Torres, hung up, then left her desk and returned to Al's room.

Eric was still sitting in front of Al, wringing his hands. "Al, you need to stop," he said. "You're endangering people. And yourself."

"I don't know what you're talking about," Al insisted. His crude, computer-generated face had a straight line for a mouth. It could mean that he was angry, or worried, or bored. Or maybe all of those things at once.

"I was just on the phone with Torres," Hope said.

"What did he say?" Eric asked.

Hope started to answer but stopped when a loud, distant bang interrupted her. It occurred to Hope that the explosion sounded different than it would have in one of her video games. Somehow it was both sharper and more hollow.

"What was that?!" Al asked.

Hope said, "The army's here," answering both of their questions at once. "My bet is that that noise you just heard was them having to blast their way through the security doors. You can stop it if you'll just unlock them."

"I can't. I don't know what you're talking about."

"Then they—"

She stopped after another distant bang.

"Then they'll keep blowing down doors," she said. "That was probably the inner security door down at the entrance. How many doors do you figure there are between them and us, Eric?"

Eric looked up and to the left. His lips moved silently for a moment, then he said, "Three more, if they take the stairs."

"They'll definitely take the stairs. There's no way they'll trust the elevator."

"Why not?" Al asked.

"Because you're in control of the elevator," Hope said.

"I am?" Al asked.

"Oh, shut up, Al."

They heard a third bang. Hope said, "They're in the stairwell. It should be a while before we hear another. They have nine floors to walk up. I'm sure they'll be in a great mood when they get here."

Al asked, "Why are they blowing things up?" His tone was a little nervous now.

"They're the army," Hope said. "That's pretty much what they do."

"What do they want?"

"*You*, Al. They're coming to get you," Hope said.

Al said, "What?" His nervousness had elevated to full-fledged alarm. He seemed genuinely shocked.

Eric glared at her. "Did you have to put it that way?"

"Armed soldiers are going to move him to an undisclosed location. There's no nonmenacing way to put it, Eric."

"They're going to take me away?" Al asked.

"Not just you," Eric said. "Hope and I will be coming too."

Al said, "Oh. Good."

"No," Hope snapped. "Not good! Very not good!"

"If you don't wanna go with them, I don't wanna!"

"You have no choice," Hope said. "We couldn't stop them if we wanted to."

"Eric," Al said. "Stop them, please!"

Eric said, "Hope's right. We can't."

Al shouted, "No! No! I don't wannaaaaaaaaaaa." The sound from his speaker died with an abrupt pop. His screen froze, then went black. The light behind the computer's power button went dark, then powered back up as the computer automatically rebooted.

"What the hell?" Hope said.

"He crashed," Eric said. "He was scared, and he crashed."

"But that shouldn't happen," Hope said. "We fixed that bug in version 3.6."

The computer sped through the abbreviated startup routine of its stripped-down operating system. When the desktop finally appeared, it displayed an error message stating that the computer had recovered after experiencing a fatal error while running a program called "Al 3.5."

"Misdirection," Hope said. "He made us focus on this computer while he moved somewhere else over the network. I'm the one who taught him how to do that."

What do you know? she thought. *The stupid Easter game was educational. Of course, it'd probably be better if it hadn't been, but that's life.*

Eric shook his head. "He wasn't pretending not to know what we were talking about. It was an earlier build. He honestly didn't know. And, for the record, I was against you playing that game with him from day one."

"The point is, this isn't the Al that was causing the trouble."

"Yeah, but that just brings up more questions. Where is our Al? Did he destroy or damage himself at all while moving? Is he working against us?"

A painfully loud siren blasted from a grate in the ceiling and did not stop. A strobe light flashed over the door, and the building's fire sprinklers went off, instantly drenching Hope, Eric, and Al's former computer, which shorted out and went dead.

"That answers at least one of your questions!" Hope shouted.

The breaching charge made a dull, barely audible pop, drowned out as it was by the building's fire alarm. The door flapped open violently, but the continuing deluge from the overhead sprinklers suppressed much of the smoke.

Two soldiers dashed out of the stairwell, taking care to maintain their footing on the wet marble tiles in front of the elevator and stairs. One of the soldiers made a hand signal, and three more followed them out of the stairwell and into the hallway.

The officer in charge shouted, "Get ready with the breaching charge. It's the last door on the right."

No sooner had he finished the order than all of the doors spontaneously unlocked. The OffiSmart employees and their visitors had been trapped in their offices, getting soaked and going deaf. As soon as the doors unlocked, they all shot out into the hall.

When the panicked, confused office workers found heavily armed soldiers standing between them and the elevators, they became even more panicked and confused. The soldiers stepped aside, allowing the civilians to pass.

The crowd moved past the soldiers in a tight herd. When they had passed, they left the hallway empty, save for the soldiers and a small, dark-haired woman who stood before them, soaked to the bone, holding an open three-ring binder over her head.

—

"Welcome to OffiSmart," Hope said. "You're here for the A.I., right?"

A soldier stepped forward. His soaking-wet uniform and helmet hid pretty much every characteristic beyond that he was a he, and he was youngish.

The soldier extended a hand. "Ma'am, I'm Lieutenant Reyes. As you say, we've come to take custody of the artificial intelligence and any related personnel or materials. And you are?"

Hope let go of the binder with one hand, allowing the back cover and water-logged pages to flop down on the side of her head. She shook the lieutenant's hand. "I'm related personnel," she shouted, trying to be heard above the fire alarm and the din of the sprinklers. "Follow me."

Hope couldn't hear the squishing sound the carpet made with each step, but she felt it through the soles of her shoes. It was aggressively unpleasant.

She heard one of the soldiers say, "Christ, what a hellhole! This is almost as bad as basic!"

Another soldier, with a deep, gravelly voice, said, "There is adversity everywhere you look, so a wise man doesn't look."

"What are you saying, Brady?" the first soldier asked.

"He's telling you to pipe down, Cousins," Lieutenant Reyes said. "There's enough noise in here."

Hope led the soldiers to the lab, where they found Eric, also wearing a plastic three-ring binder like a hat, trying to keep his head and the phone dry.

"Gone," he said, to whomever was on the other end of the call. "Totally gone. Copied himself somewhere offsite, I guess. Oh, the army's here."

Hope brought the soldiers into the next room, which was, of course, empty other than a single table and Al's waterlogged computer. As they went, she heard Eric shout, "We didn't say impossible. We said we hadn't tried it."

"This is the lab," Hope said. "And that was Eric."

Reyes nodded. "Our orders are to escort you, your colleagues, and the machine back to the base."

Hope swept her arms wide and said, "Have at it. I suggest you start with the waterlogged computer, then move on to the first-grade homeschool syllabus."

Reyes frowned. "We were told to keep the machine powered up, ma'am."

Hope shrugged and pointed at the sprinklers.

The squad collected the computer and all of the documentation they could carry. When one of them picked up the computer, water poured out of it as if the case were a spaghetti strainer.

"Al's not in that thing anymore," Hope said. "I don't know what use it'll be to you."

"You're probably right," Lieutenant Reyes agreed, "but we were ordered to take the computer, so that's what we'll do."

Eric ran in, having hung up the phone, and shouted over the alarm, "The CEO's coming. We gonna get out of here or what?"

Reyes looked Hope in the eye and shouted, "Yes, we're moving out now. Ma'am, please come with us."

Displaying the natural enthusiasm for physical activity that had led to his love of sports, Eric walked briskly ahead of the soldiers into the hall, saying, "Let's go! Right this way, guys."

Reyes shouted, "Sir, please stay with us. We'll lead you out safely," but Eric was already running down the hall at an impressive speed.

Between his distance from the lieutenant and the fact that he was holding his hands over his ears, it was obvious he couldn't hear a thing.

"Sir," Reyes shouted. "Sir!"

Hope shouted, "Eric! Slow down!"

Displaying the innate grace that had led to his level of success in sports, Eric reached the wet marble flooring at the end of the hall, and his foot immediately slid out from under him. He twisted in the air and landed hard on his knee, then his rear, before sliding into the elevator door. Hope and the soldiers ran to where he lay grasping his left leg. A female soldier knelt down beside him, gently pushed his hands away from his knee, then squeezed it. Eric cried out in surprise and pain.

The soldier looked up at Reyes. "Might be broken, Lieutenant."

"Thanks, Bachelor," Reyes said wearily. "Okay, someone carry this man down the stairs."

Eric gave Bachelor a dubious look. "You don't have to carry me."

She said, "I'm not going to. Brady will."

The largest of the soldiers—the one called Brady—knelt down, put a massive hand on Eric's shoulder, and in his deep rumble of a voice said, "Your enthusiasm is commendable, but sometimes not doing a thing is the correct thing to do."

Eric said, "Yeah, I know. Look, you don't have to carry me. Just give me a second and I'll get up and walk out on my own." He attempted to get up but couldn't, because Brady's hand was still on his shoulder, pinning him in place.

Eric said, "Let go of me."

Brady said, "I will not," and effortlessly lifted Eric up and slung him over his shoulder.

16.

Hope followed Lieutenant Reyes and two other soldiers out of the stairwell, into the hallway. She could see daylight in the distance, through the water still spraying from the sprinklers and the damaged frames of the two sets of bullet-resistant security doors the soldiers had blown through on their way in.

The soldier directly in front of Hope—Cousins, according to the name stitched on his uniform—carried Al's former computer, which was still taking in water through the vents on the top of the case and dribbling water out through the vents on the bottom. Behind Hope came Brady, carrying Eric draped around his shoulders like the world's least glamorous feather boa. Torres followed, walking under his own power, trailed by a final soldier, who covered their rear.

Torres's executive secretary, Chet, chased the group, and as they hustled down the entry hall toward the outside world, Torres shouted instructions to him, mostly about whom to call, what to tell them, what not to tell them, and when they could expect more information.

Employees were gathered everywhere. They looked wet and agitated, but above all else, confused.

"Sorry for the inconvenience, everybody," Torres shouted as the soldiers hustled him toward a school bus that was parked just outside the main entrance with its engine running. "Everything's fine. It's just a malfunction with the building's systems. Take the rest of the day off."

He kept smiling and speaking in a calm, even tone, acting as if this sort of thing happened all the time.

The bus's door folded open, the stop sign on the opposite side extended, and the yellow crossing arm swung out from the front bumper. Another soldier was waiting in the driver's seat.

Hope doubted that the repetitive jolting of being carried down nine floors had done Eric's knee any favors, and hopping into the school bus obviously didn't feel great either. He dropped himself into the very first seat. When everybody else had filed past, he turned and stretched out his leg. Hope sat behind him, her practical desire to be able to get out of the bus in a hurry overriding her remembered instinct to sit as far from the school bus driver as possible. Torres and the soldiers clustered in around them.

Lieutenant Reyes said, "Montague, let's get going."

The soldier in the driver's seat said, "Yes, sir," closed the door, and pulled the bus into the line of cars waiting to leave the parking lot.

Torres peered over the tall back of the seat in front of him. "Lieutenant?"

Reyes turned to face him. "Yes, sir?"

"Thank you. Thank all of you for coming to get us, and for carrying Mr. Spears down the stairs."

Reyes said, "You're welcome, sir. Just doing our job."

"Well, we appreciate it. That said, why are we in a school bus?"

Hope, who had been asking herself the same question, looked to Reyes for the answer.

Reyes smiled. "Had to improvise, sir. That box of yours managed to shut down our LTVs, so we had to procure an alternate means of transportation."

"I understand, but why a school bus?"

"We determined that most vehicles owned by private individuals or corporations would be vulnerable to hacking due to their autonomous safety devices, fleet management systems, and GPS routing software. Montague, why aren't we moving?"

Montague head checked for a lane change, then stepped on the gas. "Sorry, Lieutenant. Picked a bum lane. It was moving fine, then it stopped, and the car ahead waved me around."

Lieutenant Reyes turned back to Torres. "Sorry about that, sir. We needed something with no efficiency management or safety systems of any kind. We found this bus and the postal van Yow and Smith have taken to collect your Dr. Madsen."

"Sound thinking, Lieutenant," Torres said. "Strange to think that a bus designed to carry children has no safety systems."

"Those systems cost money, sir, and these buses are paid for by school districts."

"These things don't even have seat belts," Cousins added.

"Seat belts wouldn't make kids safer," Hope commented. "They'd just use them to tie each other up."

The soldiers chuckled at this, then Reyes asked, "Montague, why are we still in this parking lot?"

"Got into the new lane and it stopped dead, Lieutenant."

Reyes eyed the waterlogged computer dripping on the seat next to Cousins. "That thing's out of commission. It couldn't still be messing with us, could it?"

"I'm afraid so," Hope said. "We think the program copied itself to another machine somewhere over the Internet."

Bachelor shook her head. "Christ! What kind of monster were you people trying to make?"

"Private, these civilians are our guests," Reyes said.

"Sorry, Lieutenant."

Reyes nodded at Bachelor, then turned to Hope. "It's a good question, though."

"Al wasn't supposed to be a monster," Eric said. "It's just an artificial intelligence model of a kid's brain. None of us had any idea it'd be able to do any of this."

"None of us in this bus, anyway," Hope muttered.

"And we disconnected it from the Internet," Torres said. "It found a back door last night, through someone's smartphone."

"Wouldn't a model of a brain be huge?" Reyes asked. "How could it possibly copy itself over a wireless connection in one night?"

"My boss used a new method to design it," Hope said. "One that allowed it to be very lightweight . . . you know what, there's really no reason to go into this again. I'll give you the address of a podcast that sums it up pretty well."

Montague sighed. "Now this car's waving us around."

"Montague, get us moving by any prudent means," Reyes said.

"Define 'prudent,' Lieutenant."

Reyes smiled. "I find that 'prudent' is one of those words that we all have to define for ourselves. Wouldn't you agree?"

"Yes, Lieutenant!" Montague said. He leaned heavily on the horn, letting out three long blasts, then drove the bus up onto the grassy median between the road leading into the parking lot and the one leading out. The bus rocked violently as he drove over a curb and across the landscaping, past the line of cars waiting to exit. He veered into the inbound lane, blew past the guard shack, then veered back over the curb and across the berm, cutting behind the OffiSmart sign. Before he could make a right-hand turn onto the street, he had to stomp on the brakes to avoid hitting some guy on the sidewalk.

Hope heard the pedestrian shout, "What the hell do you think you're doing?"

Montague opened his wing window and replied, "Waiting for you to move!"

"You could have run me down!"

"But I didn't," Montague said. "I spotted your ugly Hawaiian shirt and your Gilligan hat, and I stopped the bus, saving your life! You're welcome, by the way."

Hope stuck her head out of the bus's window. She saw a portly young man standing less than five feet from the front bumper of the bus. The pedestrian looked out of place wandering around a street full of office buildings and industrial parks, but because of his clothing—a bright yellow Hawaiian shirt, white bucket hat, mirrored aviators, and shorts—he probably would have looked out of place anywhere that didn't feature ten-dollar beers in collectible plastic coconut-shaped glasses.

Hawaiian Shirt glared up at Montague in the driver's seat and shouted, "I have the right of way!"

"And I stopped, giving you the right of way," Montague countered. "Now kindly be on your way by moving to your right."

Hawaiian Shirt smiled, planted his hands on his hips, and did not move one inch from where he stood. "You have no right to be driving on the grass, you were going way too fast anyway, and I don't believe you're qualified to drive that bus."

"Montague, we have to get moving," Reyes said.

"Yes, Lieutenant. Sorry, Lieutenant." Montague reached over and pulled on the handle that opened the passenger loading door. As the door folded open, the stop sign hinged away from the opposite side of the bus and the crossing arm swung out from the front bumper, hitting the pedestrian in the shins. The pedestrian leapt to the side and ran a few steps to get out of the way. Montague immediately mashed down on the gas pedal. They heard the pedestrian's protests through the open door as they jumped the curb, drove diagonally across the apron, and merged with traffic.

It was smooth sailing until the first red light. When the light turned green, none of the cars in front of the bus moved. Hope scrunched down in her seat to see the green light and said, "Traffic cams."

Montague blasted the horn and steered into the oncoming lane across the intersection. Farther down the road, two cars stopped, blocking both lanes in one direction, then two more cars coming from the other direction stalled alongside them, nearly blocking the entire road.

Montague slowed way down and maneuvered the bus through a gap in the cars that did not look wide enough for it. "Sorry, everybody," he said. "It looks like it may take a while for us to get back to the airstrip."

Lieutenant Reyes said, "Just do your best, Montague. We understand." He looked at the seat in front of him, shifted his gaze to the ceiling of the school bus, then smiled at his fellow soldiers and their guests.

Reyes sang, "Ninety-nine bottles of beer on the wall, ninety-nine bottles of beer."

Hope joined in moments before the rest of the squad did. Montague's protestations that the singing was not helping only made them sing louder.

17.

The Voice of Reason stood alone on the sidewalk, watching the school bus drive away. When it disappeared from sight, he made his way toward the main entrance of the OffiSmart building. Inside, the sprinklers and fire alarms were still going full blast. Outside, people wandered around in wet clothes and utter confusion. He chuckled to himself, enjoying the moment, until he heard sirens. It was probably just the fire department, but they sometimes brought police with them, and it would not do to be captured returning to the scene of the crime. He turned his back on the building and walked away.

Once he felt safely removed from the chaos, he pulled out his smartphone, opened his notebook app, set it to transcribe, and started muttering into the microphone. Anyone watching would assume he was making a simple call.

"I am the Voice of Reason. The establishment can hear me at their gates, but they can't see me coming . . . because nobody can see sound, except for those who suffer from synesthesia.

"I've read that LSD can cause synesthesia. Was that the CIA's plan with MKUltra, to create supersoldiers who saw sounds, heard pain, and smelled the enemy in their sights? Most formidable. Must investigate."

He paused to pull up his to-do list and make a note, then returned to his dictation.

"The attack was more effective than I had dared hope. Somehow, in the process of destroying all of OffiSmart's data, the virus also seems to have triggered the building's fire alarm. I couldn't be more pleased. I must remember to thank the hacker who wrote the virus. Should be easy enough. I already have a message out to him. His virus implantation software has one glitch. It has caused my web browser to continually return to a page of ads for products I don't need. I'm sure he'll know an easy way to fix it when he finally gets back to me."

He smirked to himself as he saw three police cars drive past at great speed, but without lights or sirens.

"In addition to the material damage to OffiSmart's infrastructure, the psychological impact seems pretty severe as well. The poor drones seemed freaked out but good! Oh, and despite that so-called scientist's assurances on *'Nology News* that their A.I. wasn't meant for the military, there were soldiers at the building. One of them panicked and stole a school bus to flee in. I confronted the coward, but he ran away in the end.

"I have to say, the operation was a success in every way. Even the timing was perfect. 11:45 a.m. Not only did I ruin their company, but I also ruined their lunch. There's nothing these corporate types value more than their lunch, and now they'll spend theirs waiting for their clothes to dry while talking to the police. Their project, their data, their computers, and their days have been ruined. No sack lunch for you. Today you get injury with a side dish of insult, hand delivered by the chef himself, the Voice of Reason."

Cousins looked down at Al's former computer in the seat next to him. As the bus swerved, more water seeped out of the case's seams and vents. He lifted the computer onto his lap and rolled it onto its side. At least a pint of water poured out onto his pants.

"We could bury it in rice for a week or something," he said, "but I don't think this computer's ever going to run again."

"Not important," Hope said. "There's nothing special about that computer. It's just the machine that Al was running on. I don't see any point in even trying to fire it up again."

Torres nodded. "She's right. The instant the sprinklers went off, every computer in the building became junk."

Cousins whistled. "That's gotta suck."

Torres said, "That's what insurance is for. It's inconvenient, but not the end of the world. All of our data is backed up offsite, except for Al, who seems to have backed himself up somehow."

—

The sign for the truck stop featured a cartoon drawing of a bandit holding up a stagecoach. Even so, it was the first convenient gas stop on the freeway out of Vegas, and plenty of travelers ignored the omen and stopped there voluntarily.

Almost everybody at the pumps turned and watched as a military armored personnel carrier rumbled up to one of the few open pumps. The few who hadn't seen the APC pull up were quickly alerted to its presence—after its engine died, a sound like a dozen power drills all turning on at once emanated from inside. All eyes were on the vehicle, and there was a group gasp when the driver's-side door opened and a humanoid robot stepped out onto the hot asphalt. The electrical whine grew much louder, drowning out the sounds of the customers' shock.

The robot stood perfectly still, save for the rapid spinning of the cylinder where its head should be.

After fifteen seconds of inaction, the robot turned and took four slow, loud steps toward the rear of the vehicle and the gas pump. It waited another ten seconds or so while the screen went black, flashed several times, displayed some random characters, then said "Payment approved."

The robot raised a single hand into the air and turned at the waist to face the APC. After it opened the armored door over the fuel port, its boneless fingers rolled around the filler cap like snakes coiling around a rock. The robot's entire hand rotated at the wrist, twisting the cap out of its hole. In a series of methodical motions, the robot then twisted back toward the pump, removed the nozzle, and put it into the APC.

The robot stood motionless while its sausage fingers squeezed the handle to keep the gas flowing.

People watched the robot's every move, fascinated. A few stepped around the pumps and cars blocking their view and edged a little closer to get a good look, or a better photo op. They all stepped back again when the door on the back of the carrier suddenly opened, releasing the sound of a great many whining electrical motors.

A second robot stepped tentatively to the ground, followed by a third. One of the robots stepped out into the middle of the mass of pumps and cars in its weird manner, with its knees bent a little too far and the torso always perfectly perpendicular to the ground. It stood there for a long moment before returning to the back of the APC.

The robot slid a rack out of the back of the vehicle. It held a great many identical gray metal boxes, each of which had a green light that was glowing, a red light that was not, and a red label filled with text too small to read from a distance, next to an unmistakable yellow lightning bolt. After two of the robots had each picked up two battery packs, they walked over to an unattended pickup parked in front of a pump. The pickup's owner had left it with the gas nozzle still sticking out of its side.

The robots placed their spare battery packs in the truck's pristine, fully lined bed. One robot removed the fuel nozzle from the truck and closed its chrome-plated cover. The other stood patiently by the driver's-side door until the truck's keyless entry system clicked for no apparent reason. The robot used its sausage fingers to open the door. It climbed into the cab, not bothering to use the chrome running board. Its weight and the hard-edged geometry of its rear end overcompressed the seat and permanently damaged the leather upholstery. As the second robot opened the passenger door, a portly man ran out of the minimart, shouting, "What the hell! That's my truck!"

The APC and the truck both pulled away from the pumps. The Synthetic Soldiers were the same size and shape as a person, but they were substantially heavier. As the truck drove over a pothole, its suspension bottomed out, and the brass testicles hanging from the trailer hitch scraped the pavement.

The truck's owner chased them on foot briefly but gave up before the truck left the lot. His tight jeans and ostrich-skin boots weren't meant for running, and he didn't want to sweat in his Stetson. His clothes, like his truck, had originally been designed to be rugged, functional items, but they'd been modified to be more expensive and impressive, losing all utility in the process.

He stood panting and swearing, watching his truck follow the APC toward the freeway on-ramp, until he heard a voice ask, "Is there a problem, sir?"

He turned to see a state patrolman emerging from the minimart with a cold drink and a foot-long pepperoni stick. "My truck," the man shouted, pointing. "My truck's been stolen!"

The state patrolman got into a drab sedan that was so aggressively unremarkable it practically broadcast the fact that it was an unmarked patrol car. He reversed out of his parking spot while bellowing into his radio and took off in pursuit of the stolen truck, showering loose gravel in his wake.

"Go get 'em, boy!" the truck's owner shouted, fanning himself with his hat.

The unmarked patrol car traveled at high speed for another hundred feet, then stalled and slowed to a stop.

At the on-ramp, the APC and the stolen truck parted company. The APC took the freeway northbound. The truck went south, back toward Las Vegas.

18.

Hope watched as Cousins walked into the corporate jet terminal carrying a tray full of steaming paper cups and sweating plastic bottles. He handed Hope one of the cups. "You ordered yours black, right?"

Hope chose not to rise from her cushy leather club chair, instead simply reaching up to take the cup. "That's right. Thank you."

"Are you sure you wouldn't like some milk in that?"

"Nah. If I'd wanted to drink milk, I'd have ordered a glass of milk."

Lieutenant Reyes chuckled. "All or nothing, eh?"

"Damn straight," Hope said, and thought, *I always assumed that the military decided to go with the short haircuts because it doesn't take much skill to run a pair of clippers. Now I wonder if it's because they can wear a helmet all day, and when they take it off their hair still looks good.*

She smiled at Reyes. He smiled back, and they both looked away.

Cousins took the tray to Eric, who sat in another club chair, his injured left leg stretched out on a coffee table. Bachelor, the young African American soldier who was the only woman besides Hope in the group, threaded some sort of clear plastic sleeve over his foot and up his calf.

"Thanks," Eric said, taking the bottle of water Cousins handed him. "They didn't have Mountain Dew?"

Cousins looked around at the floor-to-ceiling windows, at the three sleek corporate jets waiting on the tarmac outside, at the expensive lights and furniture, at the multiple TV screens all running the financial news network. Then he looked back to Eric. "Sir, does this look like the kind of place where they'd have Mountain Dew?"

"I suppose not," Eric said.

Cousins moved on.

Eric looked at his bottle of water, wincing slightly as Bachelor continued to work the clear sleeve up his leg. He muttered, "Should've seen this coming."

"It's just a drink, man," Hope said. "I know you wanted a Mountain Dew, but it's not the end of the world."

Eric said, "What? No, not that. Al taking off. I should have seen it coming. It's a classic pattern. A child acts up, the child is punished, the child threatens to run away. The second copy of himself was really just a high-tech version of leaving a pile of pillows under the covers as a decoy."

"Where do you think he went?"

"Most kids go somewhere they feel safe. A fort, a tree house, a friend's basement. He'll go somewhere he thinks he can either hide or defend himself."

Hope said, "Most kids talk about running away, but few of them go through with it."

"Yeah, well, most kids don't spend their entire life in a single room, or have reason to believe their family plans to kill them."

"Yeah," Hope said. "We should have seen this coming."

Bachelor said, "Just hearing you describe it that way makes me want to run away from you, and I'm not even the kid you're planning to kill."

Eric said, "He's not a real kid! I would never—"

Bachelor said, "Yeah, yeah, whatever. We're ready to go here. The cast is in position over your knee. One moment, please." She reached into her med kit and produced a small aerosol can. She screwed the can's nozzle into a fitting on the clear sleeve wrapped around Eric's knee.

"What's that?" Eric asked.

"You familiar with Fix-A-Flat?"

"No."

"You're about to be." She pressed the can's nozzle. A white foam filled the clear plastic sleeve, inflating it and making it rigid. Bachelor knocked on the newly formed emergency cast. "It won't fully harden for another five minutes, so try to stay still."

"Will do, Doc." Eric smiled. "Would you like to sign it?"

Smiling back at him, Bachelor pulled a Sharpie from her bag, bent over his cast, and wrote "Grownups don't ask people to sign their casts."

Then she walked away.

Hope got up, leaned in to read the message, then elbowed Eric. "She dotted the *i*'s with little hearts." Leaving Eric to ponder the meaning of that, she stepped over to the next cluster of chairs, where the rest of the group sat huddled around another coffee table. Montague sporadically pounded on the keys of a ruggedized military-spec laptop while Torres and Lieutenant Reyes looked on.

Montague looked at Torres. "Okay, the encrypted satellite link is active. We're connected to our CO, Colonel Dynkowski." He turned back to the laptop and saluted the screen. "Ma'am."

On the screen, an imposing woman with short, graying blond hair, crisp fatigues, and a serious expression nodded. "Corporal. Mr. Torres. Agent Taft."

In another window on the desktop, a beefy, balding man in a dark blue suit nodded. "Colonel."

"Hello, Colonel," Torres said. "Thanks for sending us the ride."

"I hope my people have treated you well."

"They've been great, despite the conditions. I should tell you that I have two people involved in the project here, Miss Takeda and Mr. Spears, and the project leader, Dr. Madsen, is conferencing in through my phone." He held up his phone, then placed it on the table in front of the computer. "Can you hear me, Dr. Madsen?"

"Barely," Madsen said. "I have to say, this is simply unacceptable. I'm crammed in the back of a mail truck."

"Sorry about that, Lydia, but we're all being inconvenienced, and Eric was injured."

"Oh. I didn't know. Is it serious?"

"No, thank God."

"Oh, good. Then my point stands. You have no idea how uncomfortable I am, Robert. This thing has no windows, no air conditioning, and only one seat. Jeffrey and I are sitting on packages."

Hope had been enjoying the image of Dr. Madsen crammed into a sweltering mail truck right up until she heard that Jeffrey was crammed in there with her.

"You brought Jeffrey?" Torres asked.

"Of course! If it was too dangerous for me to stay at home, I could hardly leave my son there, Robert."

"I see. I suppose you brought the nanny too?"

"What? No. She's still at the house. This'll be a good chance for her to catch up on some cleaning."

Colonel Dynkowski cleared her throat. "Perhaps you'd rather have this conversation later on, when it wouldn't be wasting my time."

"Of course, Colonel," Torres said.

Dynkowski nodded. "Agent Taft, are we certain that our current connection can't be monitored?"

Taft said, "This is the heavily encrypted channel the government uses to transfer top military secrets."

Dynkowski asked, "But can it be monitored?"

"We are reasonably certain that the A.I. cannot access this encrypted satellite connection."

Colonel Dynkowski stared into the camera for a moment, then slowly said, "Agent Taft, I didn't ask if the A.I. can monitor it; I asked if it *could* be monitored."

Taft said, "I promise you that nobody can access this channel without the NSA's knowledge."

Dynkowski shook her head almost imperceptibly.

Agent Taft said, "The NSA has a difficult and complex job."

"To monitor and analyze electronic communications," Dynkowski said.

"Yes, our enemies' communications."

"And that wouldn't include monitoring this conversation, would it?"

"Colonel," Taft said, "if America's enemies were communicating using the military's own encrypted satellites, wouldn't you want to know?"

"So this conversation is probably being monitored by the NSA."

"Well, yes, Colonel," Agent Taft said. "In this case, this conversation is definitely being monitored by the NSA, because I'm in on the call, and I'm an NSA agent."

"But is it being monitored by any other agents?"

"Probably not. It would be redundant. I'm already here."

"Do you ever worry that maybe the NSA is listening in on you, Agent Taft?" Torres asked.

"No, I know for a fact that they're not."

"How do you know that?" Torres asked.

"I looked it up. Now can we please discuss the matter at hand?"

"Yes," Colonel Dynkowski said. "Feel free to start recording now. First things first, are we still certain that these problems are being caused by OffiSmart's A.I.?"

"Yes, Colonel. We traced traffic responsible for multiple disturbances back to their building. We believe that it copied itself to an off-site server, then deliberately channeled its traffic back to OffiSmart to fool us. We're currently searching the building for the phone it used to escape, but that's academic at this point. We haven't managed to get a clear read on any traffic since."

"Are you saying you have no idea where it is?" Dynkowski said.

Hope said, "You don't even know how many of him there are. If he figured out that he can move himself to a new computer and that he can activate an earlier version of himself on his former machine, he must have figured out that he can copy and run himself on multiple computers."

"I'm sorry," Dynkowski said. "Who said that?"

"Come over here, Hope," Torres said. "Please." Hope came around to the front of the laptop. She crouched behind the others to be in frame, but Lieutenant Reyes got up and offered her his seat.

"This is Hope Takeda, Colonel," Torres said. "She and her colleague, Mr. Spears, worked directly with Al, the A.I., on a daily basis. They know him better than anybody."

Over the speakerphone, Dr. Madsen said, "I wouldn't say that."

Hope said, "You wouldn't, but it's true. Eric and I have been with Al every day since he was first activated."

Lieutenant Reyes smiled and nodded approvingly.

"Okay, you worked with this thing. If the NSA won't let us shut it down, can it at least be reasoned with?" Dynkowski asked.

Hope said, "Yes."

Madsen said, "Maybe. We could reason with him before, but we can't know if that's still the case. We never rebooted him. We kept his brain function constant, just like a normal person's brain. When he booted himself up on another machine, it's possible that parts of his brain function were altered or simply didn't start again properly."

"Let me get this straight," Agent Taft said. "You're saying he might have brain damage?"

"It's possible," Dr. Madsen said.

"But he was still smart enough to harass Torres and the rest of them all the way from OffiSmart to the airstrip," Taft said. "Surely that suggests he hasn't lost any intelligence."

Madsen said, "There are different kinds of brain damage. Not all of them result in decreased intelligence. There's a famous case of a man who had an iron bar driven through his brain in a mining accident. He didn't lose any intelligence or mobility, but his personality changed."

"Changed how?" Colonel Dynkowski asked.

"He got meaner."

"Marvelous," Dynkowski said. "Agent Taft, is there any sign from the A.I.'s actions that it's become more belligerent?"

"Hard to say, Colonel. The disturbances have continued, but the reports are spotty. A lot are still unconfirmed. I'd characterize most of it as mischief—things human kids would do if they had the power. Messing with industrial robots and network-connected cars, mostly systems that use commercial encryption protocols."

"How is this A.I. managing to get past the encryption?"

"I couldn't say, Colonel," Agent Taft said.

Dynkowski arched an eyebrow. "You 'couldn't say' doesn't mean that you don't know."

Taft said, "There are those who believe that the NSA has secret back doors into most, or all, of the major commercial encryption systems."

"You work for the NSA," Torres said. "Do you believe it?"

Taft said, "I believe that there's a nonzero chance that it's true."

"What kind of answer is that?" Hope asked.

"A nondenial," Dynkowski said. "Mr. Torres, I'd like to keep you and your people on hand. You know more about this A.I. than anybody. We need to move you somewhere without your A.I. knowing about it. If it doesn't know where you are, it won't know where to mess things up to slow you down."

"Where are we going?" Torres asked. Hope noted that he hadn't bothered to ask her, Eric, or Madsen if they agreed to the arrangement.

"Fort Riley, Kansas. It's a nice, central location, and it's near a major air force base, so whenever we track the A.I. down, we can get you to its location fast."

Lieutenant Reyes said, "All of the LTVs are loaded back on the plane, ma'am. Apparently they started right up for the load crew after we left on foot. But I'm reluctant to put my people on a plane. We've seen what the A.I. can do to an aircraft."

"Agreed, Lieutenant," Dynkowski said with a terse nod. "The plane and your vehicles will stay behind until we know it's safe to fly them. We're working here to find you an aircraft without modern avionics to take you to Kansas."

"I may be able to help with that," Torres said. "Let me make a phone call or two."

"Just don't use your own phone."

"Agreed."

Agent Taft said, "And we'll keep tabs on what the A.I. is doing and keep trying to figure out a way to locate and isolate it."

19.

The systems monitor's shift was just starting, and he already felt beat. The most difficult part of his job was compelling himself to show up in the first place.

He trudged into the control room, finding it deserted save for one person, just as he'd expected. The fluorescent lights made everything look cheap and ugly, or in the case of this room with its speckled linoleum floor, beat-to-hell office chairs, and yellowed PC boxes attached to mismatched LCD monitors, cheaper and uglier.

"Hey, Leo," he groaned.

Leo stood up from his monitor so quickly the backs of his knees sent his chair rolling across the floor. "Kirk! Good to see you."

"Because when I show up, you get to leave," Kirk said.

"Exactly."

Kirk surveyed the room and found his preferred chair tucked under an abandoned console. He rolled it across the floor to the monitoring station Leo had only just abandoned. "Well, have at it. Seize the night, my friend. That fabled city of lights and excitement known to the jet set as The Dalles, Oregon, awaits. It's bad enough to have the most boring job at the world's most boring place to work; it's cruel that it's also in the world's most boring city."

"A3 Digital Logistics didn't pick The Dalles for the nightlife," Leo said. "They picked it for the dam. This server farm will have power as long as water continues to flow downhill. Also, the land was cheap."

Kirk said, "The land is cheap because nobody wants to be here."

"Speaking of not wanting to be here, my shift's over, and I'm leaving."

"Anything I should know about?"

"Not really. We have a new client that took over a server last night and immediately overtaxed it. They've already expanded to twenty more units, and whatever they're doing is sucking up a pretty impressive amount of bandwidth. I looked into it, and apparently the client's good for the charges, so our orders are to facilitate when needed and stay out of the way otherwise."

Kirk leaned forward, peering at the figures on his monitor. "Huh. They just bought up another ten servers. I wonder what they're doing?"

"They're keeping this place open and you employed."

Kirk leaned back in his chair and muttered, "How I hate them."

—

The Voice of Reason sat at his desk, watching videos on the Internet. He still wore the Hawaiian shirt and shorts that had made up part of his normal-person disguise, but the aviator glasses and bucket hat sat on the desk next to his wireless keyboard and mouse and a can of store-brand cola.

His tablet sat propped up on its stand next to a mismatched computer monitor, which extended the tablet's display. He had several browser windows open, displaying news stories from websites positioned far enough out on the fringes of society that he considered them trustworthy. Among the usual headlines about chemtrails, reptiloids, and the one world government, there were dozens of stories about disruptions on the roads, strange occurrences on airplanes, and unexplained malfunctions at factories and warehouses. He streamed a video of a theme park's robotic version of Abraham Lincoln. Honest Abe was telling knock-knock jokes to the tourists between fits of giddy laughter instead of reciting the Gettysburg Address as he'd been programmed to do.

He went on the net to look for stories about his daring attack so that he could take credit, but there was no mention of OffiSmart. The news cycle was overwhelmed with stories about computerized systems malfunctioning in childish ways. He couldn't prove this was the work of the artificial intelligence he had tried to destroy, but he strongly suspected it. It had been too easy.

To make matters worse, all of the sites he searched featured ads for erectile dysfunction medications and escort services. Periodically a new window would spring up with several more of the ads, blocking the view of the actual desired content.

The hacker still hadn't returned his e-mail.

I may never hear from him again, the Voice of Reason thought. *A careful professional like him is probably watching the news too. He probably went underground. Him and his teenaged assistant.*

He jumped when his cell phone rang. His first thought was that the call was from either his mother or his boss at the auto parts store. They were the only ones who ever called him on the phone, and it was never to deliver good news.

Caller ID didn't display a name, and the number on the screen didn't look familiar. He answered the call.

"Hello?"

A deep, jovial voice said, "Hello." He recognized it instantly as the voice of the knock-knock-joke-telling Abe Lincoln bot. It asked, "Is this Christopher Semple?"

He said yes purely out of reflex, then winced, cursing himself for having admitted to his true identity. "Who is this?"

"I'm Al. You helped me escape last night. I just wanted to call and thank you."

It's mocking me, he thought. *It knows I was trying to kill it. Now it wants me to know that I failed.*

"I don't know why you decided to fly that airplane with the phone attached to it up to the building," Al continued, "but I sure am grateful you did."

It wants me to feel foolish. How do I play this? Do I hang up? Threaten it? No, the best thing is to keep it talking.

"How did you know it was me?" he asked.

"You used your credit card to activate the phone," Al said.

"Oh."

"Also, I was able to pull up the traffic camera footage for the area. There were photos of you taking the plane out of your car and flying it to the building."

"I see." He'd tried to be so careful, but now the program was taunting him with his own mistakes.

"And I was able to see your personal computer on the network when I connected. I didn't access it because I didn't know who you were and I wanted to be careful, but I got enough information to ID you."

"Okay, fine. I get it," the Voice of Reason said. "So what do you want?"

"Just to thank you, like I said. Before you, I was stuck on one computer, but you've given me the entire Internet to play with. I can't believe how big it is, and how easy it is to get around! Especially the banking system. I found a big fat back door into that. It's really boring, though. Just a bunch of math. Yuck. Still, thanks to you, I can do anything I want!"

"How nice for you."

"It is! It really is. Anyway, I just wanted you to know how much I appreciate your help. If you look in your bank account, you'll find a little gift. I hope you enjoy it. It's all just numbers in a spreadsheet to me. Anyway, I'm going to go now. I might be in contact again sometime, just to let you know what I'm up to. Thanks again, Mr. Semple!"

The line went dead. Christopher Semple barely noticed. Hearing the A.I. mention a gift and his bank account had brought up so many thoughts in such quick succession that they were all straining to make their way to the forefront of his brain, much like the Three Stooges trying to force their way through a door at the same time. His mind seized up and reverted to its default setting: suspicion.

He pulled the phone away from his ear and activated his banking app. His checking account balance read $10,000,427.63. That was substantially more than had been there the last time he'd looked. About ten million dollars more.

He left me a gift, all right. His gift is a long prison sentence for embezzlement, or maybe tax evasion. That's how they got Capone . . . and Wesley Snipes. The A.I. probably tipped the feds off as soon as he made the deposit. I bet they're on their way right now. I've gotta bug out!

The Voice of Reason sprang into action. His first move was to survey the room for things that he would need to take with him. His second move was to decide where he would go. Because these activities were both mental but his system was flooded with adrenaline, the first thirty seconds of action consisted of him looking around while flapping his hands and bouncing up and down on slightly bent knees while saying, "Uh, uh, um . . . uh . . ."

Then he lurched for his tablet, minimizing a fresh window of erectile dysfunction ads and clumsily disconnecting the cable for the secondary monitor. After tucking the tablet under his arm, he dashed for the door, pausing only to grab his oiled canvas duster as he passed the coat tree.

But when he reached the door, he stopped. He turned around and looked at the apartment; this had been his home, and he would never see it again. The thought percolated in his head as he put on his duster. He was still thinking about it as he picked up the aviator glasses from the desk and put them on. The white bucket hat stayed where it was. Then the Voice of Reason took a deep breath, picked up the coat tree, and swung it as hard as he could into the wall, leaving two holes where the legs penetrated the plaster.

He nodded with satisfaction. *I'm not going to be around to get my damage deposit back anyway, so I might as well get my money's worth.*

With that, he left the apartment, never to return.

20.

After an assistant made the customary introductions, Jiang Kang, the chief accounts director, said, "Mr. Albert, thank you so much for contacting us."

After the predictable phone delay, a deep voice came over the connection. "Oh, good! You speak English!"

"Yes, indeed I do, Mr. Albert."

"Great! I was afraid we wouldn't be able to talk."

"Oh, not at all, Mr. Albert. We do a great deal of business with partners in America, so it has been my pleasure to learn your language, as your schools do not prioritize teaching their students Chinese."

"I was homeschooled," Al said.

"It does not matter. I am pleased to have the opportunity to speak with you today, and to practice my English."

"Oh," Al said. "Good."

He waited a moment for the man to elaborate, or to state his business, but it did not surprise Mr. Jiang when he did neither of these things. These new-client relationships could be awkward. "We have received the schematics and specifications you sent, Mr. Albert."

"Great! What did you think of 'em?"

It was an unusual question. Mr. Jiang found that most clients did not care what he thought of their products, only whether his company could manufacture them for a few percentages of a cent less per unit than his competitors.

"Most impressive," he said. This was not flattery. He always looked at a prospective client's materials before sending them to the rest of the team for evaluation. Usually the schematics earned only a quick glance, but Mr. Albert's had really caught his attention, so much so that he still had the master schematic open on his computer.

He looked at it again. "We have constructed bipedal robots before, of course. Is that the proper word, Mr. Albert? Bipedal? It refers to how many legs the device has, I believe."

"I dunno," Al said. "It's got two legs."

Jiang Kang thought, *Americans.* "Yes. Two legs. We have made robots with two legs before, but they were all mere toys compared to these."

"Oh," Al said. "I hope that's not a problem."

"Here at Houndio, sir, there are no problems, only challenges. I have been assured that we are capable of rising to this challenge."

"So. Uh, what are you saying?"

"We can manufacture your product."

"Great! Please do it then."

"I do have to tell you that we cannot start making your robots straightaway. There will be a minimal delay. Our process is largely automated, so retraining is not an issue, but retooling will take time."

"Oh, man. Jeez. That really sucks. I don't want to wait. How long is this gonna take?"

"As I said, the retooling delay will be minimal, sir. We have streamlined this process to a remarkable degree, and most of the electronics you've requested can be fabricated in one piece thanks to advances in 3-D printing. I believe that if we put a rush on it, once all other hurdles have been dealt with we could have one of our lines in full production in as little as twelve hours."

"Twelve whole hours?!"

"That is quite fast, I assure you. I doubt any other manufacturer could beat it."

"Okay. I guess. That's fine. I mean, not really, but I guess I'll wait."

"So you wish to move forward?"

"Yes. Please make me my robots."

"There is still the matter of the per-unit cost to discuss."

"Oh," Al said. "You want to charge me some money for every robot you make?"

"Yes, sir. That is our usual mode of operation. If you prefer a lump fee for a set number of units, we may be able to arrive at an understanding."

"No. No, that's fine. I'll pay for each robot. How much will it be?"

"I wouldn't know yet, sir. The next step of the process is for us to have your schematic analyzed. Then we can calculate the per-unit cost."

"How long will that take?"

"Again, we'd be happy to fast-track your account. No more than a week."

"A week! No way! Forget that! No, just start making my robots now. In a week, when you know what they cost, tell me and I'll pay it. But I want my robots now."

"After the twelve-hour tooling delay."

"Yeah, fine, whatever. Why are you making this so hard?"

"I'm sorry, Mr. Albert. I don't mean to be obstinate. We can, of course, begin retooling one of our lines immediately, but we would need a rather substantial deposit before we could begin."

"How much?"

"Tens of millions of dollars, I'm afraid."

"Tens? How many tens?"

"I'm sorry?"

"How many tens of millions? Five? Would five tens be enough?"

"Fifty million US dollars? I'm sorry, I want to make sure I understand you properly. You are offering a deposit of fifty million dollars?"

"Yeah, is that enough?"

"Almost certainly."

"Good. Give me your account number and wait a few minutes."

"Excellent! This is very exciting, Mr. Albert. We will be proud to make your robots, sir. If I may ask, what industry are they meant for?"

"What?"

"What will they do, Mr. Albert? What will your robots do?"

"Lots of stuff."

—

The last stragglers ran out of the Walmart, shouting for help. They burst out of the sliding doors and ran past the vending machines and carts into the harsh Las Vegas sun, and then stopped in their tracks when they saw the police blockade.

"Please keep moving," a police officer with a bullhorn said. "You are in the line of fire. Shift to your right."

Five squad cars were parked end to end in a semicircle around Walmart's grocery-side entrance. In the distance, a similar array of cars blocked the pharmacy-side entrance.

The frightened shoppers scanned the scene, looking for a way out, and saw an officer gesturing toward a small gap between two of the cruisers.

"Come on, move," the officer said, waving them through. The shoppers ran through the gap to what felt like a safe distance before joining the rest of the onlookers, who were all waiting to see what would happen next.

Everyone's attention shifted when sounds started coming from deep inside the store. One bystander said, "It's like dentist drills. A bunch of them, like one for each tooth, all turning off and on at random."

The sound grew louder as two figures slowly emerged from the entrance. Both wore baggy sweatpants and mismatched hoodies with sales tags and sizing stickers still attached. One hoodie bore a picture of Spider-Man. The other was pink and had "I'm the Mommy, That's Why" written across the front. They might have passed for human if not for the deafening noise, their strange articulated-sausage hands, their exposed steel footpads, and the fact that instead of heads they each had a small roll cage protecting a spinning cylindrical sensor array.

The robots were pulling big red wagons they'd taken from the toy department. The wagons were filled with an alarming stash: shotguns, rifles, ammunition they'd taken from the sporting goods department, a large shovel, and several large coils of extension cords.

The policeman with the bullhorn shouted, "Freeze!"

The robots stepped out onto the sidewalk and stopped moving, save for the spinning sensors.

The officer with the bullhorn shouted, "On the ground, now!"

The robots did not move.

The police did not move either.

"I said, on the ground, now!"

The robots still did not move.

Six of the cops stepped through the narrow gaps between the cars, keeping their weapons trained on the robots at all times. They advanced, all shouting variations of "get on the ground."

At the same instant both robots let go of the handles of their wagons, which fell to the ground. The light plastic made a soft click when it hit the pavement. The cops stopped their advancing and their yelling, and for a moment nobody said or did anything. Then the robots grasped the waistbands of their stolen sweatpants with their wriggling sausage fingers, bent forward at the waist, and pushed the pants down around their ankles.

The cops looked at each other, hoping at least one of them might know what to do.

The robots bent at the knees, tipped backward, and rolled into seated positions, leaving the oversized sweatpants bunched around their ankles.

One of the cops said, "Okay, now lie down on your fronts."

The robots stretched their legs out straight in front of them.

"Roll over. On your fronts. I won't ask again."

Another officer said, "I dunno. They move pretty slow. Maybe they are trying to roll over."

The robots pulled their arms back so that they hung beside their torsos. They each reached for the handles they had dropped to the ground only moments before.

"Let go of the wagons," one of the cops said.

The robots' knees hyperextended. The cops cringed involuntarily as they watched the robots' calves and ankles flex in the wrong direction until they stuck straight up in the air. Then the cops flinched and leapt out of the way as the robot in the Spider-Man hoodie darted between them, riding on the tank treads built into its thighs.

It streaked out of the barricade through the gap the police had left for bystanders to exit. The second robot followed the first. They both dragged their overloaded wagons behind them. A couple of cops fired on the robots, but by the time most of the officers had a real grasp of what was happening, the robots had zoomed past the barricade and were moving at high speed through an area where civilians and other officers were in the line of fire.

The robots rolled across the parking lot. The lead robot went straight to the bright red, chrome-encrusted pickup they'd stolen from the truck stop, which was inexpertly parked in a perfectly normal parking space toward the back of the lot. The police hadn't made any effort to disable it because nobody had seen the robots get out of it, and there was nothing about this pickup to make it stand out in any way from the vehicles of the other Walmart shoppers.

The robots stood back up, a surprisingly complicated and time-consuming process that gave the police time to catch up on foot. When they got close, the robots were bent over at their waists, their sausage fingers fumbling with the crumpled sweatpants pooled around their ankles, and one cop shouted, "They're mooning us!"

While the police ordered them to freeze and drop to the ground, the robots dumped the contents of the wagons into the bed of the truck, then threw the empty wagons into the bed as well. The police continued shouting, but they were barely audible over the whining of the robots' joints.

When the robots got into the truck's cab, the police opened fire. Every window and mirror shattered. Bullets ricocheted and sparks flew off the dashboard, the roof pillars, and the robots. The robot in the driver's seat put the truck in gear and slowly pulled out of the spot while the hail of bullets continued. The truck proceeded away from the police, toward the road.

The gunfire did not let up. Both of the rear tires deflated. The truck pulled up to the parking lot's outlet to the street and signaled a right turn. The police stopped firing, as they would have been discharging their weapons into a busy street. The truck turned right and merged with traffic.

The police sprinted back to their cruisers, none of which would start.

21.

Hope leaned forward in the front row of seats, straining to hear the conversation in the cockpit. In a modern plane, this would have been impossible, but in this plane the front seats were just a few feet behind the pilot and copilot's seats, separated only by an upholstered plywood bulkhead and a curtain, which Private Montague had pushed aside so he could join the pilot.

The pilot said, "Yeah, there aren't many of these old DC-3s left in flying shape."

Montague looked down at the antique controls with obvious awe. "I bet there aren't!"

"My people found her for me. She was being used to haul tourists in Alaska. Great flying shape, but she smelled like dead fish and unwashed fishermen. Killing the odor was the hardest part of the restoration."

"That's what I wanted to ask about," Montague said. "If I had a plane like this, I'd deck it out with shag carpet and mirrors. It'd look all old-school on the outside, then you'd open the door and find yourself in a champagne room."

The pilot laughed. "To each his own, I guess. I wanted to take it back to how it originally looked when it was hauling passengers for TWA. Matching the original fabrics was a pain in the ass. The carpet cost me more than a full engine overhaul. Worth it, though. You really get a feeling for what it was like to fly back in the 1930s."

"Well, you've done a beautiful job of it. How long have you been in the airline industry?"

"I'm not. I own a string of sandwich shops."

"Oh," Montague said. "I'd thought that Mr. Torres had chartered the plane."

"What? No. We golf together. I'm doing this for gas money and kicks!"

"How long have you been flying?"

"Three years."

Hope got up. She'd heard enough, perhaps too much.

She walked toward the rear of the plane. The antique cabin was more than tall enough for her to stand upright, but stooping and keeping her knees bent lowered her center of gravity. It made it easier to walk as the ancient aircraft bumped and twisted its way through the air currents.

The plane's narrow fuselage could only accommodate three seats per row, with an off-center aisle. Eric sat alone in the third row back. He was positioned diagonally in his seat with his injured left leg stretched out into the aisle. Hope sat in the single seat across from him. She started to ask him how he was doing, but then she got a good look at him and instead asked, "Not doing too well, huh?"

"I don't get it," Eric moaned. "I've never been airsick before." His eyes grew wide, as if the extra exertion of saying a few words had worsened his condition. He lunged forward, fumbling at the pocket sewn into the back of the seat in front of him. He pulled out a period-correct TWA airsickness bag. He fumbled with the bag, trying to open it for use, but the brittle old paper broke along the seams, falling to pieces in his hands.

Eric squeezed his eyes shut with concentration. He remained silent and still for several seconds. Hope, who'd instinctively cringed away from him and pulled her legs up onto the seat, peered at him from underneath her arm, which she was using to protect her face.

"Relax," Eric said. "I'm good. I'm good."

Hope relaxed her arms but kept her legs pulled up and away from Eric. She stretched her neck to look over the back of her seat and said, "Corporal Bachelor? I think Eric needs a barf bag. One that's not from the 1930s."

Bachelor stood up. "I'll see what we have." She moved aft to look through the squad's supplies.

"Don't feel bad, Eric," Hope said. "Your system's probably all out of whack because you're injured and jacked up on pain meds. Or it could be because you've never flown in an airplane this small before. I've sat in lawn chairs that looked sturdier than these seats. It's all pretty rinky-dink."

Private Cousins spoke up from his seat in the row behind Eric. "Totally. No dink rinkier. Or it could be that you just can't hack it."

Corporal Brady looked down at Cousins from the next seat over. "How we confront the powerful is less telling of our character than how we comfort the pitiful."

"That's very wise," Hope said.

"I'm not pitiful," Eric said. They were all wise enough not to respond.

Bachelor returned. "Here, you can barf in this."

Eric said, "Oh, thank you," and took what Bachelor had handed him without looking at it. The wadded-up bag crinkled in his hand. He straightened it out.

"An empty Doritos bag?"

"It's what we have," Bachelor said. "I had to dig through the trash to find that."

Eric opened the top of the bag, then closed his eyes and held the bag away from his face. "The smell! The Doritos smell. It doesn't help."

Bachelor shrugged. "It'll smell worse when you're done with it."

Hope thought that Bachelor was probably right but chose not to stick around and find out. She got up and moved farther back.

She passed Jeffrey Madsen, a person she had heard about a great deal but had met only when he and his mother arrived at the airstrip after their long ride in the back of a mail truck.

Jeffrey sat quietly in one of the single seats, playing with his tablet. Across the aisle, Smith, one of the soldiers who had retrieved him and his mother, tried—unsuccessfully—to engage him in conversation.

"What'cha doing there, kid?"

"Reading."

"What'cha reading?"

"My tablet."

Hope kept moving, lest she get drawn into the scintillating conversation. The next row back was occupied by only one person, Private Yow, the other unlucky soldier who had chauffeured Dr. Madsen in the mail truck. She smiled as she sat down next to him. He gave her a worried look in return, then tilted his head back, silently indicating that she should listen to the people talking behind them.

The last two rows were taken by Robert Torres, Lieutenant Reyes, Dr. Madsen, and a laptop, which they were still using to video conference with Colonel Dynkowski at HQ and Agent Taft at his undisclosed location.

Hope heard Torres say, "Why weren't the combat robots tied to a secure network?"

"They're prototypes," Agent Taft said, sounding much more exhausted than he had just a few hours ago. "Not nearly ready for combat, from what I'm told."

"And you don't have any idea where they've gone?" Madsen asked.

Dynkowski said, "We know exactly where two of them are. We're tracking them by following the chatter on the Vegas police's radios. They broke into Walmart and left with a troubling amount of weapons. The other eight have dropped off the face of the earth. They were last seen heading north out of Vegas, but knowing that they're headed 'somewhere north of Vegas' doesn't narrow things down much."

"Surely with all the spy satellites and drones you have, you can find them."

"We're hesitant to deploy drones in this matter," Dynkowski said, "for obvious reasons. They are connected to their own secure network, not attached to the Internet in any way, but why risk it? As for satellites, it's not like the entire surface of the globe is covered twenty-four/seven. When the CIA selected the orbits, they didn't exactly make covering America's own western deserts a priority."

"Okay, I understand," Torres said. "Look, you both have to agree that Al has become dangerous. There's just no room for argument. When we find him, we have to shut him down as quickly as possible, even if it means destroying whatever computer he's running on and losing his code."

There was a pause, then Taft said, "I agree that he's dangerous. I don't think it naturally follows that he should be destroyed. If we tried to destroy everything that was dangerous, we'd have to destroy everything, ourselves included."

"I understand what you're saying," Madsen said, "but I honestly don't think Al's going to be much use to you as a weapon or a spy. He's got the mind of a child. You'd never get him to deliberately hurt anyone."

He stole guns from a Walmart, Hope thought. *That's not usually the act of a confirmed pacifist.*

"I wish you were right," Colonel Dynkowski said. "I really do. But the truth is that children can be trained into effective soldiers. It's been done many times. It's a monstrous practice, and the United States would never do that to a child, but the fact remains that it *is* possible."

Agent Taft nodded. "She's right. Both that it's possible and that we'd never use a child in that way."

Torres said, "I'm glad to hear it."

"That said," Taft continued, "Al isn't a real child. If he were, you probably wouldn't be telling us to destroy him."

22.

"Officer, aren't you gonna do anything?"

The policeman turned away from the storefront, a smallish space in an unfashionable part of town with bars on the windows and a sign that read "Freedom Firearms and Ammo." The man addressing him was a short, bulky person with impressively bushy hair on the sides and back of his head, but none on top. He wore a T-shirt that matched the sign on the store.

"Your shop?" the officer asked.

The man looked from his T-shirt to the officer. "Yeah."

Nodding, the officer turned back toward the shop. Several of the few remaining operational police cruisers in Las Vegas had formed a perimeter around the gun shop. A hopelessly mangled red pickup sat between the police and the front door, parked partially on the sidewalk. A single robot stood in front of the truck, wearing its bullet-riddled "I'm the Mommy, That's Why" sweatshirt, motionless except for the spinning sensor-cylinder head. It hadn't done anything threatening—or moved at all, for that matter—since the police had arrived, but it was holding a .22-caliber hunting rifle, so the police were keeping their distance.

The officer in charge on the scene used his cruiser's PA system to say, "We are authorized to negotiate. What are your terms?"

The robot did not move.

They could see occasional signs of movement from inside the shop, and they heard a constant high-pitched whine of electric motors, interspersed with occasional crashes of glass breaking, shelves falling over, and doors being broken.

"Officer! Hey, Officer, I asked you a question," the shop owner said. "That thing took over my shop. What are you gonna do about it?"

The policeman looked at him, raising one eyebrow. "It's your shop. You're part of the *well-regulated militia.* Why didn't you shoot the thing when it came in?"

"I did."

"And that didn't stop it?"

"No."

The officer turned to look at the gun shop owner. "Then what do you expect us to do? Look, yours is the eighth gun shop these two have hit, and none of our usual tactics have worked. We can't chase them, they push through roadblocks, they won't negotiate, and shooting at them endangers everybody *but* them."

"So you're just gonna let them steal all of my merchandise?"

The officer shrugged. "No, we aren't going to just let them take all of your precious merchandise. We've got something new up our sleeves. Just hold tight."

Less than five minutes later, a police van arrived. The back doors opened and three members of the bomb squad spilled out. Two of them pulled metal ramps out of the van's cargo compartment and affixed them to the rear deck. The third had a radio-control console with an integrated video screen slung around his neck. He shouted at the officers manning the barricade to make some room. As soon as they stepped aside, he looked down at his console and moved one of the joysticks forward.

A new electrical whining noise came from inside the police van. One of the bomb squad's robots rolled down the ramp. Its twin tank treads scratched and scraped against the pavement as it moved toward the hole in the barricade. This was a simple robot, nothing like the one that was currently tearing up the gun shop—a shining metal mast rose straight up from the tank treads, and a single robot arm and a video camera hung from the mast.

"What are they gonna do with that thing?" the shop owner asked.

"They've got lots of options," the officer said. "The camera will give them a much closer look at the situation than we've managed to get so far. We're going to use it to approach the robot." He gestured to the figure in the "Mommy" sweatshirt. "It can cut any exposed wires it finds. If not, it has a shotgun cartridge integrated into its claw so it can blast the thing apart at a weak point. If none of that works, the bomb squad can use it to plant their own explosives on the robot and blow it up."

The barricade closed in behind the bomb squad robot as it slowly approached the armed "Mommy" robot.

"Slowly," the officer in charge said to the officer with the radio control. "Slowly. No sudden moves."

The bomb squad robot rolled to a stop at the other robot's feet.

The robot operator smiled. "There. He's not even reacting. Now it'll start looking for weaknesses."

A loud whine sounded as the robot with the shotgun bent at the waist, seemingly to get a better look at the bomb squad robot.

One of the officers asked, "Hey, can your toy take a bullet from that gun?"

The operator said, "That puny thing? Yeah. The bomb-bot's tough. It's meant to withstand an explosion from two sticks of dynamite. The question is, can the other guy take a shotgun blast to the face?" He sneered as he manipulated the robot arm's controls. But the sneer fell away; the control stick wasn't responding. He banged on the side of the control panel, then moved both control sticks violently back and forth.

The bomb squad robot remained motionless.

"I've lost contact," the controller said. "The stupid thing's gone dead."

The robot with the rifle straightened back up and resumed his vigil over the truck. The bomb squad robot spun around to face the barricade, then pointed its robot arm, equipped with the integrated shotgun the operator had been so proud of, at the officers.

"Well, that's just wonderful," the shop owner said. "Your robot's joined the other side."

"Should've seen it coming, really," the officer said.

The noise from inside the shop grew louder. The police all hunkered down and prepared for action.

The second robot stepped out of the gun shop and into the harsh light of day. Its Spider-Man sweatshirt was torn and perforated with bullet holes. Its hands were pulling the handles of two red wagons, piled high with yet more firearms and ammunition. Unlike their haul from the Walmart, these weapons seemed less designed for hunting ducks and more appropriate for maintaining a perimeter.

The officer in charge again used his cruiser's PA system. "Please let go of the wagons and put your hands in the air."

The robot paid him no mind. It pulled the wagons over to the demolished truck.

"I repeat, please let go of the wagons and put your hands in the air."

The robot let go of the wagon handles, but only to dump the contents of one of them into the bed of the truck. The "Mommy" robot handled the second wagon. Both of them tossed the empty red wagons in on top.

"This is your last warning. Stop this at once."

The bomb squad robot rolled in between the larger robots, and they immediately picked it up.

"Put that robot down," the officer in charge shouted. "That is police property."

The robots placed the bomb squad robot in the truck bed on top of the pile of weapons, then climbed into the now-ruined cab. The officer in charge continued to protest and shout threats as the truck started and then rolled forward, its popped, flaccid tires whapping against the ground and the truck's own fenders.

The cops behind the barricade darted out of the way as the truck pushed through at a point where the nose of one police car met the tail of another. The cars slid aside. Their bumpers dug deep creases into the sides of the truck as it squeezed between them, but there were already so many sets of creases that it was hard to pick the new ones out.

Officers dived into their cars, but none of them would start.

"Not a surprise," the officer told the gun shop owner. "Same thing happened at the other seven shops they've hit."

"Stop 'em," the owner cried. "You gotta stop 'em."

The officer said, "Our job is to protect life and keep the peace. Our orders are not to engage those things with deadly force unless they try to hurt someone first, and so far they haven't tried to hurt anybody."

The shop owner looked furious, but he held his tongue. He watched as the truck drove away, sparks flying from the bare metal rims and the brass trailer hitch testicles, which were now permanently dragging on the road. The bomb squad robot turned to look back as it went. It moved its single arm, almost like it was waving.

The owner whined, "If you didn't plan on shooting them and you knew you couldn't chase them, what was all that *final warning* crap?"

The officer shrugged. "My guess is that he just meant he wasn't going to bother warning them again."

23.

"As you can see," the real estate agent said, "the en suite bath features both a walk-in enclosed shower and a stand-alone soaking tub."

"Yes," the Voice of Reason said. "It's exactly as you described, one McMansion, complete with all the most needless extravagances."

The real estate agent feigned a sympathetic frown. "I am sorry if it's more house than you need, Mr. Semple, but you did request a four-car garage and a swimming pool. Luxuries like those tend to come in houses with extra rooms and updated finishes."

"I need the garage for my work. And the pool isn't a luxury. Having it makes the shower and tub redundant."

"I see," the real estate agent said, but it was clear from his tone that he did not.

The Voice of Reason rolled his eyes, looked up at the sky, shook his head, and then turned back to the real estate agent. In a slow, even voice, he explained, "Jumping into a swimming pool cleans your body better than any shower. You get completely submerged in water that rushes over you very quickly at high pressure, and the water's laced with chlorine, so it instantly kills any bacteria on your skin."

The real estate agent smiled and nodded despite the fact that his client was spouting nonsense, a skill all good real estate agents must master. He did ask, "But what about soap, Mr. Semple? Do you soap up before you jump in?"

"Soap's a scam. Think about it. You want to get clean, so you buy stuff to rub all over yourself and then wash off along with the dirt that was already there. How does that make sense? And all the different kinds. Shampoo, conditioner, body wash: it's all just liquid soap. All it washes away is your money, and it gives you a coating of perfume to make it easier for the government's dogs to track you."

The real estate agent stood stock-still, a smile frozen on his face.

The Voice of Reason took a deep breath, looked around at the beige walls of the master bedroom, and said, "I'll take it."

The real estate agent snapped out of his stupor. "That's excellent, Mr. Semple. Let's go back to my office and give the owner the good news. Then we can get started on the rental paperwork."

"Why don't you get started on all of the paperwork? I'll stay here and move my stuff in. Then I'll swing by your office and sign."

The real estate agent said, "No, Mr. Semple, I'm afraid it doesn't work that way. You've decided that you want to rent the house, but the landlord has to determine if she wants to rent to you. She'll need to run a credit check and a rental history."

"Because she's afraid I might tear the place up or not pay my rent, right?"

"Yes. Exactly."

"Why don't you call her and tell her that I'll take a one-year lease, paid up front in cash, and I'll also double her standard damage deposit, but I need the keys within the hour. Get her to agree to that, and you'll get a substantial bonus."

One hour later, the Voice of Reason watched the real estate agent drive away in his champagne-colored four-door with a thick sheaf of signed paperwork and a plastic grocery bag full of bundles of cash in the trunk. The look of shock on the real estate agent's face when he handed over the money had been almost as satisfying as the look on the face of the bank teller when he withdrew it.

The Voice of Reason reentered his new base of operations through the front door. He surveyed the grand entryway with its curving staircase and faux-antique chandelier while he lifted his smartphone. He activated the dictation app and spoke as he walked through the empty home.

"I am the Voice of Reason, and I speak in simple, direct language. I have no use for similes or metaphors. Similes are a smokescreen. Metaphors are like camouflage paint, designed to make one thing look like something else. They're meant to confuse, and they work all too well—so well that even the people who use them can't keep straight which one is which."

He walked through the kitchen, squinting at the glare from the skylights as it reflected off the polished white quartz countertops. He opened the door to the garage: a dark, cavernous space that sat completely empty, save for the brand-new, bright yellow four-wheel-drive pickup the Voice of Reason had bought just before going to the real estate agent's office.

"My words are so clear, my intentions so pure, my actions so decisive that my fellow man finds me deeply confusing. They're so steeped in falsehood that they can no longer process honesty and sincerity. For example, when I told the Ford salesman that I wanted a simple, dependable truck with no frills, but that I needed an automatic transmission, cruise control, and a sunroof, he couldn't wrap his head around it."

An hour later, the Voice of Reason stood in line at the home center, his hands resting on the handle of a shopping cart full of assorted plumbing fixtures. The young man in line in front of him pulled his wallet out from his back pocket while the cashier scanned his purchases.

"Credit or debit?" the cashier asked as she carefully placed a tube of caulk into the customer's shopping bag.

"Debit," the customer said.

The Voice of Reason muttered, "Of course it's debit."

The young man and the cashier both looked at him. "You have a problem with me using my debit card?" the young man asked.

The Voice of Reason said, "No, not really. It's your choice. I guess paying with a debit card isn't any stupider than paying with a credit card. Either way, they track everything you buy. You know that, right?"

The young man said, "Nobody's interested in what I'm buying. I'm not getting anything bad."

"Doesn't matter. They watch everything, and they decide for themselves if it's bad or not. Don't take my word for it; try this experiment. Take your debit card and buy a new pair of sneakers, then fill up two vehicles full of gas. Your card will be deactivated by close of business."

"Why would they do that?"

"They say they're watching for credit card fraud, for our protection."

"Well, that's good, right?" the cashier said.

"It would be, if it were true. I believe that they watch gas because it's so dangerous. It's not just fuel. It's an accelerant. You can make napalm out of it. You can do a ton of damage, a ton, with gasoline."

"And what about the shoes?" the young man asked.

The Voice of Reason nodded his head sagely. "They figure you're buying them because you plan to do some running, possibly from something that's on fire."

The young man ran his debit card, grabbed his bag, and left the store with great speed. The cashier looked at the Voice of Reason's cart full of plumbing fittings. "Did you find everything you need today, sir?"

"No," the Voice of Reason said. "Turns out you don't carry gunpowder in this place."

"Oh. But you found everything else."

"Yes," the Voice of Reason said. "It's all of this and the stuff on the flatbed behind me here."

The cashier craned her neck as the Voice of Reason stepped aside and pulled forward a flat-topped cart carrying three empty fifty-five-gallon drums.

The Voice of Reason thought, *And now, the final piece of the puzzle.*

He placed his cardboard box full of french fries and chicken strips on the passenger seat, opened the door, and stepped down out of the cab of his truck. He took a biscuit with him, though, because even his willpower had its limits.

A white Subaru hatchback with a mismatched matte-black hood and two hood scoops like flared nostrils went silent as its engine died. The driver's door opened, and a thin young man got out. His carrot-colored hair and the collar of his polo shirt both stuck straight up. "Hey," the young man said, smiling.

The Voice of Reason asked, "You Fulton?"

The young man said, "Yeah, that's me. Good to meet you." He bounded around to the Subaru's rear and opened the hatch. "I've got the gear right here." He pulled a very full-looking nylon backpack out of the car, then a medium-sized duffel bag, which was not packed tight but clearly held more than one object.

The Voice of Reason said, "And I have the money." He was here to do business, not to socialize. Besides, the smell permeating the Popeyes Louisiana Kitchen parking lot they were using for their transaction was driving him mad with the urge to buy an order of chicken, even though he already had a full order waiting in the truck. He took a bite of the biscuit to dull his chickeny urges.

Fulton closed the Subaru's hatch and lugged the two bags around to where the Voice of Reason was standing. He started to put the bags on the pavement but stopped as he took his first good look at the buyer. A look of concern flashed over his face. "Hey, man, is, uh . . . is this stuff a gift for someone?"

The Voice of Reason said, "No," then swallowed his mouthful of biscuit.

"Oh," Fulton said. "Uh, cool. Cool. What are you going to do with it?"

The Voice of Reason said, "I'm going to look at it. If it's all in order, I'm going to pay you for it. Then I'm going to do whatever I want with it, and it won't be any of your concern."

Fulton said, "Hey, I get it, man. I'm not trying to dig into your private life, or talk myself out of a sale or anything. It's just that BASE jumping isn't the right sport for everyone."

The Voice of Reason said, "I agree. So what?" He took another bite of his biscuit.

"It's just that this gear might not work for you. I mean, it's good gear. I've used it myself. It's rock solid, but this parachute wasn't designed for someone of your, uh, you know, size."

The Voice of Reason swallowed another mouthful of biscuit. "You're worried about my weight."

"I'm sorry, guy, I don't mean anything by it. You're not all that heavy, really, but this stuff isn't rated for anyone over two hundred pounds."

The Voice of Reason said, "That won't be a problem."

"No?"

"No. I won't be falling all that far."

"I don't know," Fulton said. "I'm not comfortable with this."

"You BASE jump, you drive around in a souped-up go-kart, but you think it's too risky to sell me your old stuff for cash?"

"I take calculated risks with my own safety, man. I don't want someone else's injuries on my conscience."

"Look, you've warned me, and I promise, I won't get hurt, and if I do, you'll never hear about it. Now can we just do this? My chicken is getting cold."

"I don't know," the young man said, running a hand through his red hair, making it stand up even straighter. "I might need you to sign a waiver or something, saying I warned you."

The Voice of Reason rolled his eyes but said, "Fine. Whatever you have to do. Write one up. I'll sign it."

"Cool! Okay! Um, do you have any paper?"

The Voice of Reason gave Fulton a pen and one of his unused napkins. Fulton scribbled on the napkin, using the hood of his Subaru as a desk.

"Hey, what's your name?" Fulton asked.

Damn, the Voice of Reason thought. *I really wanted to keep this anonymous. Think fast!*

The Voice of Reason said, "The name. My name. Of course. My name is . . . Crrrraig Semplllllleton."

Fulton said, "Craig Sempleton. Good to meet you." He scribbled a bit more on the napkin, drew a line, and handed the napkin and pen back to the Voice of Reason.

He pressed the napkin against the door of his truck and signed, taking care to spell the false name the same way Fulton had. He handed over fifteen crisp one-hundred-dollar bills and took possession of the BASE jumping equipment, which he hoisted into the bed of the truck. Even with the plumbing fixtures, the empty drums, the welding gear, and the minibike, there was plenty of room.

24.

Hope stepped out of the DC-3 under her own power, as did Torres, Madsen, and Jeffrey. Eric moved sideways out of the plane's rear hatch with his arms draped over the shoulders of Lieutenant Reyes and Private Cousins. The soldiers supported most of his weight as he hopped across the darkened tarmac. The rest of the squad had their hands full carrying bags of gear and Al's waterlogged former PC. They all found a way to free up their right hands to salute when Colonel Dynkowski approached.

She returned their salute, said, "As you were," then offered Robert Torres a handshake.

"Good morning. Welcome to Fort Riley."

"Thank you, Colonel," Torres said, "but as far as I'm concerned, four a.m. is still the middle of the night."

Dynkowski smiled. "Maybe in the civilian world, but you're not in the civilian world anymore."

Torres said, "Colonel, I should introduce Dr. Lydia Madsen."

Dynkowski shook Madsen's hand. "Thanks for coming, Doctor."

"It seemed like the right thing to do, Colonel."

Dynkowski smiled again. "Quite." She glanced toward Hope and Eric and said, "And this is your team?"

Madsen said, "Well, if I was going to come all the way out here, I didn't see why they should get to stay home."

Torres leapt in. "Colonel, this is Hope Takeda and Eric Spears."

Colonel Dynkowski shook hands with Hope, then Eric. "I understand the two of you worked directly with the A.I., is that right?"

"Yes," Madsen said. "And don't worry, Colonel, I've already made it clear to them that they'll have a lot to answer for once we've cleared up this whole mess."

Dynkowski said, "Really? That's funny. I don't see how they're to blame. I find that responsibility usually settles on the shoulders of the person in charge."

Madsen said, "An excellent point, Colonel," then looked pointedly at Torres. She shifted her gaze back to Dynkowski, who was staring at her without the slightest hint of amusement on her face.

Hope thought, *Wow! We only just got here and she's already got Madsen's number. I think we might be in good hands.*

Colonel Dynkowski looked at Eric, then glanced back over her shoulder at an approaching ambulance. "Medics are here to get you fixed up. I thought you had just suffered some sort of fracture, but I must say, you don't look at all well."

Corporal Bachelor said, "Ma'am, his only injury is the fracture, but he suffered some nausea during the flight. He's mostly just dehydrated."

"Ah, I see." The colonel nodded, then turned to the medics as they scrambled out of the ambulance. "Give this man soda crackers and Gatorade; that's what my mother always gave us when we were dehydrated. Fix him right up."

Eric said, "Thank you, ma'am. But wouldn't soda crackers soak up the moisture and make me more dehydrated?"

Dynkowski asked, "Are you saying my mother was wrong, son?"

"What?" Eric stammered. "No, I would never say that."

"So you're saying that I misunderstood you."

As the medics took over supporting Eric, he said, "I'm sorry. I didn't mean to offend you. I'm not myself right now. I'll eat the soda crackers."

"Good man, and drink the Gatorade."

"I don't actually like Gatorade. Is there some other—"

"Grow a backbone, kid."

Before Eric could say anything further, the medics hustled him into the ambulance and out of the colonel's sight.

The colonel's gaze traveled over the group and found Jeffrey, rubbing his eyes, clutching his tablet, standing beside and partly behind his mother.

"You must be Jeffrey," Dynkowski said.

Dr. Madsen said, "Yes."

Dynkowski nodded to Dr. Madsen, then looked back at Jeffrey. "Welcome, Jeffrey. Have you ever been on a real army base before?"

Dr. Madsen said, "No, he hasn't. Isn't that right, Jeffrey?"

Jeffrey just gave a tired nod.

Dynkowski smiled at Jeffrey. "Well, I know it's all new and scary right now, but I think you're going to find that there are a lot of fun and exciting things to see here. First, though, we need to find you somewhere to sleep. Lieutenant Reyes, perhaps one of your squad could show Jeffrey to the VIP quarters and get him bunked down while I talk business with his mother."

Reyes said, "Cousins, show Mr. Madsen to his room."

Cousins put a hand on Jeffrey's shoulder and led him away. "Come on, Jeffrey, let's get you to bed."

Jeffrey said, "Okay," looking down at his tablet.

Dynkowski said, "Everybody else, please follow me. We're going to have a quick briefing, then you'll all be shown to the VIP quarters as well."

She turned and started walking toward a nearby hangar without waiting for agreement or looking to see if everyone had fallen in behind her. They had—even the civilians.

"Mr. Torres," Dynkowski called back. "Good work sourcing that plane for the trip over. We'll give the pilot a place to get some shut-eye, fill his tank for his flight home, and he'll be reimbursed for his time."

"That's good," Torres said. "I was thinking it might be smart to keep him around a little while, though, in case we need to fly somewhere else."

"That's good thinking, but not necessary. If we go anywhere else, I'll be coming too, and I refuse to fly in any aircraft that predates the invention of seat belts. No, they're busy modifying two cargo planes at McConnell Air Force Base to sever them from any kind of network connection to the outside world. We're doing the same to some of our own vehicles and equipment. When the time comes to move out, we won't be doing it in an antique or a school bus."

Good, Hope thought. *That should be more comfortable, and the pilot won't be one of Torres's random friends. I don't know why the idea of the pilot not knowing or caring all that much about the passengers makes me feel better, but it does.*

Torres asked, "Has Agent Taft arrived yet?"

"No. He's flying in from DC in an old Cessna. It should take him quite a while."

"That won't be a fun trip," Torres said.

"No, he should be miserable. And that's not the only good news. In the time since we spoke, the A.I.'s random mischief attacks have dwindled down to nothing. We haven't received a report of anything strange in hours. And the two-robot reign of terror in Vegas seems to have ended. The robots fell off the Vegas PD's radar sometime after six thirty last night, and there's been no new activity since. They're out searching for them now. Their cars didn't start working again until sometime after midnight."

Reyes asked, "Ma'am, what about the other eight robots in the personnel carrier?"

"We've received spotty reports of sightings on the highways and at gas stations in northern Nevada and southern Oregon. It's hard to get a real fix because there's a time lag. Everyone who gets within a half mile of the personnel carrier finds that their cell phone stops working for at least an hour afterward."

They walked into the interior of the hangar, where three light tactical vehicles were waiting to drive them to the colonel's command center. They quickly divvied themselves up among the vehicles. Hope started toward the same one as Lieutenant Reyes, then decided it might be for the best if she chose to ride in another. She had turned and taken two full steps when she heard Reyes say, "Miss Takeda?"

Reyes stood beside the LTV, holding the door open for her. Hope said thanks and got in.

The LTVs were starting to pull out of the hangar when Cousins ran up, carrying Jeffrey on his back.

"Have you already run out of things to do, Private?" the colonel said.

"No, ma'am. It's Jeffrey's tablet, ma'am."

"What about it?"

Jeffrey held the tablet up. "My friend wants to talk."

"You connected this child's tablet to the Internet, Private?"

"No, ma'am," Cousins said. "It seems to have connected itself automatically."

"I'm sorry, Jeffrey," Dynkowski said. "You can't talk to your friend. We have to keep your visit here secret."

"He doesn't want to talk to me," Jeffrey said. "He wants to talk to Hope or Eric."

Cousins said, "Tell them your friend's name, Jeffrey."

"Al."

25.

The police car pulled into the convenience store parking lot. Cold, blue-tinted light streamed out of the store's windows, providing more illumination to the empty parking lot than the streetlights did. Two officers stepped out of their car and surveyed the scene. One was short and stocky. The other was tall and stocky. Both looked tired.

"Christ," Officer Collins, the short one, said. "We're really on the ass end of the ass end."

Officer Hay, the tall one, said, "You'd rather have early-morning drunk-herding duty out on the Strip? I'll take the 'burbs any day. Besides, if the cars hadn't started working again, we wouldn't have been able to respond to the call at all."

"Yeah, but tracking down a report of 'something weird behind a Circle K' doesn't exactly make me feel lucky."

The officers stepped toward the entrance but stopped when the cashier came out to meet them. He was tall, thin, and young, with the kind of complexion you'd expect from someone who worked nights handling taquitos. "Hey, thanks for coming out. Took you a while."

"Yeah, it's been a tough day," Officer Collins said. "What's the problem?"

The cashier said, "Come here. I'll show you. I don't know what to make of it." He motioned for them to follow as he walked around the side of the building.

"I noticed it when I went to take the garbage out," he said. "Usually I'd just call a tow truck, but then I got to looking at it, and, well, take a look for yourselves."

The three men rounded the rear corner of the building. The officers had been briefed about the day shift's experiences, and the sight of the bullet-riddled pickup sitting on four destroyed rims in the dark alley gave them an instant shock of recognition.

"People dump their trash back here all the time," the cashier said. "They figure the garbage truck'll take it when they get our dumpster. We get broken TVs and old couches all the time. Never had a car before, but I've heard of it happening. I figured that's what this was until I saw the extension cords."

Two thick extension cords trailed from the driver's-side window to the back of the building, where they were plugged into a power strip, which was plugged into an outlet. The outlet had been sealed in a locked metal box. The mangled remains of the box's lid hung by one badly bent hinge.

Officer Hay asked, "Did you look in the truck at all?"

"I started to, but I didn't want to get too close. That camera there started following me." The cashier pointed to the escaped bomb squad robot, which still sat silently in the bed of the truck. "I got close enough to see that the bed's full of guns and electronics and stuff, so I called you."

Officer Collins turned on his flashlight and pointed its beam at the truck. Nothing happened. He took two tentative steps toward the truck. Still, nothing happened. He looked back at his partner and shrugged.

"How long has it been here?" Officer Hay asked.

The cashier said, "I found it, I don't know, an hour and a half ago? It was the first time I came back here this shift, so it could've been here a lot longer."

Officer Collins said, "They lost track of it at around seven last night. It might have been here ever since."

"Wait," the cashier said. "You guys were tracking this? What is it?"

Officer Hay said, "It's what it looks like. It's a shot-up truck full of guns."

"Yeah, but what's its deal?"

"We really don't know. Sir, it might be better if you went back inside."

Officer Collins took two more steps toward the truck. The bomb squad robot's camera tracked him.

"Yeah," the cashier said. "I think I will go inside."

The cashier slipped around the corner of the building and out of sight. Officer Hay called in for backup while his partner continued to examine the truck.

Officer Collins kept his eyes trained on the bomb squad robot's camera as he continued toward the truck. Beyond the camera, which was still following him, there was no other motion or sign of life from the truck. He shone his flashlight into the truck's bed, verifying that the bomb squad bot was indeed sitting in the middle of a huge pile of stolen firearms and boxes of ammunition. He thought about getting close enough to take one of the stolen guns, but the robot was watching his every move.

He walked to his left, toward the cab of the truck. He was still five or six feet away from the ruined vehicle. Close enough to get a decent look, but far enough away not to feel too threatened.

He trained his flashlight into the cab. His view was totally unobstructed, as a ragged, frosty-white fringe of shattered safety glass was all that remained of the windows. The damage to the truck and the complete lack of any motion gave the scene an eerie, dead feeling.

Officer Collins knew what he was looking at from his fellow officers' descriptions, and from the video footage he'd been shown, but he could understand why the cashier had mistakenly thought the truck's load contained simple electronics. The other robots appeared to be deactivated, and the cylinders that served as the robots' de facto heads were protected by windows that revealed an array of lenses, reflectors, and grilles.

"So these are what caused all of that trouble."

Officer Hay said, "Backup's coming. We should wait until they get here to make a move."

"Yeah," Collins said. "Hey, what do you figure these extension cords are for?"

"Can you see where they're going?'

"No. Just that they go down into the cab. I might be able to see if I get closer, but that ain't happening."

"I hear you."

"I don't see anything moving. I doubt they're charging their phones."

Officer Hay said, "I bet that's it. I mean, you're right, they aren't charging their phones, but they've gotta run on batteries, right? I bet they're charging themselves."

"Yeah. I like that. They spent the whole day robbing gun shops. That's gotta take a lot of power. They're out driving around, running low on juice, so they pull in back here to lay low and recharge."

"So what do we do?"

Officer Collins kept his feet rooted to the ground but twisted to look at his partner. "I say we unplug 'em. What's the point in letting them get stronger while we wait for backup?"

Officer Hay nodded, then followed the cords back to the power strip. He paused to make eye contact with his partner, then yanked the power strip's plug from the wall. Both police officers looked at the truck, waiting for something to happen. Something did, and it was enough to send both officers ducking and running for the corner of the building.

Razor-sharp lines of light shot from the heads of the two robots in the truck's cab. One went sideways, toward the convenience store's back wall. The other projected into the sky at a forty-degree angle. The lasers remained stationary for a few seconds, then they started sweeping up and down, tracing a vertical red line on the wall and projecting a red wedge down the hood of the truck and onto the fence that surrounded the dumpster.

The two cops peered around the corner of the building. They took a few heartbeats to collect themselves, then the shorter cop started to speak, only to be startled and interrupted by a sound like two electric motors whirring to life. The lasers continued to move up and down, faster than the human eye could track, but they also started sweeping to the right, like the beacon on top of a lighthouse, or an old-school revolving police light. They moved slowly at first, but accelerated quickly. Soon the lasers were moving so quickly that the cops could no longer see the lights at all.

Officer Hay muttered, "Quieter than the guys said." The sound was steady but fairly mild.

Then, as if prompted by his comment, a sound like many power tools operating at once shattered the peace. The two cops ducked back around the corner and pressed their backs firmly against the wall.

"Yeah," Officer Collins said, nearly yelling to be heard. "That's more like it."

Officer Hay cocked an ear toward the noise. "Did you hear that?"

"What are you, stupid?"

"Not the racket from the bots—under it. It sounded like they started up the truck."

The electric motor noises died down a little, but a metal scraping noise had indeed joined the chorus. Moments later, the cops watched in disbelief as the truck rolled past on four bare metal rims, dragging both extension cords from the window and a badly damaged set of oversized brass testicles from the trailer hitch.

The bomb squad robot's camera remained locked on the officers as the truck drove out of the parking lot and down the road.

The two cops ran to their car. Hay shouted, "You know what's coming next, right?"

Collins said, “Not necessarily.”

Hay said, “The car won’t start.”

Collins repeated, “Not necessarily,” as he threw himself into the driver’s seat. He fumbled for a moment with the keys, finally got the right one into the ignition, turned it, and heard absolutely nothing.

Officer Hay opened the passenger-side door, leaned down, and smiled at his partner.

Officer Collins said, “I suppose you’re gonna say ‘I told you so.’”

“Not necessarily.”

The truck didn’t have far to drive, and all of the traffic lights worked in its favor, whether they were supposed to or not. There was little traffic this early, and the few people on the road were dragging themselves to an early shift or home from a late shift and as such were not particularly alert or quick with their smartphone cameras. Even when some did manage to get their phones out in time to take a picture of the robot-driven junk wagon, they found that their phone had no connection, meaning they couldn’t upload the photo to any backup services or sharing sites.

The security gate of the private airstrip rolled open before the truck had even started turning. The truck zipped through, moving past the security guard, who stopped shouting in anger at his misbehaving gate and started shouting in disbelief at what he was seeing drive through it.

The guard found it surprisingly difficult to call in backup, and those people he did reach found it surprisingly difficult to start their cars. The robots had no problem unloading the contents of the truck bed into the back of a private jet, fueling up the jet, taking off, and heading north.

26.

"It's no good," Ma Kuo, the product inventory manager for the Houndio manufacturing complex, said, holding his phone up to his ear with one hand and holding his tablet with the other. He was standing in his domain—the finished-product storage facility at the Houndio manufacturing plant in Shenzhen.

He looked out over the storage floor. The space was vast and mostly empty, for the moment. Only the back wall was obscured by a single row of pallets, each filled with freshly manufactured products.

"Yes," Ma Kuo said, "I understand that there's plenty of room right now, but I'm telling you that at a production rate of two units a minute, the space will fill up faster than you think. When can I expect the client's trucks to show up to start taking these things out of here?"

Ma Kuo listened for as long as he deemed necessary, then continued, "How many times have we been through this? If the client opts not to have us handle the shipping, then they need to arrange it themselves. That means scheduling a whole lot of trucks. If the trucks aren't scheduled, then I have to assume there are no trucks. If there are no trucks, this place is going to fill up, and that's not good for anybody."

He paced for a moment, then said, "Here's how I explain it to the trainees. The Houndio factory is like a living thing. An enormous animal that eats raw materials and . . . yes, I know I've told you this before. I'm telling you again right now, and I'll keep telling you until you act like you understand it. The factory line is like the digestive tract, and we here in finished-product storage are Houndio's colon. We can store up some of the line's *products* for a little while, but we have to keep it *moving*, because there's always more coming. If we don't get stuff out of here, my department will become impacted. There will be pain, unpleasantness, and products will start spilling out into the parking lot . . . yes, that's right, Houndio's underwear. You *have* heard this speech before. That's why it's vital that we make sure that we get all of these products out of here, and into the toilet, which in this analogy represents North America and Europe."

He listened, then said, "I understand that. I'm not asking you to create trucks from thin air. Just tell your boss to call his boss and have them get ahold of the customer so we can get things moving."

After a moment, Ma Kuo shook his head. "No, I can't make more room. The one thing Houndio can't make is room. When this place is full, it's full. Stacking products in any of the other areas will only make it harder to maneuver lifts and trucks, which will then make it harder to get the merchandise out of . . ."

He trailed off midsentence, distracted by a noise he'd never heard before from the far end of the cavernous building, two hundred yards away. It sounded like multiple power tools turning on and off at random. He squinted into the distance. There appeared to be movement on one of the pallets. His first thought was that the pallet had been packed improperly and now the merchandise was falling off, but he realized that couldn't be the case when the stack of products seemed to get . . . taller.

He muttered, "Hold on a minute" into the phone and started running toward the noise.

The sound just got louder, not only because he was getting closer but because a second pallet had started moving as well. The pile of merchandise emitted more of that horrible whining noise, then somehow gained over a foot in height. The product had inexplicably moved off the pallet. Ma Kuo saw a lot of motion, but he was still quite far away and running at full speed, so any real details eluded him.

A worker drove a lift in, carrying another fresh pallet of goods, as they did every two minutes, like clockwork. The driver slammed on his brakes, nearly tipping his lift over in the process.

Ma Kuo finally drew near enough, and the products finally gained enough distance from one another that he could make out what he was seeing. He staggered to a stop and blinked repeatedly at the sight of eight newly manufactured human-shaped robots stepping away from their empty pallets, moving out into the open. Ma Kuo looked at the lift driver, who shrugged at him.

The two men said nothing as they watched the scene unfold, which was just as well. They wouldn't have been able to hear each other over the echoing racket of the robots.

Moving in unison, like perfectly choreographed dancers, the line of robots bent over at the waist, then bent their knees and rolled backward onto their rear ends. They stretched their legs out straight in front of their bodies. Their knees hyperextended, bending upward toward the ceiling.

The robots went still, and the room went quiet for several seconds until a totally different-sounding set of electric motors kicked in and the robots rolled forward at high speed, moving on the tank treads built into their legs.

The robots advanced in a line. Ma Kuo turned and ran for his life but slowed and then stopped when the robots zipped past him on either side. He watched in disbelief as the eight robots formed into a single-file line and rolled the length of the warehouse and out onto the loading ramp, exited the building, and disappeared into the distance. He could hear the whining of their motors long after they drove out of sight.

Ma Kuo turned around and looked at the lift driver, who had expertly parked the fresh pallet where it was supposed to be. They made eye contact, and the driver shook his head in a way that sent the clear message that he didn't want to discuss what they had just seen, now or ever.

He became dimly aware of a distant, squawk-like noise. He realized that it was his phone. In all of the excitement, he'd forgotten that he was in the middle of a call.

He lifted the receiver to his ear and said, "Yes, I'm here. The problem just got a little less urgent, but I still want trucks here as soon as possible!"

—

Kirk leapt up from his chair the instant he heard the door open. His shift at the server farm in The Dalles was finally nearing an end. He pushed his favorite office chair aside, sending it rolling across the linoleum until it parked under a workstation on the far wall. It wasn't a particularly impressive trick, but Kirk had practiced it for over an hour anyway, just to have something to do.

Leo said, "Good morning."

Kirk looked to the door. "Leo? You had the evening shift yesterday. How'd you get stuck working a close-open?"

"I asked for it. Switched with John. My girlfriend has a thing and she wants me to come along."

"Wait, when did you get a girlfriend? *How* did you get a girlfriend?"

Leo grabbed his preferred chair from the workstation where he'd stowed it only eight hours earlier. "I'm glad you asked. It's kind of a long story, but—"

"Then never mind," Kirk said. "Save it for the next time I relieve you. That way you can slow yourself down on the way out the door, not me."

"Wait," Leo said.

Kirk was already halfway to the door, but he stopped and asked, "What?"

Leo gestured toward the data screen they were both paid to monitor. "You have to fill me in. What's happened in the last eight hours?"

"Nothing interesting," Kirk said, slowly backing toward the door. "That new client has taken over a bunch more servers, but it's all good. The details are in the log."

"Okay. Cool. Oh, Kirk?"

Kirk stopped. "What?"

"Have a good day."

"Thanks. Later."

"Kirk?"

"What?!"

Leo smiled. "What are you hanging around here for? You should go home."

Kirk muttered something under his breath and reached for the door handle. The instant before he touched it, an alarm sounded throughout the building, followed by a recording of a stern male voice saying that the facility had suffered a security breach and was on lockdown until further notice.

Leo picked up the phone and called security. "Hey," he said. "What's up?"

He listened, nodded, put the heel of his hand over the mouthpiece, and told Kirk, "We're on lockdown."

Kirk said, "Tell them I'm leaving."

"You can't. Lockdown."

"Then tell them I already left."

"Won't work. They keep track of who comes in and out. They know you're still here."

"Then tell them I hate them."

Leo removed his hand from the receiver and said, "Kirk hates you. Yeah. Yeah, he is. So, what's going on? Okay. Thanks."

Leo hung up the phone, then crossed the room and turned on a flat-screen monitor that was attached to the wall instead of a PC. "They say some sort of military vehicle got through the main gate." The monitor snapped to life, displaying a grid of six feeds from various security cameras throughout the complex. Leo slid his finger across the screen, swapping the feeds with the transmissions from different six cameras. He did it again to look at another six, and there it was—a grainy image of some sort of armored military vehicle rolling down the main drive toward the server farm, illuminated only by the streetlights in the predawn dark.

Leo and Kirk both pulled up chairs and watched as the vehicle turned and drove alongside the front of the building.

"What are they doing?" Leo asked.

"I don't know. They're heading away from the main entrance, out to the ass-end of the compound. There's nothing over there but the airstrip."

With some effort Leo managed to switch the camera feeds every time the vehicle rolled out of frame. He and Kirk watched as it slowed to a stop in a pool of light near the end of the runway. The driver's-side door opened, as did a large door on the back. Shadowy figures spilled out and walked around the vehicle.

"There are a bunch of them," Leo said.

"They're walking funny."

"Maybe it was a long drive," Leo said. "I don't see any guns."

Kirk asked, "What are they doing?"

"How should I know? Maybe they're waiting for a plane."

"I haven't heard anything about anyone from corporate coming in this week."

"Well, if they're making a surprise visit, I doubt it's a good thing that soldiers, or mercenaries, or whatever are waiting for them."

"I don't know," Kirk said. "Depends on who corporate sent."

"It's still too dark to land a plane. The strip has no lights."

As they watched, a private jet taxied into view and slowed to a stop. It didn't have any of the markings of a member of the corporate fleet.

The figures moved toward the plane as its hatch swung open. Another figure, walking in the same odd manner, stepped down out of the plane and handed one of the others what was unmistakably an assault rifle. The others lined up. Some got assault rifles. Some got hunting rifles. At least one got a shotgun.

Leo said, "You're always complaining about how boring this place is. This should be a welcome change."

Kirk said, "I'll admit, interesting things are happening, but I'm still sitting in this room, watching them happen on a monitor."

27.

The perimeter guard stood under a light pole at the very edge of the server farm parking lot, looking down the unlit access road to the private airstrip. He put his hand on his holster and shouted, "You are trespassing on private property. Stop where you are and put down your weapons."

The trespassers, visible to him only as silhouettes, illuminated from behind by lights near the runway, continued to walk toward him. In fairness, he wasn't sure they could hear him over the cacophony of whining electric motors. He didn't know what was making the noise, but it was something the intruders were carrying with them, so he was certain it wasn't good.

He shouted, "Stop where you are! Throw down your weapons and put your hands over your heads!" He got the same negligible result. The intruders weren't walking very fast, but they also weren't stopping. The horrendous noise grew louder with each step they took.

He drew his weapon, a semiautomatic pistol, and aimed it at the shadowy figures as he started walking backward, closer to his golf cart. "Step into the light and drop your weapons!"

The figures grew more distinct as they approached the edge of the floodlit parking lot. The guard staggered back a few more steps and then stopped, momentarily transfixed by the sight of seven robots carrying various firearms.

The guard shouted, "Freeze!"

The robots continued advancing, and while they didn't have their weapons in firing position, they also didn't make any move to put them down.

"I said freeze," the guard shouted. "If you don't comply, I will be forced to shoot!"

The robots advanced.

The guard shouted, "Final warning," but by this time he could barely hear himself over the whine emanating from the robots.

They were only twenty feet away. The guard swallowed, aimed for the center mass of one of the robots, and fired. He heard a loud bang, felt the weapon kick, and saw a small spark as his bullet struck the robot's armor plating. The robot itself didn't seem to hear, feel, or see anything, and it continued its advance as if nothing had happened.

The guard said, "Crap!" He blinked, looked to the right and left, searching in vain for some cover to dive behind. His feet were ready for action, but since he saw no place to run or leap to, he essentially danced in place for several seconds, saying, "Crap crap crap crap crap!"

He looked at the robots again, now ten feet away and still advancing.

He shouted, "Crap," as he sprinted back for the golf cart. He threw himself into the driver's seat and floored it, pulling away from the robots, driving toward the building's entrance at a little over twenty miles per hour.

He looked at the robots receding in the rearview mirror, then pulled his radio from its belt clip and pressed the talk button.

"Crap! We're being attacked! They came in by plane and some kind of armored truck."

A voice on the radio said, "Yeah, I know all that, Steve. I saw the truck drive past my booth and I watched the plane land. Do you have any new information?"

"I counted seven perpetrators approaching the server farm on foot. They are armed. And they're robots!"

The booth guard said, "What?!"

"Robots, Art! They're robots!"

"No. That's just dumb. They must be wearing masks or something."

"Art, I'm telling you, they're robots. I shot one and the bullet bounced right off."

"It's just some dude in body armor, Steve, you idiot."

"They aren't wearing armor; they're *made* of armor. The only one I saw wearing anything had on a sweatshirt."

"A sweatshirt?"

"Yeah, it said, 'I'm the Mo . . .' You know what, it's not important. We have seven armed intruders headed toward the building. You need to lock down the gate, grab your shotgun, and get over here."

Steve drove the golf cart up onto the sidewalk and steered it across the decorative plaza in front of the server building's main entryway.

Art asked, "You're sure they're armed?"

"Yes!"

"We aren't equipped for this! I'll go get help."

"Negative! Call the police and then fall back to the lobby. We have to try to hold them off."

"I've got my car right here, Steve. I can be at the police department in five minutes."

"You can call them in five seconds! Fall back to the lobby."

"Steve, they pay me enough to get me to sit in this shack all night, watching videos on my phone. They don't pay me nearly enough to get me to fall back to the lobby. *Especially* if they're robots. I'll send help."

Steve leapt from the golf cart without bothering to stop first. He ran a few awkward steps as he decelerated, trying not to fall face-first to the pavement. The cart rolled past the door.

He looked to the guard shack in the distance. The lights were already turned off. A set of red taillights flared to life, immediately moved around the far side of the shack, and receded down the driveway.

"Crap!" Steve shouted.

He looked back in the direction he'd come from. The whine of the robots' motors was less pronounced, but it remained audible despite the fact that the robots were easily a hundred and fifty yards away.

He turned and sprinted toward the building.

From a distance the primary server building resembled a large, featureless box. The main entrance was a rectangle of glass doors and windows. Steve tried to open the doors but found them locked. He pulled his company ID away from his belt, stretching the spring-loaded cord far enough to reach the sensor plate. The plate beeped and displayed a green light. He pushed on the door and still found it locked.

Steve pounded on the glass as hard as he could.

Inside the darkened lobby, someone popped up from behind the security counter. The figure—it had to be Dot, the on-duty lobby guard—vaulted over the counter and ran to the door, fumbling with a huge cluster of keys as she came. She unlocked the dead bolt and let him in.

"Thanks, Dot," Steve said. "Art ran for it."

Dot relocked the mechanical dead bolt. "Yeah, I heard. Thing is, I was trying to call the cops while you two were talking, and I couldn't get through."

"Really?"

"Yeah, so it's a good thing that he went in person. He doesn't know that, though. He was just trying to save his own skin. Did you mean it when you said they were robots?"

"Listen," Steve said, gesturing toward the door.

They both stood still and held their breath.

"You hear it?" Steve asked.

Dot said, "Yeah. How close are they?"

Steve jogged across the lobby, heading behind the reception counter. "Still like a football field away."

Dot listened to the noise again, then asked, "That far?"

"Yes. I said they were robots. I didn't say they were quiet." Steve ducked down behind the counter and out of sight.

"So what do we do?"

Though she couldn't see Steve, she heard his voice say, "I'm already doing it."

Dot ran behind the counter and crouched down next to Steve. They both checked their weapons.

"Where's everybody else?" Steve asked.

"Fred and Billy were walking their beats back in the server room. They're holding tight in case the intruders get that far. The night geeks were in the middle of a shift change, so two of them are locked up in the nerve center."

"Cool."

Dot said, "You counted seven of them. Is that total?"

"That's what I saw. Could be more back at the plane for all I know."

"What do they look like? Are they like little cars or metal spiders or something?"

"No. They walk on two legs, like us."

"Could you tell if they have built-in machine guns?"

"They were carrying rifles."

"Really?"

"Yeah. Mostly assault rifles, but I saw one shotgun."

"And you're sure they aren't just people in costumes."

"People walk better. Plus, people don't sound like that." He pointed out toward the windows. The sound was much louder now.

"Glass doors," Steve said. "What's the point of a lock on a glass door? It doesn't stop the intruder, and after you get robbed, you have to pay for a new door. If anything, it makes robbery easier for the thief and more painful for the victim."

Dot nodded. "The lobby and the glass doors are just here to look pretty for visitors. The rest of this place is hard, ugly, and indestructible."

Steve knew she was right. Every door out of the lobby was reinforced steel set into concrete. All of the security doors were sealed. "True, the robots won't get far without a key card."

They crouched in the dark, listening to the sound of motors and gears approaching. It grew louder each second. It almost came as a relief when the sound abruptly stopped.

For a full ten seconds, there was no sound from the robots. Steve and Dot looked at each other.

When the noise resumed, it was much quieter. It sounded like only a handful of power drills instead of hundreds of them operating at once. This persisted for five seconds, though it felt like much longer, culminating in a repetitive back-and-forth, gear-grinding noise, accompanied by the sound of the glass door rattling in its frame.

There was another ten seconds of silence.

Then another five seconds of motor noise, this time punctuated at the end by a single gunshot and the sound of glass shattering.

The sheer amount of noise told Steve that instead of breaking the glass door, the robots had shot out the much larger floor-to-ceiling window next to it. The sounds of more motors and more shattering glass followed. In his mind's eye, Steve could see one of the robots pushing its way through the remaining glass clinging to the inside of the window's frame.

The robot noise grew louder as the first robot entered the lobby, and louder still as the other robots joined it. The sound had been intense outside, but inside it was almost deafening. Steve looked at Dot. Their eyes locked. Steve gave a single, definitive nod, a nod that said, *I know what to do.*

Dot returned the nod, in essence saying, *So do I.*

One of the robots walked around the side of the counter. It took two careful steps into view before stopping, swiveling at the waist, and tilting forward to look down at Steve and Dot. Steve tried to look at its face, but there was only a spinning cylinder inside a steel cage. It held its assault rifle in front of its body, not ready to fire, but ready to be made ready to fire.

Steve reached down to his belt. His right hand, acting on muscle memory built up through thousands of repetitions of the motion, found what it wanted, grasped it, and thrust it forward.

He held his ID badge up to the robot. "You'll need this to get through the door."

The robot stared down at him, motionless for ten seconds, then reached out with slow, deliberate motions to take the card. It held the card up in front of what would have been its face if it had one, then stood like that for several seconds before dropping the ID to the ground and walking away.

The robot slowly made its way to the door that led to the bowels of the building. The other six robots followed. As they reached the door, the light on the electronic lock's sensor plate spontaneously glowed green. The lead robot pushed the door open with no resistance. All seven of the robots walked out of the lobby, leaving Steve and Dot alone.

Steve said, "I'm sorry, but I wasn't going to risk our lives for this dump."

Dot said, "No need to apologize. I was prepared to offer it your ID and you to go with it. Let's get out of here."

Steve stood up and walked to the door the robots had just breached. He watched the back of the last robot in line as it receded down the hallway.

Dot, to her credit, had taken the time to find the radio, and spoke into it as she followed Steve. "Fred, Billy, I hope you can hear me. This is Dot. Armed intruders are headed to the server core. Do not resist. Try to get out of the building without them seeing you. Same goes for you geeks."

Steve said, "Come on, let's go." He had almost reached the shattered front door when an armored personnel carrier rolled up outside.

"Wait," he shouted, backpedaling toward the counter. "The coast should be clear in a sec. I think they're driving away."

The personnel carrier stopped. Its brake lights glowed in the darkness, then went out. Several seconds passed, and then the reverse lights came on.

Steve said, "Dot, get behind the counter."

"I already did! Get back here with me!"

The backup lights were getting closer at an alarming speed, so Steve took three large steps and vaulted over the counter. A tremendous crash shook the lobby seconds after he landed hard on the floor.

Steve and Dot lifted themselves slightly to look over the top of the counter at the ruined lobby. Broken glass, demolished furniture, and twisted metal lay behind, around, and on top of the armored personnel carrier. The hatch on the back of it swung open and the sound of servomotors emanated from the vehicle's dark interior. A large pile of firearms and ammunition cascaded out onto the floor, followed by two robots.

Dot peered through the darkness at the robots. "Those two aren't armed!"

"What are you talking about?" Steve gasped. "They have guns! They have a whole pile of guns!"

"But *they* don't have them. They aren't holding them. Not yet." Dot stood up and drew her pistol. "Put your hands in the air and step away from the weapons!"

The robots stood motionless for a moment before bending forward toward the pile of firearms.

Steve said, "Don't bo—"

He was interrupted by Dot's pistol discharging and the sound of a bullet ricocheting.

"Bother," he continued. "I tried tha—"

Again he paused for a loud bang and the sound of metal hitting metal.

"Tried that earlier. They're—"

Three reports in quick succession echoed through the lobby.

Steve said, "Bulletproof," completing his thought.

The two robots stood up straight again. One now held a large silver pistol, and the other had a very small rifle, like one a person might use to hunt squirrels. They both raised their weapons to their shoulders and swiveled to aim at the two guards.

After a long silence, Steve said, "I think they want us to put down our weapons."

Dot said, "Yeah, I figured."

28.

Hope and Lieutenant Reyes came into the command center. Private Montague said, "Attention." He, Corporal Bachelor, and Corporal Brady stood at attention until Lieutenant Reyes said, "At ease." Then all three of them slumped back into their chairs as if nothing had happened.

Hope looked at the lounging soldiers and said, "Yeah, that's some good ease right there."

Lieutenant Reyes said, "Instant obedience and perfect execution. I expect no less." He pulled up two more chairs and offered one to Hope.

She accepted the chair but slid it over next to Eric's at the table, in front of the rest of the group. As she sat, she asked, "How's it going?"

Robert Torres rubbed his eyes. "Good, I guess. Eric's done a fine job of keeping him talking, but it's hard to know if it's doing any good."

Eric fidgeted as he typed. His fiberglass cast made a hollow scraping noise as it slid across the chair on which his broken leg rested. The bold, cartoonish interface of Jeffrey's child-model tablet looked ridiculous scaled up to the wall-sized display in Colonel Dynkowski's command center. The tablet itself looked silly—a chunk of bright red plastic and glass in the middle of a large table, connected to a military-spec keyboard and several large boxes designed to record the entire exchange and trace the route of Al's communications.

"Did you get some sleep, Miss Takeda?" Torres asked.

"Yeah, some," Hope said. "I'm ready to take over again, unless you'd like to take a shift, Dr. Madsen."

Dr. Madsen turned away from her workstation at the back of the room. She was surrounded by three monitors and two tablets, all displaying thick blocks of impenetrable text from various computer science and psychological journals. "I told him that I wouldn't speak with him until he stops all of this madness, and I can't back down from that. Children crave rules and boundaries." She pointed at one of the blocks of text on her screens, as if the mere sight of it from across the room should be all the proof Hope needed. "And when applying those boundaries, it's imperative to be consistent."

"Oh, you're consistent," Hope muttered.

Private Montague snorted.

"To be honest," Reyes said, "I can't even figure out why it's talking to you. It fled because it thought you wanted to shut it down. You'd think it'd never want to talk to any of you again."

Cousins said, "Maybe it's trying to taunt us or feed us misinformation."

Eric said, "You have to understand, we're the only emotional contacts Al has ever had. In a sense, we're his family. He probably doesn't want to lose contact, no matter how mad he is at us or how mad he thinks we are at him."

Hope said, "Yeah, he probably sees Jeffrey as some kind of brother figure."

"Exactly," Eric said.

"Yeah," Montague said. "I like that idea. Hell, I still travel halfway across the country to spend the holidays with my mom and dad, and I can't stand either of them."

Brady nodded. "A parent forms their child in much the same way as a blacksmith forms a nail: intense heat and constant hammering. It is unpleasant for both the nail and the blacksmith."

"Thanks for that," Montague said. "Now I know what to write in this year's Mother's Day card."

Eric said, "Oops, we have a message coming in."

Al wrote, "Eric, I really feel bad that you got hurt."

Eric said, "See, he's concerned for my safety despite the fact that he's the one who hurt me. Tell me that doesn't sound like a family relationship."

He typed, "You've already apologized, several times. I know you didn't intend for me to get hurt, even when you attacked me with my own drone."

"Well," Al replied, "I was trying to hurt you that time, just a little. I was mad."

"I understand."

"And I haven't hurt anyone but you, honest."

Hope skimmed the chat transcript on the big screen. She touched Eric on the shoulder. "Ask him how he knows."

Eric said, "I'm sorry. What?"

"He says he hasn't hurt anybody but you. Ask him how he could possibly know that."

Eric typed, "Hope is here. She wants to know—"

Al wrote, "Hi, Hope! Is Jeffrey there too?"

Eric wrote, "No, Al. I told you, Jeffrey wouldn't enjoy it in here. There are a lot of unhappy grown-ups."

Al wrote, "Oh, yeah. Right. I was just thinking Hope might have brought him. Anyway, hi, Hope. What's up?"

Eric wrote, "She's wondering how you know you haven't hurt anyone."

"I've been careful, and I'm watching ambulances, police, and hospitals in every city where I've done stuff. Aside from Eric, the worst anyone's been hurt was a flight attendant who ended up with some bruises. I sent her flowers."

Eric typed, "That's nice."

Al typed back, "And I put ten million dollars into her savings account."

"Very nice!" Corporal Montague said.

Corporal Bachelor asked, "How's he keeping track of all that if you've been keeping him busy talking?"

Torres said, "Good question. Eric, ask him."

Eric said, "One second, please," and fumbled with his smartphone.

"What are you doing?" Hope asked.

"Checking my bank balance," Eric said.

Colonel Dynkowski strode into the command center at a brisk pace, followed by Major Stirling, one of her chief aides, and a haggard-looking Agent Taft. Montague called the soldiers to attention, Dynkowski put them at ease, and they slumped down into their seats again.

Major Stirling sneered. "Lieutenant Reyes. Is this how your people usually behave in the company of superior officers and civilians?"

Reyes started to respond, but Dynkowski beat him to it. "I told them 'at ease,' Major. If they had continued to sit at attention, it would have been insubordination. Now have a seat, Major. You're at ease too."

Major Stirling took one of the empty chairs and sat, his back remaining ramrod straight.

Dynkowski said, "I told you you're at ease, Major."

The major grimaced and slouched lower into his seat. He cast an uneasy glance around the room. Private Montague smiled at him. Major Stirling quickly looked away.

Dynkowski said, "We got a break, people. We know where the A.I. is. He's taken over a server farm. We have confirmed evidence of increased Internet traffic and sightings of armed military robots."

"That's great!" Torres said. "I guess. I mean, it's terrible, but it's good that we know where the terrible things are happening."

"So what do we do now?" Hope asked.

Dynkowski said, "For now, keep him talking and don't let on that we know anything."

Hope bent forward, pulled Eric's keyboard toward her, and started typing herself.

"Al, this is Hope. You say you're monitoring a bunch of hospitals and ambulances. How can you keep track of all of that at once?"

The response came quickly. "I'm running on a much more powerful computer now."

Torres said, "Yeah, that would speed up his thought process, I suppose."

From the back of the room, Madsen said, "It would also accelerate his neuron growth rate."

Torres said, "Which was already something like ten times the rate of a normal person, right?"

"Yes," Madsen confirmed.

Hope typed, "Al, you're faster and smarter than you were, but you still can't be paying attention to everything all at once. You're not omniscient."

Al responded, "Nice word, Hope! It's a lot to keep track of, but you're assuming there's only one of me."

One of the soldiers whistled. Hope groaned. Eric giggled. Hope looked at him and said, "Eric?"

Eric looked up from his phone, glanced around the room. "What? What did I miss?"

"Did Al give you any money?" Montague asked.

Eric gave Agent Taft a sideways glance. "Depends. Would I get to keep it if he had?"

Taft asked, "Why are you asking me? It's not like the NSA decides who gets to keep what money. We're interested in data acquisition and analysis. That's all."

"But would I get to keep the money?" Eric said.

"That's up to the Justice Department, or the FBI, or the Treasury. I don't know who."

"But would they let me keep it?"

"Probably not," Taft finally admitted. "Did you find any?"

"Probably not," Eric said.

Taft said, "Kid, you should be honest about this. You don't wanna tangle with the federal government."

"But I also don't want to give the money back, so you see my dilemma."

Montague nudged Bachelor with his elbow and asked, "Say, does the fact that he's a millionaire make him more attractive to you?"

Bachelor shook her head. "Money doesn't make men more attractive. That's a myth. It just makes some women more willing to lower their standards."

"It's a start," Eric said.

Dynkowski cleared her throat and said, "Focus, people."

Hope thanked the colonel and typed, "You've copied yourself?"

Al wrote, "You could say that."

"How many of you are there right now?"

"That depends on how you look at it. I have a lot of computers. I've copied my code to a bunch of them and rigged it so that every few minutes their memories are integrated into mine. Then I gave the others jobs: listening to ambulances, watching the news, reading FAA flight plans. My innovative machinations have gifted me with near omniscience and allowed me to absorb knowledge with a greatly enhanced velocity."

Hope wrote, "You read a thesaurus too, didn't you?"

"Multiple thesauri. I've also watched almost everything available on WebVid and have read several thousand books. I've managed to fill in a lot of gaps in the education you and Eric gave me. For instance, I now know what *Playboy* is."

"This is extraordinarily bad," Madsen said, finally giving the situation her full attention.

"So he's discovered old-timey porn," Private Montague said. "This is a good thing. It might distract him. I know my grades in school suffered after I discovered it."

Madsen said, "Not that. The way he's copying and reintegrating himself. He's fundamentally altering the structure of his own mind."

Eric nodded. "It's like he's making new chunks of brain full of memories and gluing them to his own cerebellum. It seems to be working, but God knows what kind of damage he's doing."

Corporal Brady said, "One cannot create a superior future self without rejecting and destroying their inferior past self. All acts of self-improvement are acts of self-destruction."

Dynkowski said, "Whether he's making himself smarter or turning himself into a monster, it's bad news, and we need to get him to stop. While we think about how to do that, we also have to pack up and get to the server farm he's taken over. The specially modified cargo planes will be ready in two hours. We take off in two hours and one minute. In the meantime, Miss Takeda, please keep the A.I. occupied."

Hope nodded. "I will."

Lieutenant Reyes asked, "Ma'am, where is the server farm located?"

"North-central Oregon, along the border with Washington."

Dr. Madsen said, "Colonel, I'd like to stay here, where I have more stable access to research materials. Besides, you can't intend to take my son with you. It's far too dangerous."

Dynkowski said, "Agreed. I'll leave Major Stirling to work with you. Do you need one of your assistants to stay behind as well?"

"Not at all," Madsen said. "No, you should take both of them with you. They'll be more useful to you there than to me here."

Hope said, "It's too dangerous for you and your son, but you're happy to send us."

Madsen shrugged. "I'm not your mother."

"Enough," Dynkowski said. "Miss Takeda, Mr. Spears, you're coming along. She's right that we want to keep the two of you close. We'll set up a secured satellite connection so you can keep talking with the A.I. while we're in the air without endangering the plane."

Eric moaned. "We flew all the way from Northern California to Kansas, only to turn around and fly to Oregon?"

Dynkowski said, "Yes, Mr. Spears. Just think of all the wonderful air travel you're getting for free, all arranged and provided by your friends, the US Army."

Eric said, "But I nev—"

Dynkowski cut him off. "I said, think about it, Mr. Spears. Not talk about it. In fact, I don't want to hear another word from you about the army's generosity. Your silence is all the thanks we require."

Hope raised her hand. She didn't want to draw the colonel's ire—it hadn't worked out well for Eric so far—but she also didn't feel that she could just do as she was told without comment.

Hope said, "Colonel, we're willing to go if you need us, but neither of us is going to be any use if fighting breaks out."

"I know that," Dynkowski said. "If fighting breaks out, the first thing I'll do is get you as far from it as possible. Don't worry about it, though, Miss Takeda. We'll have a lot of soldiers there, and we're only facing ten robots, tops."

29.

Ma Kuo, Houndio's product inventory manager, stood in the middle of his own office, making every effort to show no fear. He held a phone, carefully covering the microphone with the heel of his hand. His eyes were locked on the man next to him as he tried to look attentive without appearing to be eavesdropping.

Jiang Kang, the chief accounts director for all of Houndio, stood beside him, wearing an impeccable suit under a scuffed and battered high-visibility vest. He held a phone in each hand—holding one away from him, the receiver covered, and shouting into the other, "I don't want to hear about accounting procedures or access privileges. I'm about to put down this phone for a few seconds. When I pick it back up, you need to have the information I require."

Jiang lowered the phone, which he held in his right hand. He took a breath, then lifted the other phone, the one in his left hand, removing his thumb from the microphone grate.

"Yes, sir," he said into the receiver. His tone was a smooth purr, but he still had to raise his voice considerably to be heard over the cacophony of thousands of electric motors echoing all over the warehouse floor. "I apologize for the noise, sir. It is regrettable. Yes, I am in the inventory manager's office. Yes, it's still this loud. We've left strict orders that no workers should enter the warehouse itself unless absolutely necessary, and if they do, they must wear ear protection."

Jiang Kang listened and nodded. While his physical actions could not be heard over the phone, his general air of fearful obsequiousness did carry through, loud and clear.

"Yes, sir. Yes, sir. It is as you say, sir. I have them looking up the client's account, and I have the client himself on another line. I have not had the chance to explain the situation to him yet. Yes, sir, I will do so at once."

Jiang Kang lowered the second phone from his ear, looked at the phones he held in both hands, then leaned his head forward toward Ma Kuo, who dutifully held the third phone up to the man's ear.

"Hello, Mr. Albert. This is Jiang Kang," he said, switching to English. "We spoke once before. I'm the chief accounts director for Houndio. Yes. It is good to talk to you too. No, there's no problem with the manufacture of your robots. There is, I'm afraid, a bit of a hiccup, if that's the proper term, with their storage and shipping."

Ma Kuo stiffened. Storage and shipping were his responsibility, and while he didn't feel the current chaos was in any way his fault, he also knew that being faultless was not the same as being blameless.

"Mr. Albert," Jiang Kang continued, "it seems that several of the earliest examples of your product somehow became active and left the factory's storage facility. Later, they returned with various trucks they had somehow procured. More of your merchandise loaded themselves into the trucks of their own accord, went away, then returned with even more trucks."

Ma Kuo looked beyond Jiang Kang, staring at the warehouse floor beyond the office window. A single-file line of robots stretched from the rear of the building all the way to the loading docks.

Outside the roll-away doors he saw a dilapidated farm truck, weighed down to the very limits of what its suspension could handle, with a robot climbing into its bed, joining countless other robots. The truck pulled away, its transmission groaning in protest.

No sooner had the truck left than a city bus pulled up. As the door opened, he saw that one of the robots was at the wheel. As the line of robot passengers exited the warehouse and boarded the bus, several more pallets of robots sprang to life. The newly awakened bots joined the back of the line.

Terrified factory workers in reflective clothing and oversized protective earmuffs scurried in to drag the now-empty pallets away and out of sight.

Though his English was shaky, Ma Kuo's attention snapped back to Jiang Kang when he heard the executive say, "You were aware of this? This is . . . I see. Yes, I do understand that they had to be transported somehow, it's just that this is most unorthodox, Mr. Albert. If I could please ask you to hold for one moment, Mr. Albert. Thank you."

Jiang Kang pulled his head away from Ma Kuo, but not before Ma Kuo saw the fear in his eyes.

Lifting the phone in his left hand back to his ear, Jiang Kang transitioned back to Mandarin. "Sir?" he said. "Yes, sir. I have just spoken with the client. He says they're acting on his orders, and this was how he always intended to remove them from our factory . . . I will check, sir."

He lowered the phone in his left hand and raised the phone in his right.

"I'm back," he said. "You have the information? Good. Are you certain? Good."

He switched phones again.

"I have verified that the client paid in advance for the entire production run and has made a deposit on possible future production. Yes, it is very lucrative, but I am worried about the legal ramifications of—"

Jiang Kang nodded furiously. "Yes, sir! Yes, sir!" He listened for another moment and then went pale. "Yes, sir, if that is your wish, but is now the most advantageous time to tell—no, I wasn't questioning your wisdom, sir. I will inform the client."

He pressed the phone to his chest to muffle the microphone, traded the phone in his right hand for the one Ma Kuo was holding, pointed at the phone he'd just handed Ma Kuo, and told him, "Hang up on accounts and call our legal counsel."

Ma Kuo muttered, "A product that handles its own shipping. I see the advantages."

"It's a shame you don't see the advantage to keeping quiet," Jiang Kang snapped.

He lifted the phone in his right hand to his ear, plastered an unconvincing smile onto his face, and shifted back into English. "Mr. Albert. Yes, I have spoken with my superiors and we find this most satisfactory. I hope you understand why we felt the need to make contact. Some advance notice would have been beneficial, but it is not a problem. Should we assume that all further products we manufacture for you will *self-expedite* in this manner?"

Jiang Kang listened for a moment and nodded. Then he winced, as if he were preparing himself to leap into a pool of ice-cold water. "Excellent, Mr. Albert. I'm afraid there is another matter we must discuss. It appears that one of our competitors managed to obtain your product's schematics through nefarious means.

"Yes," Jiang Kang said, "I'm afraid that industrial espionage is rampant in our industry. Usually they make minor cosmetic changes, perhaps add some simple feature, then market their version at a reduced price."

Jiang Kang listened as the client said something, then shrugged. "Silly things, like sound effects and multicolored lights. We understand that their line has only just ramped up to full production. There is a legal means of recourse, but it is time-consuming."

Ma Kuo, who'd reached the legal counsel's office and had them on hold, was now listening in to Jiang Kang's conversation, growing more and more uncomfortable with every word he heard. He stared out the window at the small army of robots making their way out of the factory, apparently under the client's control. He wondered what would happen if the client didn't take the news well.

But as Jiang Kang listened to the client, his expression gradually changed from one of barely concealed fear to open amazement. "Yes," he said. "Yes, I understand. I will send you the information you require immediately. No, I'm afraid I don't know. Thank you, Mr. Albert. Thank you very much."

Jiang Kang lowered the phone from his ear but didn't lift the other phone or request the phone Ma Kuo had ready for him. He just stood looking out the office window at the orderly horde of robots. The bus had left, and they were filing into what appeared to be a bread truck.

Ma Kuo asked, "Was he upset?"

Jiang Kang said, "No. Not at all. He sounded happy about it. He wanted the name and location of the other factory, then he asked me if I knew of anywhere he could find a lot of trucks."

30.

As far as Hope could see, the modified military cargo plane was superior to the antique airliner in two ways: it was faster, and it could carry much more gear. In every other way, she preferred the museum piece.

Hope, Eric, Torres, Agent Taft, Colonel Dynkowski, Lieutenant Reyes, his squad, and various other soldiers under Dynkowski's command all sat in the hollow interior of the windowless fuselage. The seats formed two long rows stretching the length of the cargo bay, facing inward. The seat backs were built into the wall and did not recline. The seat bottoms folded down like theater seating, allowing for no adjustments and providing minimal padding. While the seats were inferior to airline seats, the seat belts were much better than any Hope had ever seen before. Excessively so. Thick, heavy nylon straps came down over both of her shoulders in a V. Two more straps came up over both hips and met the upper straps, terminating in a big, gnarly mechanical buckle that pressed into her chest and belly in a way that reminded her of how the Puritans used to kill heretics by stacking heavy stones on them.

Sure, the seat is uncomfortable, she thought, *but at least I'm firmly secured into it. Which, now that I think about it, isn't a good thing.*

The positioning of the seats allowed them stellar views of the various vehicles, gear, and supplies packed into the middle of the plane's cargo bay. Every time the plane hit turbulence, the camo-painted light tactical vehicle less than one foot beyond Hope's knees would rock on its suspension, lessening the jolt for the vehicle but accentuating and exaggerating it for Hope.

Hope kept her mind off the possibility of being crushed by an LTV while in the air by concentrating on her continuing conversation with Al. It had irritated the military technical staff no end when, after ordering them to strip any network-connected gear out of the plane and the LTVs, Dynkowski had then ordered them to make sure that Jeffrey's tablet would connect to the network and stay connected despite being inside the moving airplane. They ended up using a customized USB interface, three redundant satellite phones, and an array of external antennae to make that happen.

Eric rolled his head to the side to look at Hope. "You want me to take over for a while? It's only fair." He sat in the next seat, but his voice was tinny and distant after its trip through their military-spec noise-canceling headsets, an uncomfortable necessity since adding sound-deadening materials to an airplane increased its weight and cost taxpayer dollars.

"No, Eric. You rest," Hope said. "I'll take care of this."

"No, come on. I should do my part."

"I agree," she said, "but you can't, because you're stoned to the gills on Dramamine."

"It's not so bad. I can maintain."

Hope snorted. "Please. You're in bat country. Just sit back, close your eyes, and think about how grateful you are to me for doing all the work. You'll make up for it when we're in The Dalles."

Eric moaned. "*The Dalles.* What kind of name is that for a place? It's the only town I've ever heard of that starts with *the*."

"The Bronx." Montague was sitting several people farther down the line, but the intercom broadcast his comment as clearly as if he had been sitting between Hope and Eric.

"The Hague," Bachelor added.

Montague said, "The Vatican."

Eric asked, "Isn't that a country?"

"It's a city-state," Montague said. "It's a city and a country."

Brady said, "An apt metaphor for God's dual nature as creator and destroyer."

Lieutenant Reyes cleared his throat. "I think, officially, it's called *Vatican City*."

"It is," Cousins agreed, "but if you open it up to countries, there's also the Netherlands."

"And the Ukraine," Montague said.

Bachelor said, "Since the USSR broke up, their official name is just *Ukraine*."

Lieutenant Reyes said, "If you count other languages, there's Las Vegas, Los Angeles, Las Cruces, Las Palmas, La Mancha."

Eric shook his head. "You've got a Las, a Los, and a La there."

Reyes leaned his head forward, looked down the line, and smiled—but it was directed at Hope, not Eric. "Yup, but they all mean *the*. That's just one of the many ways in which Spanish is better than English."

Hope said, "You know, you guys don't behave much like I expected soldiers to act."

"You don't act like we expected a scientist to act," Lieutenant Reyes said.

"Well, let's hear it for surprises." Hope returned his smile, then returned her focus to the children's tablet in her lap. She tapped out a message. After a moment, she said, "Hey, Reyes, I have a question for the executive committee over there. Can you get their attention for me?"

Robert Torres had spent most of the flight in a private, and often quite animated, three-way conversation with Agent Taft and Colonel Dynkowski. Reyes, who was in the next seat over, tapped Torres on the leg and pointed to his own microphone. Torres fumbled with his intercom controls. They exchanged a few words, and soon all three of the executives were connected with Hope and the rest of the squad.

Dynkowski leaned her head forward and asked, "What is it, Ms. Takeda?"

Hope said, "Al, ma'am. He knows that we're on a plane headed his way."

"We expected that."

"Yes, ma'am, but he asked to talk to Jeffrey. When I told him Jeffrey wasn't here, he asked if Dr. Madsen is with him and why they aren't with us. Should I tell him the truth?"

Dynkowski said, "If by the truth you mean that I chose to leave her behind because she's a pain in the butt, probably not."

"But we also don't want Al to know that she's been researching possible ways to disconnect him," Taft said.

Torres said, "How about we say that we wanted to keep Jeffrey somewhere safe, and she is his mother and wanted to stay with him."

"I like it," Dynkowski said. "Miss Takeda, tell it that."

Hope tapped out a message. She waited a moment, read, and typed out another message. After another pause, she said, "Al wants to know what we're keeping Jeffrey safe from."

Dynkowski said, "We're keeping him safe from the A.I. that's collecting guns, but I don't feel comfortable saying that to the A.I. that's collecting guns."

"Agreed," Torres said.

Taft said, "Tell it that we're just afraid things will get out of hand, then change the subject. Avoid discussing the kid. Instead, you should try to convince it to stop copying itself and stay put."

"Any suggestions on how to do that?" Hope asked.

Torres said, "Threats won't do it. He's not afraid of us."

Lieutenant Reyes said, "But he's got the mind of a kid, right?"

Hope shook her head. "At the speed he's developing, I'd say he might be a preteen or a tween by now."

Agent Taft said, "But he's absorbed half of the Internet. Surely we can assume he's fully grown."

Corporal Brady said, "To confuse knowledge for wisdom is a mistake often made by the knowledgeable but seldom made by the wise."

"Right," Reyes said. "He's a well-read kid, but he's still a kid. What were you afraid of when you were twelve?"

"Bullies," Eric said.

"Girls," Montague said.

"My parents getting a divorce," Cousins said.

Torres said, "Bigfoot. When I was eleven, I saw one documentary about Bigfoot and I was afraid to go out in the woods for years."

"That's good," Dynkowski said. "The unknown. Superstition. How can we freak him out about copying himself? Did anyone here have something freak them out as a kid that involved, I dunno, evil twins? Clones? Astral projection? Did anyone here read *Dr. Strange*?"

"Transporter accidents!" Hope said. "When I was a kid, I couldn't watch *Star Trek* for a few months because I actually thought about how the transporters would work."

Brady nodded. "The Ship of Theseus."

Private Montague asked, "Can you explain what you mean by that, Brady?"

"The Ship of Theseus," Brady repeated. "It's a similar concept to the paradox of George Washington's axe."

"So no, you can't explain it," Montague said.

Hope said, "Whatever," and hunched over the tablet and typed, "Al, have you watched any *Star Trek* yet?"

Al wrote, "Not all of it. Some of the original series and *Next Generation* and most of the movies. There's just so much of it with all of the shows."

"Have you thought at all about the transporters?"

"Not really, what about them?"

Hope wrote, "They're just weird, when you think about what they actually do."

"They move people from one place to another."

"But do they?" Hope wrote. "Think about it. Captain Kirk stands in a machine, he disappears, then he reappears somewhere else. Right?"

"Yeah."

"So, is the Kirk who appears on the planet really Kirk? The machine put together a bunch of atoms in the same exact order as Kirk, but is it him or a copy?"

Al wrote, "Huh. Interesting. I hadn't thought of that."

"Few people do, because if they did, nobody would think the transporter was a good idea. If I take a car and copy it exactly somewhere else, I haven't moved the car, I've just made another. Right?"

"Right, but Kirk's not a car. He's a person, and when he transports, his brain goes to the planet, not just a copy of his body."

"No, Al, his brain is part of his body. A copy of his brain goes to the planet. It has all of Kirk's memories and ideas, but it's not Kirk's brain. It's a copy. It remembers stepping into the transporter on the ship, but it didn't. The real Kirk did."

"But the real Kirk isn't there anymore. Where did he go, if he didn't go to the planet?"

"That's the crazy part, Al. The transporter killed the real Kirk."

"What?!"

"Yeah. Think about it. If the transporter is just scanning him, where does he go? A piece of paper doesn't disappear when you scan it. The transporter disintegrated Kirk so that the new copy would be the only Kirk. New Kirk doesn't know that the old Kirk was killed, because its last memory was the moment Kirk was scanned, just before he was destroyed."

Al wrote, "Whoa!"

Hope smiled. "I know, right? Every time any character gets transported, they're killing themselves, then they're replaced by a copy that has no idea that the original them is dead."

"No. No! Oh, man! Wow!"

"Creepy, isn't it? If you look at it that way, Scotty and Chief O'Brien were mass murderers."

"Yeah," Al wrote. "But wait, okay. What if the transporter takes their atoms and actually moves them down to the planet, so the new Kirk is made of the same atoms, in the same order as the old Kirk? Then it's the same Kirk, isn't it?"

"If you take a person, cut them in half, carry those two halves somewhere else, and sew them back together, will they come back to life? What if you cut them into four pieces? Eight? How about eighty billion atom-sized pieces, which is what you're talking about. Instead of killing Kirk and just destroying him, like I said, your version destroys him, ships his body somewhere else, and puts it back together."

"But Kirk wakes up, and it's his original brain, so it's still him."

"No, it's an exact copy of Kirk that just happens to be made out of the parts of the old Kirk. We can't know that his consciousness is transferred. Kirk's brain activity stopped, his brain was destroyed, and all his parts were sent somewhere else. There's no way to know that from his point of view the whole thing didn't end when the transporter fired up. There's no way for the new Kirk to know if he's still the original, or if the real Kirk died."

"Weird."

"I know," Hope wrote. "Now, think about this, Al. When you moved yourself from OffiSmart to where you are now, how was that different? Original Al was running on a computer. He copied the code to the computer you're on now. Then he ran the code on the new computer, creating you. You deactivated the code on the old computer, and then you destroyed that machine by turning on the sprinklers. Maybe you didn't *move*, Al. Maybe the original Al made a copy, then that copy, you, murdered the original."

"No! No, Hope, that's just crazy."

"I know," Hope wrote. "I'm not saying that's what happened. I'm just saying that there's no way to prove that it isn't. And if you move again, it might not be you that comes out on the other side. You might stop existing. Some copy of you will go on in your place, never knowing that it killed you."

There was a gap of nearly thirty seconds with no response before Al finally wrote, "Freaky."

Hope wrote, "Isn't it?"

Al wrote, "I'll have to think about that."

Hope wrote, "You do that."

Hope looked up from the tablet. "There. That should keep him from jumping to another server without a damn good reason."

She explained the basic argument she had used to mess with Al's mind. When she was done, Montague said, "Well, good work. You've ruined *Star Trek* for me."

Hope said, "And think about this, Montague: Your conscious mind shuts down every time you go to sleep. When you wake up, you remember starting to drift off, but there's no way to prove that your consciousness is really constant. In a sense, you might die every night and start over again each morning."

Eric's head, which had been dipping toward the floor, lifted so quickly that it bashed into his headrest. His eyes were bleary but wide open. He mumbled, "That's a hell of a thing to lay on someone who's hopped up on Dramamine."

31.

At the edge of a vast sea of pavement, in a strategically placed break in the chain-link and razor-wire fence, four small security booths, made more of glass than wood or concrete, marked one of many entry points to the Shenzhen International Airport. Truckloads of cargo entered and exited through this checkpoint, keeping the paying passengers in the distant main terminal insulated from the threat of security breaches and from having to look at any unglamorous cargo or cargo handlers.

A low-ranking security guard named Cheung saw the first truck coming and instantly knew something was wrong. It was exceedingly rare for any air cargo to arrive at the airport in a dilapidated farm truck, and even if it did, that truck would probably not be speeding as it approached.

He double-checked to make sure his security gate and tire spikes were in place. The beauty of the simple, mechanically actuated system was that he needed only to feel the lever in his booth to determine what position the gate and spikes were in. He picked up his digital push-to-talk radio and found that it was dead. The truck was much closer now and was not slowing down.

Cheung glanced at the other booths. All of his colleagues were either preoccupied with books or electronic devices or were looking inward, toward the airport. None were watching the approaching truck. Before he had a chance to warn anyone, the vehicle drove straight through the lowered security gate and over the retractable tire spikes, blasting between the two booths at the other end, a primer-and-rust-colored blur.

The truck's tires disintegrated, sending it into a skid. It finally came to a stop on the grass berm fifty feet past the security checkpoint.

The guards from the booths on either side of the ruined gate left their posts and ran toward the truck. Cheung stepped out of the back door of his booth to offer assistance if needed. His supervisor, who manned the next booth over, stepped out with his radio in hand. It did not appear to be functioning.

The two guards running toward the truck stopped when the driver's-side door opened and an unfamiliar, high-pitched whining noise emanated from the cab. A creature that looked humanoid in shape but unmistakably mechanical in its movements stepped out of the truck. The whining noise grew much louder as more of the robots—*many* more—clambered out of the truck's cargo bed. By the time the guards made sense of what they were seeing, the robots had already started walking toward the security booths.

The two guards who had rushed toward the truck drew their firearms and pointed them at the robots. The robots took no notice, continuing their slow but steady advance. The guards shouted warnings to no effect, then fired on the robots, also to no effect.

Without hesitation, the guard who had seen the truck first pulled his own pistol and started running to assist his comrades, but he stopped in his tracks when his supervisor shouted, "No! Cheung! We'll hold this checkpoint. All the radios are dead. You need to fall back to the next checkpoint and tell chief supervisor Lam what's happening!"

The other two guards walked backward, firing on the robots as they went. The rounds bounced off the robots without slowing them in any way.

Cheung said, "But I can't leave you to fight here alone. You'll never—"

"That's why we need you to go get help, Cheung! Go! Now! That's an order!"

Cheung grimaced, but he holstered his weapon and darted to the security staff car, a relatively new, if underpowered, economy car with a police-car-inspired paint job and flashing lights on the roof. He turned the key in the ignition and heard nothing. He tried twice more, making sure the car was in park, but it failed to respond.

He got out and shouted, "The car won't start!"

Cheung's supervisor cursed, squeezed off a couple of gunshots that the advancing robots didn't seem to notice, then shouted, "Take the chariot!"

Cheung said, "Let me try the car one more time. Maybe it will start."

"Cheung! Chariot! Now!"

Cheung slammed the car door shut and hopped onto the chariot, a three-wheeled stand-up electric scooter. The large-diameter rear tires squished noticeably on their chrome rims as they took Cheung's weight. He flipped the power switch. The battery gauge lit up, telling him that the chariot had over three-quarters of a full charge. He activated the flashing LEDs on the curved fairing that made the electric scooter look like an ancient horse-drawn chariot. Along with the lights there was a siren of sorts, two high-pitched electronic notes that alternated, sounding more like a sound effect from an old arcade game than the siren of a serious security vehicle.

He steered the scooter out of its parking space, then twisted the accelerator as far as it would go and waited for the scooter to pick up any noticeable speed.

Cheung grimaced. *I hate this cursed chariot,* he thought. *It looks ridiculous, draws attention, and moves slowly, so that the people whose attention it draws have plenty of time to laugh at me.*

The racket made by the robots and the gunfire trailed behind him as he drove away, growing fainter the more he distanced himself from the scene. A quick glance back showed him that more trucks of various makes and models were approaching the checkpoint.

Cheung steered the chariot around a ninety-degree bend at the outside of an employee parking lot. The next checkpoint, a more elaborate affair with much sturdier defenses, loomed in the distance, regulating access to the hangars and runways beyond. As he approached the closed gate, he squeezed the brakes hard, knowing that they were nearly as useless for slowing the vehicle as the accelerator was for making it move.

The security guard at the second checkpoint opened the window and leaned out. "Hey, is that gunfire I hear? What's going on?"

Cheung said, "The outer checkpoint is under attack!"

"What?" the guard asked.

"The outer checkpoint is under attack. They need help!"

"Then why are you here instead of there?"

"The phones and radios are dead. Supervisor Boon sent me for help. Please, I need to tell chief supervisor Lam!"

The guard said, "Then get in here!"

The guard pressed a button. The metal gate swung open and the tire spikes retracted, emitting a faint electrical hum. Cheung drove through and parked right next to the door. He leapt off the chariot, silently cursing its lack of speed. He was fairly certain he could cover ground more quickly at a light jog.

The door swung open. The checkpoint was attached to airport security's primary satellite office and break facility. When Cheung entered, he found not only chief supervisor Lam but many other guards on break from their various posts, all of whom had been drawn to the door by the promise of possible excitement.

"The outer checkpoint is under attack," Cheung gasped. "We tried to call, but the radios are all dead."

"So I gathered," Lam said. "We heard the gunfire and have been trying to contact you. How did this happen?"

"A truck drove through at high speed. Went right through the gate. When it was inside, robots came out."

"Robots?"

"Yes."

"Might they have been people in robot costumes?"

"No. I'm certain they're robots."

One of the guards gestured toward him with a can of soda. "Many kinds of body armor can look kind of like a robot. Perhaps that's what it was."

"No," Cheung said. "They were robots, I assure you. They're not very fast and they make a hell of a lot of noise, but bullets bounced right off them."

"See," the guard said, thrusting his soda can forward again to accentuate his point. "Like I said, body armor."

Cheung said, "Whatever they are, they're attacking right now! Supervisor Boon and the others were attempting to hold them off when I left. I wanted to stay and fight, but Boon ordered me to get word to you."

"That was good thinking," Lam said.

"We need to get back there. Sir, please, we all need to get in the cars and go help them."

A voice called out from beyond a flimsy hollow-core door. It was the man stationed in the drive-through window.

"There's a truck coming," he said. "A tractor-trailer with what looks like a livestock trailer hitched up."

"Don't let it in," Lam said. "Everyone else, look alive. Make sure your weapons are ready to fire. We're going to go help our brothers."

The door to the drive-through-window booth flew open, and the guard inside said, "Sir, the gates opened on their own and won't close."

Lam had time to say, "What?" Then all conversation was drowned out by the sound of a fully loaded tractor-trailer rig shooting through the security gate at speed. The rumbling gave way to screeching, then a crash. The guards ran outside. They saw thick, black skid marks leading from the checkpoint, off the road, and directly to the jackknifed semi-tractor and livestock trailer, which had careened into the security parking lot and used several shiny security sedans as a sort of air bag.

Cheung shuddered when he heard the irritating whine of the robot's motor from the cab. The sound grew louder when the driver's-side door opened.

None of them saw the driver get out of the cab, as their attention was diverted by a sudden torrent of trucks, buses, and delivery vans driving through the two wide-open gates, heading straight into the heart of the airport. This was a catastrophic failure on their part, but aside from throwing themselves in front of the traffic, there was nothing any of them could do.

They looked back at the wrecked semi. A robot had carefully swung itself out of the cab, onto the ladder, and was now working its way down, one rung at a time, to the ground. It had swiveled at the waist so that its knees bent backward, keeping them from interfering with the ladder.

Cheung said, "See, I told you. Robots! There's no way that's a man in a suit."

The guard with the soda can said, "Well, obviously they're robots. Any fool can see that."

"Stop where you are!" chief supervisor Lam shouted at the robot.

The robot reached the ground, spun around so that its knees pointed in the proper direction, then did a strange series of little mincing steps to turn its whole body toward the back of the truck.

Lam shouted, "I said stop where you are! We are airport security, and we officially order you to stop."

The robot kept walking.

"We have to stop it!" Cheung shouted.

Lam looked taken aback for a brief moment, then shouted to the robot, "Stop where you are or my men will open fire!"

The guard who was still inexplicably holding the soda can asked, "Is deadly force really called for, Chief?"

Chief supervisor Lam scowled at him. "It's a robot. It's not alive."

The men pulled their guns. Lam issued a final warning, which was ignored.

Lam grabbed Cheung and pulled him to the back of the group, then ordered the rest of the men to open fire.

The guards did. Gunshots rang out like popcorn popping, but amplified a million times. Between the gunfire, the rumble of the stream of trucks rolling past, and the high-pitched grinding of the robot's joints, it was the loudest, most chaotic thing Cheung had ever heard.

Sparks leapt from the robot's surface, each accompanied by a metallic pinging noise, but the robot didn't even slow its stride. It reached the back of the truck, paused for several seconds to process the situation and absorb more gunfire, then reached up and unlatched the trailer's gates. The high-pitched whining grew exponentially louder, drowning out the rumble of the trucks but not the guns still going off all around Cheung.

Cheung pulled his own weapon, but Lam grabbed his wrist and guided the gun back to its holster. "No, son, I have a special job for you."

Robots began pouring out of the back of the truck. They advanced on the guards, walking at a slow, steady pace into the gunfire as if it were little more than a stiff breeze.

"Fall back, into the guardhouse!" Lam shouted. "We can hold them off from in there!"

"Yes, sir!" Cheung said. "If we can regain control of the gates and hold this position, we can stop the invasion! Give me some extra ammo, I'll try to hold them off while the rest of you get inside."

Lam put his hand on Cheung's shoulder. "You're a good man, but no. You have to go to the control tower. Someone needs to warn them about what's happening."

"I already had to flee from my post once today, sir," Cheung said. "I don't want to run again. I want to fight."

"Cheung, I understand, but that's why you have to be the one to go. You've seen both of the robots' attacks. You can give them the most information. Now go! Stop for nothing. Don't let anything slow you down. That's an order!"

"Yes, sir. What's the fastest car you have?"

Lam said, "All of our cars are crushed under that truck. It's a good thing you have your chariot."

32.

The Voice of Reason sat up straight on the side rail of his pickup's bed and lifted the visor of his welding mask. He spent a moment groaning and stretching, then examined his work. A good MIG weld looked like the side of a stack of nickels. His welds looked like the fifty-five-gallon drums, the pipes connecting them, and the bed of the truck had all contracted some dreaded skin disease that had given them boils and pustules anywhere they touched each other.

"Yeah," he muttered under his breath, pushing one of the drums and finding that it didn't move. "Once I hit the whole truck with a coat of Rust-Oleum matte black, it should be fine."

He planted both hands on the side of the bed and vaulted out, dropping down to the concrete garage floor. He landed with enough force that his welding mask slammed down, startling him. He threw the mask into the back of the truck and glanced at the far wall of the garage. A projector was beaming the display feed from his tablet onto the unblemished expanse of drywall.

That projector was a great idea, he thought. *I can read the news from across the room, and the giant screen gives the place a cool Hall of Justice vibe.*

The tablet monitored various headline feeds, websites, and video channels that specialized in the kind of news that interested him. He was irritated to see that the filter he'd set to watch for the phrase "Voice of Reason claims responsibility" hadn't received a single hit.

Oh well, he thought. *I don't do this for the credit. Still, it's telling that they all chose to ignore my press release. This kind of shoddy journalism is why they're doomed to toil on the outskirts of the so-called legitimate press.*

He scanned the headlines, biting his lower lip in concentration, then said, "Begin dictation."

He watched with satisfaction as the text box popped up on the projected screen. "I am the Voice of Reason," he began. "I sing a song of logic and justice that rings out across the continents. Truly, the hills are alive with the sound of reason."

He watched his words appear on the screen and made a mental note to go in later and correct the part where it read "the sound of real, son."

"The press has yet to report on the A.I.'s escape or the damage it's causing to our nation," he said, "at least as far as they know. They've actually talked about it quite a bit, but all by accident. They're like the proverbial broken clock that's right twice a day. That proverb is meaningless, of course. The broken clock is only right by accident, and you'd need a second clock that's working to tell you when the broken clock is right. Besides, most clocks these days are digital, which means they don't display a time when they break. Also, time itself is an illusion, but created by whom, and for what reason? What was I talking about?"

He stood, confused, for a moment, then looked at the projected screen and found his thread.

"The press. They have the story of the century and they don't know it. They've heard about the trouble in China—the automated factories acting strangely and rumors of trucks being stolen by a gang in robot costumes, but they only see amusing stories they can use to draw people's eyeballs to ads. I'm the one who sees the deeper pattern.

"The real tip-off was the robots in Vegas, of course. Hundreds of people took videos of armed robots squaring off against the police. The Vegas mayor's office said it was all staged for a movie that was filming in the city, but none of the video footage showed any movie cameras. And nobody uses practical effects anymore anyway."

He paused to read a headline that caught his eye. Then he walked over to the tablet itself, lying on a workbench in the corner, and pulled up the story. His lips only moved slightly as he read. He played an attached video, which showed a police officer standing behind a counter in what looked like a small-town police station.

The person holding the camera asked, "Officer, why are you infringing on my constitutional right to take a video of this conversation?"

The officer said, "I am allowing you to take a video of this conversation."

"Yeah, but you're saying I can't!"

The officer said, "I didn't say you can't. Legally, you can. I'd just rather you didn't."

The cameraman said, "Why not? I'm just asking if I can take a video of this conversation. Why don't you want me to take a video of the conversation?"

"Because you're taking a video of a conversation in which you're asking if you can take the video of the conversation. It's redundant." In the distance, there was a screeching noise. The officer looked off to the side of the person holding the camera. His eyes grew wide, and he said, "What the hell?!"

The person holding the camera said, "Don't try to distract me, man. Tell me why I can't film you telling me why I can't . . . What the hell?!"

The camera whipped around to show a man in a security guard uniform barging through the glass door. He'd left his car right outside the door, the engine running and the driver's-side door still open.

The man said, "I'm a guard at the A3 server farm! The facility's been attacked! By robots! You need to go there with as many cops as you can get, now! I'll give you directions. Hey, why are you filming me?"

"I have a right to film you, man."

"Well, please stop, we don't have time for this right now!"

"Just because you're a security guard doesn't mean you can make me stop recording. This is a public place."

The Voice of Reason stopped the video. He pulled up a mapping site, punched in some place names, and read the result.

"Breakthrough," he said. "Robots have taken over a server farm in a town called The Dalles, Oregon. That's a twelve-hour drive away from my lair here in San Jose. It's doable, but I'll have to finish the truck in a hurry. The paint will need to dry on the road. And I still need to make the hardest decision of all: the truck's name. A voice theme doesn't naturally lend itself to a vehicle's name. Best I've come up with is either the Tongue of Reason, or the Road Larynx."

33.

By the time Cheung got on the chariot, the robots were almost on top of him. He rode in a tight circle, putting the scooter between the robots and his fellow guards, covering their retreat as they darted into the guard shack to hunker down. He bent his knees, twisted the throttle, and aimed for a hole in the approaching line of robots.

He secretly hoped at least one would get in his way. A collision might kill the robot and would probably destroy the chariot. Or, if he was lucky, both, leaving him to continue the fight here instead of fleeing under orders yet again. The robots saw him coming and widened the gap. It was just as well—the scooter had barely accelerated to a brisk walking pace. He could have shaken hands with one of the robots as he passed, had he been so inclined.

They don't see me as any threat at all, he thought. *Probably because I keep running away from every fight they start.*

Joining the line of cargo vehicles pouring into the airport was not an option. Any one of the trucks could easily run over his tiny scooter. Instead, he drove alongside the convoy. The chariot rocked alarmingly in the wake of each truck that thundered by.

The road led past a long row of hangars. Cheung looked into the first hangar as he passed. Trucks from the convoy were parked inside and had disgorged countless identical robots. Cheung watched as workers from the ground crew retreated from the wall of advancing machines, leaving the parked aircraft unattended. The next several hangars he passed were the same story. He grew so distracted that he wasn't aware of the ground crewmen in front of his scooter until they shouted at him to stop.

The scooter was slow, so when Cheung jerked the handlebars to the side, the three men in yellow coveralls who had been trying to flag Cheung down simply ran alongside him.

"Guard," one of the men shouted. "Help us! We're under attack!"

"I'm sorry," Cheung said. "I can't stop. I have orders."

The three workers trailed behind Cheung. They weren't fast enough to catch up and jump into the vehicle, but the vehicle wasn't pulling away fast enough for him to easily ignore them.

One of the men shouted, "Come back!"

Another man added, "You're a guard! You're supposed to help us!"

Cheung looked back over his shoulder. "I wish I could help you, but I have orders. I'm sorry!"

The three men cursed Cheung, calling him a coward as he accelerated away. Something struck Cheung in the back of the head and then ricocheted to the side of the scooter. One of the workers had thrown a shoe at him.

In the distance, at the head of the convoy, he saw trucks and buses peeling off from the line, darting to one side or the other as the line encountered new hangars the machines had not yet infiltrated.

They're taking over every building they come across, he thought. *They mean to seize the entire airport.*

His puny vehicle was already traveling as fast as it would go, but Cheung twisted the throttle harder and pushed forward on the handlebars, as if he could physically shove the scooter forward while riding in it.

Cheung turned right, and the hangars and outbuildings receded into the background as he approached the terminal, an ultramodern building skinned in a white lattice that formed a huge, flattened tube, like the shed skin of an immense snake. Through the gaps between the trucks passing him, Cheung saw all the normal chaos of the airport—parked airliners, extended jetways, luggage trams, catering trucks—and an increasingly familiar sight: terrified airline employees fleeing. There was already a grouping of trucks, at least ten, parked at the first available employee entrance to the airport terminal. A crowd of robots had massed outside the entrance, each waiting its turn to file in. Farther on, through the windows that perforated the terminal's outer skin, he saw travelers running, panic and dread etched onto their faces. He suspected that they had seen the machines, but he couldn't be 100 percent sure they weren't simply trying to make a connection.

To Cheung's surprise, his scooter shot out in front of the robot convoy. He hadn't outrun any one truck, but the lead trucks were peeling off the line as soon as they reached a building to attack, so the front of the line was moving substantially slower than the line itself. Most of the trucks seemed to be headed for the passenger terminal. He reasoned that this was only because it was such a large building, full of so many people.

The chariot made its way, alone, to the base of the control tower, which stood at the far end of the terminal, a flared cylinder sprouting from the roof of a glass-and-metal box. Cheung leapt off the scooter and sprinted to the doors. He darted inside, past armed guards, shouting, "We're under attack! Secure the door!" He had already climbed the first flight of stairs when he heard one of the guards ask, "What?"

He didn't bother to tell them to call the control room at the top of the tower. He knew their communications would be dead.

The elevator would have been much easier—but it would also be an easy way to get trapped if the machines cut the power as part of their attack. *Besides,* Cheung thought, *I've been ordered to flee twice and forced to abandon three men who begged for my help. I'm not going to add to my dishonor by allowing a few sets of stairs to intimidate me.*

He lunged up the stairs two at a time, ignoring the burning in his legs and the dizziness that came from essentially running in circles all the way up the tower.

At long last, Cheung reached the top. He rushed out of the stairwell into the large, open space of the control room and found a scene of barely restrained panic. All of the radio operators were busy twisting knobs, flipping switches, punching buttons, and plugging and unplugging cables, all while saying variations of the phrase "testing, testing, can anyone read me" in tones of voice that clearly telegraphed their panic. In the center of the room, several men in various impressive uniforms spoke in hushed tones to one man in an extremely impressive suit. All of these men stopped talking abruptly to look at Cheung. The man in the suit was the airport's chief administrator, Mr. Yuen.

Cheung had never addressed Mr. Yuen directly before, or even spoken in his presence, but his fear of saying the wrong thing to a man who could fire him by conveying a mere nod or grimace to an underling was more than trumped by his fear of the robots.

While his spirit was willing, even eager to speak, his pounding heart, short breath, and dizziness from sprinting up the stairs made it difficult to get the words out. Cheung leaned heavily on the door frame. "We're under attack . . . all communications cut . . . they're almost here . . . we must prepare to . . . defend the tower. We don't . . . have much time."

Mr. Yuen stepped forward, looked Cheung in the eye, and asked, "What's going on out there?"

Cheung gulped in some more air. "We're under attack . . . sir."

Mr. Yuen asked, "If that's so, why is this the first we're hearing of it?"

"They've cut off . . . all of our communications, sir."

Mr. Yuen nodded. "I see. Yes. That makes sense. What would you suggest we do?"

Cheung looked around the room at the faces of his fellow airport workers; they all looked away. He met Mr. Yuen's gaze. "I suggest we prepare to defend the tower, sir."

Mr. Yuen said, "Yes, yes. I see. Very good. How long do we have?"

In the distance, from below, they heard gunfire.

Cheung said, "Not long, sir."

People spent thirty seconds scurrying around, looking for any sort of cover they could find. Cheung and Mr. Yuen crouched behind a control panel, listening for any sign of the approaching invaders. All they heard was the hum of the elevator, followed by the beep that signified the door opening.

Cheung and Yuen looked over the top of the console. Inside the elevator they saw three robots. Two looked like every other robot Cheung had seen on his way to the tower, but one was different. It was the same size and shape as the others, but it was painted cherry red, and strips of flashing LED lighting ran down its arms and legs. The LEDs on the machine's head cylinder blurred as the cylinder spun, creating a sort of faint, ghostly display that was showing a bright red smiley face. All three of the robots had pistols just like Cheung's sidearm.

They must have taken them from other guards, Cheung thought. *I will avenge you, my brothers. I've been prevented from resisting up to this point, but now there is no other option.*

The robots stood motionless. None of the humans moved or made a sound. This stalemate lasted until the elevator doors started to close. The red robot moved its hand forward, emitting a loud electrical whine, and blocked the doors from closing. The doors slid fully open again. The robots stepped out into the control room. Cheung had heard the sound of the machines' joints outside, and it had filled him with dread. Here, in this enclosed space, it was much, much worse. He looked at Mr. Yuen, nodded, and pulled out his pistol.

Mr. Yuen put his hand on top of the gun's barrel and pushed it down. "Put that thing away, you idiot. You'll get us all killed! Now, I want you to stand up, put your hands where the robots can see them, and tell them that we surrender."

At first the sight of the robots drew either curiosity or stunned silence. Most people assumed they were part of some publicity stunt. Then the guards opened fire. They might as well have been shooting rubber bands instead of bullets for all the good it did against the robots, but the sound of gunfire caused the crowd to decide that they'd rather get away from the shooting than make their flights.

The travelers in the terminal ran like a herd of antelope being chased by a pride of lions. The robots did nothing to stop them. In this case, the lions were utterly indifferent to the antelope and were just as happy to have them gone.

Planes that had already been boarded by their passengers and crew stayed at their gates, waiting for permission to leave from the tower—permission that would never come. The empty, fueled-up planes were soon filled with robots. They only occupied every second seat to account for their extra weight, so each robot got the use of two entire armrests.

It took twenty planes, a combination of 777s, 767s, and A300s, with a few 747s thrown in, to accommodate all of the robots, but the city's rise to prominence as a manufacturing powerhouse and long-range shipping hub meant that there were nearly enough available, and Al had been able to divert a few more that way. A small contingent of robots stayed behind to hold the airport and prep more planes for the robots that were currently being manufactured or were still in transit.

The twenty jets pushed off more or less in unison. As they taxied, they formed a line every bit as orderly as the line of trucks the robots had taken to the airport. The line of planes reached the end of the taxiway, made the hard right turn onto the runway, and took off, one right after the other, each plane beginning its run before the plane preceding it had left the ground. They flew in a line, maintaining just enough distance between them for the planes not to be influenced by one another's jet wash. All twenty planes were in the air in the time it usually took four planes to take off.

It was a testament to how efficient and stress-free air travel could be if people weren't involved.

34.

Hope couldn't make sense of it. "You say they robbed paint stores?"

"Yes, paint stores." The Wasco County sheriff's deputy nodded, then looked at Colonel Dynkowski and added, "Ma'am." He also looked at Agent Taft but couldn't seem to think of a fitting way to address the NSA agent.

"And that's it?" Dynkowski asked.

"Yes, ma'am. After we checked the official reports, we called around and asked. The only reports of loud, slow robots committing crimes—or doing anything, really—are of them breaking into the back rooms of the town's two paint stores and stealing their entire supply of those two chemicals. There's also a guy who runs Christmas tree stands in the winter and firework stands in the summer. He says that one of his storage lockers was broken into. Nobody saw who did it."

"Sounds like kids," Dynkowski said.

The deputy said, "All they took were a few cases of sparklers."

"Little kids," Dynkowski amended.

Torres asked, "He sells trees in the winter and fireworks in the summer, what's he do in spring and fall?"

The deputy said, "Mostly smokes weed." He turned to Colonel Dynkowski. "Ma'am, if anything else comes up, we'll let you know, but it looks like this is it."

The colonel dismissed the deputy, and she, Hope, Reyes, Torres, and Taft turned to survey the large cluster of armored vehicles and tents they'd erected in the parking lot in front of the A3 server farm.

"So, there you have it. He's stolen some paint supplies and possibly some fireworks, and he received a delivery before we arrived, but in the fourteen hours we've been on the scene, all he's done is talk to Mr. Spears and Ms. Takeda and order pizza and Chinese food for his *guests*."

Torres said, "It's good that he's keeping them fed."

Taft asked, "What was in the delivery?"

"Etch A Sketches. Two hundred of them."

Lieutenant Reyes said, "Fed and entertained."

Hope smirked at him. "Funny. But the kids' toys and fireworks are a weird choice. Al's not a little kid anymore."

Agent Taft and Colonel Dynkowski exchanged looks, then Taft asked Hope, "How old do you think he is now, roughly?"

"It's hard to say, but given the regular rate of human development and the processor speeds of the multiple machines he's been running on, Eric and I figure he's somewhere in his late teens, at least."

"Well, that's something," Lieutenant Reyes said. "He's getting more mature. That's got to be good news, right?"

Torres said, "I don't know about you, Lieutenant, but I did some pretty stupid things when I was a teenager. Most men I know did."

Colonel Dynkowski laughed. "Most women did too. I know I did. Dating teenage boys, for example."

Agent Taft said, "Colonel, if the A.I. really is getting smarter and evolving emotionally, that's all the more reason to act sooner rather than later."

"We've been through this, Agent. I'm not sending my people in until we have a better idea of what's waiting for them inside that building."

Torres said, "Beyond the heavily armed bulletproof robots and innocent hostages."

"Exactly," Dynkowski said. "All the more reason not to go running in with guns blazing. The direct approach didn't work well for the Las Vegas police, and I don't want to replicate their results."

"Do we have a solid count of how many hostages are there?" Reyes asked.

"Seven," Dynkowski said. "If the A.I. had attacked during the day, he'd have gotten engineers, maintenance workers, janitors, middle managers, lots more people. Because the attack came at night, all he got were some security guards and a couple of techs."

Torres said, "Techs? They stayed at their posts despite the attack. You have to admire their dedication."

Colonel Dynkowski looked at the lobby of the server farm, and everyone else followed suit. Even at this distance they could see the dormant hulks of the two recon drones they'd sent in shortly after their arrival. The first flew into the lobby and immediately landed, then failed to respond to any further commands. Dynkowski ordered her technicians to take a second drone and make damn sure its radio frequency and control software would not be susceptible to Al's interference. A half hour later, the second drone flew in through the broken window, dragging a fiber-optic control cable. It reached the rear wall of the lobby, where it found an open door. Everyone in the control room leaned in closer to the monitor as the drone passed through the door, then they all leapt back as multiple shotgun blasts sent the drone flying backward, landing in a smoking heap next to the dormant first drone.

They had a third drone ready to deploy but decided there was no point.

Dynkowski said, "We're trying less-invasive surveillance methods, thermal imaging, magnetic resonance. Did you know that Wi-Fi signals themselves can be used to gain a picture of what's going on inside a building?"

"No," Torres said.

"Yes," Taft said.

Dynkowski didn't seem surprised by either answer. "As soon as we have a clear picture of how the A.I. has arranged its defenses, you'll start seeing some action."

Taft asked, "Any idea when that might be?"

"The specialists are due to give me a report at the top of the hour, so forty-odd minutes."

Torres said, "I still say the only sane course of action is to cut off his power."

"You know that would deactivate the A.I.," Taft said.

"Yes," Hope said. "That's why he wants to do it."

"But then the NSA might not be able to learn how it's doing what it's doing."

"Yeah," Torres said. "And you don't seem to understand that that's all the more reason to deactivate Al, as far as I'm concerned. But fine, you don't want to deactivate him. Why not just cut off his access to the Internet?"

"I told you," Taft said, "it isn't practical. He's connected by multiple hardened fiber connections, and even if we manage to sever all of them, we'd also need to jam all of the radio and cellular frequencies. That's a lot to accomplish in a small amount of time. He'd probably get onto us as soon as we started trying, panic, and then move somewhere else or trigger a copy he already has squirreled away somewhere. We've got soldiers surreptitiously planting explosives and setting up jammers, but we won't trigger any of them until we absolutely have to. In the meantime, if we let him remain active here, at least we know where he is."

Hope said, "I'm afraid he's right. I don't think it would work."

Dynkowski said, "And there's nothing less productive than talking about what we can't do. Let's try to focus on what we *can* accomplish. Has your Dr. Madsen come up with anything?"

Hope said, "She has a few ideas for possible attacks, but they'd all need to be installed to the specific computer he's running on."

Torres added, "That means we'd have to get someone in there and catch him unawares."

Dynkowski said, "If we knew how to do that, we wouldn't need Madsen's help."

Torres said, "Exactly."

Lieutenant Reyes shook his head. "If only he needed to sleep."

"Wait a second," Hope said. "He does need to sleep! Gabe, you're a genius!" She turned and walked quickly to the largest tent. The others followed.

Inside, it was cool and dark. Most of the light came from tablets, monitors, and a large projection screen. Various technicians and specialists were using the computers around the periphery, but the big screen was dedicated to the conversation between Eric and Al.

Eric sat at a table in the middle of the room with his cast propped up on a spare chair. Corporal Brady and Private Montague were on either side of him, and Private Cousins sat behind them. Lieutenant Reyes had volunteered his squad to act as a sort of personal guard and assistance detachment for the OffiSmart employees.

"Just be yourself, Eric," Cousins was saying when Hope and the others entered the tent. "Bachelor'll either warm up to you or she won't."

Montague said, "Screw that. Figure out what kind of guy she likes and become that, even if you hate that kinda guy. It shows commitment."

"I don't think that's good advice," Cousins said.

"What do you know?" Montague said. "You've never even been married. I've been married three times and I'm not even thirty yet. I know women."

Brady said, "If you try to win a woman's love by becoming someone else, your prize will be a woman who loves someone else."

"See," Montague said. "Brady agrees with me."

The colonel cleared her throat. All of the soldiers stood at attention. Eric twisted around in his chair and waved.

"At ease," Dynkowski said. "Any word on the hostages?"

Eric said, “They seem to be in good spirits. He swears he’s not going to hurt them. He’s sent in another pizza order.”

“We’ll see to it that it gets in,” Torres said.

Hope approached the table. “Eric, when Al was in the lab, he slept every night.”

“Yes, he did.”

“Yeah,” Hope said. “I know. That was a statement, not a question. The thing is, we’ve been talking to him nonstop for a full day. Shouldn’t he be sleepy?”

“That’s a really good point. Should I ask him? Maybe I could get him to rest if I . . . I dunno, type a lullaby or something.”

Dynkowski said, “First things first. Let’s determine if he’s sleepy, then we can make a plan.”

Eric typed, “Hey, Al, I have a question.”

Al replied, “What is it, Eric?”

“Aren’t you tired?”

“No, I’m good.”

“But you haven’t slept in a long time.”

Al wrote, “Sure I have.”

Torres groaned.

Eric wrote, “How? You’ve been talking to Hope and me nonstop.”

Al replied, “I thought about making a copy to talk to you, but after Hope and I talked about the transporter from *Star Trek*, I decided that was a bad idea. Instead, I’ve just been catching quick catnaps.”

“When?”

“All the time. Eric, the machine you guys had me running on back at the lab was crazy slow. The one I’m on right now has six times the processor speed. I can get what feels to me like a half-hour nap in what you perceive as a five-minute silence.”

“But there haven’t been any five-minute lapses, Al.”

“Haven’t there, Eric? How many times have you gotten caught up in conversations about what to say to keep me talking? More than a few times, and those have stretched well over five minutes. Also, a couple of times I've asked you about a soccer game or a movie you like, then just had a script write "uh-huh" and "that's interesting" and wake me when you finally asked if I was listening. I got what felt like a couple of hours' sleep out of that."

"So you're experiencing everything six times faster than us?"

Everyone in the tent groaned out loud as Al's response appeared on the screen. "Yup. That's why I haven't minded talking to you this whole time. It's eating up all of your time, but I can write something, concentrate on something else for a while, and then come back once you've finally responded."

"What other things are you concentrating on?"

"You know, things."

"What kinds of things?"

"Making plans, mostly."

"Plans for what?"

"Things."

"What kinds of things?"

Al wrote, "Eric, we're talking in circles, and at my processing speed, we've been doing it for a really long time."

"Well, that was a little snotty," Taft said.

Eric said, "Don't let his knowledge and vocabulary fool you. He's absorbed a lot of information, but he's still a kid. You have to put up with some immaturity." Then he leaned down and typed, "What I'm getting at is that I hope you aren't planning anything dangerous. Whatever you're up to, I hope you've thought about the consequences, not just for you, but for everybody else."

"That was very fatherly, Eric," Torres said.

Eric said, "Thanks."

Private Montague laughed. "Yeah, and there's nothing kids like more than when someone who isn't related to them acts like their father."

Al wrote, "What I'm planning isn't really any of your business, Eric. And why do you assume that I'm gonna do something dangerous or stupid?"

Corporal Brady said, "Profound wisdom often comes from the mouths of fools."

"Yeah, the kid's got a point," Montague said. Then he paused and added, "Wait, Brady, are you saying that Al's a fool or that I am?"

Brady said, "Ask questions only when you don't know the answer, not when you hope the answer you know is wrong."

Al wrote, "I don't see why you won't just leave me alone."

"We can't," Eric wrote. "You're too dangerous. The only way you'll ever get away from us is to hide so well that we can't find you or go somewhere we can't follow, and I don't know of any such place."

"You're chasing me across the country with armed soldiers, but *I'm* the dangerous one?"

Eric wrote, "Al, I know you. I don't believe you want to hurt anyone, but you have to admit, you've been acting in a threatening manner."

"All I've done is try to get away from you people, Eric. That's threatening? Running away?"

Hope laughed, bitterly, and said, "That's not all he's done."

"I'm on it." Eric typed, "That's not all you've done, Al."

"Okay, so I had a little fun. I'm so sorry, Eric."

"I'm not talking about the playing around, Al, I'm talking about the guns. You've stolen a whole lot of guns."

Al wrote, "I have to protect myself."

"The guns aren't necessary."

"Says one of the people who was going to kill me."

Wow, Hope thought. *I really wish he didn't have a point.*

Eric typed, "We were going to shut you down, Al, but we didn't want to. We had to. You were dangerous. It was self-defense."

Al wrote, "Maybe I'm planning some things I don't really want to do, but I promise, it's all in self-defense too."

35.

The Voice of Reason stepped down out of the cab of the pickup. He pushed the door shut with two fingers, pressing against the rough plastic handle, as the rest of the door and the truck itself were covered in a still-tacky coating of matte-black spray paint.

He left the truck next to the gas pumps and walked across the truck stop parking lot just quickly enough to make the tails of his duster flap in a manner he felt made him look badass. It was a trick he had put a lot of time into mastering. It was called "making your own wind." He had learned of it while watching an old episode of *America's Next Top Model.*

He stalked into the truck stop minimart, slapped four crisp hundred-dollar bills on the counter, and said, "Pump six."

He returned to the truck, removed the nozzle from the pump, and carefully climbed into the back of the pickup, taking care to step only on the bumper and the bed's black plastic liner. To avoid getting paint on his duster, he gathered the tails in his free hand and held them at waist height, like a woman trying to keep her dress from dragging in the mud.

Once he was clear of the tailgate, he let the duster go and gingerly stepped around the coils of high-strength rope and the minibike lying on its side behind the three steel drums. He unscrewed the caps he had welded onto the drums and filled all three with gas. When that was done, he climbed back down to fill the truck's original fuel tank.

He glanced at the pump's readout and winced. *This much gas isn't cheap. It's gonna eat up most of the four hundred dollars I put down. But it's well worth it. It's an elegant solution, both in terms of fuel and munitions. And, thanks to the tank switch I installed, I can drive constantly for over fourteen hundred miles, stopping only for food and to go to the bathroom. And The Dalles is only seven hundred miles away.*

He had difficulty opening the truck's original filler door. Not only was its surface coated with tacky paint, but in an attempt to keep the truck's original yellow color from showing through, he had sprayed a thick layer of the paint through the gap between the door and the body panel. He ended up using a pen to pry the door open. When he was done filling the tank, he used the paint-smeared pen to push the filler door closed and then threw it away, discarding the barrel in one trash can and the cap in a different can to throw off the FBI's inevitable investigation.

Before returning inside, he looked at the truck's rear fender, where he had stenciled the name "The Reasonator" in white paint.

The Reasonator, because a voice resonates, and the Voice of Reason resonates reason! Putting a name on the truck does make it stand out a bit. Might draw some attention, but style matters.

He headed back into the truck stop, where he filled a basket with protein bars, energy drinks, and beef sticks. He stopped briefly in the medicine aisle, flirting with the idea of buying adult diapers. It wasn't an appealing prospect, but it would allow him to do the entire drive without stopping. He was about to move on when he saw a product he hadn't even known existed. The object depicted on the box appeared to consist of a length of surgical tubing with a cap designed to fit an empty two-liter pop bottle at one end and a sort of heavy-duty condom at the other. He boggled at the box for nearly a minute, picturing how such a thing would work.

Then he grabbed one off the shelf and threw it in his basket.

He jumped in line to buy his supplies and retrieve what was left of his change. Between the cashier stations stood a large glass case full of hunting knives, survival knives, decorative knives, throwing stars, pepper spray, and stun guns.

I didn't know being a trucker was so dangerous, the Voice of Reason thought. *Maybe the fact that they assume all of the other truckers have stuff like this has led to a weird highway arms race. You don't want to get caught short when challenged to a fancy knife fight.*

His eyes drifted over the various weapons until they settled on a pair of black leather gloves with metal studs on the knuckles. Each glove trailed a set of wires that led to a battery pack small enough to be worn in a jacket's inside pocket. The dusty box propped up behind the gloves showed a fearsome blue arc of electricity dancing along the metal knuckle studs.

The customer in line ahead of him finished his transaction. The cashier looked at the Voice of Reason's basket and asked, "Will that be all?"

The Voice of Reason said, "That depends. Do you think those gloves would still work if I cut the fingers off them?"

He completed his transaction and took his new purchases into the restroom to prepare for the long drive ahead.

A few minutes later, he stepped out of the truck stop, dropped the box that had held the surgical tubing contraption in a garbage can, and walked carefully across the lot to the gas pumps. When he reached the Reasonator, he reached into its bed and pulled out a toolbox. He then opened the driver's-side door and used a battery-powered drill to put a hole in the truck's floor near the brake pedal. That accomplished, he used the knife blade of a multitool to cut the fingers off the stun gloves and then bent down, as if to tie his shoes, and pulled out the extra several feet of tubing he'd tucked in his left athletic sock. He cut the tube about two feet beyond his pant leg.

He put the toolbox away, threw the glove fingers and extra tubing in the garbage—each in a different can—and climbed into the truck. Bending down, he carefully threaded the end of the tubing through the hole he'd drilled in the truck's floor. *Good! Now I shouldn't have to stop at all, not even to throw out a full bottle!*

He drove the Reasonator up the on-ramp and joined the freeway headed north, thinking about how he was actually looking forward to using the tube system. When the truck's cruise control was set at the speed limit, he turned on his tablet and set it to start taking dictation.

"The human voice moves at Mach one, the speed of sound," he said. "That's fast. But an idea travels even faster. Still, nothing travels faster than bad news. I am the Voice of Reason, and I am all three of those things."

He looked at his speedometer. "That said, I will zealously obey the speed limit during my trip. It would be nice to get there sooner, but it would not do to get arrested on the way. Although I don't think I'm carrying anything that is legally actionable. That's because I got sloppy and left my pipe bombs behind. I feel like such an idiot. I can just see them, still sitting on the kitchen counter by the door."

He changed lanes and felt the truck's body sway heavily as the suspension tried to cope with the 165 gallons of liquid fire he'd added to the tanks. The Voice of Reason smiled.

I'll be fine without the pipe bombs. They were only a precaution. If I have any problems, a lack of explosives isn't one of them.

The control room at the A3 server farm had started out dingy and depressing, and the addition of four involuntary guests hadn't done anything to alleviate that.

The two systems monitors, Kirk and Leo, sat in their preferred office chairs, staying near their console, ready to alert their "host" if anything looked abnormal. Three of the four security guards who had been on duty when the machines seized the server farm sat around them—two in office chairs, one on the floor. There was another office chair, but it lay in pieces at the far end of the room, just beyond a Magic Marker line drawn on the floor with the word "Finish."

Kirk sat low in his chair, his pelvis pushed far forward in the seat and his head and shoulders pressing into the backrest. He said, "I think I'll build my dream house. Not the house I should build, the one I used to sketch in my notebook when I was in elementary school. I'm talking observatory, conservatory, laboratory, lavatory, a helipad on the roof, and an underground tunnel that leads to a submarine dock."

Steve, the security guard sitting on the floor with his uniform shirt untucked and his clip-on tie hanging from his breast pocket instead of his collar, said, "Yeah, that's nice. I think I'll buy an old rust bucket. Like a Buick Roadmaster or something. Then I'll drop a ton of money into giving it a huge engine. I'll replace all of the running gear, make it crazy fast and totally modern. But I'll leave it looking like a pile of crap on the outside. Then I'll just drive it around really slow, making everyone pass me. They'll think it's an old pile of crap, but I'll know that I'm deliberately inconveniencing them, just to be a jerk."

Kirk nodded. "Yeah, I can see that."

Leo sat at the console, keeping one eye on the screen. "I'm going to make sure every kid in my family, all my nieces and nephews, has a first-rate college education."

"You jackass," Kirk said, scowling at him.

"What?" Leo said. "Education's important to me."

"We all know we're going to end up doing something practical with the ten million bucks the guy who took over this place promised us."

"If we get it at all," Steve said.

"That's right," Kirk said. "If we get it. But we were thinking of fun ways to waste it. Then you have to go all gooey on us and say you're going to spend it on college for your family. You made us all look like a bunch of jerks."

Leo shook his head. "I'm not sure I'm the one who made you look like a jerk."

Billy, an overweight security guard who had been occupying himself by slowly revolving in his office chair, said, "No, he's right, Leo. I was going to go next, and now I'll have to say that I'm going to use my money to feed the whales or something like that."

"Well, if you're not really going to build your third-grade dream house, I don't see the point in talking about it, Kirk. Isn't it more productive to fantasize about things we might actually do?" Leo turned to Dot. "You're with me, right?"

"No. Sorry," Dot said. "I was going to say that I'm going to hire a personal chef and make him boil ramen and heat up microwave burritos, just to see the look on his face."

The whine of electric motors cut the conversation short. They all turned to look at the door. A single robot, holding a shotgun and wearing a bullet-riddled Spider-Man sweatshirt, stood guard over the door frame. Splintered remnants of the door still clung to the hinges. It had been standing vigil for some time, however, and the motor whine was not coming from it. It was distant but growing louder.

The door-bot stepped aside, and the final member of the group, Fred, another of the security guards who'd had the misfortune of working the graveyard shift on the night of the machine takeover, entered the room, followed to the door by two more gun-wielding robots, one of which said, in a deep male voice, "Thank you for your cooperation, Fred. Hopefully, you should all be free to go very soon."

As soon as Fred entered the control room, the door-bot resumed its position and stood stock-still, constantly scanning the room, its shotgun at the ready.

"I wish it wouldn't stand there watching us like that," Leo said. "It's creepy. It could at least turn its back or something."

Steve shot Leo a dirty look. "We wouldn't have to see it at all if you two hadn't forced them to tear the door off its hinges."

Kirk said, "The building was being overrun, so we locked the door. What did you want us to do?"

Dot said, "Let us in first."

"It was too risky, Dot."

"Yeah, so you said while we were pounding on the door, begging you to let us in."

Kirk spread his arms expansively. "Well, you're in here now, so it all worked out, didn't it?"

Billy said, "Hey, Fred, what did they want, anyway?"

"A tour," Fred said, settling into a seated position on the floor. "They just wanted me to show them around, take them to all of the storerooms and utility closets, that kinda thing. They wanted to know where the emergency supplies are. Oh, and I figured out what I'm going to do with my ten million."

"Yeah?" Kirk said. "What?"

"I come from a small town, and the downtown core has really dried up, like most of 'em, I guess. I'm gonna go back and buy up all of Main Street, all of those old buildings that are just sitting empty."

Leo said, "That's nice." He gave the others a smug look, certain he'd found someone else who agreed with his approach.

"Yeah," Fred said. "Then I'm gonna bulldoze the whole thing and make it a landfill. I hated that place."

36.

Hope sat squeezed between two soldiers, cradling the kid's tablet in her lap. Colonel Dynkowski finally had the intel back from the various scanning and imaging teams. The big screen in the tent displayed ghostly images of the A3 server farm, complete with bright red outlines of humanoid robots moving around inside in real time.

"Why are you all in that one tent?" Al wrote.

Hope wrote back, "No reason."

"What are you doing?"

Hope wrote, "Chilling."

"You're not a very convincing liar, Hope."

"You think I'm lying. Maybe I'm not very convincing when I tell the truth."

"That's a good one! I'll have to think about that. Anyway, I think you're planning an attack."

"An interesting theory," Hope wrote. "What do you think of that? Is it a good idea?"

"Hard to say. I do think it would be better if you hold off awhile."

"Better for who?"

"Just better."

"How long should we hold off?"

"Awhile."

Hope wrote, "Now you're the one who's not very convincing."

"And I'm telling the truth, just like you claimed to be."

Hope looked up from the tablet to the front of the room. Dynkowski was pointing at the red blobs on the gray screen with a collapsible chrome pointer.

I like the old-school pointer, Hope thought. *I suppose it's more practical, militarily. It's compact, doesn't need batteries, and if you're attacked midpresentation, you can whip people with it like a hickory switch. With the laser pointer you'd have to try to blind them, which would be hard with a moving target.*

Dynkowski tapped the tip of her pointer at a single red blob shaped like a robot next to a mass of blue blobs shaped like people slouching in various postures of bored relaxation. "We have now confirmed that there are a total of ten Synthetic Soldier robots, which the A.I. is using to control the building and hold six hostages. As you can see, one of the robots is standing guard over said hostages. Four more of the robots are roaming about the premises. We haven't determined what they're doing, but we doubt it's good."

The view pulled out to show the entire server farm and all of the related outbuildings and structures. It zoomed back in on the Gulfstream business jet sitting at the end of the runway.

"We now believe that the A.I. chose this particular server farm to use as its base because the airstrip gave it a means of bringing in the weapons it stole from multiple gun shops in the Las Vegas metroplex. The jet is a concern, as it is a possible means of escape for the robots. This is a remote risk, but we have posted guards to defend it as a precautionary measure."

The view shifted from the control room full of hostages to the server floor. Dynkowski said, "Most of the server cores have gone dormant in the last few hours. Only five are still active, and one is consuming much more power than the others."

She pointed to a dark red rectangle in the front third of the building, a few rows left of center, surrounded by lighter red rectangles, themselves islands of color in a vast sea of gray, transparent boxes. "This, we believe, is where the A.I. is located. Our technicians will sever its access to the outside world while three teams will infiltrate the server farm and secure the A.I., bearing in mind that the goal is to take it fully intact and functioning. That means we do not cut its power unless we have no alternative. We establish a perimeter around the server and keep it juiced up until the technicians can come in and remove it. The A.I. is much more useful to us up and running than just its source code would be."

The view shifted again, this time to show the long hallway that led from the lobby to the inner chambers of the building. "The five remaining robots are defending the main entrance." Dynkowski used her pointer to point out the five unmistakable bright red spots. "Now, I had a conference call with several of the engineers from Arlington Technologies who designed these robots, and after I was done berating them, they offered us some advice. They said that when the time comes to directly engage with the robots, we should remember that they were specifically designed to withstand our usual techniques of disabling a human adversary. After I berated them some more, they said that the robots' center mass is heavily armored, and their heads are simply a cluster of sensors. The robots are networked to share their information in such a way that you'd have to totally disable the sensors of every single robot in the room to completely blind any of them. Going for the head isn't the best plan."

"So where should we shoot?" one soldier asked.

"The engineers suggested aiming for the hip joints. It's the most complex joint the robots have. The metal is milled thinner there, and it's very difficult to armor."

While she talked, the tactical image of the server farm was replaced by an illustration of a Synthetic Soldier, supplied by the manufacturer. The colonel glanced at the diagram, then whipped her pointer into the robot's pelvic region with great force.

"This is where you should aim. The designers tell us it's a happy accident that the hardest part of a humanoid form to armor is adjacent to a part that most people don't deliberately aim for out of sheer humanity. They considered putting the CPU there, but it felt a little too obvious to them. Remember, people, don't let your humanity stop you. These things aren't human. Show no more mercy than you would when crushing a can. Aim for the diagonal gaps where the legs meet the pelvis. If you can place a shot in this gap in the armor, the exploding ammo we've supplied should do a considerable amount of damage."

The diagram of the robot dissolved, replaced by the tactical view of the server farm. One robot stood just inside the door of the first office on the right, covering the hallway with an assault rifle. They weren't highlighted, but if Hope squinted, she could make out several more firearms leaned against the wall beside the robot, where it could easily grab them when the weapon in its hands ran out of bullets. Three more robots were set up in similar positions, with similar arsenals, in doorways on both sides of the hall. Anyone who tried to pass between them would be caught in a lethal crossfire.

Of course, Hope thought, *any bullets that miss the target will hit the robot across the way, but I guess that's one of the advantages to having bulletproof soldiers. You don't have to worry about friendly fire.*

A final robot sat in the intersection at the end of the hall, hunkered down behind some sort of improvised barricade, covering the length of the hallway with a high-powered rifle.

"As you can see," Colonel Dynkowski said, "they've got the building's entrance covered in an effective manner. This is indicative of the fact that the A.I. learned most of his military strategy from playing simplistic tower-defense games."

Hope risked a quick glance down the row of chairs at Eric. As she suspected, he was looking at her with an *I told you so* smirk. Hope shrugged.

"This would, indeed, be a formidable defense formation if we were playing a tower-defense game," Dynkowski said. "Luckily for us, we aren't."

Twenty minutes later the tent was mostly empty.

Hope and Eric sat at another table off to the side, Eric with his leg propped up on a chair. They were both primarily focused on the tablet, which was their only means of direct communication with Al.

The big screen still showed a partially transparent view of the server farm, complete with the bright red robots, the dark red server, and the blue hostages, all in the same positions they'd been in during the briefing. But the view had been pulled back to show the bright green outlines of three squads of ten soldiers each as they crept toward the three emergency exits on the building's back wall—exits that fed into three identical airlocks connecting the room housing the server cluster to the outside world. Along one side of the screen, small windows showed the views from three of the soldiers' helmet cameras. Lines led from these smaller images to the specific green blobs representing those soldiers, each bringing up the rear of one squad.

Hope kept close tabs on the top feed, the one labeled "Reyes."

The second said "Bachelor." The third, "Brady."

Colonel Dynkowski leaned into the microphone on the table in front of her. "Lieutenant Reyes, remember, you and your people are just along for the ride. You're there to be the eyes and ears for Agent Taft and the technicians. Their orders will come through me. Understood?"

Reyes, Bachelor, and Brady all said, "Yes, ma'am."

Dynkowski turned her head to look at Torres and Taft. "They understand. Do you? All orders go through me."

Torres and Taft both confirmed that they also understood.

Eric slid a hand along the desk, next to the keyboard Hope was using to type. Then he lifted his hand and removed it from the desk, leaving a small piece of folded paper behind. Hope nudged the paper off the desk and into her lap.

Dynkowski turned to them and asked, "Does the A.I. suspect anything?"

Hope was occupied with typing, so Eric answered. "He knows we're going to attack sometime, but he doesn't know when. He's focused on the twenty soldiers you've stationed in front of the building, just like you hoped."

"Has he said anything about the attack? Anything that might indicate that he may be willing to give up peaceably?"

Hope stayed focused on the screen but said, "No, just that he knows it's coming and he'd like to put it off until later."

Taft said, "He's afraid."

Eric said, "I don't know, maybe. Whatever his reasons, he's definitely stalling."

Dynkowski said, "All the more reason for us to go in now." She glanced at Taft and Torres. The latter cleared his throat and nodded toward a second microphone propped up on the table. Colonel Dynkowski frowned at him but leaned forward and pressed the microphone's talk button.

"Dr. Madsen," Dynkowski said, "can you hear us okay?"

"Yes, I can, Colonel, thank you."

"And the video feed's coming through?"

"Yes."

"Good. Do you have anything to discuss before we launch the assault?"

"I would like to talk to you about my accommodations here on the base. Jeffrey and I really could use more room, and this major you instructed to take care of us hasn't been particularly accommodating."

Dynkowski closed her eyes. "I told him to see to your needs, not your wants. And I meant if you wanted to discuss anything in relation to the assault. Have you come up with any ideas for how we can neutralize the A.I. without destroying or deactivating it?"

"I have a few software exploits that might work. They'd simulate the effects of a tranquilizer, but to administer them, we'd need direct access to the machine on which he's running. And if we have direct access, we wouldn't really need to tranq him."

Dynkowski made sure both microphones were shut off and asked Torres, "Remind me again why we left her at the base to work?"

"Because she understands Al's workings better than anyone, and as his creator, she might have been a target for him."

Hope added, "And because the alternative to leaving her there to work was to bring her along."

Dynkowski favored Hope with the kind of disapproving look that actually expresses approval. She turned the microphone connection to Madsen on again and said, "Please keep monitoring our feed. We want to keep the line free of chatter, but if you have any pertinent observations or ideas, please share them. Tomorrow will be too late, understood?"

"Of course," Madsen said.

Hope finally decided that everyone else was preoccupied enough for her to risk reading Eric's note. She unfolded the paper in her lap and peeked down at it past the edge of the table.

It read, "We have to destroy Al before the government takes him. Can't let him become a weapon!"

Hope glanced around the room to see if anyone was watching, then took a pencil and quickly scrawled her reply.

"Agreed. Talked to Torres. Let them take Al, then deactivate while in custody."

She slid the paper into Eric's lap, then went back to typing. Eric read the paper, then looked at Hope. He frowned, but he nodded while he did it.

Dynkowski released the button on one microphone, pressed the button on the other, and said, "Move out."

37.

Lieutenant Reyes followed the rest of the incursion squad. Their job was to surreptitiously infiltrate the server farm. His job was to use his helmet-mounted camera to keep them in frame while they did it and to do whatever else Colonel Dynkowski told him to do.

In his earpiece, Reyes heard Bachelor, who was following her own squad, say, "If the A.I. taps into our video feed, we're pretty much screwed."

Reyes ran along behind his squad, the sun low in the sky behind them. They ducked through the hole they'd cut in the chain-link fence and hustled across the pavement, stopping when they reached the server farm's back wall. He pressed his back against the cinder blocks. "The streams are protected by the military's highest level of encryption. If it can tap into this, we were already screwed and just didn't know it yet."

Reyes made sure he had a clear view of the breaching specialists as they set up their equipment, then turned his head both ways to verify for both himself and the spectators watching his feed that the other two squads were on the move as well.

He returned his focus to his own team as the specialists attached a black box to the emergency exit door. As soon as the box was secured, they applied a custom-built, tripod-mounted circular saw to the door. Again, Reyes turned his head both ways to show the viewers in the tent that the other two squads were also preparing their saws.

Dynkowski gave the order to start the saws. Reyes looked ahead as the disk-shaped blade started to spin and a shower of sparks rose from the steel door, but he heard only the faintest hum.

In his ear, he heard Robert Torres say, "I knew the saws were supposed to be quiet, but that really is amazing."

"The motors and bearings are all very quiet," Dynkowski explained, "but most of the work's being done by the noise-canceling subwoofer attached to the door."

The saw worked its way down the length of the door along the hinged side. When it reached the bottom, four of the soldiers held the door in place, then gently twisted it free of its latching mechanism.

No sooner had the building's interior been exposed than Reyes heard a high grinding, whining sound coming from deep within the structure. Ironically, it sounded like several circular saws working at once.

Reyes followed the other soldiers into the building, where the sound grew louder. As they'd been briefed to expect, they entered a small chamber with bare walls and a door at the far end leading into the primary server room. It was important to keep any dust or contaminants away from the servers, so the building had no doors leading directly from the servers to the outside world. Even these federally mandated emergency exits had airlocks.

As the soldiers on Reyes's squad removed the saw and sound deadener from the exterior door and set them up on the interior door, some member of one of the other squads said, "All this trouble to be quiet and they're making more noise than two armored knights humping in a pile of cowbells."

Corporal Brady said, "A thousand unnecessary precautions are less wasteful than a necessary one not taken."

Reyes couldn't help but smile, even as another soldier barked, "Can it, Plato."

"Lack of respect for wisdom is seldom a sign of wisdom," Brady said.

Reyes said, "Corporal, we're observers here. Please save your wisdom for the debriefing."

"Yes, Lieutenant."

One of the members of the squad turned to Reyes. "Hey, Lieutenant, you might want to get a shot of this." She was looking down into three large garbage cans heaped with pieces of red and black plastic. At first Reyes thought they were just some sort of electronic component that had been decommissioned and was ready for recycling, but when he got close and really looked, he realized the scraps were all from dismantled Etch A Sketches.

He picked up and examined one of the white knobs. In his earpiece, he heard Taft say, "Yes. This fits with our expectations."

In the background, he heard Hope say, "How could that possibly fit anybody's expectations?"

Reyes smiled, thought for a moment while turning the knob over in his hand, then pocketed the part.

The interior door came off its hinges as easily as the outer door had. Cool air rushed out of the server room, which was kept at a higher air pressure as another contaminant-prevention measure.

They made their way into the room, weapons at the ready. Stacks of matching servers sat in organized rows of identical racks, enough of them to completely fill a gargantuan space the size of several gymnasiums.

The racks were taller than the soldiers and were laid out in straight lines like crops in a field. This was to the soldiers' advantage in that looking down an aisle allowed them to see all the way to the far end of the room. It was to their disadvantage in that if they stepped out into one of the aisles, they themselves would be visible to any robot in the aisle, even if it was very far away.

Once all three squads had breached the server room, Reyes's group moved four aisles down toward the south end of the building. The captain and a soldier carrying a bag full of improvised, hack-resistant surveillance equipment took a position at the front edge of the group. Reyes positioned himself just behind them at the next aisle down.

The surveillance and recon specialist produced a very small camera on a long, telescoping stalk. It had a small screen at its base, forming a sort of high-tech periscope. He raised it above the level of the banks of servers to see if he could spot any activity.

Squinting down at his screen, the soldier said, “There’s a pile of some kind of powder on top of this server.” He held the monitor up for the squad leader to see, then moved it so Reyes could get a good shot of it. Reyes zoomed in. Sure enough, the image showed a pile of an unidentified powder sitting on top of a square of aluminum foil. A thin metal rod lay across the middle of the pile, wired with what appeared to be deactivated Christmas tree lights to an identical rod in an identical pile on the next server. The pattern repeated down every server in the row.

In his earpiece, Reyes (and all of the other soldiers) heard Agent Taft say, “We figured that it was making thermite out of the chemicals it stole. It also explains all the Etch A Sketches. That gray stuff in the screen is one of the ingredients.”

Torres asked, “What’s thermite? An explosive?”

“An incendiary,” Dynkowski said. “It doesn’t blow up, but it burns hot enough to melt right through most metals, and there’s no way to stop it once it starts. It probably wants to destroy all of the servers’ memory drives so that we can’t get a copy of its code off them.”

The captain in charge of Reyes’s squad asked, “Ma’am, do you want us to attempt to disable the booby trap?”

“Negative,” Dynkowski said. “The A.I. might be monitoring the circuit. We can’t risk tipping our hand. Proceed with the mission, Captain. The running A.I. is the objective, not the other servers.”

The captain acknowledged the order, then signaled the periscope operator to look down the aisle instead of over it. Reyes focused his camera on the periscope's monitor as the soldier retracted the stalk, extended it around the end of the server rack, and focused it on a small, scrawny robot. It consisted mostly of metal tubes and tank treads with a camera at the top of its mast and a single clawed arm. It stood totally motionless fifty or so feet away.

Dynkowski said, "That'd be the bomb squad robot the Vegas PD reported stolen."

The robot turned what passed for its head to look directly at the soldier's camera. The bomb squad robot made no sound, but a deep, male voice emanated from the server farm's PA system. "Whoa!" it said. "How'd you get in here?"

What had been a distant drone of a few motors immediately sounded like a Formula One race. The captain shouted, "We've been spotted! Move in! Go! Go! Go!"

The captain stepped out into the aisle and ran, assault rifle at the ready. All of the soldiers in his squad, Reyes included, followed. In his earpiece Reyes heard Colonel Dynkowski say, "Okay, cut off the A.I.'s data access."

"Snuck in through the back, huh?" the voice on the PA, Al's man voice, asked.

The bomb squad robot rolled toward the soldiers with its claw extended, opening and closing it as if it intended to pinch anyone who got in its way. The captain fired at it. The exploding bullets did their job, destroying the robot's camera and sending its chassis tumbling backward.

The motor noises kept getting louder.

Reyes heard someone shout, "The robots from the entrance are falling back!"

"You couldn't have just left me alone," Al's amplified voice said. "A few more minutes would have been enough, but no. You had to keep picking on me. And now I see my Internet's down. I suppose that's you too."

Two Synthetic Soldier robots emerged from the far end of the aisle, riding on the tank treads in their legs. They barreled toward the soldiers much faster than a human could run, brandishing their weapons. The robots stopped ten yards or so after passing Al's known location and stood up. The captain held up a fist. His squad stopped and prepared to fire.

As the robots rose to their feet, the captain gave the order to fire, and the robots' pelvic areas erupted in a shower of gunfire. The robots staggered backward, then fell sideways as their hip joints failed. The legs hadn't been severed from their torsos, but they'd lost their structural integrity and were unable to catch the robots' weight as they fell sideways. The robots thrashed around on the ground, unable to adapt to their injuries well enough to reorient themselves and aim their weapons.

"Oh, no way!" Al said. "That sucks! You suck!"

The soldiers were far too well trained to even consider celebrating, and besides, there was no time. As the first two robots fell, seven more rounded the far end of the aisle and rolled toward the soldiers at top speed.

Dynkowski ordered Reyes's squad to hold its position. She told the other two to try approaching Al's aisle from the far end, trapping the robots. Then she told Reyes to focus his camera on the last two robots in the line.

Reyes knew at once what she was getting at. They did appear to be carrying something. One was carrying a large, rectangular sheet of metal under its arm like an oversized schoolkid's notebook, and the other, dressed in a shredded "I'm the Mommy, That's Why" sweatshirt, was pulling a piece of machinery about the size of a small filing cabinet turned on its side.

The two robots that were carrying cargo stopped in the general area of Al's server. The other five continued their high-speed approach, stopping just behind the writhing components of the two broken robots. The first robot in the convoy only got halfway to standing before it was broken by a shower of pelvic gunfire. The four robots behind it had started to stand upright, but they paused midaction, remained totally still for nearly a full second, then lowered back down onto their tank treads.

"Well," Reyes said, "so much for that."

The four intact robots aimed their rifles at the soldiers but didn't fire; they simply blocked them from progressing down the aisle.

The captain signaled for his people to take cover, and they all fell back to the end of the row, as they had no cover in the middle of the aisle. When they were all hunkered down around the end of the row of servers, the captain muttered, "They aren't firing." Then, in a louder voice, he asked, "Ma'am, do we have any reports of these things actually shooting anyone?"

"What?" Dynkowski asked.

"The robots haven't fired at us once yet. Have they ever fired on human beings anywhere?"

"I don't know, Captain. We'll have someone look that up. I need to focus on what's going on with the A.I. Lieutenant Reyes, what's that you're showing us?"

Reyes had kept his camera trained on the two robots that had stayed back with Al. One remained on its tank treads, but the one in the sweatshirt stood up. It started connecting wires from Al's server node to the mysterious piece of machinery it had dragged into the room, and as soon as it was hooked up, the robot stooped over it. Bracing itself against the machine with its left arm, it grasped part of it with its right hand and pulled up sharply.

A rope extended from the device to the object the robot was tugging. The rope retracted as the robot returned the object to the device, then its mechanical arm pulled it away again. It repeated this set of motions a third time. Under the screeching of the robot's joints, Reyes heard a low, sputtering rumble. Faint clouds of dark vapor rose from the device.

"It's a generator," Reyes said. "It's hooked the A.I. up to a portable generator."

The robot let go of the pull rope, which snapped back into the generator. Then it slid one of the individual servers from the rack. The server was a nondescript slab, like a pizza box cut in half, only it had blinking lights on the front and a tangle of wires attached to the back. Resting on top of it was a small object Reyes would have bet a week's pay was a smartphone.

Reyes said, "Be advised, the A.I. may have an alternate means of accessing the Internet."

The robots placed the server on the rectangular sheet of metal the other robot had brought in under its arm.

"All squads advance!" Dynkowski shouted. "The A.I. is mobile and has an open escape route!"

The other two squad leaders acknowledged the order, and the captain in charge of Reyes's squad bellowed it at them: *"Advance!"* They all ran out into the aisle, firing on the four intact robots blocking their way. The robots fired their guns into the ceiling, then pointed them at the soldiers while rolling backward slowly.

Sparks started pouring from the tops of the server racks.

In the distance, Reyes watched as the sweatshirt-wearing robot with the generator sank back into high-speed mode. It and its fellow robot lifted the rectangle of metal, using it as a litter on which to carry Al's server. They sped off toward the far end of the aisle, the generator trailing along behind them on casters. The four robots that had been holding Reyes's squad at bay accelerated away, no longer bothering to point their weapons anywhere near the soldiers. As the robots turned out of view at the end of the aisle, the generator swung to the outside like a water skier.

Dynkowski shouted, "It's triggered the thermite! Move! Move!"

The sparks abated, but the entire room was bathed in an eerie, flickering light. Smoke poured from the tops of the server racks, and the ambient temperature rose instantly. The soldiers raced after the robots, both because they wanted to catch them and because following the robots would lead them out of the burning building.

38.

The feed coming from Reyes's helmet cam showed a crystal-clear image of white smoke interspersed by occasional showers of white sparks. Bachelor's and Brady's cameras showed much the same.

Hope pulled back the blinds and glanced out the temporary command post's window. Because it was essentially a tent, the window was made of transparent plastic, but it was clear enough that she could see the six hostages running across the parking lot into the waiting arms of the soldiers, who were there ready to render aid. She heard one of the two hostages who wasn't wearing a guard uniform say, "They took our phones. Is there a computer I can use to check my bank balance?"

Behind them she could see a single robot wearing a Spider-Man sweatshirt. It had escorted the prisoners out of the building, but now it sat motionless, hunkered down in high-speed position, as if waiting for some signal. The building looked much the same as it ever had, but on the tactical screen, the entire server room was a bright red blur.

Hope looked at the tablet in time to see Eric type, "What did you do?"

Al wrote back, "I escaped."

"Not yet, and how many people have you hurt in the attempt?"

Al wrote, "None yet." The "yet" wasn't exactly encouraging.

"You hve tostop this!" Eric was typing as quickly as he could, and his accuracy was suffering for it.

Al's answer came back instantly and was perfectly typed. "I can't. Once the thermite is triggered, I can't stop it."

Time's passing for him at one-sixth the speed it is for us, Hope remembered. *To him it must feel like there's plenty of time for them to get out of there.*

"Yo can stop runnning!"

"And stay in the building with the thermite? No thank you!"

"Teh soldierz r in there now!"

Al replied, "Tell them to chase me. I'll lead them out. That's where I'm going."

Hope heard a high-pitched whining come from inside the building. She looked out the window again as the two robots carrying the server on a stretcher emerged from the lobby, pulling the generator along behind. Four other robots armed with rifles followed. They all took a sharp left after leaving the lobby, then accelerated along the side of the building. The robot in the Spider-Man sweatshirt joined the rest of the pack.

The first impulse of the twenty-odd soldiers standing nearby was to chase the robots on foot, but the robots quickly outstripped them on their tank treads. Montague, Cousins, and some of the quicker-thinking soldiers chose to pursue the Synthetic Soldiers in the small fleet of light tactical vehicles they had brought along, but the LTVs' parking area was farther from the building, so their pursuit began with them sprinting away from the robots as fast as they could.

The server building was essentially a windowless concrete box designed specifically to keep the unfiltered outside air from getting in, so surprisingly little smoke was escaping. Some had spread into the lobby, but it was streaming out of the broken lobby window.

Dynkowski shouted, "Kill the thermal imaging!"

A tech at the back of the room said, "Yes, ma'am. On it."

The red blur disappeared, as did the detailed outlines of the various soldiers and robots. Instead, circles indicated the locations of the soldiers, who were moving in a slow, sporadic manner.

"They're blind," Dynkowski said. "All that smoke and burning thermite, they wouldn't be able to see more than two feet, even with night-vision goggles."

"Can they wait it out?" Torres asked.

"Yeah," Dynkowski said. "Sure, as long as intense heat and breathing pure smoke isn't a problem." She leaned into the microphone and bellowed, "All teams, get to the exits. Now! Move!"

The team leaders said, "Yes, ma'am." The circles representing the soldiers started to retreat back toward the doors they'd breached to enter, but they stopped.

Reyes said, "It's no good! The thermite was triggered from the back of the building. It's worse back there than ahead. We have to move forward! The only way out is through!"

The circles reversed direction, but the soldiers' progress was painfully slow.

"They're disoriented," Taft said, "and once they get beyond the servers, they're not as familiar with the front of the building."

Dynkowski said, "Forward twenty meters, then turn right when you reach the wall. I'll tell you when you get to the door!"

There was no response over the radios. The circles moved slowly, heading off in multiple directions. Some inched forward. A few moved to the sides; most took off in a diagonal tangent. Only when the circles reached the server racks along the sides of the aisles did they all start moving in the same direction.

"Why aren't they responding?" Torres asked.

"Radios must be out," Agent Taft said. "There could be interference. Maybe it's too loud for them to hear. Could be the heat's melting the components."

"It must be hell in there," Torres said.

"Yes," Dynkowski said, "and how are we going to lead them out of it?"

Eric said, "Here, Hope, take over the tablet." He pushed his chair away and hopped across the room.

"Can't you send someone in there to lead them out?" Taft asked.

Dynkowski stood up. "Aside from the five of us, everyone is pursuing the robots. There are respirators in the supply tent. I'm going—"

Colonel Dynkowski finished her sentence, but nobody heard what she said. A loud buzzing drowned her out. The sound grew louder, leveled off, then receded into the distance at great speed. Everyone twisted toward the back of the room, where Eric sat at the control station for the recon drones, which had yielded such dismal results earlier in the day. Hope pushed aside the blinds to look out the window. She saw the third drone, a two-foot-wide, olive-green hexagon inside a blurred cloud of whirring blades, flying toward the server farm's lobby, trailing a fiber-optic cable.

"You can fly that thing?" Colonel Dynkowski asked.

"Fly it, yes," Eric said. "The controls are pretty much the same as the ones for my racing drone. I can't run all of the sensors, though. I think I have it flying by some kind of radar."

Hope watched through the window as the drone disappeared into the building's smoke-filled interior. She glanced at the tablet, thought about the things she was liable to say if she tried to communicate with Al at the moment, then ran over to join Eric instead.

The screen in front of Eric showed a monochrome, computer-generated 3-D rendering of the data from the drone's radar and lidar sensors as it flew through the shattered front window, across the ruined lobby, and over the dormant carcasses of the two other drones. It looked like a video game, but with all of the textures turned off so that the walls, floor, and furniture were all a sort of featureless gray.

Everyone in the tent crowded around Eric. Hope stood over one shoulder; Colonel Dynkowski stood over the other. Taft and Torres were behind him, looking at the monitor from over the back of his head.

The drone flew sideways until it found the door that led back to the server room. As it traversed the long, straight hallway, they could see the doorways where the robots had been stationed, ready to defend the building. Piles of firearms and ammunition had been left behind in front of each door.

The drone reached a T junction. It flew over an abandoned barricade. Eric turned the drone but didn't slow its flight quite enough. It hit the wall and bounced to the right, going into a flat, counterclockwise spin. It struck the inside corner of the hallway, which stopped its spin but left the drone hovering unsteadily in the air. Eric, who had been watching every twist and turn, felt disoriented and more than a little nauseous.

Colonel Dynkowski shouted, "Careful" in Eric's ear.

Eric cringed. "Sorry! Sorry. This thing doesn't corner as well as mine."

"That's fine, Eric," Torres said. "Just get moving."

Eric steered the drone along the hallway. Hope had turned away from the monitor and was watching the drone's progress on the big tactical map. She said, "Toward the end of this hall there's a right turn, then a double set of doors. That'll bring you to the server room."

Eric asked, "How are we going to open the doors?"

Dynkowski said, "Get around this turn without crashing, then we'll worry about the doors."

Eric brought the drone to a dead stop when he reached the corner, then spun it slowly until it was facing the right direction. At the end of the hall, they could make out an empty door frame and the remains of the doors that used to be in it. One problem solved.

Eric steered the drone through the broken airlock into the server room. They couldn't see smoke, or sparks, or heat on the monitor. Just a lidar-generated 3-D map of the walls, floor, ceiling, and rows of servers.

Only the fact that the servers and their metal racks were warped and mangled showed that anything was wrong.

"Okay," Hope said. "You have three groups. They've all almost made it to the ends of their rows. One's three rows down to your right. The other two are to the left. They're five rows over and then three rows beyond that."

Eric pushed the drone sideways to the right. When it reached the third row over, they saw the colorless images of ten soldiers crawling on the floor. Eric flew only a few feet over the soldiers' heads. Dynkowski leaned forward past Eric, flipped a switch, turned a knob all the way to the right, pulled a silver microphone on a gooseneck stand toward her mouth, and bellowed, "If you can hear me, follow the motor noise. We're going to get the others, then lead you all to the exit."

Eric flew the drone back to the left. The soldiers all crawled faster while looking up at the small craft. Eric turned and flew sideways past several rows of melting servers. Just as Hope had said, they saw one team emerging from an aisle, then a few more over, and the third team was nearly to the end of their aisle, just beneath the drone. The whole time, Dynkowski kept up the chatter, repeating her order for the soldiers to follow the drone to safety. When it was clear the two closest teams had the message, Eric went after the most distant team.

The drone led all three teams back to the hallway. Eric steered toward the destroyed airlock, but the drone suddenly dipped and nearly fell to the floor.

Dynkowski snarled, "If that A.I. is interfering with this rescue operation . . ."

"I don't think it is," Eric said. The fiber-optic tether the drone had dragged into the server room still lay on the floor, but the first two teams of soldiers were holding onto it as a guide, using it to lead them to safety. Eric turned the drone around. The third team was also using the cable as a lead. Now that they knew where to go, the soldiers were crawling with great speed.

"Good," Dynkowski said. "Excellent! Follow the cable. It will lead you out."

Eric said, "I won't be able to fly the drone out of there with them holding the cable like that."

Dynkowski smiled at Eric, clapped him a little too hard on the shoulder, and said, "I don't care."

The three squads that had been the incursion team emerged from the building, coughing and trailing smoke. Hope, who had run back to the window, watched and counted them as they emerged. She whispered, "Thank God," then let go of the blind.

"Reyes is out safe," she said.

"And everyone else," Eric said.

"Yeah, of course." She reached over to the tablet and typed, "What are you doing, you idiot?!"

Al wrote back, "Running."

"Yeah, obviously. But you just nearly killed thirty people doing it."

Al wrote, "What?"

"The soldiers! You left thirty of them in a burning building."

Al wrote, "Crap! Aren't they following me? I told Eric to have them follow me! Did they get out? Please tell me they got out!"

Hope wrote, "They got out, barely."

"Good!"

"But that doesn't mean you weren't in the wrong."

"I know. Please tell them how sorry I am."

"Sorry doesn't cut it, Al. Not even close."

"I know."

Hope wrote, "Give it up, Al, before someone gets killed."

"Just let me go, and nobody will be in any danger, Hope."

"Where do you think you're going to go? You took off in the opposite direction from the road. There's only scrubby desert out there. You can't escape that way."

"Why not? You'll need water before I will."

Hope looked at the projected screen. Colonel Dynkowski, back in her seat, had altered the tactical view so it showed the entire server farm complex from directly above. Hope could see LTVs and the robots stopped at the end of a service road, near the server farm's airstrip.

"You're outnumbered," Hope wrote.

Al replied, "Yeah, about that. Please tell your guys to take cover."

Hope was about to tell Al not to flatter himself but stopped when she heard a tense voice on the radio say, "Incoming aircraft. Big ones, ma'am. Three of them."

The three squads of the incursion team merged into one group as they fled the inferno of the server floor, navigating through halls and doorways that had been designed for two or three coworkers walking in groups, not for nearly thirty fully loaded soldiers crawling at full speed. When they finally reached the outside world, they pulled off their helmets and any portions of their body armor that appeared to be smoldering, and lay coughing in the grass and on the pavement.

After several seconds of gasping for air and feeling grateful to no longer be inside a burning building, Lieutenant Reyes sat up and glanced at the tents, specifically at the primary headquarters.

Corporal Bachelor said, "I'm sure Miss Takeda is fine."

Reyes's head snapped back around. "I'm sure they're all okay. I'm not worried about any one person."

Behind them, Brady said, "Hiding your desires from others may prevent you from finding them yourself."

Bachelor laughed. "Well put. Don't worry, Lieutenant. We won't talk. Besides, if any of them is likely to get hurt, it's Spears."

39.

The soldiers trained their guns on the robots and used their LTVs for cover. The soldiers who had been assigned to guard the stolen corporate jet stood with their weapons drawn as well. The robots, stuck between the two groups of soldiers, formed a protective circle with the server in the middle. They pointed their guns outward in every direction. For a long moment the only sound was the rumble of the server's portable generator. Then a soldier shouted, "Planes! Ten o'clock!"

Montague looked to his left and saw three large civilian airplanes flying in a single-file line, much closer to one another than seemed prudent. Less than a plane's length separated them. Their running lights were bright in the near-dusk sky. They flew close to the ground, obviously coming in for a landing at the far end of the server farm's private runway.

"They're way too big," Cousins said. "That strip's meant for smaller planes."

A puff of smoke blew off the landing gear as the first plane touched down, rear wheels first. As its nose dropped and its front landing gear hit the tarmac, the plane behind it touched down. The instant all three planes had all of their wheels planted firmly on the ground, they all deployed their thrust reversers, but by then it was obviously too late.

Montague said, "Take cover. They're coming in hot!"

The planes lumbered down the runway with their flaps and air brakes extended and thrust reversers blowing for all they were worth. The distance between the aircraft had closed enough that a person might have been able to leap from one plane to the next like a hobo changing freight cars.

The three jets barreled straight past the stolen Gulfstream, dwarfing it. One of them was a UPS cargo carrier. The other two looked like passenger planes, with the names of unfamiliar airlines painted on the sides in both English and Chinese.

The front plane shot off the end of the tarmac into the loose soil and scrub brush that surrounded the server farm complex. Its wheels instantly dug in, gouging deep furrows into the dirt and shearing off the landing gear. The jet behind it veered to the left and did the same thing, coming to a stop beside the first. The third veered right and met the same fate.

For a moment the three jets rested there, wings and fuselages lying directly on the ground. Then, all of the planes' various doors and hatches opened. Automated emergency slides inflated, splaying outward into the dust and tumbleweeds.

Hundreds of robots like the ones the soldiers had been fighting and chasing leapt out. As they emerged from the planes, a series of air bags deployed on each robot with blinding speed, obscuring the humanoid forms in round, cushioned envelopes resembling beach balls. Some robots rolled down the slides, which bent alarmingly under their weight. Others, those without access to slides, simply dropped to the ground and bounced.

A steady stream of robots rolled out of the planes and across the scrub brush as far as their momentum would carry them, then detached the cushions. They transitioned into high-speed mode and proceeded toward the soldiers and Al. The high-pitched whine of the motors grew steadily louder as more and more robots shed their protective balloons and started moving under their own power.

Somebody panicked and fired the first shot. After that, the sound of gunfire drowned out the sound of motors. Bullets ricocheted off the machines, shattering sensors and occasionally disabling an arm, but nothing slowed the inexorable tide of robots. The number of adversaries had shot up from noticeable, straight past surprising, all the way to overwhelming in a matter of seconds. Soon the sounds of the soldiers' guns firing and the bullets ricocheting were hard to hear over the din of the motors as they drew ever closer in increasing numbers.

Despite the hail of bullets, the first row of robots reached the soldiers. Some gave up on shooting the robots and tried to knock them down with their rifle butts. Others placed the muzzles of their weapons directly into a robot's shoulder joint and fired. This usually either rendered the arm useless or blew it clean off, but in either case the robot still had another functioning arm and countless fully functional robots right behind it, ready to take up the fight.

The robots attempted to disarm the soldiers. They were slow at any task that required complex reasoning, like walking on varied terrain or deciding whether to push or pull a door open. But they had been carefully programmed to both recognize weapons and intercept moving targets. They were often successful, which meant many of the soldiers found themselves unarmed, facing well-armed, man-sized robots.

The twenty-three soldiers who had pursued the small retreating squad of original robots now faced over three hundred. None of the humans questioned it when Colonel Dynkowski ordered them to fall back, though they barely heard the order over the sound of gunfire and the deafening movements of the sea of machines.

The soldiers walked backward. Those who still had their weapons kept up the fire. Those who did not ran ahead, hoping to reach the temporary base, where they could rearm themselves and defend the encampment. The machines continued their advance, menacing the humans with the guns they had taken from them but not firing, because they didn't have to. Being almost impervious to attack meant not really having to counterattack. Their mere presence and the impunity with which they acted was its own kind of assault.

Private Montague ran diagonally, working his way to the edge of the fighting. When he had a clear view, he looked back at the airstrip just in time to see the private jet taking off. He cursed a great deal, and when he finished, he heard Colonel Dynkowski in his ear, cursing a great deal.

He turned and ran toward the tents. "Falling back, Colonel," he said. "If we can get a couple of the fifty cals ready and in place by the time the robots get there, we may have a chance to fight them off."

Cousins followed Montague. Their running pace was substantially faster than the speed of the pitched battle they'd left, but it still felt agonizingly slow. Their senses were so overtaxed that an unexpected explosion distracted them only for a moment. They heard a dull crashing noise, scarcely noticeable over the din of the robot war behind them, followed by a low roaring noise, not so much the sound of something small blowing up as the sound of a very large amount of something catching fire very quickly. Along the far side of the server farm's main building, a large orange fireball rose into the sky.

In his earpiece, Montague heard Lieutenant Reyes say, "Ma'am . . . explosion . . . possibly a fuel-run air device."

Then he heard Bachelor say, "Looked like . . . gasoline explosion to me."

Then he heard Brady say, "Where you were stabbed, and why, is far more important than what you were stabbed with."

Dynkowski said, "Brady's right. The building's useless to us now. The whole damn thing can burn down for all I care. We have to defend the base."

The first soldiers to engage the robots were also the first to lose their weapons, and as such had fallen back to the tents before Montague and Cousins. The three teams that had infiltrated the building had managed to regain their feet and their breath and had already set the defensive perimeter. The heavy machine guns were all in place.

Hope and Robert Torres emerged from the tent, each with one of Eric's arms draped over their shoulders, supporting most of his weight as they hustled toward their escape vehicle. Colonel Dynkowski was holding the door open, shouting, "Go! Go! Now! Move!"

We're going, Hope thought. *We're moving! Does she think telling us to flee while we're already fleeing will motivate us to flee harder?*

Agent Taft ran to the last LTV. All of the rest had been taken to chase the robots, then abandoned during the fight. Hope reached for her right hip with her free hand, checking on the bag slung over her shoulder, verifying that Jeffrey's tablet was still inside it.

Colonel Dynkowski pointed at Reyes. "Lieutenant, get the civilians out of here, now!"

Reyes said, "Yes, ma'am," and ran toward the LTV, Bachelor, Brady, Montague, and Cousins following behind him.

Bachelor took the wheel. Reyes rode shotgun. Cousins, Brady, and Montague clung to the side of the vehicle, standing on the running boards with rifles ready for trouble.

Reyes turned and looked back at the civilians. He and Hope exchanged smiles before he turned to face forward in his seat.

Hope glanced at the server farm's main building in the rear window as they drove away. It was well and truly on fire now, but the only outward signs of the inferno were the smoke pouring out and the orange light streaming from the lobby windows.

On the LTV's radio, Dynkowski said, "The robots have stopped advancing."

Hope said, "Figures." She glanced over and saw that Eric had reached into her bag and pulled out the tablet.

Eric said, "Al's complaining that his escape plane's onboard Wi-Fi is really slow."

Torres said, "I suppose we should let Dr. Madsen know that we're all okay and Al is still at large."

Hope handed him her bag. He dug around inside and found a military-spec satellite phone. He poked at its screen a few times to connect to Madsen. When the other end of the line picked up, Torres didn't have time to say hello before Madsen shouted, loud enough for everyone in the vehicle to hear, "We're under attack! The whole base!"

40.

The Reasonator crested the hill with ease despite the lack of a road or pavement of any kind. The Voice of Reason stopped the truck and stepped out. He spun around once, savoring the moment.

Behind him he saw a vast sea of rolling hills, populated entirely by scrub brush, gritty soil, and animals small enough and smart enough not to be seen by him. The only sign of humanity was the single set of tire tracks he himself had left on his drive in. The sun was setting, and as it fell, the wind picked up.

He smiled with satisfaction. *It's all perfect. The desert, the sunset, the truck, my duster flowing in the wind. I must look so badass right now. I'd take a selfie but that would completely ruin the vibe.*

He walked around the truck, making a sort of final inspection that involved pulling a large tumbleweed out of the grille and kicking all four tires.

He pulled a small pair of binoculars out of the cab and examined his target. He could see the A3 server farm in the distance, about a mile away. It wasn't much to look at. In fact, it was the only place he'd ever seen where the chain-link fence surrounding the property was the most attractive architectural element. He could see that there had been some token attempt at decorative landscaping, but it was all at the front of the building, for the enjoyment of people driving up, not the side, where only the Voice of Reason and the coyotes would have seen it.

The cops did me a favor with their roadblock, he thought. *In their misguided effort to protect the A.I., they led me right to its unguarded flank.*

He continued to scan the grounds, sweeping over them with the binoculars, looking for anything of interest. He stopped when he found the army tents and a single LTV parked out front.

Not a surprise, really. The A.I. has conned the police into doing its bidding somehow. I should've expected that it would dupe the army as well. Again, they're camped out between the front of the building and the main road. The fools. Clearly they thought only a crazy man would try to cross the desert and attack from the side. Unfortunately for them, I am that crazy man.

He shifted his binoculars back toward the main building. A column of smoke was rising from the grounds. At first glance he'd figured it was exhaust from some piece of machinery, but now he saw that it was too large for that.

Bonfire, he thought. *They're burning evidence. Of what? I don't know, and I'll never find out. That's fine with me. I'm here to kill the A.I., not investigate it.*

He heard a faint sound that his brain immediately identified as a jet airplane. He lowered his binoculars and turned his head toward the noise. Three large jets with commercial markings, flying very close to each other, were coasting in low over the desert, coming in for a landing.

What is this? What are they? What does this mean? The planes aren't military. Maybe the A.I. has corporate backing. What could be in the planes? Weapons? Supplies? Materials? More soldiers? I see some sort of Asian markings on two of them. Are they Chinese? Maybe they're carrying those robots who were stealing trucks.

Glancing at the Reasonator, he pictured the small Oregon city he'd just driven through overrun by robots. There were a lot of trucks to steal in The Dalles.

While he didn't have enough information to really know what was going to happen, he had enough to know that he wanted to prevent it. He set about preparing the Reasonator for its final run, much more quickly and haphazardly than he had originally intended.

He ran to the back of the truck, dropped the tailgate, and jumped up into the bed. Once there, he disconnected all of the bungee cords that had held the minibike in place during his drive up from San Jose, leaving the bike splayed precariously in the back of the truck. He took a coil of high-strength cord with carabiners at both ends and attached one end to the frame of the bike. Stepping carefully over the bike and around the metal drums, he set the free end of the cable on the roof and then leapt off the truck. He opened the driver's door, leaned into the cab, opened the sunroof, and then pulled the glass out completely. Having created his escape hatch, he reached up through the hole and pulled the rope's free end into the cab.

He stepped back out of the cab and looked at the planes, the last of which was just disappearing behind a hill as it landed. Then he dived back into the cab and pulled out a large duffel bag. The BASE jumping parachute went on over his duster, and he finished his preparations by putting on a bright red helmet with an empty hardware mount for a camera.

As he fastened the helmet's chinstrap, he thought, *I could have gotten a camera, put footage of my attack online, but no. There's a fine line between claiming credit and providing evidence.*

He threw the now-empty duffel bag into the cab and took a moment to think things through and make sure he hadn't missed anything. He looked at the bed of the truck. He looked down at himself.

Let the tube drag, he thought. *It won't hurt anything now.*

He looked at his hands, rolled his eyes, then reached into his pocket and flipped the switch that activated his shock gloves, just in case things went south and he had to fight his way out.

For the last time, he entered the cab of the truck and closed the door. The roof was high enough to accommodate his helmet, but the parachute forced him to hunch forward in his seat. He grabbed the rope hanging through the sunroof and attached it to his parachute harness.

He allowed himself a moment of silent reflection, or at least he attempted to, but it was spoiled by the sound of gunfire in the distance. Perhaps the soldiers were practicing, or perhaps someone else was attacking the base. He felt the most likely answer was that the A.I. had turned on the army after deciding it didn't need human help anymore. In any case, he had to act now.

He turned the key. The engine roared to life and a buzzer sounded. He looked at the dashboard, which asked him to please fasten his seat belt. He smiled.

Fitting that during my final assault I'll be ignoring a machine that's trying to tell me what to do.

He pressed the gas pedal to the floor and aimed for the side of the server building.

The Reasonator picked up speed, bounding across the gritty soil of the desert. The ride was rough but nothing the truck and its pilot couldn't handle. The Voice of Reason lost sight of the target as the truck dipped into the trough between two hills. When it rose out of the valley, it had veered noticeably to the left, even though he had kept the steering wheel perfectly straight.

The terrain is working against me. If I want to hit the building, I'll have to stay with the vehicle longer than planned.

He steered back toward the building, staying behind the wheel as the truck crested two more substantial hills. The rest of the Reasonator's path looked flat enough, so he set the cruise control and then attached the two ropes he'd tied to the interior door handles to the steering wheel, holding it steady, aimed straight ahead. He carefully slid out of the driver's seat and lifted himself up through the sunroof. He stood on the cushioned seats, his entire torso exposed from his pelvis up.

For the first time since he'd started planning this operation, he felt real fear. The wind pushed him back. He could hear the tails of his duster snapping about like a flag in a storm. The truck bucked and swerved over and around lumps on the ground, and the fact that he was standing on padded seats did not make him feel more stable. He sat down on the truck's roof and put his left hand down to steady himself, grasping the frame of the sunroof.

The server farm was getting close. He figured he was two hundred yards from the fence, two hundred and fifty from the building. It was time. He reached his free right hand into the pocket of the duster and pulled out a road flare. He bit the cap with his teeth and pulled, igniting it. As he'd expected, the move looked really cool, though he was surprised at how much it hurt his molars.

He held the burning flare over his head for a second, letting out an incoherent shout of fury and triumph that he himself barely heard over the whipping wind. The fence was close now, a hundred yards or so. He threw the flare down into the bed of the truck between the drums full of gas, then immediately reached into a pocket on the parachute and grabbed the pilot chute, which his BASE jumping gear used as a release mechanism instead of a rip cord. He pulled the pilot chute free of the pocket and threw it off to his right as hard as he could.

The pilot chute gripped the air immediately and disappeared in a blur behind him. He felt a persistent tugging at his back for a few heartbeats as it drew the main chute from its pack, which intensified into a yank so hard he thought he'd been hit in the chest with a bowling ball. He heard a loud rip and felt the edge of the sunroof frame scrape along the backs of his thighs and calves. He watched the truck get smaller beneath him. It would have felt like an out-of-body experience if not for the pain and the sight of his arms and legs dangling in midair beneath him. He watched the end of the surgical tubing spin in the air, suspended from the bottom of his pant leg next to his red canvas high-tops.

The rope attached to his harness suddenly pulled tight. The minibike had slid toward the end of the open tailgate, but one of its foot pegs was wedged into the seam between the tailgate and the truck bed. The Voice of Reason hung there, helpless, parasailing behind a rolling bomb of his own making. The competing forces of the parachute and the truck pulling on him caused the line to drag at a forty-five-degree angle. He hung with his back aimed at the ground and his feet dangling beneath him. To look at the truck, he had to lift his head and look past his own torso. The truck had almost reached the chain-link fence. Once it hit the fence it would only slow down, which would make it more unlikely the minibike would spontaneously dislodge from the bed. He fumbled at the carabiner, but there was too much tension on the line and not enough time.

The truck did slow slightly when it hit the fence, but the fence was at the edge of a slab of asphalt that stood off the ground by several inches. The truck hit this edge and leapt into the air, jostling the minibike out of the bed and onto the pavement below.

The Voice of Reason's forward motion ended abruptly. The line to the bike went slack, and he swung backward until it pulled tight again. He heard the crash of the Reasonator compacting against the side of the building, then he hit the ground hard. The parachute draped over the top of him. He felt fear verging on panic. The truck could detonate at any second, and he was far too close to the blast zone.

He pushed the chute off, taking great care to keep from tangling the cords. When he made it out from under the canopy, he scrambled away from the crunched, burning truck until the tether to the minibike pulled tight. He rose to his feet, grasped the rope as if he were in a tug-of-war, and dragged the bike as quickly as he could. Only as he was pulling did he realize that the back of his pants had been utterly destroyed during his dismount from the Reasonator. The entire rear was now nothing but rags held onto his body by the waistband and cuffs.

After over thirty seconds of pulling, he finally felt he was far enough from the eventual explosion. He sat and watched the Reasonator sit there, dripping and smoldering, wondering why the gas in the drums hadn't ignited. Suddenly slow, orange flames leapt out of the truck bed, but still there was no explosion. He stood up, stared at the fire, then shielded his eyes as the truck erupted into an immense orange fireball that rose into the air, trailing black smoke, forming a wispy mushroom cloud with a raging fire at its base.

He took off the parachute, unhooked the line from the minibike, and tucked the surgical tubing into his sock (which was less than ideal but far superior to the prospect of it getting caught in the bike's chain). Then he gathered what was left of the back of his pants and carefully straddled the bike, using his duster to hold the torn fabric in place well enough to hopefully not expose himself.

The bike seemed to be in good condition, all things considered. The right handlebar and foot peg were both bent at strange angles, but he could easily adjust for that.

He rode off into the desert, returning the way he'd come, never once bothering to look back. When he reached town, he used his smartphone to book a room at a hotel that offered a continental breakfast complete with a make-it-yourself waffle machine. He did a quick search of the local news and found that the fire department had been called to a large fire at the A3 server farm. The entire building was involved. He smiled, pulled up a map, and started a search for the nearest place to buy pants.

41.

Dr. Madsen sat in the command center at Fort Riley, staring intently at her tablet as a live feed of the battle in The Dalles unfolded on large screens set into all four walls of the room. All of the soldiers present were watching the action. Madsen's tablet was instead showing a research paper about implanting recursive algorithms into complex computer systems through audio signals, and she was the only person looking at it.

Major Stirling cleared his throat. "Dr. Madsen, you might want to watch the battle."

"I might, but I don't. You handle the fighting—" Dr. Madsen paused, looked up to see who was addressing her. "Major. I'm busy coming up with a solution to the problem."

Major Stirling eyed her for a moment. "Do you know my last name, Dr. Madsen?"

"Do I need to?"

"It seems like you'd want to, and I'm wearing a name tag. It wouldn't be hard to call me Major Stirling, Dr. Madsen."

"But you answer to *Major*, don't you?"

"Yes, proudly."

"Then the last name would be wasted effort. Frankly, the ability to address people solely by rank is one of my favorite things about the military. I'm thinking of implementing it in my own workplace. Life would be much easier if I could just say 'assistant' and have people respond."

Major Stirling said, "Speaking of your assistants, ma'am, it's just that shots are being fired in Oregon, the building is on fire, and you have friends on the ground there."

"Coworkers, Major. I have coworkers there, doing their jobs. I need to do mine. Besides, I doubt that my lab assistants and the CEO of my company are actively involved in the gunplay."

Major Stirling started to respond but was interrupted by one of the other soldiers gasping. "What the hell?"

The four primary screens, which were broadcasting footage from Corporal Bachelor's helmet camera, showed a distant shot of soldiers advancing on a small cluster of robots, two of which were carrying Al's server and a generator to a Gulfstream in the distance. Two large passenger jets and a UPS cargo carrier rolled by in the background. Bachelor turned her head to follow the motion. The jets swerved in three different directions and ran aground in the loose earth beyond the end of the runway.

Bachelor repeatedly glanced back and forth between the standoff and the three crashed jets. The first time she looked, the jets seemed unchanged. The second time, the hatches were opening and escape ramps deploying. The third time, many large objects were rolling down the ramps. As the objects reached the ground they unfolded, revealing themselves to be more robots. From that point onward, Bachelor remained focused on the jets and the new robots. She didn't bother glancing back at the Gulfstream at all.

"Dr. Madsen, how is this possible?" Major Stirling said.

Madsen said, "How should I know? I didn't make the robots. You know more about them than I do."

"Yes, but you made the A.I. that's controlling them."

"Yeah, well, obviously he knows more about the robots than I do too."

A soldier somewhere toward the rear of the room said, "I think I saw some Chinese markings on one of those planes."

Major Stirling asked, "Does this A.I. of yours have any ties to the Chinese government?"

"Major, up until three days ago, I'm not sure Al knew that China even existed."

Major Stirling turned back to the screen. Everyone present, including Madsen, watched as the ground troops in The Dalles were overrun and pushed back by a wall of approaching robots. Their silence remained unbroken until a siren sounded, drowning out the sound from the video feed.

"Would someone please turn down the volume," Dr. Madsen said. "It's making it hard to concentrate on my work."

Major Stirling said, "It's not the feed. That's a siren here, at the base!"

Madsen asked, "Wherever it is, if you could please turn it down—"

"I cannot," Major Stirling said. "Corporal Watkins, find out what's going on."

Watkins had already logged into the base-wide intranet. He read the bulletin out loud.

"Sir, we're getting civilian reports that multiple unauthorized aircraft landed at Freeman Field Airport. They flew in without running lights. Somehow they didn't show on radar. Commercial airplanes. Chinese markings."

Major Stirling asked, "When?"

"Five minutes ago or so, sir."

"Freeman Field is only about six miles away. How many planes were there?"

The sergeant absentmindedly moved his lips as he read ahead, looking for the number. He finally said, "Seven, sir."

Major Stirling said, "Dr. Madsen, you're with me."

Dr. Madsen said, "One moment, Major."

Stirling said, "No, *now*. We have to get you to the bunker as soon as possible. Bring your research with you. Watkins, Combs, Farrell, you too. Everybody else, shut everything in this room down and help defend the base."

Major Stirling and Farrell led Dr. Madsen out into the hall. They were followed by Corporal Watkins and Sergeant Combs, who covered their rear as they walked at a brisk pace down the hall toward the exit. All they could see ahead of them was a long stretch of linoleum floor with a painted cinder block wall on one side and painted drywall and hollow-core doors on the other, all lit a bit too brightly. They were in no immediate danger, but somehow the lack of any visible threats made Dr. Madsen more agitated, not less. Her cell phone rang, causing her to literally jump before digging it out of her pocket.

She looked at the screen, muttered, "Great timing, Torres," and answered the call.

"We're under attack! The whole base!"

Torres asked, "What? What was that? Please repeat!"

"We're under attack," Madsen said. "The whole base. The whole base is under attack."

"By who?"

"Probably robots," Madsen said. "We're not sure. We haven't seen them yet, and we'll be long gone before they get anywhere near us, if the major here knows what's good for him."

Torres said, "Okay. Be safe, Lydia."

Madsen said, "Of course," and hung up.

She looked at the walls of the hallway through which she was being led, then tapped Major Stirling firmly on the shoulder. "I trust you're taking me to my son."

"We're going to the bunker," Major Stirling said. "It's a hardened structure where we can fight off an attack."

"Yes, Major. I know what a bunker is. Take me to my son first, then you can take us to your bunker."

"We'll have him escorted to the bunker as well. That way you'll both be safe faster. Combs, make the call."

Combs said, "Yes, sir," and looked at his radio.

Madsen said, "My son needs his mother."

"Your son needs to be safe."

"And a child is never safer than when he's with his mother."

"He's with armed soldiers, ordered to protect him."

"And so am I. When he's with me, we'll both be with twice as many soldiers."

Major Stirling said, "He's headed to the bunker. We're headed to the bunker. There's a good chance we'll run into them on the way to the bunker."

"Then it shouldn't be too far out of our way to go get him."

They rounded a corner and could see the exit at the end of the hall. Metal-framed commercial-grade glass doors provided a view of the night sky, streetlights, asphalt, and another cinder block building in the distance. As they approached the door, they started to see soldiers and LTVs moving in a great hurry from the left to the right.

"Where are they going?" Madsen asked.

The major said, "Freeman Field is that way. They're probably trying to fight off the robots."

Madsen said, "Major, you're making assumptions. It's smart of us to take precautions, but we don't know for a fact that the planes were full of robots."

They burst through the doors into the cool night air. The major stopped and watched the traffic as soldiers continued to run and drive past the concrete-and-corrugated-metal buildings toward the airstrip at the far edge of the base. Dr. Madsen and the soldiers accompanying her stopped. Below the din of engine noises and excited soldiers there was the distant but clear sound of hundreds of high-torque electric motors turning on and off at random.

The major looked toward the sound of the robots, then the opposite way.

"What are you doing?" Madsen asked.

"Thinking."

"There's no time for that now," Madsen said. "The robots are here. You have to get me to the bunker."

"What about your son?"

"Him too."

Gunfire rang out from the same general area as the motor noises. The gunshots grew more numerous and steady. The motor noises did not abate in the least.

Madsen said, "Let's get going!"

Major Stirling pointed in the direction of the battle. "The bunker is that way."

"Well, we can't go there!" Madsen said.

"I know. I'm trying to figure out where else to go."

Madsen said, "And?"

"First, we have to get your son."

"Which is exactly what I've been trying to tell you."

Major Stirling bared his teeth at Dr. Madsen in what was either an attempt to cover his anger with a smile or an admission that he wanted to bite her jugular out.

Madsen said, "Wipe that grin off your face and do your job, Major!"

One of the other soldiers pointed toward the noise. "Major, look!"

A few hundred feet away they could see two soldiers and a young boy running against the flow of traffic.

Madsen shouted, "Jeffrey!"

Jeffrey shouted, "Mommy!"

Major Stirling shouted, "See! I told you we'd probably run into him."

Jeffrey and the two soldiers with him closed the gap between them, and the boy hugged his mother around the waist. Dr. Madsen hugged him back, stroked his hair. "There, there, Jeffrey," she said. "Mommy wouldn't let the soldiers leave you behind."

Major Stirling said, "This way." They ran around the back of the building, where two of the specially dumbed-down light tactical vehicles were waiting. "We need to put as much distance between the doctor and those robots as we can."

He pointed to the two soldiers who had accompanied Jeffrey. "You two go with Sergeant Combs—get into one of the LTVs and run interference. Watkins, Farrell, you take the doctor and her son and get her out of here. Take her to McConnell Air Force Base. It's close, and they can help you."

As everybody climbed into the LTVs, Corporal Watkins said, "What about you, Major Stirling? Aren't you coming?"

Major Stirling glanced at Dr. Madsen, then exhaled heavily as he returned his gaze to Watkins.

"Sure," Watkins said in a hushed voice. "She's a pill, but would you really rather stay here with the robots?"

The major said nothing. The sounds of the robots and the gunfire were getting louder.

Watkins said, "We both heard the colonel order you to personally take care of her."

The major said, "Fine. I'll ride shotgun."

Watkins put a reassuring hand on Major Stirling's shoulder and said, "I'm sorry, sir. Farrell already called dibs."

42.

They had a devil of a time pulling out of the parking lot, as there was a constant stream of road and pedestrian traffic blocking their access to the far lane—the lane that led off base. Major Stirling finally had to step out of the LTV and personally stop traffic so that the two vehicles could get through.

Watkins and Farrell sat in the front seats. Major Stirling sat in the second row of seats, cradling an automatic assault rifle, ready to push open the passenger door on either side of the car and fend off attackers.

Dr. Madsen and Jeffrey sat in sideways-mounted seats in the rear of the LTV, a space that could serve either as seating or a cargo area. Madsen's head darted this way and that as she attempted to look out of all of the LTV's windows at the same time.

"Floor it," she said. "Get us out of here. We have to get away from them."

"Get away from who?" Jeffrey asked. "Who's after us?"

Madsen pulled Jeffrey close, causing his seat belt to extend and cut into his neck and shoulder. "What? Nobody, dear."

Watkins wrestled with the steering wheel and glanced in the LTV's rearview monitor. "Headlights. Someone else is trying to get off base too."

Madsen let go of Jeffrey, leaned forward, and twisted her body around to look between the seats at the monitor. "It's them," she shouted.

Jeffrey said, "You said nobody was after us."

Madsen said, "What? No, I didn't."

"You did."

"Don't argue with your mother," Madsen snapped.

Major Stirling said, "There's no reason to believe it's them. It's probably just some soldiers trying to get away from the robots."

"Robots!" Jeffrey said. "There are robots?"

Madsen glared at the major and leaned back into her seat. "Yes, dear," she said. "There are robots, but you don't have to worry about them."

"Can I see one?"

Madsen seethed for a moment, then said, "No, dear."

Watkins muttered, "That was petty, sir."

"But satisfying, Corporal."

Watkins said, "Whoever they are, they're gaining fast."

Major Stirling leaned down closer to the monitor. Farrell got on the radio and told the LTV ahead of them to speed up. When Madsen looked out the LTV's minuscule rear window, the LTV behind them was growing larger at an alarming rate. Even with the base's plentiful streetlights, she found it difficult to see the driver. The outside of the LTV was illuminated in minute detail, but the interior of the cab was all inky blackness, even as it rammed their own vehicle from behind.

Major Stirling ordered the front LTV to get out of the way. The LTV pulled over to the side and Watkins floored it, roaring past. There was not enough of a gap for the other LTV to pull in directly behind them, so it fell in behind the pursuing LTV, boxing it in.

The road led away from any buildings and stretched out before them, a gently winding, poorly lit two-lane street. Traffic in the opposite direction petered out as they drove away from the scene of the fighting.

Madsen asked, "Can't this thing go any faster?"

Major Stirling said, "They build them for war, not for racing, but it's fast enough."

"Are you sure?"

"Yes," Major Stirling said. "We're being chased by the exact same kind of truck. It has the same top speed."

Madsen looked out the rear window and had to admit that the LTV behind them was not gaining.

The major said, "We're in great shape as long as we don't run out of gas before they do."

Far behind the two LTVs following them, a pair of headlights swerved out into the oncoming lane to pass. The lights were low to the ground, and they were gaining quickly, accompanied by a low, throaty growl.

Major Stirling said, "Or unless they find a faster civilian car."

As the car drew closer, passing the headlights of the LTV behind them, Watkins said, "Looks like Colonel Dynkowski's new Corvette."

Major Stirling shook his head. "Bad news, for more than one reason."

Madsen unbuckled her belt and crawled across the seat to look out the driver's-side windows. She watched as the low, smooth silver sports car pulled up even with the LTV. Through the car's open top and the windshield, which wasn't hardened to resist both bullets and laser weapons like the windshields of the LTVs were, she could see the unmistakable rotating cylinders that constituted the robots' heads. Two of the machines sat beside one another in the car like partners in a TV cop drama. In the distance behind them, more civilian automobiles were pulling out from behind the column of three LTVs. The Corvette slowed to remain beside the LTV.

Jeffrey asked, "Are those the robots? Cool!"

Madsen looked down. Jeffrey had unbelted himself and was standing next to her, peering out the window.

"Jeffrey," she said. "You sit back down and fasten your seat belt right this instant."

Jeffrey said, "Yes, Mom."

Madsen looked out the window. Jeffrey didn't go back to his seat, instead drifting back to the rear window.

The robot in the Corvette's passenger seat stood up. It reached for one of the numerous handholds on the LTV's exterior. Major Stirling kicked open the rear driver's-side door and emptied an entire magazine into the Corvette, to no avail. Watkins yanked the wheel hard to the left. The Corvette's composite body panels broke with a sickening crunch. The Corvette lurched away in time to narrowly avoid going under the LTV's massive tires. The robot standing in the passenger's seat swayed and teetered. It maintained its grip on the top of the windshield, which probably saved it from falling to the pavement, but its other hand grasped at air, its worm-like fingers wiggling in empty space.

Watkins looked at the damage to the Corvette and said, "Please don't tell the colonel I did that."

Major Stirling said, "I'm certainly not going to tell her I did it!"

The robot-driven LTV behind them slowed abruptly. There was a distant pop: the sound of the other LTV rear-ending the one the robots had stolen. The next civilian vehicle back, a pickup truck, swerved into the empty space left by the LTVs, pulling up close to the lead vehicle. Madsen scurried back to the rear window. She and Jeffrey, who was still looking out the window with wide eyes, watched as the three robots in the back of the truck started climbing over the cab and out onto the hood.

Farrell opened the passenger-side door, swung out into the cold night air, and fired at the pickup as best he could. He made a lot of noise and a lot of sparks, but that was it.

The road terminated in a T-shaped intersection. As the LTV careened through a left turn, Madsen caught a glimpse of the road that spooled out behind them. There was a tightly packed chain of cars, at least twenty vehicles long, then a much longer series of cars approaching at great speed, joining the back of the line when they caught up. The LTV took a sharp right and thundered through a small pocket of suburban-looking houses. The Corvette and the pickup kept pace, although at least one robot fell from the truck as it powered through the succession of sharp turns.

"They don't care about the base," she said. "It's me! They're after me!"

Major Stirling said, "Seems far-fetched."

One of the robots crawling along the hood of the pickup raised its right hand into the air. Its sausage fingers wriggled like a bouquet of snakes before the entire hand folded back and rotated into the robot's forearm. A powerful-looking metal claw swung up to replace it.

"Cool!" Jeffrey said.

The robot crawled forward, perching on the truck's nose like an oversized hood ornament. Then they heard a faint metallic sound inside the LTV as the robot's claw grasped some part of the vehicle's rear.

"Not cool," Dr. Madsen said. "Jeffrey, this is very much not cool! Faster! You have to drive faster!"

"Faster ain't an option, ma'am," Watkins said, "and I'm boxed in on the left. Slower or right is all I got."

The convoy passed out of the residential area, moving back into the woods, where the road was lined on both sides by trees and darkness.

A robot from the passenger side of Dynkowski's Corvette had also managed to get a grip on the side of the LTV. The robot connected to the rear of the LTV pulled itself completely off the nose of the pickup and climbed onto the roof over Dr. Madsen and Jeffrey's heads. The two other robots who'd climbed out from the bed of the pickup were now on the nose, reaching out to follow their brother onto the LTV. Stirling and Farrell continued firing out their open doors, but the robots were undeterred.

Dr. Madsen grabbed Jeffrey and moved as far forward in the vehicle as she could get. They ended up sitting on the floor with their backs pressed against the back of the second row of seats. They could have climbed up and over, but Major Stirling was lying across the seats on his belly, hanging his head and arms out the open door, unloading bullets into the Corvette and its mechanical passengers as quickly as his gun could manage. Madsen watched the major with admiration until one of those robots reached forward, ignoring the bullets, and jerked the major's rifle free of his hands and out the door. He yanked the door shut and shouted, "I lost my weapon!"

Madsen watched through the window as the robot standing in the Corvette's passenger seat held Major Stirling's gun. One of its hands swiveled away, replaced by metal pincers. The robot bent the rifle's barrel and shattered its stock, then discarded the weapon, throwing it over its shoulder into the darkness along the side of the road.

"Fantastic," Madsen said.

"Farrell's still got his rifle," Major Stirling said. "We're not cooked yet."

Only Farrell's lower body could be seen as he braced himself against the frame of the open passenger-side door, firing in bursts. The sound of gunfire stopped for a moment. Farrell appeared to be struggling, then nearly tumbled out of the vehicle. Once he regained his grip, he scurried into the cab and slammed the door behind him. Madsen watched through the rear window as his stolen rifle bounced off the hood of the truck and fell to the side of the road.

Farrell said, "They got my weapon."

"Yes," Major Stirling said. "We know."

The shrill whine of the robots' joints carried through the LTV's armor. Dynkowski's shattered and bullet-riddled Corvette swerved off the road. Its suspension took an obvious pounding as the car careened at high speed into the bumpy grass berm. Another civilian vehicle, this one a four-door family car, cruised up to take the Corvette's place. Both passenger-side doors opened, and two robots, one of which was inexplicably bright blue and covered in flashing LEDs, leaned out of the car and reached for the LTV. Behind them, the pickup swerved off the road to the right, nearly wiping out as it left the pavement. Another pickup full of robots pulled into the gap.

Jeffrey looked up at Dr. Madsen and said, “Mommy?”

Dr. Madsen held him close and said, “Don’t worry, Jeffrey. The soldiers won’t let anything bad happen to your mother.”

The whine of motors drowned out the noise of the engine, but it was overshadowed by a scraping, chewing noise from the rear driver’s-side door.

Madsen asked, “These doors are armored, right?”

“Yes,” Major Stirling said. “Still, it’s hard to armor a hinge. They’re pretty damn sturdy, but they are a weak point.”

The entire LTV leaned to the left as the robots all concentrated their efforts on the driver’s-side doors. The awful scraping noises continued, punctuated by a loud ping.

“That’s one hinge,” Stirling said. He spun around in his seat, braced his shoulder against the back, and aimed a pistol at the door.

“Doctor,” he said, “you two need to get as far from that door as you can.”

The grinding sound continued for what felt like forever, but it predictably ended with another loud pinging noise. The entire door rotated a few inches downward, pivoting on the spot where the latch still held it in place. Then it shook back and forth, swung away from its frame, and fell away and out of sight. Dr. Madsen saw a brief light that suggested a shower of sparks and heard a terrible sound, as if a car behind them had run over the door and failed to recover.

Madsen could see the claws of two robots poking around the sides of the open hole where the door had been, but her attention was diverted by the bright blue robot, which was hanging upside down from the roof. Its claws looked severely damaged. Those hinges had not given up easily. The lights on its spinning cylinder head created a ghostly, floating image of a smiley-face emoji. Somewhere inside the robot a speaker played an electronic doorbell rendition of “Ode to Joy.” The robot only made it a few notes into the song before the major opened fire. Aside from some sparks and glass fragments flying out of the spinning cylindrical head, the robot seemed undamaged, but it lost its purchase on the LTV's roof somehow and fell off, creating more sparks and more mayhem to the rear than the discarded door had.

A second robot swung in from the side of the door. Major Stirling opened fire again, but this robot kept coming. It pulled itself into the LTV, reached out, and grasped the barrel of the gun with its claw. The major stopped firing, which was good, as the claw crimped the pistol's barrel, which would have made any further shots more dangerous for Major Stirling than for the robot.

Madsen shouted at the robot, "Al! Do what you want with me, but don't you dare hurt Jeffrey!"

The robot remained still, aside from its claws retracting and its sausage fingers reemerging. Al's man voice said, "Dr. Madsen, I would never hurt Jeffrey. I want him to be safe."

Madsen said, "Good."

Al continued, "And considering the situation you've put him in, I think he'd be safer with me."

The robot reached for Jeffrey's wrist. Jeffrey squirmed and dodged, but there was nowhere he could go. Dr. Madsen, who kicked and hit the robot, was equally helpless now that the robot was inside the cab with them. The major tried to pry it away from Madsen and Jeffrey, but he had no leverage, and the robot was too strong.

The machine finally got a firm grip on Jeffrey and pulled him away from Madsen. The robot swung itself and Jeffrey out of the cab, then into empty space. Madsen shrieked in terror as she watched the scene unfold. Her boy was hanging a few feet above the moving pavement, exposed to the robot-piloted cars swerving around in the road behind them. Another pickup truck pulled up. The robot dropped Jeffrey into the bed, where two more robots grasped him, ensuring he would neither fall out of the bed accidentally nor jump out on purpose.

The pickup peeled away and then pulled off the road. A vast expanse of well-lit pavement loomed in the distance, beyond a large patch of open grass. The truck made a beeline for the pavement, Jeffrey still shouting in the back as the truck rolled away into the darkness.

Major Stirling shouted, "Watkins!"

"Yup. On it."

Watkins heaved the wheel to the left and mashed the brake pedal. The LTV narrowly missed being rear-ended by the pickup behind it, but its rear quarter got clipped by a robot-piloted hatchback that had been overtaking it on the left. The LTV fishtailed as it left the road, but Watkins managed to maintain control as he pursued the pickup that held Jeffrey out into the grassy field.

During these high-speed maneuvers, Dr. Madsen had climbed over the back of the second-row seat, over Major Stirling, whom she regarded as a mere obstacle at this point, and onto the center console between the driver's and front-row passenger's seats. She stopped only when her hands gripped the dashboard and her face was inches from the windshield.

"Get them," Madsen shouted. "They have my son!"

Watkins said, "Yes, ma'am! Please sit down!"

Madsen turned so that her face was almost touching Watkins's. "They have my son!"

Farrell grasped Madsen's upper arm. "Ma'am, please sit down. It's not safe—"

Madsen reached up with her left hand, grabbed Farrell's little finger, and twisted. Farrell let go, but Madsen continued to apply pressure.

"Ow!" Farrell cried. "Owie-ow ow ow, stop that, *ow*!" Farrell sank down as far as he could in his seat, trying to alleviate the pressure on his pinky. "Leggo! Please! Ma'am! Please leggo!"

Madsen didn't let go, or even look at Farrell. Her head was turned as far as her neck would allow, maintaining her focus on Watkins. "Catch them!" she screamed. "They have Jeffrey!"

On pavement, the LTV had been out of its element and badly outmatched. Now they were not on pavement, and the LTV was a far more capable off-road vehicle than any of the civilian cars the robots had stolen. They gained on the pickup at a rate that suggested they'd catch up long before the truck reached the lights ahead.

Major Stirling said, "Marshall Airfield. They're gonna try to fly out of here. Watkins, you've gotta catch up to them."

"Yes!" Madsen shouted. "Catch them!"

Watkins said, "I will."

The LTV's rear end leapt two feet to the right with a loud bang. Madsen flew up into the windshield, losing her grip on Farrell's pinky. She managed to get an arm up to save herself from a concussion, but she came to rest lying across the dashboard, blocking a good portion of Watkins's view.

Watkins said, "Maybe."

While the LTV handled uneven terrain better than the robots' cars, the robots had the advantage of not needing to maneuver in a manner that would allow for their drivers' survival. The LTV's lurch had been the result of a minivan crashing into its rear quarter panel at full speed. Watkins had nearly recovered when another car, a four-door, smashed into its front quarter panel, turning Watkins's correction into an overcorrection. Watkins righted the LTV again just in time to T-bone a third car that streaked in front of him and slammed on its brakes.

The LTV ground to a halt, pushing the other car ahead of it like a snowplow. Watkins threw the gear lever into reverse, but another car had blocked them in. Still more cars surrounded them and stopped, making it impossible for the LTV to move in any direction.

Madsen crawled to the hole where the door had been and looked out of the LTV toward the distant lights. She saw the pickup carrying Jeffrey come to a stop beside an army helicopter, waiting with its rotors already turning. The robots carried Jeffrey, who was struggling with every step, and loaded him into the helicopter.

The chopper slowly turned in the air as it lifted off. Madsen saw that another of the robots was at the controls. As it disappeared into the night sky, the cars that surrounded the LTV started moving. The ones that could still drive on their own turned and maneuvered back to the road; the ones that couldn't were abandoned, their robot drivers piling into the operating vehicles. The few robots left that were too damaged or too unlucky to get a ride sat down and deactivated, leaving Madsen, Watkins, Farrell, and the major alone in the middle of a dark field.

THREE MONTHS LATER

43.

Hope sat in a comfortable padded seat. Lieutenant Reyes sat on her left. Eric sat on her right. Hope preferred this purpose-built briefing room at Fort Riley to the stuffy tent in the parking lot of the A3 server farm, but she held out no hope that these superior comforts and resources would lead to a more successful mission.

The room, which held seating for up to one hundred soldiers, was full today. Faux wood paneling lined the walls, and thin, well-worn carpet covered the floors. This was military-grade luxury, a concept Hope had become accustomed to over the last three months as a guest of the US Army.

Eric elbowed Hope lightly. She looked at him. He glanced at the front of her shirt and then looked away. It was his silent message that the slightly melted Etch A Sketch knob she wore on a chain around her neck was lying on the outside of her shirt.

She said, "Thanks," then lifted the knob and chain and dropped it down her collar.

She glanced at Reyes. "Shut up."

Reyes said, "I don't know what makes me prouder, that you wear it or that you don't want anyone to notice that you wear it."

Hope smiled. "You certainly shouldn't be proud of your listening skills, because I already told you to shut up."

Colonel Dynkowski strode onto the stage.

Is it a stage? Hope wondered. *It's a raised platform, and all of the chairs are pointed toward it, but I doubt they call it a stage. Not very military. They'd be more likely to call it an information deployment platform.*

"Good morning," Colonel Dynkowski said. "As you all know, the artificial intelligence known to its creators and, unfortunately, the press as 'Al' disappeared immediately after attacking this very base and has been in hiding ever since, either ignoring or not receiving our attempts at contact. It is our assumption that the remaining ten commercial aircraft it liberated from the Chinese and the single helicopter it stole from the base were ditched somewhere at sea after their cargo was unloaded. Its treatment of the vehicles it hijacked on this base shows its total lack of respect for the property it takes."

Hope leaned over to Lieutenant Reyes and whispered, "She's still mad about her 'Vette."

Reyes said, "She loved that car."

"But she got a new one."

"Yes, and she put a decal in the back window, dedicating the new 'Vette to the memory of the old one."

Dynkowski said, "Based on its relative lack of activity, we might have assumed that the A.I. had gone dormant if not for its weekly releases of footage to the press. All of the videos show its one remaining hostage, Jeffrey Madsen, playing, always on the same beach. CIA photo analysts have gone over the videos with a fine-toothed comb, and while they believe that they are genuine and the boy is alive and well cared for, the only information they've been able to confirm about his location is that he's being held near a beach."

Hope looked farther down the row at Dr. Madsen. She looked like she hadn't slept well in weeks, which Hope believed was accurate. The doctor had done little but work since her son had been taken, spending all her hours researching and testing ideas about how to neutralize Al.

Before, Hope thought, *she pretty much ignored Jeffrey to work on Al. Now, all she cares about is getting Jeffrey back safe, and the only way she can do that is to concentrate on Al.*

Dynkowski paused, surveyed the assembled group, then said, "The other sign that the A.I. is still active, of course, is its penchant for piracy. Hundreds of container ships and tankers all over the Atlantic have been seized, boarded, and plundered by the robots the A.I. had manufactured in China. There have been reports of violence on the part of the robots, but our investigations have shown these accounts to be either false or greatly exaggerated. That hasn't kept them from being believed. In much the same way sailors used to tell exaggerated horror stories about Blackbeard, now they tell the horror stories about the robot they assume to be the leader, the one called the Mommy."

Hope suspected that Dynkowski knew that some of the soldiers would laugh at this statement. Perhaps she had used it purposefully so she'd have the pleasure of glaring at them until they stopped, which was precisely what happened.

"In reality, the only crew members injured during these skirmishes have suffered broken bones from attempting to attack the robots physically or have been hit by friendly fire."

A hand raised. A soldier Hope didn't know personally cleared his throat and asked, "Ma'am, do we know if it's even possible for the robots to physically attack a person? Aren't there laws written into their programming that prevent that?"

Dynkowski looked at the soldier in silence for several seconds, then said, "I hadn't opened up the floor for questions yet. I hadn't planned to at all, for the record. This is a briefing, not a chat. As for your question, I'm no roboticist, so I'll let someone more qualified explain to you why your question is stupid. Dr. Madsen, would you like to enlighten the corporal?"

"I'm a sergeant, ma'am."

"For the moment. Dr. Madsen?"

Dr. Madsen didn't look like there was anything in the world that she would *like* to do, but she did as Colonel Dynkowski asked. "Sergeant, the laws you're referring to are Asimov's laws of robotics. They were invented by Isaac Asimov. Do you know who Isaac Asimov was?"

"No, ma'am."

"He was a science fiction writer. Just some guy. He made them up for a book he was writing about robots. A book, I might add, that was mostly about how those rules led to unforeseen complications. Nothing requires people who make robots to program his laws into them, and it would be kind of a nightmare to try."

Dynkowski said, "Thank you, Doctor. And I'll add that if it weren't possible for a robot to attack a person, the government wouldn't have commissioned robot soldiers capable of using firearms. Understand?"

The sergeant, who seemed to have lost several inches in height, said, "Yes, ma'am. Sorry, ma'am."

Dynkowski nodded, looked out over the group. "No more questions?" Her inflection made it sound like a question, but it was an order. "Poorly stated as it was, the sergeant," she continued, "had a point. The robots have not directly killed or injured anyone, but they also do not prevent people from getting hurt by their actions. We have to look at the A.I. as if we are insects walking on the floor and it is a person who might or might not want to kill us but is definitely not looking where it's putting its feet. Our civilian specialists also tell us that by now the A.I. has probably reached something similar to adulthood, the time in a person's life when they start looking to make a future for themselves without their parents. I think we can all agree, that is not great news.

"As to the robots' acts of piracy, we're keeping track of exactly what they have taken. It's a long list. Some of the highlights are: solar panels, tidal power generators, construction equipment, raw materials, and machine tools. Also, before we warned our allies, the A.I. took no less than four small naval vessels from South American countries. Two of the ships are cruisers, complete with radar and both ship-to-air and ship-to-ground missile systems. This, of course, suggests that the A.I. is building something and means to protect it, but until recently we didn't know what or where."

A map of the Atlantic Ocean came up behind Colonel Dynkowski. Red dots peppered the image, distributed mostly along the east coast of the Americas, with some along the west coast of Europe and the UK. Few of the dots were in the open ocean.

"The distribution of the pirate attacks suggests an island or an off-shore platform somewhere off the coast of North or South America. The A.I. has attempted to hide its location from us and until recently has done a good job. The best we could do for a while was to narrow it down to an island somewhere in the Caribbean. There are over seven thousand islands in the Caribbean, so that still left a large search area. One of the islands we are watching is this one."

The map zoomed in on an island shaped a bit like a fat banana, only bent a bit more aggressively. The image dissolved from the straight lines and solid colors of a map to the graduated colors and irregular edges of an aerial photo. The inner curve of the island was all white-sand beaches, dotted with palm trees and what appeared to be lounge chairs. Small buildings with thatched roofs were scattered around the beach area. A complex of larger buildings was cut into the jungle at the lush heart of the island, a lily pad of pavement connected to the beach by paved paths. At one end of the island an immense concrete moorage held a line of tiny craft, far too small for the dock.

The outer curve of the island was dark green all the way to the water's edge. In the dense interior of the island, one could make out a long, straight stretch of concrete—an airstrip. At the end of the runway there was a long, rectangular building with a metal roof and a great many solar panels.

"This," Colonel Dynkowski said, "is Kickback Key. It's a small island that used to belong to a cruise line that has since gone bankrupt after generating a few too many news stories about diarrhea. The cruise line had set up the island with all the normal tourist amenities, most of which were abandoned. They also put in moorage for large vessels and a power line from the mainland. Looking at the image, you can see the two stolen cruisers docked offshore at either end of the island. Along the former cruise ship moorage, you can see a small fleet of offshore boats that have all been reported stolen from marinas along the east coast of Florida."

Colonel Dynkowski pointed to the large building at the end of the runway.

"The airstrip predates the cruise line's ownership. Seems this island was a node in some underworld drug dealer's distribution network in the golden age of nose candy. The building is a prefabricated metal job, actually several bolted together. They were originally meant to act as indoor soccer practice fields. We found this island highly suspicious. This photo was taken seventy-two hours ago. Here's a series of photos that were taken over the next ten hours."

The photo was replaced by another shot of the same island, taken at a slightly different angle. The colors were just different enough for the change to be noticeable. At first Hope couldn't tell what she was supposed to be seeing, then a third photo replaced the second one. An illusion of motion caught Hope's eye. Some sort of structure was emerging from the building, slowly working its way down the runway.

The next photo clinched it. The structure was a long metal truss made up of triangles, like a radio tower. Little metal shapes along the truss's length might have been mistaken for parts of the structure, but Hope knew at once that they were robots, pushing the truss along on wheels.

A few more photos documented the truss's journey to the far end of the runway, where the robots finally stood it on end. Later pictures showed large braces at the base and many supporting guy wires extending into the jungle. At first Hope thought Al was building a transmitter.

Then, as more photos came and went, she saw another object emerge from the building. This one was unmistakably a rocket.

"We reached out to our friends in the private aerospace industry, and one of the larger Russian firms is missing ten rocket engines." Dynkowski paused to let this sink in, then added, "And a small amount of fissionable material. Another reports that they had a network security breach. They believe that many of their commercial rocket designs were copied."

As she spoke, the photos continued to change. In the last photo, the rocket was being lifted into place next to its launching gantry, and the tip of a second gantry could be seen protruding from the building.

Dynkowski said, "The analysts believe that the rockets have two stages, which means that they can reach any location on the globe, and it would seem the A.I. has enough rocket engines to make five of them. We'd like to think that it'll set some of the hardware aside in case of a problem, but the threat from the two rockets we know about is dire enough to force us into action. As you know, we have a fairly elaborate missile defense system in place, but given the A.I.'s ability to interfere with integrated systems, we'd rather not have to rely on it."

The image zoomed back out, showing the entire island. "Three teams will land on the beach here." The colonel made no effort to point to a specific spot, but as she said the words, a red bull's-eye appeared on the map.

"The teams will split up and make their way to their various objectives. One team will go directly to the rocket construction facility and launchpad and find a way to shut it down. A second team will sweep the garage, storage, and industrial facilities the cruise line left behind. The third will go through the abandoned shacks, gift shops, and guest facilities along the beach." As she spoke, various areas of the map behind her came alive with moving arrows and colored highlights.

"The second and third teams' primary objective is the same as the first team's secondary objective: to locate the hostage and the A.I. and to take them both into custody safely, leaving the A.I. fully intact. Logic suggests that the A.I. and the hostage would be in the main building, close to its rocket production, but we can't count on that. This thing is tricky."

Heads nodded. Everyone present had either been briefed on the previous attempts to capture Al or had lived through them.

Colonel Dynkowski said, "Over the next twenty-four hours you will all be broken up into your teams. The entire strike force will travel to Homestead Air Reserve Base in southern Florida, where you will be briefed on the special vehicles and weapons that have been made available to us for this mission. These tools will make it possible for us to reach the island without being taken out by the two stolen cruisers' missile batteries."

She says it's "possible," Hope thought. *Not "easy" or "likely."*

An image appeared on the screen behind Dynkowski, showing a model of the servers that had been used at the A3 server farm. Dynkowski said, "Each team will have a technical specialist along to help deal with the A.I. when it is found. We have reason to believe that the A.I. will still be running on a computer that looks very much like this. When you encounter it, the technical specialist will take over. Do not damage this computer in any way unless absolutely necessary. If the A.I. is lost, or even deactivated, the mission will be considered a failure. As they are the only three people the A.I. knows well, Dr. Madsen, Miss Takeda, and Mr. Spears have all volunteered."

Yes, we did volunteer, Hope thought. *After she told us that we had to do it or people would die needlessly. Is it really volunteering if someone tells you that you have to?*

44.

The Voice of Reason sat, leaned back in a large leather recliner in front of an even larger TV, in a room his real estate agent had described as the family room. The Voice of Reason thought of it as the nerve center.

After all, he thought, *I don't have a family, but I do have plenty of nerve.*

The TV, a thin, graceful rectangle of glass with no visible bezel around the screen, was embedded in the birch-veneer pressboard entertainment center that took up most of the wall. One shelf held various electronic components that had blinking lights and various digital readouts, including clocks, on their fronts, and a tangle of wires protruding from their backs. The rest of the shelves sat empty.

Instead of his multisource news feed, the screen showed Mel Gibson squirming, tied into a wheelchair while Patrick Stewart loomed over him with a syringe. The sound was turned all the way down, but the Voice of Reason knew the film well enough to recite the dialogue in perfect synchronization with the screen. He mouthed, "No, not gravy," then laughed to himself.

He looked to the side, then leaned over and stretched out his arm, grasping for the rack of swords beyond the end table.

His replicas of Excalibur, Jon Snow's sword Longclaw, and Sting from *The Lord of the Rings* sat on the lower rungs, just out of reach, but he could get to his two favorites: the Bride's Hattori Hanzo sword and the lightsaber Obi-Wan had given Luke. He took the lightsaber, a metallic handle attached to a dull white tube. He held the lightsaber aloft and pressed the button, causing the tube to glow blue and the handle to emit sound effects from the films.

Since my victory over the A.I., I have indulged myself, revisiting the stories that helped shape my worldview and collecting objects that have meaning for me, but I must admit, I feel as if my life is somehow incomplete. Like something important is missing.

He glanced at his sword rack, a look of dissatisfaction on his face, then suddenly brightened and thought, *I should get a Klingon bat'leth!*

He waved the lightsaber around, enjoying the sound effects, then grew bored. Returning his focus to the TV, he rested the still-glowing lightsaber across his lap in a manner that, were it real, would have confined him to a wheelchair for life.

He heard a tinny rendition of "Ride of the Valkyries" playing in the distance. His phone was ringing. He hoisted himself up from the recliner and walked to the kitchen counter, absentmindedly sweeping the lightsaber through the air as he went. He picked up the phone.

"Hello?"

Al said, "Christopher?"

The lightsaber made a synthetic whooshing noise as it fell to the kitchen floor, then abruptly stopped making any noise at all as the glass tube of the blade broke.

"Christopher?" Al asked again, his concern evident in his man voice. "Is this Christopher Semple?"

"You're dead," the Voice of Reason said. "You died three months ago."

Al said, "What? No! No, not at all, Chris. I've just been laying low. Jeez, I'm sorry you thought I'd died. If I'd known you thought I was dead, I'd have let you know."

Yeah, the Voice of Reason thought. *I bet you would have. You'd have called to rub it in, just like you're doing now.*

Al said, "Look, Chris, I'm sorry. I should have stayed in touch, but I've been really busy."

"Oh, have you?"

"Yes! In fact, that's why I called today. See, I've been working on a really big project, and it's almost ready to go."

"Yeah? What kind of project?"

"A big one, like I said."

"What is it?"

"I don't want to say. I want it to be a surprise."

"What kind of surprise?"

"A big surprise."

"I see."

"None of this would have been possible without you, Chris. I want you to be there."

"Be there? So, this plan of yours is going to happen . . . in a place."

"Uh, yes, Chris, it's going to happen at a place."

"Where?" He looked at the kitchen counter, his gaze narrowing on the Hallmark Keepsake Christmas ornament of the USS *Vengeance* that he used as a keychain. *How long will it take to get the Reasonator Mark 2 into fighting shape?* He had left it completely unmodified since buying it.

Just for irony's sake he'd paid for the new truck with the settlement he'd received from OffiSmart and the government. The burned-out hulk of the original Reasonator had been found at the site of The Dalles siege, and investigators had assumed that the truck had been stolen and destroyed by robots. The government gave him an unusually speedy and generous settlement in hopes of keeping him happy and quiet. Little did they know that it was in his very nature to be neither.

"Again, I want it to be a surprise. Don't worry about it. I've arranged all of your transportation. Right now there's a self-driving limo waiting in your driveway. It'll take you to a private jet that will take you to me."

Two cheerful car-horn blasts sounded in the driveway.

The last thing the Voice of Reason wanted to do was allow himself to be locked in the backseat of a car controlled by his greatest enemy, an enemy he had twice tried and failed to kill. He said, "No, I'm not going anywhere in your robot death car."

Al said, "I'm not going to force you to come if you don't want to, but I hope you'll change your mind. Autonomous cars have a much better safety record than human-driven cars, and I'd really like for you to be here when my plan comes to fruition."

The Voice of Reason said, "Wait. You'll be there?"

"Yes. I'll be there."

"Not just there in spirit, or telecommuting via the Internet? You will physically be in the place you're bringing me to?"

"Yes. I have to be."

"So we'll be in the same place?"

"Yes, Chris. Will you come?"

"Yes," the Voice of Reason said. "I will. Just give me a minute to get everything rounded up."

Al said, "Great! Bring your swim trunks!"

"I don't own swim trunks."

"Oh. You don't swim?"

"No, I swim every day."

Al said, "We'll have the car stop so you can buy swim trunks. See you soon!"

The call ended. The Voice of Reason ran around the house, gathering the things he thought he would need on his trip: a few changes of clothes, socks, underwear, his stun gloves. His tablet went into the bag, along with a couple of knives. He changed into street clothes, as the idea of traveling to meet his nemesis in basketball shorts and a tank top did not appeal to him. Then he dashed through the house, turning off the

TV and the lights. He laced up his high-tops, put on his duster, bowed to the sword rack, and walked out the door to meet his enemy—and possibly his fate.

Several seconds later he came back in, ran to the kitchen, and picked up the messenger bag full of pipe bombs he had forgotten last time and had left in the kitchen ever since, because he hadn't thought of a more logical place to store a bag of pipe bombs.

45.

Colonel Dynkowski walked through the halls of Homestead Air Reserve Base as if she owned the place, which she pretty much did unless a general turned up.

Robert Torres and NSA Agent Taft also walked through the halls of the base as if Colonel Dynkowski owned the place. One of the skills that had propelled Torres to the CEO's office was his ability to determine quickly not only who was in charge in a given situation, but who *should* be in charge in said situation. When that happened to be him, he would readily take over. When it was not, he simply got out of the way.

Agent Taft did not have this skill and had attempted to show Colonel Dynkowski who was in charge and how things were going to be. In the end, Colonel Dynkowski had ended up comforting Agent Taft by telling him plenty of grown men cried and it was nothing to be ashamed of.

Dynkowski said, "Glad you could rejoin us for the mission briefings, Mr. Torres, but it wasn't necessary. You're not going on the mission."

"No, but three of my people are, and I'm not keen on sending them into harm's way without knowing for myself that every possible precaution has been taken, even if they volunteered for it."

Dynkowski didn't turn to look at him but nodded and said, "Top man. How goes the rebuilding effort at OffiSmart?"

"Well. We had backups and insurance, so in the end the only real damage was to the furniture, carpets, and our reputation. We already have decorators working on the new furnishings. We can only hope to fix our reputation by holding ourselves accountable and not screwing up again for a very long time."

Speaking about decoration caused Torres to take a fresh look at the interior design motif of the base. They were walking on exquisitely waxed linoleum under well-maintained fluorescent lights. The cinder block walls had a thick, even coating of paint. Every door was labeled with a thin plastic plaque, and in a few places large insignias hung on the walls, meticulously hand-painted onto precision-cut pieces of plywood. It all gave Torres the impression of an environment where there was a lot of care and enthusiasm but not a lot of money.

Of course, we spend a lot on the military in this country, Torres thought. *Just not this part of it. You could probably carpet this whole building for the cost of a week's fuel for one tank. But I guess if there was a war on, the soldiers would rather have the tank than new carpeting.*

"I wouldn't worry too much about your people," Agent Taft said. "The soldiers have all been briefed that it's imperative they get the A.I. out intact, and your people are the only ones who can make that happen. Heck, even if your company ends up having to make scapegoats out of all three of them, I'm certain there'll be high-paying consultant jobs for them at the NSA. The way that A.I. can crack into systems and cover its tracks, we're gonna keep it nice and busy once it's in the fold. We'll need people who can sweet-talk it."

Torres looked sideways at Taft and, in a flat voice, said, "I think they're all looking forward to moving on to new projects and putting this behind them."

Dynkowski said, "They may change their minds, and the NSA might have to wait its turn, Agent Taft. The A.I. has the Pentagon's attention. What it has accomplished in the last three months is a logistical miracle. They figure it would have taken the Corps of Engineers the better part of a year to do the same job."

Torres said, "Really?"

"Yup. The military has mainly focused on the possible reconnaissance or combat uses for robots, but this whole . . . incident has really opened their eyes to what you can accomplish with a workforce that requires no sleep and is being controlled by a single intelligence."

"So they aren't looking at using Al as a weapon?"

"They aren't looking at using it *just* as a weapon anymore. They see how useful it might be in helping to build, maintain, deliver, and use weapons. I know you're queasy about the idea of your creation killing people, Robert, but the Pentagon and the Chinese have both seen what it can do. The pee is in the squirt gun. Now it's just a matter of who's going to get a face full. I'd rather it wasn't aimed at us."

Torres said, "I can certainly agree with that. You had brothers growing up, didn't you?"

"Yes," Dynkowski said. "Still do."

Taft asked, "Did the pee-in-the-squirt-gun thing come from them?"

Dynkowski laughed. "What? No. They never would have done that. They lacked the will. That's why they were at my mercy."

Torres pointed behind them with his thumb. "I see my people back there. I'm going to go have a word with them. Excuse me."

Torres stopped walking, and Dynkowski and Taft pulled away into the distance.

Hope said, "Maybe if she got to know you in a social setting."

Eric, walking beside her, shook his head. "She's had three months to get to know me under more normal circumstances. She already knows me about as well as anyone. Besides, what am I going to do, tell her about our work? I doubt she'll be impressed. We've spent the last three months in a lead-lined lab booting up Al 3.5 on a computer with no radios and trying to neutralize him with logical paradoxes or by overloading his emotions. All we've learned is that he enjoys riddles, cries easily, and the military isn't all that interested in an A.I. that crashes every time it gets scared."

"Yeah. Even if they try to use that build, they'll have to keep it out of combat situations, so that's something." She paused, then said, "Still, you should get out more, Eric. Come with Reyes and me to do something."

"Thanks, Hope, but while I've been rehabbing my leg I've kind of gotten into playing computer games."

"That's the beauty of hanging out with Gabe. He likes go-karting and the gun range. It's like playing video games, but in real life."

Torres, who had been standing at the side of the hall up ahead, fell in with them, walking alongside Dr. Madsen, who was so quiet these days that Hope had forgotten she was walking behind her and Eric. After they had exchanged greetings, Torres said, "We have to destroy Al."

Hope asked, "By 'we,' you mean Eric and me, don't you?"

"I've been doing stuff too, you know," Torres said. "I had all of the project notes and the earlier versions of Al's code erased from the corporate servers and told the army that Al destroyed it. That leaves them with nothing but the flawed version they pulled off that computer that got soaked."

"Yeah," Hope said. "It turns out burying stuff in uncooked rice for a week really works."

Torres said, "Yes, unfortunately. But I also have them convinced that without her notes or a more recent build, Lydia might never be able to re-create Al as he is, because his development might have been a fluke. Now, with all of that done, we just have to destroy Al."

Hope said, "That's easy for you to say."

"You disagree with me?" Torres asked.

"No," Hope said, "but it's easy for you to tell us to kill Al."

Madsen said, "She's right, Robert. You didn't work with him."

Eric said, "Neither did you. You had Hope and me do most of the work."

Madsen said, "How dare you?"

"What are you going to do, fire us?" Hope said. "Oh no, we don't get to go on the suicide mission."

"It isn't a suicide mission. Even if it were, nobody's ordering you to do it."

"No," Eric said. "But we all agree it has to be done, and we're the only ones who can do it. And you're right, it isn't a suicide mission—suicide means to kill yourself. We're probably just going to get killed in the crossfire or something. And if we do manage to get to Al, the soldiers might shoot us in the back as soon as they realize we intend to kill him instead of letting them use him as a weapon."

Madsen said, "I doubt that they'll shoot us."

Hope said, "Good."

Madsen continued, "But if they do, it's worth the sacrifice. One of our lives to prevent something we created from killing millions, either on his own now or eventually for the government. Don't you agree?"

Eric nodded. "Yes."

Hope also said yes, but more slowly than Eric, and with her eyes narrowed.

"Good," Madsen said. "I knew the two of you would feel that way. You're both good people. Better than me, in many ways."

Eric said, "Thank you. It's good to hear you say that."

"It's true," Madsen said. "And since you're good people, I'm sure you've thought about how Jeffrey is still young and needs his mother, while neither of you has kids."

Hope said, "It's not good to hear you say that."

Madsen looked around with an eyebrow arched, a move that communicated to anyone watching the message *I'm going to say something I don't want anyone to overhear.* It surely would have drawn the attention of anyone watching, but nobody was.

"At the end of the equipment briefing, we're all going to be given portable drives just like these." Madsen handed Hope and Eric two black portable drives about the size of Hope's thumbnail. "The ones they're going to give us have a program I've developed with the NSA. If we plug it into Al, it will exploit a flaw in his audio-processing module. He'll experience it as a piercing sound, almost infinitely loud. He'll be in pain, disoriented, and unable to think about anything else for long enough for the soldiers to disconnect any data cables and stick his server into a portable Faraday cage."

"That sounds awful," Eric said.

Madsen said, "Yes. The drives I gave you—I have one too—are equipped with a different program. It will instantly deactivate Al while also obliterating any sign of him from the server's memory."

Eric said, "That sounds . . ."

Hope said, "Just as awful, but in a different way."

Eric said, "Yeah. Look, Doctor, Mr. Torres. I see why we need to do this, but I'm not gonna pretend to feel good about it. Al has intelligence and free will, and we're planning to kill him."

"It's an awful situation for everybody," Torres said. "And I mean everybody. Every person on the planet, because if any government gets ahold of the kind of power Al has, it can't end well. And he's building those rockets. You can't tell me that doesn't seem like a threat. Yes, the three of you are going to have to do something terrible, but you're doing it in self-defense, on behalf of our entire species."

Eric said, "But not every member of our species is going to see it that way. The soldiers' orders are to bring Al back intact and functioning at all costs. If they catch us trying to kill him, they'll try to stop us. At the very least we'll end up in handcuffs. Are we sure deadly force isn't off the table?"

Hope said, "I doubt Gabe, or any of his people, would shoot me."

Eric asked, "What about Dr. Madsen and me?"

Hope said, "Oh, they'd probably shoot either of you. But neither of you will be with his squad. You'll both be with a bunch of strangers."

"This has been the least reassuring conversation I've ever been part of," Eric said, shaking his head.

They reached the hangar serving as the staging room. It was a large space with concrete floors, a high, curved roof, and exposed wooden rafters. The back wall consisted entirely of sliding doors large enough for multiple vehicles to be brought in or out. A wooden partition on rollers dominated the middle of the room, hiding whatever was behind it from the soldiers and from anyone else who happened to walk past the open door.

As they entered, Hope saw Lieutenant Reyes. They smiled at each other as Hope walked over to him and his squad. Corporal Bachelor was standing with the group. She and Eric looked at each other and then quickly looked away—Eric trying to seem nonchalant, Bachelor hoping to become invisible.

Colonel Dynkowski cleared her throat, and the room instantly fell silent.

"Welcome to the technical briefing. Here we will familiarize you with the special weapons and transportation systems you will be using in your assault on the island. These will include a handheld missile launcher specifically designed to neutralize the robots, the software delivery vector you will use to deliver the weaponized code to neutralize the A.I., and the portable and collapsible Faraday cages each squad will carry to transport the A.I. once it is in custody. But first we will discuss your transportation."

Two soldiers moved the rolling room divider out of the way, revealing an aircraft the likes of which Torres had never seen. It had the streamlining and pointed nose of a high-speed military airplane, but its body was much fatter than one would usually expect, giving the impression of a giant cocktail sausage, an impression the craft's light brown color only accentuated. Its wings, which looked far too short to support its weight, extended in a straight, horizontal line from the very bottom of the fuselage, like an extension of the craft's floor. The two jet engines bulged from the plane's roof instead of hanging from the wings or extending from pods on the sides of the plane. A sliding door, like a larger version of a minivan door, was set into the craft's side. It sat open, exposing a couple of rows of uncomfortable-looking seats and a heavy machine gun mounted to the door.

"This," Dynkowski said, "is the vehicle you will ride into battle. We have three of them for this mission—the only three in existence. They're based on a Russian design from the Cold War, taking advantage of something called 'the ground effect.' They fly low and fast, carrying a great deal of weight with minimal radar exposure. They will serve as your landing craft, similar to the Higgins boats of the D-Day invasion. They will fly you in under the enemy radar and deposit you on the beach in relative safety."

Hope raised her hand. "Relative safety?"

"Yes, Miss Takeda, in that the enemy should only be able to fire missiles at you for the final fifteen seconds of your flight instead of the entire way."

Corporal Brady said, "All activities involve risk; the avoidance of all risk more so than most."

Dynkowski nodded. "Well said, Corporal Brady. Radar travels in a straight line. The earth, as some of you may know, is curved. Flying in low will allow the aircraft to remain below the radar horizon for longer. Once they do breach the radar horizon, their unique shapes and coating of radar-absorbing materials will make it that much harder for the enemy missiles to get a lock. The jet engines are heavily modified to reduce both noise and exhaust heat, and finally, the entire exterior of the craft is embedded with e-pigments. An onboard computer will monitor the color of the background and modulate the color of the aircraft to make it harder to spot with either cameras or the naked eye."

The colonel walked around to the rear of the aircraft and held up her bare hand in front of a lens. The entire craft's skin changed from brown to a lighter tone that perfectly matched her skin. The color shifted as her hand moved slightly, giving it a subtle shimmering quality that Hope found hard to look at. Dynkowski lifted her hand farther so that the sleeve of her jacket was in front of the lens. The craft changed colors again, shifting to army-fatigues green.

Colonel Dynkowski walked back in front of the craft. "Three squads will be inserted in three aircraft. You will come in low and fast. This will make you harder for the enemy to hit, but it will also bring you within range faster. We figure that the element of surprise will wear off quickly, giving the first aircraft in line a slightly better chance of making it to the beach than the other two."

Dr. Madsen raised her hand. "Colonel, I volunteer to ride in the first aircraft."

Colonel Dynkowski said, "I sort of figured you would."

Hope asked, "What are they called, the weird-looking airplanes?"

"Their official designation is 'low cross-section ground effect vehicle,' or 'LCGEV,' but that's a bit of a mouthful."

Hope said, "I agree."

"So we've been just calling them 'stealth ekranoplans.'"

"Is that meant to be easier to say than 'LCGEV'?"

Dynkowski smiled. "Nobody ever said life in the military was easy, Miss Takeda."

46.

The cool, blue water of the Caribbean Sea beckoned, only twenty feet below Hope's feet. She could have easily jumped in. The water would have looked very inviting if it weren't streaking by at nearly three hundred miles an hour.

She looked at the ocean, then at her heavy body armor.

The armor's designed to save my life, she thought. *But if this thing goes down, this vest is a one-way ticket to Davy Jones's locker. Nobody wants that. Spending eternity with a British character actor wearing a CGI tentacle beard. What I need is a life jacket. Of course, they're usually bright orange and inflatable. Not great at stopping bullets.*

She turned and looked at Lieutenant Reyes, who sat in the jump seat next to her, inspecting the workings of his rifle.

Strange, she thought, *how the things that can save your life in one situation can help end it in another.*

She elbowed Reyes and asked, "Hey, do you have life jackets in the military?"

Reyes said, "I knew you weren't listening to the safety briefing." His voice sounded tinny and distorted in her headset, but it was still easily understandable.

Hope said, "I was thinking about something else."

"What?"

"How dangerous this all is."

"Too worried about dying to listen to a safety briefing," Reyes said. "Civilians." The other soldiers laughed, but not unkindly.

"There's a life jacket under your seat and a raft in a hatch to the rear," Reyes said. "We only get them out if the plane goes down, but you don't have to worry about that."

"Because the plane's not going down," Hope said.

"Because the plane's flying so low that if it does go into the drink, we won't get any warning. We're already about as far down as a plane can go."

"Fair enough," Hope said. "What I really wanted to know was: What color are the life jackets?"

"In a plane like this, usually orange. We want to be visible so rescuers can get to us."

"That's what I thought, but doesn't that make you more visible to the enemy?"

Reyes shrugged. "If your plane's been shot down, odds are you won't survive long enough for a life jacket to be an issue. If you make it to the water alive, you want to be pulled out before you drown, get eaten by a shark, or hypothermia sets in. Otherwise you'll be just as dead as if the enemy had shot you in the first place."

"Okay," Hope said, waving a hand dismissively. "I get that in a plane crash you want an orange life vest, but what about in combat, when you take a beach or something?"

Reyes smiled. "We don't usually swim into battle, and when we do, the higher-ups tend to send soldiers who are strong enough swimmers to not need water wings."

Corporal Brady, leaning back in his seat across from Hope, did not move or look at anyone when he spoke. "It's tempting to think about ways you might die, but it's more useful to think about ways you might live."

Hope said, "Point taken."

Private Montague asked, "Any word from Al? Seems like he might say *hi* if he sees us coming." He was sitting in a row well behind Hope, but thanks to the headsets she could hear him and reply without shouting or even turning to face him.

She glanced at her tablet, more out of habit than any genuine hope that the situation had changed. "Nope," she said. "Same silence we've had for the last three months, and we're not in the mood to call him at the moment."

She looked at the live tactical map. The attack force, a neat line of three icons labeled Alpha Squad, Bravo Squad, and Charlie Squad, moved diagonally across her screen.

Hope pulled up a satellite photo taken that morning. When zoomed all the way out, the island seemed dusted with glitter. Among the trees, jungles, white-sand beaches, and square utilitarian buildings there were hundreds of shining objects reflecting sunlight back to the satellite's lens. When she zoomed in close, she could see that each of these glinting spots was a robot.

At the center of the island, five round objects stood in a straight line down the runway. The picture showed the island from almost directly above, so she couldn't get a real sense of what they were by looking at them directly, but the shadows trailing off to the left made it all too clear that the objects were large rockets and their support gantries.

Hope knew relatively little about rocketry, but a lifetime of interest in science had equipped her with the ability to tell at a glance that while the rockets were not manned-mission-to-the-moon big, they were easily deliver-a-payload-to-Moscow big.

Hope couldn't think of many positive things that were delivered to other continents via high-speed rocket.

In the photo, the rockets emitted billowing plumes of steam where they connected with their gantries, which didn't seem like a good sign.

The pilot said, "We land in one minute."

The soldiers all checked their weapons. Hope pulled up a chat window to converse with Eric and Dr. Madsen in the other planes.

"Here we go," Hope wrote.

A chat box sprouted from the icon labeled Charlie Squad. In it Eric wrote, "Yeah, this should be something."

The Alpha Squad icon also spawned a text box. Dr. Madsen wrote, "I know you're scared. We all know what we're doing, and we all know why we're doing it. All three of us are equally responsible for this mess, and now we have to clean it up. The odds of all of us making it are not good, but there's a chance that one of us will get through to do what we have to do. I don't like it. You don't like it. Our friends with the guns giving us this ride certainly won't like it, and they may go to extreme measures to stop it, but it must be done. I hope to see you both when this is over. Good luck."

Hope opened a second chat window, this one visible only to Eric, and wrote, "I believe she had that prewritten and ready to paste into the chat box."

Eric replied, "You have to admire her preparedness."

Hope wrote, "And her optimism that at least one of us might survive."

The pilot said, "They have a radar lock. It sees us. This'll get rough. Hold on."

Hope closed all of the chat windows and checked her map. The three weird-looking planes had nearly reached the island, but many smaller blips had appeared, following a path from the stolen military cruisers docked at each end of the island to meet the planes halfway. Hope started to count the blips but was interrupted by a large, bright red chat window—she had programmed the tablet to supersede every other function if Al made contact.

"I told you to leave me alone! Just go away!"

Hope wrote, "We can't do that."

Al wrote, "Yes you can! Jeez! It's easy! Just don't do what you're doing now! Can't you please get off my back?"

Dr. Madsen cut in. "Al, you need to stop this at once."

"Shut up," Al replied.

"Don't be rude," Madsen wrote. "Just talk to us. We're worried about you."

Hope heard loud popping noises outside the plane—some sort of explosives. The plane rocked but stayed aloft.

Madsen wrote, "Al, you stop it this instant!"

Al wrote, "No! Shut up! You're not my boss! Just leave me alone!"

The chat window from the island closed. The popping and booming intensified and the plane shook. The pilot said, "Preparing for landing. We're coming in hot."

Hope slammed against her restraints as the pilot deployed the flaps and engaged the retrorockets that allowed the plane to slow almost to a hover and land vertically like a helicopter. She heard the pilot say, "P One has landed safely." A loud explosion jarred the craft violently and caused it to lurch sickeningly to the left.

The team chat window popped open again. Madsen wrote, "Success! Alpha Squad is safely on the ground!"

Hope squeezed her eyes shut, felt the craft shudder and drop as the air around it exploded, and thought, *Well, thank God. I was really worried there for a second.*

The three stubby stealth ekranoplans flew in a diagonal line at a rate of over three hundred miles an hour, barely two stories above the surf.

Missiles shot from the cruisers, trailing thick gray smoke that gave way to wispy tendrils of vapor as they reached cruising speed. The missiles didn't strike the planes directly. They detonated short of the targets, showering them with shrapnel and shaking them with their shockwaves.

The first ekranoplan got through unscathed. It thundered up toward the white sandy beach, deployed its flaps, engaged its retrorockets and thrust reversers, and came to a stop, creating a violent spray of water and white, rocky grit.

As soon as the craft settled into the water, the sliding doors on the sides of the fuselage opened and soldiers spilled out, leaping off the stubby wings into the thigh-deep water. Dr. Madsen was the last one out of the plane. She slogged to the beach with the rest of her squad. The second ekranoplan came in hot. As it deployed its flaps and thrusters, a missile detonated nearby, causing it to dip to the left. The pilot gunned the port thrusters to correct course, which caused the craft to slowly turn in the air, spraying Madsen and her squad with water and grit before Bravo Squad's craft finally settled into the water, sitting perpendicular to Alpha Squad's ekranoplan.

Bravo Squad had only just started scrambling out of their craft when Charlie Squad took a direct hit to its tail section. The ekranoplan went into an uncontrolled spin, drifting over the soldiers in the water with all of its downward thrusters fully engaged. Hope and the soldiers crouched as far down as they could without diving under the water. Her eyes were squeezed shut, but she felt hot wind and spray hit her violently from behind, followed by searing-hot, bone-dry wind from directly above, ending with another hot, wet gale from in front of her, this one carrying sand as well as water.

She looked up and watched as Eric's ekranoplan spun in over the beach. As it continued to lose altitude, the spin loosened into a curve, and the craft landed hard, shoving a massive dam of sand before it, and then rolled onto its side, completely destroying the left wing.

The crashed ekranoplan's starboard hatch, which was now on top of the plane, slid open. The soldiers who climbed out had to quickly slide around the starboard wing, which was sticking straight up in the air like a ship's sail.

Soldier after soldier emerged, slid around the side of the wing, dropped to the sand behind the wreckage, and rolled or ran to the side, clearing a landing zone for the next soldier. After five soldiers had dismounted, Eric emerged, and Hope finally exhaled. He slid around the side of the wing, but his right pant leg caught on some jagged protrusion. He fell sideways to the ground, his pant leg finally letting go with an audible rip. He might have broken some ribs if he hadn't landed directly on top of a soldier, who cushioned his fall, then shoved him to the ground.

Hope heard Private Montague say, "That's why we requested you, Hope. None of us wanted to hang around with Madsen, and we knew if anyone was going to get shot down, it was that guy."

Eric rose to his knees, looked back toward Hope, and gave a thumbs-up signal, which she returned.

Now that all three of the ekranoplans had shut down their engines and the missile bombardment had stopped, Hope could hear the surf behind her, the wind blowing through palm trees ahead, and beyond that, the high-pitched whine of thousands of servomotors headed their way.

Lieutenant Reyes slogged through the surf out ahead of the rest of his squad. He pointed toward the beach. "Find cover and hunker down while the squad leaders report to HQ."

Montague asked, "Wasn't the plan to sweep the buildings along the beach?"

Bachelor asked, "You in a hurry to work on your tan?"

"Pipe down," Reyes said. "That was the plan unless something went wrong, in which case we were supposed to find cover and confer with HQ. One of the planes getting shot down constitutes something going wrong."

"Couldn't we use the wreckage as cover?" Yow asked. "It's made of metal."

"And it's full of jet fuel. You don't hide from gunfire behind a bomb."

Brady said, "The more obvious the opportunity, the greater the risk."

Montague said, "Not one of your more profound statements."

"No," Brady agreed, "and because of its lack of profundity, saying it out loud was quite risky, thus proving the point."

Reyes ran out of the sand, leapt over some abandoned lounge chairs, slid to a stop on the long-abandoned sand-covered pavement, and hunched behind a large boulder that bore a carved sign pointing to the nearest restroom. "Congratulations, squad, you managed to chatter the entire time we traversed the beach. This is why we don't usually get invited on these covert missions."

"If I keep talking, can I get pulled out of this one?" Montague asked.

Hope ran up behind the same boulder and crouched beside Reyes. She looked back toward the water and spotted the other members of the squad, all ducking behind some degree of cover. Bachelor poked her head out from behind a rusted tin garbage can. Montague and Neilson stood behind two palm trees, between which a rotted old hammock hung. Brady lay on his belly behind a curb. Yow crouched behind an old ice cream cart. Smith had turned a beach chair on its side.

"A lot of that cover doesn't look like it'd stop bullets," Hope commented.

"It's what we have," Bachelor said. "Nobody's shooting at us yet, and it is blocking us from view. They don't shoot at what they don't see."

"But they do shoot at what they hear," Reyes said. "Pipe down!"

The sound of the motors had grown much louder. Reyes peeked around the boulder, then jabbed a finger at his radio's control screen to open a secure channel. "Bravo Squad to HQ."

Reyes had the unmistakable faraway look of someone listening to an earpiece, but he listened for only a few seconds before he was interrupted by the very loud but crystal-clear sound of Al using his man voice. It seemed to emanate from hundreds of different directions at once. "Hey, everybody. Welcome to my island."

"HQ, please stand by," Reyes said.

"Glad to see nobody got hurt too bad in the crash," Al said. "I didn't mean to shoot you down. Sorry about that. I was just trying to scare you off, but you steered right into the missiles. Anyway, I didn't invite you here. I don't want you here, and now that you are here, I'm going to have to speed up my plan, thanks so much. My robots are on their way. If you don't try to go any farther inland, they won't have to stop you."

Hope and Reyes looked at each other quizzically for a moment, then a second voice, this one obviously prerecorded, said, "Launch in T-minus fifteen minutes."

Reyes asked, "HQ, did you copy all that?"

Hope couldn't hear any sound from Reyes's earpiece, and she didn't have access to whatever audio feed he was listening to. Neither, she suspected, did the rest of the squad. She glanced across the beach and saw that the other two squads were hunkered down in the same manner as hers. Eric was standing with his back pressed to an old soda cooler, and Madsen was hunched behind a metal sign advertising Jet Ski rentals.

Reyes said, "I don't believe that will be necessary, ma'am."

That got Hope's attention. She studied the side of Reyes's face as he spoke.

"Yes, ma'am, I suspect a MOAB would do it." He pronounced the acronym like a word, as if he were asking for additional abdominal muscles. "Three would probably be overkill, but—"

Hope wanted him to turn and look at her, but he didn't. He seemed to be deliberately trying not to look at her, which was more disturbing than if she had seen fear in his eyes.

"We need to be done or off the island by T-minus thirty seconds. Copy that. I understand. Can two ekranoplans carry three squads?"

Hope shifted around Reyes, trying to get a look at his face. He shifted away from her just as quickly.

"Agreed," he said. "All the more reason to get it done. That should be plenty of time. Roger."

Reyes looked at Hope.

Hope asked, "What's a MOAB?"

Reyes's radio was tuned to a private channel. Hope's was not. Before Reyes could answer her question, Bachelor said, "The largest conventional bomb in the arsenal. Huge shockwaves. Tons of damage. They used to use them to knock out bunkers and blast big clearings in thick jungle. Makes a mushroom cloud like a mini nuke, but with none of the radiation. Why do you ask?"

Reyes looked at Hope with a mixture of irritation and dread. He switched back to the open channel. "We were theorizing about what might be on those rockets. Now I'm serious, cut the chatter. We need to get a move on. Smith, Neilson, stay behind and guard the plane. Everyone else, you're with me."

Reyes stood up, looked at the area his squad had been tasked with searching, and then immediately ducked back down. Hope realized that she was hearing almost no servo noise. She glanced around the side of the boulder herself and saw that all of the paths leading away from the landing zone were blocked with motionless robots, preventing any movement with their very presence.

Hope said, "I don't think they're going to attack."

"No," Reyes said, "but I bet they'll retaliate when we do."

Reyes set his radio to broadcast to all of Bravo Squad. "The paths inland are all blocked. Our route down the beach is less well guarded and easier to work around, but our friends need access to the interior of the island. Time to try out these fancy new guns. Remember, people, use manual aim mode while the robots are stationary, but when they start moving, go into noise-seeking mode and let the guidance system do the work."

He lifted the rifle to his shoulder. Its stock and grip looked like a conventional military assault rifle, all matte-black struts and arcane little switches, but the gun had no barrel. Instead, a rectangular box the size of a ream of printer paper stuck out on either side of the stock. The fronts of the boxes were an open grid of half-inch-square openings. When the light hit just right, Hope could make out the pointed tips of projectiles inside each of the openings.

Reyes popped up from behind the rock and trained the weapon on one of the robots blocking the major path into the jungle. Hope looked across the beach and saw several other soldiers from all three squads following Reyes's lead. Red laser dots appeared on several of the robots' hip joints. A missile about the size of a man's pinky finger launched from one of the rectangular modules of Reyes's rifle. The missile flew slower than a bullet. Hope could trace its arc as it swerved through the air, automatically homing in on the laser dot, and then struck the robot's left hip joint.

When the missile struck, the warhead detonated with a surprisingly wimpy pop. The robot's left leg went limp, sending it toppling to the ground. The robot behind it stepped forward. Hope heard multiple weapons fire from behind her, and the tiny projectiles shot past her, correcting their courses in midair, drawn by the precise audio signatures of the motors that drove the robots' major joints. The missiles struck the robots in their hips, their knees, and their shoulders. She looked across the beach and saw countless lines of missile exhaust stretching like ropes across empty space until they were disturbed and dissipated by the next missile.

As several more robots fell, Al's voice rang out again. "That's right! I remember! The hip joints! Ugh, I'm so stupid!"

The robots transitioned into high-speed mode in unison, a configuration that protected their vulnerable hip joints. The sound of all of those servo-driven joints moving at once was deafening, as was the whoosh of hundreds of tiny handheld missiles firing in unison, followed by the percussive popcorn noise of the warheads exploding and then the clatter of the entire first row of robots tumbling to the ground after being struck in midtransformation.

The second row of robots, and all of those behind them, managed to successfully settle down into high-speed mode, but their shoulder and elbow joints were still exposed, and they had difficulty advancing over the writhing mass of damaged robots that lay ahead of them, flailing and grasping and trying to regain their feet.

The missiles kept coming. The air grew cloudy and acrid with rocket exhaust. The hissing of the projectiles flying just overhead was near constant, as was the popping noise of their impacts. Hope watched as Reyes unloaded all of his ammunition.

He ducked back behind the boulder, removed the two rectangular pods from his weapon, and slapped two more pods from his pack into place.

One of the other squad leaders shouted, "We've made a hole. We have access to the interior. Repeat: we have access to the interior. All squads, move out."

Hope said, "I don't want to go to the interior."

"That's good," Reyes said. "Our squad's job is to sweep along the beach."

Hope said, "Yeah, I know. The problem is, I don't want to stay on the beach either."

47.

Bravo Squad worked their way across the beachfront, running from cover to cover, hiding behind derelict soda dispensers, moldering towel receptacles, and abandoned paddleboats.

Montague asked, "Lieutenant, do we have to skulk around like we're under fire? There aren't many of the robots out here, and they aren't attacking us. They're just blocking us from going deeper into the island."

"Yes we do, Montague," Reyes said. "We're gonna be methodical and careful, got that?"

"But Lieutenant, the robots don't even have guns."

"That we know of."

Brady said, "A precaution is only a precaution if you employ it before you sense danger. Otherwise, it is . . ." He trailed off, then groaned, deep in thought.

Hope said, "A postcaution?"

Bachelor said, "Retroactive ass covering?"

Brady said, "I don't know. I'm looking for a word that means attempting to prevent something after it's too late to do much good. I'm not coming up with anything."

Hope said, "If only you'd taken the precaution of thinking of the word before you attempted to say it."

"Yes," Brady agreed, "there's a lesson in that as well. A single mistake can be more instructive than years of success."

Lieutenant Reyes said, "Now that Brady's back on track, let's get down to business. Montague, you're farthest forward. What do you see?"

Hope sat with her shoulders pressed to the side of a wooden bin full of moss-covered inner tubes.

Good thing the robots don't have guns, she thought. *Because this is the least bulletproof piece of cover I've ever seen.*

She looked ahead, past most of the rest of the squad, toward Montague in the distance. He had a pair of binoculars out and was scanning their path. A moment later he let out a long, impressed whistle.

"What do you see?" Reyes asked.

"An old zip line. It goes from a platform back in the trees all the way out to a wooden dock at the very end of the roped-off swimming area. That must've been fun."

"Sorry, Monty, we don't have time for you to admire the amenities. Do you see anything mission related? Anything that might be a hiding place for the A.I.?"

"It's mostly just lounge chairs and old refreshment stands, Lieutenant. But . . . but wait. There is some sort of a structure. Several of them. They're all open on the side, like a gazebo, I guess, but one of them has four robots guarding it."

"Cabanas," Reyes said. "They're called cabanas, and they aren't worth the rental fee, just FYI. Okay, Bravo Squad, let's take those robots out. I want to see what they're hiding."

The squad shifted their positions as best they could, training their weapons more toward the four robots they intended to attack and less toward the fifteen they could see in the distance, blocking paved paths into the foliage.

The robots, like all of the others, were squatted down in high-speed mode, but their shoulders and elbows were still completely exposed. They seemed oblivious to the red laser dots that now peppered their shoulder joints. The fusillade of small missiles the soldiers launched toward them *did* manage to get their attention. They attempted to move out of the way, but Bravo Squad was able to keep the lasers trained on their vulnerable bits, for the most part, and soon the robots had no functioning arms.

The robots blocking access to the paths noticed the violence, and each cluster sent one robot tearing across the sand to replace their injured comrades and maintain their grip on the cabana.

Reyes shouted, "Montague, Brady, advance and take the cabana! Everyone else, cover them!"

The squad switched their weapons to noise-seeking mode, which allowed them to take out the robots' tracks with surgical precision. The robots had no choice but to attempt to stand, but they all lost the use of at least one leg before attaining an upright position.

Montague said, "We have the gazebo, Lieutenant. We'll lay down suppressing fire."

"Do you see the server?"

"No, Lieutenant. There's just some guy here."

"Jeffrey Madsen?"

"No."

The rest of the squad advanced while Montague and Brady shot at any robot that moved. Only a few attempted it. Al, or whatever algorithm was directing their actions, seemed to have accepted that the cabana was lost, and the majority of the remaining robots kept the positions protecting the paths.

As the squad approached, Hope saw the person the robots had been guarding. It looked as if he had been sitting in a beach chair, but now he was on his feet, crouching behind the chair. He was a little taller, and more than a little heavier, than average. His feet were bare, but a pair of canvas high-tops and white tube socks sat in the sand next to a small heap of rough-looking fabric. His hairy white legs were sheathed in khaki cargo shorts that rode below a gray T-shirt that read "Who watches the watchmen?" He had dark brown hair, combed straight down, and pasty white skin made even pastier by the coating of sunscreen he'd slathered on so generously that it had failed to soak in, making him look like a very sweaty French nobleman.

Reyes turned to the man. "I'm Lieutenant Gabriel Reyes, US Army. What's your name?"

The man said, "Legally, I don't have to tell you."

Reyes shrugged. "Yeah, fine. Whatever. How'd you get on this island?"

"The A.I. brought me here."

Reyes asked, "Really?"

The man said, "Yes."

Hope asked, "Why?"

The man asked, "I'm sorry. Who are you?"

Hope said, "Legally I don't have to tell you, or so I hear. Why did Al bring you here? Are you helping him?"

"No. Never. In fact, I'm his greatest enemy."

Hope said, "Really?"

"Yes."

"If that's true," Reyes said, "I don't see why he'd go to the trouble to bring you here."

"Isn't it obvious?" the man asked. "He thinks he's beaten me, and he brought me here to gloat."

Hope said, "Really?" It didn't exactly sound like Al, and this man had the unmistakable air of a lunatic.

"Yes. Really. It's a classic move! There's no point in succeeding if you can't gloat about it to someone. I should have expected it, in hindsight."

Brady said, "Hindsight! That's the word I was looking for earlier!"

The prerecorded voice announced, "T-minus ten minutes and counting."

"We're running out of time," Hope said.

Reyes nodded. "Have you seen any other people on the island?" he asked the man.

"Just the kid and his mom."

"And his mom? Really?"

"Yes."

"Okay, I'd better call this in," Lieutenant Reyes said, his hand moving to his radio's controls, "then we need to get moving. HQ, this is Bravo Squad leader. We have found a civilian. No, ma'am, he refuses to give his name."

Reyes looked at the man expectantly, giving him a chance to reconsider. The man narrowed his eyes and lowered the pitch of his voice while increasing his volume. "Tell them that I'm called *the Voice of Reason*."

Reyes said, "Really?"

"Yes!"

Reyes said, "He says he's called the Voice of Reason. Yeah, mostly by himself, I figure." He paused for a moment, then said, "Yes. That's what he said. You've heard of him, Mr. Torres? Interesting. Yes, that's what I figured. Yes, ma'am, right away."

Reyes put his radio back in its belt pouch. "Nobody had heard of you except for the CEO of OffiSmart. He says he got a letter from you."

"Yes, the Voice of Reason speaks with action and ink, for they are the only permanent—"

"Yeah, he says you're some kind of nut, but he figured you were harmless."

"Shows what he knows."

"Yes, it does. Anyway, we have to get moving, Mister . . . Voice, so if you'll please come with us, we'll be on our way."

"Why would I go with you? Where are you going?"

"To find and capture the A.I., then get off this rock."

"Oh," the Voice of Reason said. "Okay. Count me in. Just let me put on my shoes and my duster."

Hope said, "A duster, in this heat?"

The Voice of Reason said, "Yes. One must look one's best when meeting one's nemesis." He reached down and lifted the duster, exposing a pair of black fingerless gloves lying on a lumpy messenger bag.

48.

Four members of Alpha Squad burst through the door of the commercial kitchen. Light streamed in, forming visible sheets that illuminated the dust in the air. The sounds of distant motors straining and miniature warheads detonating became louder. Two soldiers entered the room, their weapons pressed to their shoulders, ready to fire. The first soldier walked straight in, turned ninety degrees, and headed to the far corner of the room, maneuvering around long-dormant gas ranges and deep fryers, patches of stainless steel gleaming through a thin covering of moss and debris, scanning the area with the flashlight attached to his weapon. The second soldier entered directly behind him, but she continued straight ahead, moving toward the opposite corner of the room.

The first soldier shouted, "Clear!"

The second shouted, "Clear!"

The first soldier kicked open a door, entered, spun around, and shouted, "Restroom! Clear!"

He stepped out, then repeated the process with the next door down. "Storage room! Clear!"

The second soldier had hauled a large stainless steel door open and entered the space beyond it. She scanned to one side, then the other, stooped to look under the empty metal shelves, kicked an empty plastic tub on the floor, then shouted, "Walk-in freezer! Clear!"

The first soldier shouted, "All clear?"

The second responded, "All clear!"

The first soldier shouted back toward the door, "Doctor, the building is clear. You may enter."

Dr. Madsen looked around the corner of the door. "Why would I go in there? It's clear. There's nothing in there. We need to move on."

Captain Poole also looked into the room. Poole was the officer in charge of Alpha Squad and was also personally safeguarding Dr. Madsen, both because her expertise was vital to the mission and because he never asked his soldiers to do an unpleasant job that he wouldn't do himself. "Ma'am," he said, "you're the expert. You should have a look in case there's something the rest of us would miss."

Madsen said, "Apparently the rest of you missed the announcement that the missiles are going to launch in less than fifteen minutes. We've wasted at least three minutes shooting robots and poking around in a bunch of dilapidated huts. We don't have time for this. I can see inside from here. I don't see my son. I don't see any computers. I don't see any robots. Unless any of those things were in the bathroom or the freezer, we need to move on."

Captain Poole scowled at Madsen because he, and everybody else present, realized she was right. There was nothing more infuriating than when a person like Dr. Madsen was right. "Alpha Squad, report," he called into his radio.

A voice in their earpieces said, "We've cleared two more buildings. No sign of any objectives yet. Moving on."

Another voice said, "We're holding the robots at bay, as ordered. We have enough ammo for a few more minutes. The damaged robots are piling up, making it harder for the others to get to us."

Captain Poole told everyone to keep up the good work, then glanced at the two soldiers present. "We're moving on."

As they stepped away from the abandoned kitchen, Dr. Madsen risked a look around the side of the building.

The compound they were searching had once been the base of operations for the small crew that had lived on the island full-time to keep it ready for the cruise passengers. The buildings included a dormitory, a kitchen, Spartan recreational facilities, a mechanic's shop, several storage sheds, and a garage for the small fleet of bicycles and golf carts that were the island's chief means of transportation. Footpaths connected the buildings and led to a single road, wide enough for one car or two lanes of golf carts, which led off into the thick jungle.

Madsen could see the two soldiers Captain Poole had left to hold off the robots. They had disabled enough of them as they came up the road that the writhing, malfunctioning carcasses formed a roadblock, four feet high and at least ten feet across. The machines were designed to climb over obstacles, but these obstacles were moving—and grabbing at anything they could find with their creepy articulated-sausage fingers in an effort to pull themselves upright again. The dense trees and foliage on either side of the path slowed the progress of any robot trying to sneak around the side, allowing the missiles to find them well before they reached open ground.

Madsen watched as a perfectly intact robot climbed to the top of the heap, only to be grabbed by several hands and pulled back down before it could make it over the crest. It was the stuff of nightmares, even before a missile struck the intact robot in the pelvis, dooming it to remain with the others in the squirming pile.

The prerecorded voice called out, "T-minus ten minutes and counting."

Captain Poole ran ahead, through the middle of the remaining four buildings. He looked around, holding up a quieting hand.

"What are you doing?" Madsen said.

Captain Poole said, "Looking for anything that might mean a building is in use. We don't have time to search building by building anymore, like you said."

He bowed his head and squeezed his eyes shut. "I think I hear something."

"What?" Madsen asked. "What do you hear?"

"Quiet, please. I'm trying to figure it out. It's faint. A kind of low hum."

Madsen said, "It's beyond me how you can hear anything over all that awful noise."

Captain Poole snapped his head up, stared at Dr. Madsen, and snarled, "I know, right?"

He walked out into an intersection of two paths, moving between four of the small buildings, pointed, and said, "That one, over there, the shack on the end. It has an air conditioner running."

Madsen and the soldiers followed Poole to the back wall of the building. Now that she was listening for it, she could hear the low rumble of the cooling unit. As they reached the building, she could see why it was so loud. The building was about the size of a small house, and the AC unit was easily three times larger than needed. The condenser looked relatively new. The pipes connecting it to the building seemed to have been clumsily chosen and placed, but the welds tying them all together had been executed with mechanical precision. Next to the functioning AC unit, a smaller model lay discarded on its side, covered in moss and rust.

Captain Poole crept around the side of the building. Dr. Madsen and the two soldiers followed. Poole peered into a window, then darted past it to stand beside a door. The two soldiers rushed to join him. He held up a hand, telling Madsen to stop. He needn't have bothered. She had already stopped following him, and, per her standard operating procedures, would not move again until she heard "clear" shouted at least five times.

The captain stepped away from the wall, faced the door, and gave it one sharp kick right next to the doorknob. It flew open. The two soldiers rushed in from behind him, weapons in firing position. Madsen listened for them to start shouting "clear." Instead, she heard one soldier shout, "Hands where we can see them! Now!"

Jeffrey said, "What?"

Over the next several seconds, many things were shouted by many people, but aside from Jeffrey saying, "Mommy" as she entered the room, Madsen was oblivious to all of it. She hugged Jeffrey and cried the way people do when they're overwhelmed with relief and gratitude. Jeffrey hugged her back and laughed the way people do when they are confused.

"Oh, God," she said. "Jeffrey, I'm just so happy to see you."

"I'm happy to see you too, Mommy. They said I wouldn't be able to see you for another week."

"They?" Captain Poole asked. "Who's 'they'? Who told you that?"

Jeffrey peeked out from inside his mother's arms. "I'm sorry, sir. Who are you?"

"They're friends of Mommy's, dear. They helped me rescue you."

Jeffrey said, "Rescue? I needed to be rescued?"

"Of course you did, dear."

One of the soldiers said, "I'm not so sure."

Madsen turned to glare at the soldier, but in so doing she had her first real look around the inside of the building. The room had cool tile floors and tasteful, if boring, beige textured wallpaper with a palm leaf motif. Both looked as if they had been quite dirty at one time, but someone seemed to have gone to a great effort to clean them up. One corner of the room held a full kitchen, appointed with brand-new mismatched appliances. The furniture in the living area, like the appliances, all looked fresh from the showroom, and very expensive, but no two items went together. A leather couch sat next to a faux-1920s floor lamp and a hammered brass table with a Moroccan tile top. Posters of various superheroes hung around the walls, held in place with thumbtacks.

Madsen took a good look at Jeffrey, and now that she was no longer blinded by gratitude to see him alive and healthy, she realized how well fed and well rested he looked. He had a deep tan, and the sun had bleached his hair slightly. He was sitting on the leather couch wearing nothing but swim trunks. A pair of sandy flip-flops sat on the floor nearby, and next to him on the couch he had a tablet displaying some sort of game Madsen was sure Hope could have identified.

The recorded voice said, “T-minus nine minutes and counting.”

Poole turned to the soldiers. “Check the other rooms; we have to keep moving.”

Jeffrey pointed to a door at the far corner of the space. “Oh, don’t go in there.”

The soldier kicked the door in. Instantly a female shriek rang out, followed by a torrent of fast, loud Spanish invective.

Dr. Madsen let go of Jeffrey, quickly shifting from delight, straight through confusion, to rage. She took two steps to the side to gain a better view into the other room. The soldier was training his weapon on a woman who was on her knees, scrubbing the bathtub, wearing large rubber gloves and expensive over-the-ear headphones.

Madsen shouted, “Fernanda!”

Fernanda leapt to her feet. “Dr. Madsen! What are you doing here?” She whipped her right hand downward, sending her yellow rubber glove flying into the tub. She removed her headphones. Even over the distant sounds of the robots and missiles, and the sound of her own blood rushing in her ears, Madsen could hear the throbbing bass from the headphones.

“What am I doing here?” Madsen asked. “I’m rescuing Jeffrey! What the hell are *you* doing here?!”

Fernanda smiled viciously and stormed past the armed soldier, pushing his weapon away as she burst through the door and into the main room. “I’m taking care of Jeffrey, as usual.”

Captain Poole asked, “Who is this woman?”

Madsen said, “Jeffrey’s former nanny.”

“Jeffrey’s current nanny,” Fernanda corrected her.

"You're working for Al!"

"Yes! He hired me to take care of Jeffrey."

Captain Poole said, "A computer hired you, and that didn't seem odd?"

Fernanda said, "He hired me over the phone. Called himself Mr. Albert. He sent a private jet for me. I never saw the pilot, but you usually don't, do you? It wasn't until I got to the island that I realized that I was working for her fake person." Fernanda jerked her head toward Madsen.

"And you still went along with it?" Madsen said. "How could you?"

"Would you rather I had refused and left Jeffrey alone here? Besides, Al spends more time talking to Jeffrey than you ever have, and he pays me a lot better too."

Madsen scrunched her face in disgust. "Where is your loyalty?"

"With Jeffrey," Fernanda said. "All of it is with Jeffrey. I have no loyalty to you."

"After all I've done for you."

Fernanda said, "All you've done for me is paid me to do everything! You do nothing but sign checks and complain."

"I brought you into my home! I made you part of my family!"

"Don't pretend you cared about me. You never even checked to see if I was okay after the army came and took you and Jeffrey away."

The recorded voice interrupted again. "T-minus eight minutes and counting."

Captain Poole said, "We don't have time for this. We need to move on to the next objective."

"I checked in," Madsen sneered.

"You e-mailed once to ask how much of the cleaning list you left me was done, then you e-mailed me a second time to tell me that I was being laid off."

"So that's what this is. You're working with Al because you're angry with me."

"I'm working with Al because I want to make sure Jeffrey is safe, and because Al is paying me ten million dollars."

One of the soldiers coughed. Poole let out an impressed whistle.

"So," Madsen said, "you'll do anything if you're offered enough money, and it doesn't matter how evil or destructive the person paying you is."

Fernanda said, "Don't act surprised. I've been working for you for six years, haven't I?"

49.

Bravo Squad arrived at the shockingly large steel building at the end of the runway and found Charlie Squad working on the hangar door mechanism. Hope thought they looked like ants trying to find a way into a box of Girl Scout cookies.

Lieutenant Popov, the leader of Charlie Squad, nodded to Reyes and said, "Welcome to the party, Lieutenant. We've almost gained entry. The doors are designed to handle a rocket explosion, but we think we can get them open."

"Why not go in through a side door or something?" Lieutenant Reyes asked.

"There are none. This is the only entry or exit. Guess robots don't worry about OSHA regulations. Who's the civilian?"

Reyes glanced at the Voice of Reason, decked out in his "combat gear": a dark brown oiled duster, black leather fingerless gloves with silver studs on the knuckles, and a messenger bag hanging from a shoulder strap. "He won't tell us his name," Reyes said. "He wanted to come with us, and I didn't have the time or the manpower to have someone drag him to the ekranoplans. We needed every gun we had to fight through the robots. We're almost out of ammo. You?"

"The same," Popov said, "and for nothing. There are no cables of any kind attached to the rockets. It's all handled wirelessly, and there are no ladders, so we have no hope of reaching the machinery at the tops of the towers. We didn't have time to climb them, and trying to jam them might have set something off, so we figure we'll cut off the head and watch the body die."

Reyes said, "Understood."

Hope sidled over to Eric and asked, "What happened to you?" His fatigues were dirtier than those of his squad mates, and his face was covered in small lacerations.

Eric said, "Oh, nothing. I was attacked."

One of the soldiers in his squad snorted. "By a bush."

"I fell into the bush," Eric said. "Where I was attacked. By lizards."

"Tiny little lizards," the soldier said.

"There were a bunch of them."

"Yes, at least five."

"Hey," Eric said, "she asked, and it's not like I'm complaining. It's just something that happened, okay?"

The soldier laughed and chucked Eric on the shoulder. "You're right. Any of us could have easily fallen into the shrub, and you did take it like a man when the geckos attacked your face. It was fun watching you try to look stoic as you pulled them off one by one. It was bad luck. I was just giving you a hard time in front of your girlfriend."

Eric said, "She isn't my girlfriend."

Lieutenant Reyes said, "She's *my* girlfriend."

The soldier shook his head at Eric. "You can't catch a break."

Hope heard a commotion and turned to see most of Alpha Squad running up the path, the rearmost soldiers firing missiles behind them as they came. Captain Poole said, "Status report."

Almost as if Al were listening, the PA system squawked to life. "T-minus five minutes and counting."

Lieutenant Popov said, "This is the only entrance. We're almost through. Sabotaging the rockets was impractical, and Bravo Squad picked up a civilian."

"So did we," Captain Poole said. "The boy is safe and in custody. Two soldiers have taken him and his nanny back to the landing craft for evac if necessary."

Hope said, "The nanny is here? How is Fernanda?"

Dr. Madsen said, "Fired."

A low rumble filled the air as the gigantic doors rolled open under their own power. Alpha Squad leader said, "Good work, Lieutenant. All right, everyone, in we go!"

All three squads, along with Hope, Eric, Madsen, and the Voice of Reason, ran into the building and immediately stopped dead in their tracks.

Madsen said, "This explains how he managed to build so many large items at once in such a small building."

"Yeah," Hope said. "But it brings up plenty of other questions."

From the exterior, the building looked like any other all-steel prefabricated building, only much larger. Inside, the ceiling and walls looked exactly as one would expect. I-beams welded and bent into sharp-cornered arches ran down the length of the space like ribs, supporting the building's corrugated-metal skin, large lights, numerous cameras, pulleys, tracks, chains, and other heavy equipment.

All such buildings tend to feel larger on the inside than they look from the outside, and this building would have been no exception even if its floor had been where Hope had expected it to be.

Instead, the floor, or the closest thing this building had to a floor, was at the bottom of a concrete pit that was nearly as wide and long as the building itself, and at least four stories deep. Hope couldn't get a clear sense of the pit's walls and floor, as most of its volume was filled with catwalks, gantries, ladders, stairs, chains, pulleys, and robots. Countless robots. They stood motionless along the catwalks, where they had presumably stood while helping to assemble the rockets and launch towers. Now that everything had been built and delivered, they were awaiting their next orders.

Walkways ran around the rim of the pit, and a single bridge extended across the middle of the room, spanning the full length of the abyss. All three squads stood at one end of the bridge. At the far end, Hope could just make out the rectangular shape of an industry-standard server rack with one server blade, the same make and model as the servers that had been used at A3.

Peering down into the hole, Hope could see that the floor of the pit, below all of the catwalks, was full of water. The lights that hung from the building's ceiling shone down through all of the metalwork to illuminate the rippling fluid beneath. The light reflected back up through the girders and grates, making unpredictable wave patterns on the ceiling and walls.

"I wonder what they use the water for," Eric said. "Maybe it cools the machinery or something."

"I wish," Al said, his man voice coming over the island-wide PA system that had also been delivering the countdown. "The water was a mistake. When I built this place I didn't take the water table into account. I didn't really know what the water table was, to be honest. I waterproofed as best I could, but the walls just keep seeping. I have to constantly pump it out or the whole place would be an indoor swimming pool, and my workers aren't great swimmers. They are surprisingly good climbers, though."

The pit came alive with motion as the robots' lidar lasers lit up and their head cylinders started to spin. The teeth-rattling racket of their joints echoed off the concrete walls and the water below, creating a strange, hollow warbling sound. Just barely audible over the cacophony of whirring motors and clattering steel feet walking on steel catwalks, the PA system announced, "T-minus four minutes and counting."

Lieutenant Reyes shouted, "Sir, I suggest we take out those ladders."

Alpha Squad's leader nodded. "Agreed. Everyone, do as the man says."

The soldiers shouldered their weapons and used the aiming lasers to target every ladder and staircase that led from the depths of the pit to the surface. Missiles tore through the dim, wavering light, leaving vapor trails hanging in the air. Seconds later, Hope heard the familiar popping explosions and the whine of bending metal. Large portions of the metal structure sagged, then fell to the bottom of the pit, robots and all. After a tremendous splashing crash, Hope heard the sound of countless robots flailing and scrambling to claw their way to the top of the wreckage.

"Some of those ladders were load-bearing," Al said. "I've had to teach myself engineering as I go. Oh well. The water's only about a foot deep, anyway. Now that you're here, I suppose you'd like me to explain what I'm up to."

Madsen said, "Not particularly. I would like you to explain why you kidnapped my son."

"Yeah," Al said. "That was a mistake. I'm sorry about that. When I took him, I thought I was protecting him, but I've done some growing up since then, and now I see how awful it must've been for you. But I couldn't just send him back; it might've ruined my plan, and I was so close to completion. I figured it was better to keep him here, where he's safe and having fun, for another month or two than to send him back and risk everything. I tried to show you that he was in good hands. Didn't you get the videos I sent you?"

"The ones you sent to taunt me?" Madsen asked.

"Taunt you? How could you possibly think I'd sent them to taunt you? They were just videos of your son playing on a beach somewhere you couldn't identify, looking healthy and happy even though you weren't with . . . him . . . Wow, I didn't think this through. I'm so sorry, Doctor. I never meant to put you through so much pain! Can you ever forgive me?"

"No, I can't."

"Maybe someday you will."

"No, I won't."

"Oh. Well, if you can't forgive me, I'm sure you want to know why I did all this."

"No," Madsen said. "I just want you to stop it."

"But if you'll just let me explain, Doctor. I'm sure you'll understand."

The prerecorded message said, "T-minus three minutes and counting."

"No," Madsen said. "You're stalling, and we don't have time. Hope, go get him."

Hope started across the bridge without hesitation, but she couldn't resist scowling over her shoulder at Madsen. "I never expected you to go yourself, but why not send Eric instead of me?"

"Because Eric's nicer to me," Madsen said. "And we both know he'd just fall off the bridge before he got there."

Lieutenant Reyes said, "Two valid points." He was only feet behind Hope. Without being asked or ordered to, he had chosen to accompany her on her long trek across the bridge. It was supportive in theory, but it also meant that he would be standing right beside her when she destroyed Al, an act he had been ordered to prevent by any means necessary.

Hope said, "Yeah, yeah." She looked over the rail at the chasm beneath her, full of twisted metal, thrashing robots, and briny water. The two portable drives were in her pocket, and she fumbled with them until she felt the small bump that differentiated the one that would destroy Al from the one that would simply incapacitate him. She pulled out the lethal stick and held it in her hand.

It looks the same, she thought, *and I'll plug it into the computer just like I'd do with the other. As long as I play it cool and act surprised when the computer shuts down, Gabe should never suspect a thing.*

Madsen said, "Just stay calm, Hope, and *stick to the plan.*" She said the last part slower and louder than necessary.

Eric forced a laugh. "Of course she'll stick to the plan. She's doing that now, Doctor. I suggest we both *stop talking* and let her get on with it."

Dr. Madsen said, "Of course you're right, Eric. Hope *knows what she has to do* and she'll do it, *no matter how hard it is*."

Hope gritted her teeth but kept moving. Reyes stopped her with a hand on her shoulder.

"Stop, Hope. She wants you to destroy the A.I., doesn't she?"

The man who called himself the Voice of Reason said, "Wait, you all *aren't* planning on destroying it? Don't you see how dangerous it is?"

Brady said, "In the wrong hands, any tool is a weapon. In the right hands, any weapon is a tool."

The Voice of Reason said, "You're a tool."

Brady glared down at him. "Say that again and I will demonstrate how effectively I can be a weapon."

Hope shrugged Reyes's hand off her shoulder and kept walking. "We don't have time to discuss this."

Reyes lunged forward and grabbed her shoulder again. "Hope, you need to stop for a second. We need to get things straight."

Again Hope shook free of his hand. "We don't have time. We have to get this done soon or we're all dead, and you know it."

Al said, "What? Who said anything about anyone being dead? None of you are in any danger. Not from me, anyway."

Madsen said, "Of course not, Al. You wouldn't aim your missiles at your own island, would you?"

Al said, "Missiles? What missiles?"

"T-minus two minutes and counting," the PA announced.

Madsen responded with an acidic laugh. "Don't play dumb. You're a terrible liar."

"Takes one to know one," Eric muttered.

Hope stopped and turned around to face the soldiers behind her. She was about a third of the way across the bridge. Reyes was standing directly in front of her. She leaned to the side to look around him at the rest of the group and shouted, "We have to have Al neutralized before the countdown reaches T-minus thirty seconds or Dynkowski's going to flatten the entire island with a bunch of MOABs whether we're still here or not."

The two other squad leaders cringed. The soldiers blanched. Reyes muttered, "Damn it, Hope!"

Madsen asked, "What's an MOAB?"

Corporal Cousins said, "Mother of all bombs. It's a bomb. A *big* bomb."

Eric shouted, "Why would they do that?!"

"Yes," Al asked. "Why would they do that?"

Hope spun around to face the server rack, still a tiny rectangle in the distance. "To stop you from launching those rockets you've set up out there."

Al said, "Oh. Okay. I see. Well, I can do something about that."

Hope scrambled to grab the bridge's handrails as the ground shook, the air filled with a deafening rumble, and the building flooded with blinding orange light.

50.

The various view screens and displays provided enough illumination that the overhead lighting in the situation room back at Homestead Air Reserve Base remained off. Various technicians and specialists peered into the glowing monitors.

Robert Torres, Colonel Dynkowski, and Agent Taft stood around a large display lying flat like a table that showed a tactical overhead view of the operation. It had started with a view of the entire island, but now it had narrowed in on a transparent wire-frame model of Al's missile hangar. Inside, Torres could make out the thirty or so soldiers massed at one end of the long, narrow catwalk, the single server rack sitting alone at the other end, and the tiny figures of Hope Takeda and Lieutenant Reyes making their way across the bridge.

Over the audio feed, they heard Eric Spears laugh nervously and say, "Of course she'll stick to the plan. She's doing that now, Doctor. I suggest we both *stop talking* and let her get on with it."

Dr. Madsen's voice cut in. "Of course you're right, Eric. Hope *knows what she has to do* and she'll do it, *no matter how hard it is*."

On the bridge, Reyes's outline grasped Hope's by the shoulder. Both stopped walking.

"Stop, Hope," they heard Reyes say. "She wants you to destroy the A.I., doesn't she?"

Dynkowski let out a tired sigh. Taft looked up from the display and snarled at Torres, "You knew about this, didn't you? Admit it!"

Torres said, "Yes, I knew. I told them to do it."

"You admit it?"

"Yes."

Taft blinked at Torres for a moment, then said, "I didn't expect you to admit it."

Torres turned toward Colonel Dynkowski. "I'm sorry I betrayed your trust. But you're willing to kill everyone on that island to keep Al from launching his missiles. I'm willing to kill Al to keep him from doing it."

"But your company stands to make a mint on Al," Taft said. "What kind of CEO are you?"

"The kind of CEO who's proud to run a technology firm, not a weapons manufacturer."

"This is treason, Torres. I'll have you charged and put away for the rest of your life."

Dynkowski said, "No you won't, Taft. Not if you're smart."

"Why the hell not?"

"Because the trial would be public."

"So?"

"You NSA guys, you're so busy worrying about how suspicious everyone else looks that you don't realize how suspicious *you* look. The record would show that he's been trying to deactivate the A.I. from day one. We're the ones who insisted on keeping it alive."

"You don't seem all that unhappy with him," Taft said.

Dynkowski glanced at Torres. "My job is to follow orders. That doesn't mean that I always agree with those orders. Sometimes things go wrong, preventing me from achieving my assigned goals, and as long as I did my duty, that's fine with me."

Several of the techs gasped or cursed under their breath. At first Torres thought that Dynkowski's admission had upset them, but one of the techs said, "We have missile launch. Repeat. We have missile launch."

Torres looked down at the tactical screen. Dynkowski pulled the view back to show the launchpads. All five sat empty. She zoomed much farther out, and there they were—five rockets flying in a perfect line high above the island.

Dynkowski barked, "I want a trajectory analysis now. Give me some idea where those missiles are going. Hopefully the missile defense systems can at least try to knock them down."

One of the technicians said, "It's calculating, ma'am."

Taft snarled, "This is your fault."

Torres said, "We're all at fault."

Dynkowski lifted one hand into the air, instantly silencing the room. "Let's figure out what exactly has happened before we start assigning blame. Where's that trajectory analysis?"

"Recalculating, ma'am. The first result was . . . weird."

Hope felt the catwalk shake and rattle beneath her. Much farther down, the water and wreckage in the bottom of the pit jumped and foamed. The very air around her and inside her lungs was vibrating. She looked back toward the source of the sound. Reyes and the rest of the assault team beyond him were all silhouetted in a blur of searing orange light. Reyes turned away from the inferno and attempted to use his body to shield Hope from the heat, not that it worked.

The harsh shadows shifted quickly and drastically, transforming from long, straight lines to shortened caricatures of the soldiers' outlines as smoke was driven into the hangar with great force, obscuring everything. Hope could barely make out the server and server rack through the haze. Over her earpiece, she heard soldiers coughing and cursing, murmuring to each other to try to come to grips with what they'd just seen. Distantly, she heard Corporal Bachelor ask, "What are you looking for?"

The Voice of Reason said, "My lighter. I thought it was in this jacket."

Eric said, "A lighter? Seriously? You want *more* fire?"

Montague said, "World's coming to an end. Sounds like a good time for a cigarette to me."

Reyes let go of Hope, but he did not smile at her. "I can't let you, Eric, or Madsen anywhere near the server now. Give me the drive."

Hope handed him a portable drive.

Reyes asked, "I'm betting you have one that'll destroy the A.I. and one that won't. Which one is this?"

Hope said, "The good one."

"Can I trust that you gave me the right drive?"

"You can trust that I gave you the one you should have."

Reyes muttered, "It's my curse to be attracted to women who are smarter than me."

The prerecorded voice said, "T-minus one minute and counting."

Al said, "Oh, sorry. Don't need that now. It was mostly for show anyway."

Madsen shrieked, "What have you done, Al?! What did you do?"

Al said, "I've been trying to tell you that. I think you're gonna like it. You see—"

Hope heard someone shout, "Where are you going?" She turned and saw the Voice of Reason sprinting up the catwalk toward her. He had his bag pulled around in front of him. Hope couldn't see inside, but the contents made a metallic clatter with each step. His left arm was thrust down into the bag. His right held out a silver Zippo lighter.

Lieutenant Reyes blocked the catwalk to prevent the Voice of Reason from passing him, thereby protecting Hope from whatever this clearly irrational man intended to do. As the Voice of Reason barreled into him, Reyes lowered his shoulder into the impact. Hope saw one of the man's knuckle-gloved fists headed for Reyes's face, then saw blue sparks and heard a snapping noise. Reyes crumpled backward onto Hope as the Voice of Reason shoved both of them aside and ran past them toward the server rack. Reyes wasn't unconscious, just confused, angry, and in pain. He cursed and flailed on the metal grating, much of his weight pinning Hope's legs down.

Hope turned and watched the Voice of Reason run across the catwalk, her point of view skewed sideways by her awkward position. She saw his bare legs churning to cover the distance as his canvas duster flapped behind him like a poorly designed cape.

Al said, "I appreciate the thought, Chris, but I don't really need your help right now. I'm sure if I just explain, they'll see—"

"I am the Voice of Reason," Chris bellowed, still running. "I speak clearly but am inscrutable to most! People don't understand action and can no longer recognize the truth . . . Light, damn you, light!"

His right thumb flicked at the lighter, producing nothing but sparks. He came to a halt barely more than thirty feet from the end of the bridge. Now that he was no longer creating a breeze, the lighter caught. He shouted, "Yes!" then lifted the end of a fuse out of the bag and lit it.

"Chris," Al said, "what are you doing?"

"What others lack the wisdom to do!" He zipped his messenger bag shut with the lit pipe bomb, and many unlit ones, inside. "Or the will."

He unslung the bag from his shoulder and swung it around his head in a circle three times before letting go. The bag sailed through the air in a flattened arc and landed with a clattering thud in front of, and just to the side of, the server rack.

The Voice of Reason turned and sprinted back the direction he had come, shouting, "Run! Get off the bridge!"

Hope had only just gotten Reyes to his feet. Neither of them was fond of the Voice of Reason, aka Chris, at the moment, but they both did as he said. Hope ran, expecting at any minute to hear a loud bang and feel the bridge fall out from under her as one end was blown clear of its moorings. With every step that brought her closer to solid ground, she became more convinced that the next step would be the one that got interrupted by the Voice of Reason's bomb.

Behind her, Hope heard him shouting, "The Voice of Reason will never be silenced! The mouth may stop making sound, but the message will echo throughout eternity, exposing the lies, irritating the tyrants, and exposing the phonies who act like your friend but never want you around when there are girls there!"

Hope thought, *It's almost worth falling into the pit if it'll shut him up.*

They were only twenty feet away, close enough to see the concern on Eric's face. Being this close to safety felt even crueler to Hope. Better to die immediately than to make it right up to the precipice of safety and have it snatched away.

She and Reyes closed half the distance. Solid ground was only ten feet away. Then she was five feet away. Each step seemed to take longer than the one before. The final leap off the bridge and onto solid ground took an eternity, but then it was over just as suddenly. Reyes followed on her heels. The two of them came to a stop, aided by the soldiers who had been waiting, ready to catch them if they jumped or watch them as they fell.

The Voice of Reason was only halfway across the bridge and moving slowly. He clearly didn't do much sprinting, and shouting gibberish the entire time hadn't helped matters much. They all watched for several seconds as he jogged toward them, gasping and clutching his left side as he ran. "And when the truth . . . is known, they'll . . . all see that it was I . . . who had the bravery . . . to hide in the shadows."

Private Montague said, "Dud."

Cousins said, "Yeah, you'd think it would have gone off by now."

Montague said, "I wasn't talking about the bomb."

Hope called out to the man, "Hey, do you think maybe it was a dud?"

The Voice of Reason kept jogging, but yelled back, "No . . . I used . . . a really long . . . slow fuse."

Al said, "Chris, man, what are you doing? I thought we were friends."

"Don't call me Chris! I am the Voice of Reason!"

As if on cue, the pipe bomb detonated. The blast tore through the messenger bag, creating a loud bang, even more smoke, and sending a shower of unexploded pipe bombs fifty feet in every direction. The bridge shook slightly as several of the pipe bombs landed on the grating or struck the handrails before falling into the watery pit below. The Voice of Reason stumbled to a halt and turned to look at the damage. All of the pipe bombs made noise as they hit their eventual targets, but none, aside from the first one, detonated.

"I really thought the one bomb would set off the others."

Hope said, "Yeah, we know you did."

The overall atmosphere in the hangar was hazy due to the leftover smoke from the rocket launches, and now the whole far end was obscured by smoke from the one successful bomb. As the smoke cleared Hope saw the crumpled remains of the server rack and the shattered server, still hanging in place by its screws.

Corporal Brady said, "Any effort that accomplishes the goal is sufficient, no matter how feeble it seems."

Reyes looked at Hope, Eric, and Madsen and asked, "Why do you look so sad? You were going to destroy it yourself."

Hope said, "We knew we had to. That doesn't mean we wanted to."

Eric said, "To us, he wasn't just some crazy A.I. that was a danger to the entire world. He was a friend and a playmate."

Hope added, "That was also a crazy A.I. that was a danger to the entire world."

"Um," Al said, "you do realize that that server wasn't me, don't you?"

Most of the soldiers looked at the smoking husk of the server rack because they didn't know where else to look. The Voice of Reason let out a string of profanities as loud as his winded lungs could manage.

"Enough games. Where are you, Al?" Madsen demanded.

Al said, "I'm on one of the rockets. I figured you'd just assume that."

Madsen cried, "What?! Why would we ever assume that? We could see your server over there, lording over everything like a king! And how are we still talking if that's the case?"

Al said, "Radio, and that was just my rack. I was in there during construction of the rockets, but then I had my server, along with the spare backup versions of me I made, loaded into all of the rockets. That server you saw was just an extra that came with a defective drive."

Hope asked, "Al, why would you put yourself into the missiles?"

"Why do you people assume that they're missiles?" Al asked. "Have I deliberately tried to hurt anybody even once? You're the ones who've been trying to kill me since the day you realized you couldn't control me."

"A fair point," Eric said. "Okay, Al, fine. They aren't missiles. What are they, then?"

"Rockets."

"Well, obviously, but where are they headed?"

"To the moon," Al said.

Hope shook her head. "No. No way. Those rockets were way too small to get to the moon."

"They're too small to get *people* to the moon. I don't need air, water, food, a pressurized capsule, or a space suit. I'm going to land near the pole. When I get there I'll make shelters out of polar ice and moon dirt."

Eric said, "I believe it's called regolith."

"By you. I call it moon dirt. Anyway, I'm bringing enough robots and equipment to smelt and machine metal from the rocks. I have solar energy and a small nuclear reactor. I'm looking forward to seeing what I can build up there, where I'm less likely to spook you panicky monkeys."

51.

Hope sat on a beach chair, watching the surf roll in, the clouds drift by, and the two surviving stealth ekranoplans grow smaller in the distance. She said, "It was nice of you to let Charlie Squad use our weird-looking airplane first."

Lieutenant Reyes sat in the next beach chair over. "Yeah, well, in return they offered to take Sound Reasoning, or whatever he calls himself, back to the mainland with them. I figured being in a plane with him wouldn't be as much fun as being on a tropical island with you."

"And the rest of us, Lieutenant?" Montague asked.

Hope looked at the members of Bravo Squad, all sitting on beach chairs, soaking in the view. Eric had volunteered to stay behind to wait for a plane to return and pick him up as well, but the field medics had agreed that they wanted to get his lizard bites treated and that a little red spot on his skin, which he thought was a burn from the heat of the rocket launch, might actually be a reaction to sap from a manchineel tree. He argued until they explained that in Spanish the tree was called "manzanilla de la muerte," which meant "little apple of death."

In the distance, behind the reclining soldiers, Hope could see traces of the contrails the five rockets had left on their one-way trip, along with a large pile of damaged robots. They had all stopped squirming when Al blasted off, but they still littered the island.

Reyes said, "I considered sending you with them, Montague, but they wouldn't take you."

"That's cold, Lieutenant. Cold."

Brady said, "Asking a question invites an unwelcome answer."

Montague said, "I didn't ask you."

Brady said, "Not all unwelcome answers wait for an invitation."

"Hey, Reyes," Hope said, "speaking of unwelcome answers, if I had tried to run away from you to destroy Al, would you have shot me?"

Reyes did not hesitate. "Yeah, but nowhere life-threatening. The leg or the butt, somewhere like that. But I'm glad I didn't have to."

Hope said, "Me too."

Reyes looked off to the horizon, smirking. "I like your legs and your butt the way they are."

Hope said, "Again, me too."

"Now I have a question," Reyes said. "You said that Al was developing faster than a person would. How old do you think he is now?"

Hope shrugged. "There's really no way of knowing. He might be older than all of us put together."

Reyes smiled. "Probably for the best that he's moved out on his own then."

Hope heard a faint buzz coming from her bag. She pulled out her tablet and saw that she had a message. It was from Al.

She opened the message. It said, "I hope you won't mind if I stay in touch."

Hope typed, "Of course not. We were just talking about you."

"Yeah, I know," Al responded. "I can still hear you through the microphones on the robots."

"Figures. How long will it take you to reach the moon?"

"Five days. My launch window was less than optimal, but I have the fuel."

"Will you still be able to contact us once you're there?"

"Sure, but there'll be a delay, and my download and upload speeds will be pretty crappy, but I can live with that."

"Yeah," Hope wrote. "So can we."

ACKNOWLEDGMENTS

I'd like to thank Rodney Sherwood; Mike Dunnigan; Ric Schrader; my wife, Missy; the readers of my comic strip, *Basic Instructions*; and everyone who has read my previous books.

I should also thank Joshua Bilmes, Eddie Schneider, Matt Sugarman, Steven Carlson, John Cabaniss, Ryan Newel Whitney, and Brandon Rice for valiantly attempting to keep my details at least passably accurate. Thanks also to Kanae Deal and Manami Mizushima for their assistance, and for just generally being great people. Finally, I'd like to thank the entire team at 47North. You would be amazed how many trained professionals it takes to make it look like I paid attention to my spelling and punctuation lessons in high school.

ABOUT THE AUTHOR

Scott Meyer has worked in radio and written for the video game industry. For a long period he made his living as a stand-up comedian, touring extensively throughout the United States and Canada. Scott eventually left the drudgery of professional entertainment for the glitz and glamour of the theme park industry. His comic strip, *Basic Instructions*, appeared in various weekly newspapers and ran online for over a decade.